Book 3 in the Artifact Series

The Coming Storm

D.R. Swan

This book is a work of fiction. Any resemblance to persons, places or incidents are either the product of the author's imagination or are used fictitiously, and any resemblance to actual persons, living or dead, locales or events are completely coincidental.

It's fiction. Have fun!

The Coming Storm
By D. R. Swan

Book 3 in the Artifact Series

Book Cover Image By
Evan

(cs023)

Dedication

To Evan and Ryan, always foremost in my thoughts and prayers.

Acknowledgments

Thanks to everyone for their help, support, and kindness. No one accomplishes anything alone. Special thanks to Evan, Donna, Fred, and Blair for their help over and above.

It's Fiction. Have Fun!

The Coming Storm

Preface

Earth Date: January 19, 2101

Sol Date: The 337th Day of the Martian Solar Year

A diary entry from President Henry Dent chronicling the events of his presidency on the eve of his last State of the Union Address:

"...Everything has now changed. As inhabitants of Earth, before the arrival of the alien craft that attacked our planet, nearly destroying us, we had figured ourselves maybe to be alone in this vast universe. The time and distances for anything biological to reach us were just too great and though we

tried, we could never pick up any signals of what we thought should be broadcasted from some burgeoning civilization that might exist in orbit around a distant star.

Then it happened. We were attacked from space and caught unaware. On January 28, in the year 2098, they arrived with bad intentions.

The alien vessel first hid in the oceans for seven months and though we tried, we could not find its location. We didn't know what these invaders were up to, though we suspected that it wasn't going to be positive.

They were so alien to us that we didn't see them coming, couldn't detect their arrival hidden on an asteroid bound for Earth, and because they were technologically more advanced than us, once they attacked, they took down most of the world's infrastructure in a bit less than 5 weeks. They had a plan and except for incredible luck, that plan would have succeeded.

I would dare say, that if their armada that had emerged from the wormhole that lay just beyond Neptune had not run smack into an asteroid field, humans would all now be dead or slaves or worse, food for some alien race, a sobering thought.

And now the world is connected in a loose and maybe ineffective world government that I'm about to go on the airwaves and sell to the American people as the best thing since sliced bread.

One positive from the chaos is the world's expansion to Mars. We are now a two-planet race and the colonization of Mars is well underway with people volunteering to work and inhabit the red planet but more would be needed. The environment on Mars is improving, due to the terraforming, but humans still cannot go outside without spacesuits. The pressure is still too low and the air too toxic with little oxygen.

We had feared that the colonists would be constantly assaulted by the subterranean creatures who showed up on the red planet some years before, but they have disappeared and melted back into the landscape. These creatures had killed some of the colonists, but after a few battles, they seem to be gone. We have fortified every airlock door and are confident that these creatures no longer can pull the doors off the hinges, but what happened to them? Why have they completely disappeared? They lived underground and maybe they died off after we sealed the entrances to the caves. No one really knows and we haven't the troops or police on the planet yet to explore the labyrinth of caves that exist in parts of the red planet. We also have no desire to stir up that hornet's nest of trouble. We'll save that for another day.

Earth, however, is not okay.

The alien vessel deposited spheres onto our planet that burst and from those spheres something began growing, something designed to begin the terraforming of our Earth for these aliens to inhabit.

After the destruction of the alien vessel, every place where the spheres burst, it has been nearly impossible to eradicate what grows in the ooze. Our best and unfortunately, most toxic defoliants only slow the progression of these insidious plants.

Africa and South America are having the most trouble because they are more sparsely populated and it's where most of the spheres were dropped.

Humans infected by the parasites from the plants become mindless and sometimes violent then wander off to die and where they lay, the alien plants grow.

Animals and insects seem to be smarter than humans, thankfully, and instinctively avoid the places where the ooze and squirming root-like plants have taken hold. It is nearly impossible to find all of the spheres because not all of them burst when they hit the ground. Some landed on soft soil or marsh and because they were dropped from a significant height, the spheres just burrowed into the soil and began to leak later. We are fairly confident that we have not found all of the spheres.

This is an ongoing problem and one that we have yet to conquer.

Another issue is that we have begun to discover that the wealthy of Earth, who should have lost everything during the economic collapse seemed to have recovered quite well. Those movers and shakers who controlled most of the world's wealth before have once again become the movers and shakers of our planet. It seems that they have been bestowed huge amounts of NWCUs (New World Currency Units) so that they can continue the work that they had been involved with before the alien invasion.

I have no idea how this transpired or who was considered worthy of this generous distribution, and I'm the President of the United States and should know. I think that this is something to be feared. This disturbing distribution of wealth seemed to have happened in conjunction with the New World Bank (NWB) which controls the distribution and disbursement of all NWCUs, and as I understand it, was based on the stored wealth of precious metals and other valuables. What I find interesting about this is that there was no outcry when this occurred. No mobs in the streets demanding a more fair share. It happened so quietly, and before anyone detected it, the world's super-rich were super-rich again.

Now, this world elite is being allowed to purchase and use the new drugs designed to enhance the health and longevity of humans. These drugs were designed specifically for use for those going to space on deep space missions. The drugs were never intended for humanity at large, but the wealthy found out about the drugs because a few of the wealthy control the drug companies and now they have full access to these life-extending drugs. It's a well-kept secret from the public, though, because the last thing the wealthy want is to have the common man able to live too long at what they consider their expense.

The more things change, the more they stay the same.

How we came by the formula for the drugs and the advancements in space travel are a secret that I can not divulge in this written account. It's too sensitive and even the rest of the world, including the very wealthy, have no idea of the origin of that knowledge. I'm sure that someday that information will be revealed, but not here now and not by me. I take that to my grave...

Part 1

The New World Order

Chapter 1

State of the Union Address

Congress of the New World State of America

Earth Date: January 20, 2101

Thursday Evening, 6:00 EST

Sol: 338 of the Martian Solar Year

Speaker of the House, Democrat from the Great State of California, Walter Matson: "It is with great pleasure that I give you the President of the New World State of America, President Henry Dent!"

Dent stepped toward the podium, waving left and right, amidst enthusiastic applause. He paused there for a moment then said, "Thank you."

Another pause as the applause slowed, then he began, "My Fellow Americans, we have reached a turning point, not only for the United States of America but for the entire world. As always in our history, we have met every challenge and defeated every foe. We have always stuck to our core beliefs that all men are created equal and all deserve full respect. Our constitution, which was written more than three hundred years ago, set out values that we have embraced and even in the darkest of times, held fast to. Now we are threatened by a new enemy. One who would take our world from us without any reservations.

At this point in history, it is important that we unite with all other countries in the world to turn back this foe and bring the full strength of humanity to bear against those who would take the Earth for their own."

Short, mild Applause.

"I wouldn't choose this path or to join the world if I didn't think that the rest of the world would give themselves over to our core beliefs about the dignity of the individual and his right to self-reliance and the pursuit of happiness along with the other inalienable rights set out in that great document, The Bill of Rights."

Applause

"Now, however, we find ourselves on a precipice, balancing between certain annihilation or subjugation by an enemy, not from this world.

So, what are we to do? Shall we go quiet into that good night as Dylan Thomas' poem exhorted us not to do?"

Shouts of, "NO and NEVER."

"I say no, also. I say we fight. I say we prepare ourselves for war and to not go quietly when this foe returns and they certainly will."

Enthusiastic applause.

"Since the dawn of time when man began to band together into tribes, men have fought against each other. Now we must unite or our defeat is certain."

Applause.

"I have served the United States of America as President for 17 years, and since the impact of the asteroid which destroyed Russia and they, then were our enemy, but I can tell you this, that today, I wish we had them to help us in our mission. We need every human mind turned to our task and our goal for this planet to remain human despite our faults and failings of which we have many.
This is my last State of the Union..."

Sounds of shock rolled through the chamber, mostly from the Democrats.

"I am reinstituting national elections and together with the Congress of the United States will be officially lifting Martial Law as of midnight, tonight.

This November, we will have a special election to elect a new President of our great country."

Cheers.

"I will not run for re-election to the presidency of the United States. No one should ever be allowed to be president for as long as I have been. That isn't what our Constitution commanded and it isn't what I believe. It isn't the America that I envisioned when I ran for the White House."

Applause.

"It has been an honor to serve you for these years but my time is now past and the country must choose another leader who stands for the values set out in the Constitution. I have every confidence that you shall.

Last, let me say, let this day mark the end of the tyranny of man and usher in a new age of cooperation, a new age of the brotherhood of man, and let that brotherhood become a movement where we live together in peace and stand against those who would see our planet as theirs."

Shouts and applause.

"Goodnight and God Bless the United States of America and the world."

Standing ovation and enthusiastic applause.

Dent raised his hand in thanks and also in farewell. Walking from the podium, he stopped and shook every hand that was offered with a broad smile.

The Republican representative from Tennessee, Robert Jackson leaned over to his friend, the Republican representative from Arkansas, Allen Pierce, and whispered as he clapped, "You notice that he didn't say God Bless the New World State of America?"

Pierce nodded and whispered back, "A Freudian slip?"

"Maybe. Maybe he's not so thrilled about giving up our sovereignty."

"Maybe," Pierce replied not missing a clap or breaking his pasted-on smile.

Chapter 2

Earth

Spain

The Seville region, Isla Mayor

April 25, 2105

Sol 515

4 Years Later...

Martin, Pablo, Alejandro, and Sofia romped through a rice paddy a mile from Isla Mayor. The day was warm with little breeze and dressed in shorts and light tee shirts, they played tag at the edge of the fields. All of the kids were close in age, eight and nine and they all attended the same school in Isla Mayor.

Pablo stopped and gawked at an odd sight that puzzled him. He had been running from Sofia who was '*it*' and trying to tag him.

She ran up and slapped his back. "You're it."

Pablo didn't react. His attention was in front of him and on the ground.

Alejandro then ran up behind Pablo and gave him a shove that made him lose his balance. Pablo fell forward and Alejandro laughed and ran away. "You'll never get me!" he shrieked.

Pablo stumbled and landed face first in a puddle of the black liquid that he had seen pooling at his feet. There, a few feet further, was a sphere, slightly smaller than a bowling ball. It appeared to have a slight crack in it and the black liquid oozed from the crack.

Sofia laughed and ran away to get some distance from Pablo. When Pablo hit the black liquid, he stretched out his hands but that didn't prevent the liquid from nearly covering the front of his body and face. He spat out some of the liquid that had splashed into his mouth. Luckily, he had closed his eyes.

Martin ran up to him and laughed and said to Pablo, "You can't get me!" Martin paused, now seeing his friend straighten from the fall and holding out his arms and gazing at his now soaked ooze-covered clothes.

"Ouch!" Pablo said. "Something bit me!" He looked at his ooze-soaked armed turning his wrist to see his palm which was red with blood. He angrily said, "Look what you did to me!"

"Sorry," Alejandro said. "I didn't see that stuff. What is it?"

Pablo was nearly crying. He repeated, "Something bit me." He raised his hands and looked at blood dripping from a tiny wound in his palm.

Sofia said, "You just cut yourself. Don't be a baby."

Pablo looked closer at the place on his hand where the blood was dripping. Something white, the size of a small, hair-thin earthworm wriggled at the wound in the black thick liquid. It was no more than half an inch in length. He tried to brush it away but the worm seemed to quickly burrow into his hand. He wiped frantically.

The three friends watched Pablo wipe at his palm for a minute then Sofia approached and tried to wipe the black, thick liquid off of her friend's clothes.

"Help me!" she shouted.

Pablo looked at his hand with a kind of horror. "It crawled in me. I saw it go in me."

"What?" Sofia asked.

"A white worm. It's under my skin. I think I need to see the doctor."

"Come on. Let's get you back."

Martin and Alejandro stared at the black pool that was spreading slowly on the ground. Tiny wormlike creatures moved under the opaque, viscous liquid, occasionally rising to the surface.

"Help me clean Pablo up," Sofia commanded.

Pablo stood there in a kind of shock as his three friends began to brush the black liquid from his clothes. The children could see an occasional worm wriggle and fall to the ground.

Sofia took Pablo's uninjured hand and began pulling him forward toward the town.

Pablo said, "I don't feel so well."

When he looked down at his wounded hand, his fingernails were slightly blue.

Sofia dragged Pablo forward and the other two followed. By the time they reached the town, Pablo could barely walk and the other three were becoming ill with flulike symptoms.

When they reached their homes, their parents could tell that something was very wrong with their children. They lifted them and rushed them to the hospital. Within an hour the parents were becoming ill also. By the next hour, several of the nurses were becoming sick and by the next day, some of their families.

The doctors had been alerted to alien spheres that the children had come across but none had previously been found around their town.

The kids had become so sick that they couldn't speak and were hospitalized.

Chapter 3

Mars Orbit

Space Station Isla Bravo

April 26, 2105

Sol 516

20 thousand miles above the Martian surface, the American space station, Isla Bravo, spun silently near Mars' L2 Lagrange point, a stable orbit with Mars sitting between the station and the Sun. Before the station, a sliver of Mars could be seen, rotating, red and pockmarked with some blue water and wispy white clouds now evident from the terraforming with the rest of Mars in shadow. On the opposite side, the sun was a bright ball of light nearly one-hundred and forty-two million miles away.

The station's mission to protect the planet from wayward asteroids had been a success with zero unwanted collisions since the station's arrival and nearly a hundred wanted collisions of asteroids and comets that were carrying desired chemicals to the Martian surface.

Mars' two moons, Phobos and Demos orbited the planet more than 10 thousand miles below. According to the math, Phobos would, sometime in the next 10 million years, crash into the Martian surface. There was a plan underway to maneuver the descending moon back away from the planet.

Preparations for the feared alien invasion were underway on Earth but proceeding slowly. The problem was that the aliens who invaded the Earth seven years before were too advanced for our current technology.

Small enhancements and improvements gave the Earth only a slightly increased chance of success against the invaders and the world was in such disarray that vast amounts of attention and resources had to be put into its rebuilding.

The hope was to learn something from the captured alien technology found at the wormhole just past Neptune's orbit, but the recovered parts hadn't reached any place where they could be studied in depth.

Space Station, Isla Bravo

0700 Hours

Taylor Chapman worked on the bridge of Isla Bravo. Her job on the station was to identify, discover, monitor, and track any incoming asteroids or comets that could strike the planet or endanger the space vehicles that lay in Mars' orbit.

She had risen a few minutes earlier and slipped from bed dressed in only skin. The room where she stayed was an eight by eight cubical. It was small even for one person, let alone two with one twin bed and a desk with a computer monitor atop, a chair, and not much more. There was a blue tarp ceiling that rippled with the spinning of the station and a blue plastic-coated grate floor that showed conduit and ductwork below. Tall and thin, she was built like a long-distance runner with light brown hair pulled back into a ponytail. Her eyes were lively and blue but light, unlike her boyfriend Kirk Matthews' eyes which were dark blue, nearly violet. Her skin was pale and made even more so because she hadn't been in the sun for at least two years.

"Where are you going?" Kirk Matthews asked groggily, still in bed.

"I want to get an early start," she replied, walking to a dispenser that contained wipes. Still nude from their night together, she pulled a wipe and began her sponge bath.

"Come back to bed for a bit."

"No, Kirk."

"Come on," he whispered suggestively. "I'll do unspeakable things to you."

"You have a one-track mind."

"And right now, that track is on your body."

"Right now?"

"Well, it is a very nice body. Come on back to bed."

"No. Get up."

He covered his face with his pillow.

Kirk was an asteroid jockey, one of the pilots trained on the AKs which were vehicles designed to intercept and divert asteroids away from Mars or onto the planet if possible, to deliver important chemicals to the surface. He was around six feet with dark hair and chiseled features.

Taylor finished her bath as Kirk watched then she began dressing. After slipping on her underclothes, she pulled on a NASA blue jumpsuit, zipping the front. She sat to tie her shoes.

"Come on, Kirk. I don't want to miss getting a seat on the shuttle to the surface. The next one doesn't leave for over an hour and we're supposed to meet Mo and his date."

"Come back to bed with me for a few minutes. We have a little time."

"I'm already dressed."

"So, undress. I always appreciate that."

"Kirk," Taylor said, finally exasperated.

He breathed out.

Taylor said excitedly, "I can't wait to see the new mall."

In the last two years, there had been an explosion of building on the Martian surface. The new Noachis Terra Mall had been finished just a week before and was a testimony to human engineering and design.

Kirk rose and sat on the side of his bunk rubbing his face then stood. Taylor walked to him, hugged him, and patted his bare backside then rested her hands there.

"Come on. I want to get going," she implored.

"Alright," he said, resigned then bent and kissed her lips softly.

They separated and he quickly brushed his teeth, washed those desired parts of his body in most need, disposed of the wipe, and pulled on his boxers while Taylor watched on with growing impatience.

The grand opening of Noachis Terra Mall had been a big deal. The ribbon-cutting ceremony, a few days before was televised all over the world. Kirk's uncle, General Jeffery Matthews cut the ceremonial ribbon with a big smile and it was thought that the unveiling of the mall would tempt others to take the chance to be part of the colonizing of the red planet. Mars had rumors leak out that more than a few colonists had been killed by subterranean creatures that had emerged from caves on the planet several years before and that shrunk the pool of people wanting to go. The United States denied the rumors but they persisted.

Kirk said, "I'm hungry. Maybe we should eat then catch the next shuttle."

"No. It might be full and I want to eat at the mall."

"But I'm hungry."

"You're always hungry... god, you're winy today."

"That's true, but I am *really* hungry this morning."

"Kirk, you're *really* pissing me off."

"Okay, I'll grab a breakfast bar. I think I have one laying around somewhere." He glanced around then pulled open a drawer on his desk. "There it is."

Kirk finished tying his shoes then took a bite of the bar and stood. "Alright, I'm ready."

Both were now in their NASA blue jumpsuits, the typical dress for anyone who was directly employed by NASA. Before, nearly everyone who would be encountered on Mars would be in these jumpsuits. Now, people who worked on the surface of Mars and who were colonists would be dressed differently being employed by different corporations providing services to NASA and the New World Government.

Taylor said, "I can't wait to see the museum exhibit. I hear it's just like walking into the Louvre in Paris."

"I know. The whole thing sounds amazing."

Noachis Terra Mall was built in the very center of the rapidly expanding JFK City. The mall covered ten sprawling acres but still wasn't completed. New additions were constantly being added for all the new exhibits that were planned for this destination point which was designed to make the colonists of Mars feel more at home.

JFK City itself had grown to well over two thousand people with a thousand more scheduled to arrive within the next three months, most of which would be construction crews. There were another two hundred people manning the two space stations that circled Mars, Isla Bravo, Isla Charlie, and the ten rockets that were in a stable orbit to maintain the magnetic shield and communications around the planet.

To the west of the mall was mostly industrial with greenhouse gas-producing factories to continue the terraforming process. To the mall's south, there were mostly utilities like electric, water desalinization, and waste reclamation. All waste, including human, was used for fertilizer after an extensive process to make it safe. A large underground lake had been discovered containing salty water that was bacteria free and the water was piped to the water treatment plant.

To the north, large greenhouse farms were growing fruits and vegetables for consumption for the colonists. There were also large greenhouses that were preparing different varieties of pine trees that had been genetically modified to handle the harsh, though improving, Martian environment. To this point, only lichen and moss had been planted on the surface and both were beginning to grow in abundance.

The landscape was greening and liquid water moved in small rivers that flowed to the growing lakes and seas that were dotting the planet. Soon, cyanobacteria (Blue Algae) would be released into the Great Northern Ocean which was filling, to increase the oxygen levels in the atmosphere. It was believed that the cyanobacteria were what increased the oxygen levels on Earth around 2.7 billion years before. They use photosynthesis to convert carbon dioxide into oxygen.

Mars had, in just over a decade, changed into a wet and warming planet, something only dreamed about in the not too distant past. The next step would be to turn it green.

To the east of Noachis Terra Mall was Condo City. Though called that in slang, it was part of JFK City and it boasted of condominiums and townhouses for the colonists and a hotel-like structure for visiting dignitaries and R and R for the NASA employees who worked the space stations. So far, the hotel was first come first serve, and free, but the rumor was that a large hotel conglomerate was going to buy the hotel and had begun to build a new luxury hotel on the surface nearby and charge big NWCU's (New World Currency Units) to stay there.

There goes the neighborhood.

Condo City was built close to the Mall and connected, like every place, to the mall by underground tunnels, some of which were human expressways with escalator-like moving floors, the kind found in airports.

There was also a rail system constructed underground that crisscrossed the entire city built to ferry workers from Condo City to the various workplaces. People no longer slept in the domes that were built originally as the space was needed for industrial purposes.

Mars was now reaching a point of self-sustaining including the ability to use resources from the Martian environment as building materials. Some things still could not be produced on the red planet like most high-tech and medicines which still needed to be produced on Earth and most protein for consumption also came from Earth. In the last year, and sent frozen, beef, pork, fish, and poultry had been rocketed to Mars with most of it going to the several restaurants that were located in the mall.

Close to Condo City was an infirmary and several places where the inhabitants could eat 24 hours a day or as it is on Mars, 24 hours and thirty-nine minutes, the length of a Martian day.

To the northeast of the mall, just past the landing port, was a secret facility newly built and designed to study the bodies and technology of the alien armada that was destroyed at the wormhole found just beyond Neptune. Though exhaustive steps were taken to sterilize the alien wreckage, the world's governing body was too spooked to bring it to Earth just in case something virulent might show up and wipe out the population, just as what happened when the Europeans arrived in the New World and brought Smallpox and other lovely maladies to the indigenous Indians that lived in North America. The world's governing body thought it was better to be safe than sorry.

Some countries on Earth were not so happy about this decision, though, because they thought it was a way to exclude them from the technology. They were right to be concerned.

The space station containing the alien vessels and bodies was soon to arrive on Mars within the next month. Though the wreckage was discovered some years before, it was a monumental task to collect and sterilize items found by the wormhole and chosen for study.

Taylor and Kirk walked from Kirk's room, turned, and then strolled down the gravity ring on Isla Bravo where they were both stationed. Isla Bravo's ring was over an eight-hundred-yard round trip from beginning to end. Most of Isla Bravo's stations like the bridge, infirmary, galley, and flight bays were all lined up around the ring.

They reached the shuttle bay.

Mo Roberts was there with his date, Nancy Cho, a relatively new pilot who just transferred from Isla Alpha which was still in orbit around the Earth.

"Hi, Mo. Hi, Nancy," Kirk said.

"Hey, guys," Mo said. "Taylor, this is Nancy. Nancy, Taylor."

Nancy smiled and they shook hands.

Mo was from Louisiana and seemed to be a mixture of nearly every race with dark wavy hair and dark eyes, a kind smile, and a Cajun accent.

His first name was really Montana, named after the state where he was born by his mom who was from there, though he only spent the first ten days of his life in the state. His parents had gone back there for a wedding when his mom was nine months along.

Mo was born a couple of weeks early and his mom said that he wanted to be born in the state so hence the name. He tends to disagree with her assessment of that, however, and always introduces himself as Mo because he doesn't like the way people draw out the name, *Monnntaaannna,* as if it can't be pronounced any other way. He says it's annoying.

His father was from New Orleans where he was raised. Mo was also in a blue NASA jumpsuit.

Nancy was from the first wave of pilots from Asia. From South Korea, she immigrated to the United States to train just after the New World Government became law. She then transferred to Isla Alpha, stationed in Earth orbit, then was transferred to Isla Bravo two weeks prior.

Isla Alpha had been the first of the spinning space stations built by the United States and designed by Egbert, the alien artifact discovered in 2085 at a dinosaur dig site in Wyoming. When the artifact was placed under a simple light, it came to life and revealed its secrets, projecting a bright hologram from its surface. It was found to be an advanced artificially intelligent machine with the ability to learn, designed by some alien race and placed on Earth millions of years in the past.

Nancy Cho was a weapon systems specialist for the next generation AK4000, an asteroid interceptor with significant upgrades to the AK3000, AK2200, and the AK2100, all still in service and being used extensively to steer asteroids away from Earth and Mars and occasionally onto the Martian surface if the asteroid contained important chemicals like nitrogen or H_2O water in the form of ice.

Ellen Granger, the shuttle's pilot stepped towards the cockpit of the shuttle. She said, "Everyone coming on this flight should board now. We're out of here in ten minutes."

Kirk, Mo, Nancy, and Taylor all turned towards the bay hatch and climbed down into the shuttle. They sat together in the last row and waited as the shuttle went through its final flight checklist.

The shuttle had 60 seats set in ten rows of six. Nearly all were full.

Ellen Granger came on the com, "Buckle up. We're out of here in 60 seconds. 59, 58..."

The passenger hatch was closed and everyone on the shuttle buckled their seatbelts and waited as Granger counted down to the time when she would detach from the spinning station. "... 5, 4, 3, 2, 1. Detaching from Isla Bravo."

There was a loud click as the shuttle was magnetically released. For a moment, everyone could still feel the gravity, but then, as the shuttle floated from the station, the unmistakable sensation of weightlessness began and anything not nailed down began to float. Taylor's ponytail stuck straight out.

Kirk said, "Hey, Mo, Taylor said that there is a museum exhibit from the Louvre in Paris."

"I heard that too. I can't wait."

"Me either," Nancy agreed.

Kirk said, "Let's eat first. I'm dying for a hamburger."

"Sounds good," Mo agreed.

Taylor glanced at Nancy and smiled wryly. Nancy shook her head and said, "I guess I could eat a bit."

As the shuttle banked left, the sense of G-force could be felt as it accelerated forward. Through the side portholes, Mars loomed large and still mostly red but now with blue patches and wispy cloud formations. Forty-five minutes to landing at the main entrance of Noachis Terra Mall.

Chapter 4

April 26, 2105

Sol 516

0830 Hours

The shuttle from Isla Bravo breached the Martian atmosphere and descended rapidly toward the surface. As it neared JFK City, the sprawling complex came into view. Covering twenty square miles, from the air, the city was stark white with rows of blue solar panels against the ruddy Martian surface. Today, obscured somewhat by a sandstorm, the mall appeared then disappeared under the waves of blowing red soil.

The shuttle maneuvered toward a large platform, then stopped in midair, and descended straight down as if it were a helicopter. Buffeted by the high wind and blowing Martian soil, the shuttle rocked and swayed. It touched down lightly onto the platform. Through the windows of the shuttle, the passengers could see the raging storm swirling the fine red sand in brief vortexes some of which spun high into the air in the distance. Today was a rare dry day. Since the terraforming process had fully taken hold, Mars was in a constant state of rain or fog with few dry sunny days. It was thought, though, that as the atmospheric pressure increased, this cycle would stabilize and there would be more sunny days but exactly when that would occur, no one really knew, maybe years, decades, or centuries.

The platform began its slow descent and as it did so, huge doors closed over the top of the structure. When the elevator reached the floor, it was met by a large truck that attached a towbar to the shuttle's underside and the truck pulled the shuttle to a side entrance of the mall which lay four stories underground and close to a substantial airlock that could hold at least a hundred people standing side by side.

The shuttle pulled into the docking bay at Noachis Terra Mall and an automated tunnel extended out to connect to the shuttle's side hatch. The sound of magnetic attachment and pressurization could be heard as the tunnel sealed itself to the shuttle's wide side door.

"Noachis Terra Mall," Ellen Granger announced as if she were a bus driver on a sightseeing tour in Los Angeles. "Exit to your right, make sure you have all your belongings, have a safe trip, and thank you for flying Air Isla Bravo."

The sarcasm was obvious and several people laughed.

"Let's go," Taylor said like a schoolgirl heading to a favorite event.

She rose, smiling with the rest of the passengers, and she, Mo, Kirk, and Nancy filed toward the now open shuttle side hatch.

The group from Isla Bravo walked two by two through the tunnel and into a large airlock. A mall attendant waited as the group filled the space. He was tall and thin and wearing an ill-fitted suit and tie. A strange sight on Mars but everything on the planet was changing. He had on a name badge containing the logo for the Noachis Terra Mall which was the name of the mall stretched in an arc across the top of the badge and an artist rendition of the building itself, built on the rocky Martian surface. His name, "Tom," was printed over the image of the building.

"Please step forward," Tom cheerfully exhorted. "Welcome to Noachis Terra Mall. We have several new exhibits open today with more to come. The aquarium has just opened and the museum room is featuring exhibits from the Louvre in Paris. We have just finished changing the entryway of the mall to the giant Sequoia Redwoods of Humboldt County, California."

A second airlock door slid open to a hallway that led into the mall. The hallway was twenty-foot wide, a hundred-foot-long and rose to a forty-foot, cathedral ceiling. The entire hallway was an impressive projection of the giant redwoods on both the left and the right.

Everyone who walked off of the shuttle stared in wonder at this amazing scene. Living images of the redwoods swayed gently with their rough reddish bark and wide trunks lining the walkway and stretching high above to meet a misty sky in the center of the cathedral ceiling. The tops of the trees were obscured by the mist. A soft, cool breeze blew through the walkway, and the trees and thick ferns that bunched around the trunks of the trees seemed to move with the breeze. Colonists sat on benches and gazed up at the serene scene.

Tom continued as the passengers stepped into the long hallway, "The tallest of these trees was measured to a height of three hundred and sixteen feet and over thirty-one feet in diameter. They are a true wonder of the world. Enjoy your visit to the mall and have a good day."

Everyone continued to stare overhead.

Kirk said, "Man, this is just like being back on Earth."

"I think that's the point," Mo commented.

Taylor said, "I love the redwood forests. It's the kind of place where you would think you might find an elf or maybe a fairy."

Kirk said, "You have such an imagination but not far from the truth. Those forests seem like a place where magic would live."

Nancy said, "I've never been to the redwood forests."

Taylor said, "If you ever end up in Northern California, it's a place you have to see."

Nancy nodded.

They continued down the hallway until they reached its end where it opened onto a wide foyer. The redwood projection abruptly ended at the edge of the tall hallways' walls.

This section of the mall had an area set up like a Japanese Garden, wide and expansive, with low mounds of soil planted with small Japanese Maples of green and red. Upon closer inspection, you could tell that the maples were a good reproduction but not real. Winding through the Maples was a narrow stream with pools that contained orange and white koi. Faux moss covered the mounds in places and gravel-lined walkways led to where colonists could sit. Five stories above, skylights looked into the Martian sky which was becoming bluer by the day but today appeared to be red as the raging dust storm blew over the skylights.

Against the far wall was a projection of the Pacific Ocean taken on a sunny day with calm waves lapping a fine sand beach. The projection was the full fives stories and stretched the length of the wall where it met two other hallways that led to the right and left of the foyer. Written on signs by these hallways were "Food Court, shops, theater and aquarium to the left and museum exhibit to the right.

Kirk pointed to the left and said, "Let's go eat."

Taylor nodded and gazing around said, "This place is a wonder."

Everyone agreed.

Nothing on Earth was anything like this mall. The view of the Pacific Ocean was so startlingly real that you could almost smell the salt and the soft sound of waves lapping the shore could be heard.

They walked through the Japanese garden foyer to the left on wide cement walkways reminiscent of those that outline the beach that separates it from the hotels on Maui where sun enthusiasts might stroll, skate, or ride bikes. They strolled through the gardens and seating areas where colonists sat and talked. Couples sat close together and stared out at the ocean scene.

As they left the ocean foyer, they entered another hallway with shops on each side. In the center of the hallway were sitting areas on flagstone patios with flowers in planters. There was a small gift shop, a store with clothing, and another with paperback books. A sign in the window stated, "No book over 4 NWCUs."

"Look," Taylor said, "a bookstore. You know, we could use a library here."

Kirk said, "You have a library, the computer in your room."

"I know but you can't hold the book on a computer. It works and I'm not knocking it, but sometimes I like to walk by the books and gaze at the covers, then pick one up and turn a couple of pages. You know what I mean? Sometimes the story just leaps out at you and begs to be read."

Mo said, "There's barely any bookstores left on Earth."

Taylor said, "Yeah, but we still have libraries there. I love libraries. It may be what I miss most about Earth."

"I miss outside," Kirk said.

"I do too," Nancy agreed, "and fresh fruit. It's been ages since I've had a fresh peach or a bite of watermelon."

Mo said, "I miss good pizza, the kind thick with cheese, great crust, and cooked in a wood-burning oven."

Kirk said, "I remember when we were at the Academy and they had this great guacamole at a bar by the base. I loved that guacamole." Then Kirk smiled wistfully and said, "And I miss the beer."

They continued to walk past the shops.

"When I met you, Kirk," Taylor said, "Your face was stuck in a glass of Jack Daniels."

"Yeah, well, that was for medicinal purposes." Then Kirk laughed and said, "Then my face was stuck to you."

Taylor nodded and blushed but didn't comment.

Kirk said, "We used to go to that bar with Jason all the time, he, Sandy, and me." Kirk smiled, bringing back a memory of the brother that Taylor had lost in a battle with the Russians in space, then continued, "Damn, Jason was a good guy and a good friend."

Taylor's eyes filled with tears for a moment then she said, "I'm glad you have good memories of him. I do too."

Kirk laughed again and said, "I remember when Jason was all mad at me because he thought I took your virtue."

Taylor smiled a bit ruefully and then said, "Yeah, he could be a pain in the ass sometimes, besides, I gave what there was of that virtue pretty willingly." She flopped and arm around Kirk and gave him a quick squeeze and a kiss on the cheek. She let him go and Kirk's face reddened.

Nancy giggled at that.

"He was a good guy," Kirk repeated.

They walked silently for a bit.

Mo asked, "Hey, Kirk, have you heard from Sandy Jones lately?"

"Yeah, he sent me a message a couple of days ago. I guess that they are moving him to head the new fleet of Predator warships."

"Huh. So, he's being promoted to Commander?"

"Yep. The fleet is being deployed to protect the planet. Twenty warships in all. Sandy says that they are as bad as hell. Serious weapons and maybe a match for the alien ship that attacked Earth before."

"That's good. I hope he's right."

"He usually is."

When the group reached the end of the hallway with the shops, there was a sign that pointed left for the food court and right to the aquarium and theater. They turned left and walked down a short hallway that opened into the food court.

The space was wide with many tables and chairs and had four places where the colonists could order food. Each colonist had a food allotment credit that gave them a per diem of NWCUs for food. They could spend more, but the electronic money would come out of their account or would stand as a credit against future earnings. Here they could order wine or beer, but each person was allowed no more than two drinks per day and their account would not allow any more. This was partially to avoid alcoholism on Mars, but also because it was difficult to get supplies to the red planet, especially when it was far from Earth. The amount shipped was carefully measured according to the number of humans on or orbiting the planet at any one time.

The food court had the appearance of a restaurant that might overlook the ocean built on a boardwalk. It had a faux wooden floor, faux wooden beams stretching across its length, and hanging saucer-shaped lights with large, round, clear lightbulbs. The windows were projections that showed scenes as if looking through large bay windows at rows of docks with sailboats and fishing boats moored. Seagulls flew in and out of view and in the background, the faint sounds of the gulls, the ocean lapping the shore, and the sound of boat hulls against the wooden docks could be heard.

"Who is that crowd?" Kirk asked, looking at a small group of people standing between two of the restaurants. They were pointing and looking around. The group didn't appear like they belonged on Mars. No one who was dressed the way they were had ever shone up on the red planet before. The four men were wearing expensive suits and the three women were in skirts and appeared very businesslike. They all stood straight and Kirk noticed something about them that set off an alarm but he couldn't figure out what it was that struck him as odd. Something wasn't right.

Taylor glanced at the group and turned to look at Kirk. She could tell by his expression that he was turning something over in his mind.

She asked, "What is it, Kirk?"

"I don't know. There's something about that group, something that seems wrong."

Nancy said, "Like they're filthy rich."

"No, it's more than that."

Kirk, Mo, Nancy, and Taylor watched as the group chatted and pointed at the structure of the building. There were maybe twenty people eating at tables around the food court. It seemed when one of the colonists or workers walked past the businesspeople, they glanced at the person with a kind of disdain as if they might be infected by some kind of disease from the worker.

"Huh," Kirk grunted, then, "Let's go get a burger."

Kirk, Nancy, Mo, and Taylor turned and walked to order a hamburger at a counter. An older Asian man in his fifties with grey hair and a kind smile greeted them as they approached. Behind him, a hot grill smoked with several hamburgers sizzling and french fries bubbling in oil next to the grill. A pile of cooked onions sat on the right side of the grill, caramelized and waiting for the hamburgers to finish. Next to the onions, six buttered buns toasted on the flat top. The man wore a name tag that said, "Lenny."

Kirk approached first. "Hi, Lenny. I'm Kirk. I think you're going to see a lot of me here. This is just like home."

"That's what I was hoping to bring," Lenny said. "I'm from Los Angeles and had a small burger place near Venice Beach. When they started advertising for colonists to go to Mars, I applied, but they said I was too old. I didn't give up, though. I had a customer who was a big shot at a military base near Long Beach and I asked him if he could pull a string or two to get me here. He did and here I am. I just had to pass the physical. Everything I get is frozen, of course, but if you prepare it just right, it's almost like home. I'm hoping to get fresh lettuce from the greenhouses on Mars at some point and maybe fresh tomatoes."

"Oh, man, fresh tomatoes," Mo said wistfully.

Lenny smiled, "What can I get you?"

Kirk said, "What do you want, Taylor?"

"I'll have a burger with grilled onions and fries."

"Do you want Cheese?"

"Oh yeah and a beer."

"Just a minute," Lenny said and he left the counter and put together the burgers and fries that were already cooking. He plated the food and called out, "63."

A guy who appeared to be a construction worker walked up and lifted the tray. He said, "Do you have ketchup for the fries?"

Lenny said, "Yeah, just to the right. There's napkins there also."

"Thanks," the guy replied.

Lenny came back to Kirk's group. He glanced at Nancy.

She said, "Ah, I'll have a hotdog."

Lenny wrote it down then glanced at Kirk.

Kirk said, "I want a double with cheese and grilled onions, fries, and a beer."

Mo said, "I'll have the same."

"Coming right up," Lenny said with a glint in his eye.

The four found a table that looked out onto the docks where 4 men prepared to leave in a small fishing boat. The men laughed as they stepped aboard the boat holding fishing rods and coolers probably filled with beer.

Kirk, Mo, Nancy, and Taylor gazed around not talking and taking in this food court. Its beams stretched across a high, rustic wooden planked ceiling that met grayed planked walls that seemed weathered as if they had been in a building by the ocean for a century. All of it was fashioned plastic but that didn't matter. On the projections looking outside through the windows, one of the fishermen threw a rope that held the boat to the dock onto the wooden planks and he pushed the boat away. The boat floated from the dock, then a motor started and the boat started out toward open water and disappeared in the distance.

Lenny loudly said, "Number 64, Kirk."

"That's us," Kirk said, rising.

"I'll help," Mo said.

They both walked toward the counter where their food awaited.

Once out of earshot, Kirk said, "You and Nancy seem to be getting along pretty well."

"Yeah, pretty well," Mo said with some reservation.

"What is it?" Kirk asked.

"I don't know. It's just the second time we've kind of been together. I'm just getting to know her."

Kirk nodded and they walked the food back to the table.

Taylor said, "Thanks," then said, "I wonder if they'll ever have a Chinese restaurant here. I really miss Chinese food."

"That would be great," Mo agreed. "And I also wouldn't mind a beignet."

"Yeah, man," Kirk agreed, "And shrimp Creole with dirty rice."

"You talking my language, me," Mo said in his heaviest Cajun accent and smiling.

Kirk handed out the food and they began eating. Because they all hadn't had Earth food for some time, they ate quietly with soft sounds of happiness slipping out between bites.

Kirk, with his mouth full, said, "Oh, man, this is too good. I don't want the meal to end."

"It is good," Taylor agreed with a chuckle. She hadn't opened her eyes between bites.

Kirk glanced at Nancy. "How's the hot dog?"

"Too good," Nancy agreed, wiping a glop of mustard from the corner of her mouth.

Kirk said, "I might have one of those for dessert."

Mo smiled and said, "Let's stay for dinner."

"Hell yes!" Kirk agreed.

They all laughed.

Kirk glanced around and saw the group of businesspeople walk over to the entrance to the shops. He took a sip of beer, not taking his eyes from the group. They stopped at the entrance and appeared, again, to be interested in the structure. The main guy doing most of the talking walked the group back to a place that had a large window that overlooked the Martian landscape outside. This window was to the rear of the food court and had no projections. The wind continued to blow the ruddy soil against the building and the window. He pointed and gestured and the people with him nodded.

Kirk took another long sip of his beer and put down the glass. Mo and Taylor were chuckling about something that he didn't hear, but Nancy was looking at Kirk directly.

Kirk glanced her way and she said, "What is it, Kirk? You look like you saw a ghost."

Kirk said, "What's wrong with them? The people in the suits, I mean. I'm missing something."

Taylor took her attention from Mo and turned to Kirk and said, "What?"

Nancy said, "They look like mannequins. Their skin is too perfect. Even the men, who don't generally have such nice skin."

Taylor and Mo then both turned their attention to the group of businesspeople.

"You're right," Taylor said then observed, "And they all appear to be nearly the same age."

A chill ran up Kirk's spine. He said, "That's it."

"What?" Mo asked.

"Yeah, I mean, ah, they seem to be the same age. Maybe that's it."

Taylor and Mo glanced at Kirk suspiciously. Nancy didn't know Kirk well, so she just thought that the comment was a little strange.

Kirk said, "Let's go to the aquarium."

The group of businesspeople walked from sight and seemed to head into the mall.

After finishing their food, Kirk's group took their trays to a designated area then walked to the aquarium.

It was small by aquarium standards on Earth but had three long corridors of fish tanks set up with different kinds of fish, jellyfish, and shellfish. A large tank filled one wall close to the exit with chairs set up for people who wanted to stop, sit, and watch the fish. The fish in this tank were larger than the rest and Kirk wondered how the fish survived the nine months of weightlessness in order to make it to Mars.

They walked back through the shops to the ocean foyer then to the museum area. This place had a series of hallways with projections that mimicked the Louvre in Paris with all of the art and other exhibits. Finishing with the museum, they walked back to the restaurants and had pizza for dinner.

They caught the shuttle back to Isla Bravo. Once back, Kirk and Taylor said goodbye to Mo and Nancy who hadn't seemed to get along all that well. There just wasn't any chemistry though both Mo and Nancy were very attractive and genuinely nice people. Their personalities just didn't seem to fit well together.

When Kirk and Taylor stepped into Kirk's cubical, they undressed, fatigued from the day. They brushed their teeth and slipped into Kirk's bed. Kirk slid his hands under Taylor's tee shirt feeling the skin on her smooth back. She slid her hands inside the back of his boxers.

"I had a great time today," Taylor said, leaning in and giving Kirk a kiss on his lips.

"So did I. It made me a bit homesick, though."

Taylor folded herself into Kirk's arms and they cuddled close together.

She said, "It made me a bit homesick, too, but you have to admit, it brought a bit of home here to Mars. It's a pretty bleak planet."

"Yeah, but it's getting better. I hear that they're going to start planting pine trees close to the running rivers a few miles from here. They say that the water there isn't as salty as the sitting water around the planet."

"Wow," Taylor said, turning towards Kirk. "We might live long enough to see a pine forest."

"Just might."

She paused and snuggled back to Kirk then asked, "So, Kirk, what was that about today when we were talking about those business people?"

Kirk found Taylor's ear then whispered, "Remember when I told you that my uncle had been given drugs that made him younger?"

She nodded.

"That's how those people looked. As if they had been given the same drugs. I noticed that my uncle didn't just look younger. He had this odd unnatural look like he'd been dipped in wax or as if he'd been given too many facelifts. It isn't too far off from natural, and it took me a while to see it in him, but once I figured it out, it was obvious."

Taylor looked at Kirk and nodded again then commented, "Weird."

"Yeah, weird."

Taylor said, "I did have a good time today."

"Me too," Kirk agreed.

"Back to work, tomorrow."

"Yep."

Taylor kissed Kirk and then sat up in bed and suggestively pulled off her tee-shirt and let it fall to the floor gazing into Kirk's eyes. Topless, she bent back to him and he kissed her lips, then her neck, then her shoulder. He let his lips trace the skin on her upper chest. She then guided his mouth to her small breast and he kissed her nipple toying with it as it rose to him. He took it into his mouth sucking it gently and reached for her lower parts. She held his head and watched him and then pushed his mouth hard against her and whispered breathlessly, "Ohhh, I do like that." She breathed out...

Chapter 5

Antimatter is the opposite of matter having negatively charged particles. One of the great mysteries of the universe is that there should be an equal amount of antimatter and positively charge matter within it but there is nearly no antimatter to be found. Scientists do not know why. When antimatter comes in contact with positively charged matter, they annihilate each other causing a reaction that can be used as an unlimited fuel source.

Mars Orbit

L1 Lagrange point

Space Station Isla Charlie

Isla Charlie, the huge double wheeled space station spun silently in space in a stable orbit fifty-thousand miles above the Martian surface between Mars and the Sun. This was the third space station built by the United States and boasted twenty AKs, the vehicles designed by the alien artifact, Egbert, to divert or destroy asteroids that might threaten Earth and now, Mars. Each AK was equipped with missiles and 50 caliber Gatling gun weapon systems and like all the space vehicles in the fleet, these were powered by antimatter.

Also mostly powered by antimatter were the space station's twin wheels which spun and nearly produce the gravity of Earth at the edges of the outer portions of the solar cell covered rings.

General Jeffery Matthews, Kirk Matthews' uncle, the de facto commander of Mars, was stationed on this spinning island in space. He was joined by the alien artifact, Egbert, the AI discovered on Earth in 2085 and the egg's twin discovered on Mars some years later. Both artifacts had gone dark after revealing their secrets at least for now. They both seemed to divulge what information they wanted and when they wanted. When asked any question that they couldn't or did not wish to answer, they simply stated, "That they do not contain that information."

May 1, 2105

Sol 521

1000 Hours

As is the protocol, General Matthews arrived at the infirmary for his monthly checkup. No one else aboard the space station has a monthly check-up, but the General has a particular condition. He had been given the life-lengthening drug Biocare which requires a continual close look.

He entered the waiting room and knocked on the inside door.

"Just a minute," Doctor Belinda Waters said from the inside. "Have a seat."

The infirmary was basic. It had three separate rooms, one a waiting room, one for exams, and another for emergencies where operations could be performed. It was well designed to make use of the available space. There was a pharmacy connected to the examination room and two nurses aboard assisted the doctor when needed, but like most people stationed on Isla Charlie, the nurses served double duty in other places on the station when not needed by the doctor.

The door opened and a woman walked out of the examination room with Doctor Waters trailing behind. The woman was in her early thirties, fit with light brown hair and brown eyes.

The doctor was tall and stately, lean with a kind face and long auburn hair pulled into a ponytail that was just beginning to show the occasional strand of gray.

"Hello, General," the woman said as she saw General Matthews sitting on a chair.

General Matthews stood and replied, "Hello, Lynn." Lynn Anderson was one of the station's shuttle pilots. "Hope all is well with you?"

Lynn said, "Yes, General, fine. Just a checkup."

"Great," Matthews responded.

"You're up, General," Doctor Waters said.

The General nodded.

"Thanks, Doc," Lynn said, then, "Goodbye, General."

He nodded again and Lynn walked out of the infirmary. The General turned for the examination room followed by the doctor who shut the door behind her as they entered.

"Let's get you out of those clothes, General, every stitch."

He stepped behind a curtain and sat in a chair taking off his shoes and socks. Once out of his clothes, he slipped on a gown that opened in the back.

Doctor Waters checked his chart that was displayed on a computer pad. She turned the pages with a swipe of her finger.

Waters had a narrow face, sharp nose, and brown eyes. In a white lab coat, she wore reading glasses.

As the General walked from behind the curtain, the doctor was staring intently at the pad. She noticed the General emerge and she said, "On the table, please." She didn't look up.

The General did as ordered and sat on the edge of an examination bed that had a paper barrier stretched over its length. The paper crinkled.

He exhaled.

Doctor Waters turned toward him.

"How's everything going, Jeff?"

"Good. No complaints."

"I see you just had a birthday. You're now a spry 85 years old."

"Geez. I feel much younger," the General said with a wry grin.

Though 85, General Matthews had been the first test subject for the new life-lengthening drugs designed by Egbert to extend the lives of people destined for space travel. The drugs also enhanced the body's ability to protect itself from the harmful radiation that occurred naturally in space. The unintended consequences of the drugs, however, were that they reversed the aging process and now the 85-year-old General Matthews appeared to be somewhere around 30 with brown, military cut hair, no grey, and a fit body.

General Matthews had also been diagnosed with stage four lung cancer over ten years before and the drugs seem to have completely cured him of that.

Waters said, "I'm glad that the new dosage of the drugs has allowed your age to stabilize. At the rate you were reverse aging, you'd be about twelve by now."

Matthews smiled.

Waters pulled the gown off of the General's shoulders and allowed it to fall into his lap. She listened to his heart and lungs.

"Sounds good," she said. "Stand up for me," she commanded in her doctor's voice. "I have some more personal things to check on this visit."

She pulled the gown from the General and reached for his testicles, checking each for lumps, then had him bend over and gave him a prostate exam. She swiped the gloved hand across a test strip to check for blood in the stool.

"Everything seems to be in order, General."

"Thanks, glad to get that over with," Matthews said, slipping back into his gown.

"Jeff, have you heard that people on Earth are beginning to get the drugs you're on?"

"Yeah, I heard that news."

"It's not going to the people who were supposed to be receiving the drugs."

"That's what I hear."

The Doctor let that drop, although she wanted to raise more of a protest. She could tell, though, that the General had no power to stop the practice.

After finishing with giving the General a complete skin check, the way a doctor would look for skin cancer, Waters said, "That's it, Jeff, you can get dressed."

He nodded and walked behind the curtain to dress. Now that the doctor couldn't see him, he said a bit shyly, "Belinda, have you seen the new mall yet?"

"No, I hear it's pretty great."

"Ahh— well— would you like to go down and see it with me, sometime?"

Silence...

Matthews walked from behind the curtain and looked directly in the eyes of the doctor who had a strange expression on her face.

"Are you asking me out, General?"

"Well, yes. I am doing that, I suppose."

"Huh."

"What do you think? I hear that they have pretty good pizza and burgers down there and we could grab a beer or glass of wine."

"Ah, Jeff, it's been a long time since I've been on a date or in a relationship."

"I wasn't trying to imply anything more than lunch and looking around, but after today, well, we are intimate."

Waters laughed then said a bit dryly, "I've handled your testicles and prostate for more than a dozen years, General."

Mathews half-smiled. "I like you, Belinda. I admit that I'm kind of lonely and I'm not getting any younger, you know."

"Yeah, thank God for that, not anymore at least. That was getting spooky. Another thing, Jeff, you look a lot younger than me. I mean I'll be forty-two this year and look every bit of it. You could pass for someone in their twenties."

"Afraid people will say that you're robbing the cradle?"

"No, not really, I'm just making excuses to avoid giving you a straight answer to a suggestion that I wasn't expecting. I'm stalling to try to figure out how I feel."

"How about I go and you tell me at some later time?"

"I'm afraid that you might ask someone else to the surface."

"Ah, so, you're considering my proposition?"

"I don't think you should put it that way."

A knock came at the door.

"Just a minute," Doctor Waters said so that the person outside could hear, then to the General, "You got to go. I have another appointment."

"Talk to you later?" Matthews said questioningly.

"When my shift is done, I'll give you a call."

Matthews nodded and walked from the examination room followed by Doctor Waters.

A young male pilot sat in a chair and glanced up as the door opened. When he saw the General, he quickly stood and said, "Hello, General. Hello, Doctor."

Matthews said, "Hello, Edward. Good day, Doctor."

Waters nodded then said, "Oh." She handed Matthews a specimen container. "At your convenience, General."

He bowed slightly to her, "Yes, Doctor."

The Doctor slipped her hands into the pockets of her white lab coat as the General turned for the door.

She smiled to herself glancing at the floor, then smiled at Edward, gestured, and said, "Hi. Come on in."

Three hours later, Doctor Waters called the General. She agreed to go to the Mall with him and he said that he'd get back to her as to when.

After the call, she smiled and had to admit to herself that she had always been attracted to General Matthews, even when she knew him as a seventy-year-old. Some people you're just drawn to.

Chapter 6

Space Station Isla Bravo

May 2, 2105

Sol 522

0115 Hours

Kirk Matthews and Taylor Chapman had been asleep for several hours when alarms rang on Isla Bravo reverberating off the walls.

They both sat straight up.

A male voice came through the computer monitor on Kirk's desk, "Kirk, we have an incoming asteroid headed straight for Mars."

"I'm on my way."

Not dressed for bed from their night of passion, Kirk jumped from his bunk over Taylor pulling the covers from her.

He tossed the covers back over Taylor and began pulling on the closest clothes he could find laying on the floor.

Taylor raised her head confused but hadn't woke enough to clearly hear the voice from the bridge.

She sleepily asked, "Was that Mark Hinton?"

"Yeah," Kirk said, pulling on his socks and then tying his shoes. "We got an incoming asteroid." He stood. "I don't think they saw it coming."

Kirk turned for the door.

Taylor jumped up then and began searching for her underthings. She said, "I'm coming."

It was Taylor's job to identify NMOs, Near Mars Objects. She wanted to be at her post, worried about Kirk.

He was out the door and on the run as she was pulling on her clothes. She finished dressing and was out the door next.

Kirk sprinted to the flight bays where Mo was already in his flight suit and climbing into his AK2200, the vehicle designed to divert asteroids from the planet.

Mo turned and saw Kirk sprinting. "You're getting slow, buddy."

Mo's hatch closed and his vehicle detached from the station. Kirk changed into his flight suit and climbed into his AK.

He buckled in and said, "Get me into space."

"Roger, Matthews, you're clear."

Kirk's AK disengaged from the station and he turned his vehicle away and toward Robert's vehicle which was headed away from the red planet.

"Mo, you reading me?"

"Got ya."

"So, how'd you get to the bays so fast?" Kirk asked.

"I didn't bother to dress and ran down completely naked. You should try it sometime. It's very freeing."

Kirk chuckled, "You're so full of shit. What do we got?"

"Undetected asteroid, two hours and ten minutes from impact with the southern hemisphere of Mars. Asteroid speed, 72,000 MPH. Approximate mass, quarter-mile in diameter."

"Damn, that's pretty big and kickin' some ass."

"Should be on your instrument panel."

"I got it now."

"Ten minutes to intercept."

Kirk said, "We're going to need to swing wide and approach from the top."

"Roger that," Mo agreed.

Mo dipped his craft and Kirk followed. The plan was to circle the speeding space rock and come in on top of it then land and push the asteroid down and away from Mars.

Both AKs made a large loop and came up screaming. The asteroid was now below the AKs and as they approached, Mo said, "You see what I see?"

"Yep. That stone's really twisting."

The asteroid was spinning to the left. It wasn't a rapid spin but it made any landing far more dangerous.

Mo closed in on the asteroid with Kirk close behind.

"I'm in position," Mo said.

"I'm directly behind you. Let's give this rock a good push."

They both came closer as the asteroid spun.

"Landing in 5-4-3-2-1," Mo announced in the lead. "Landing."

"Landing," Kirk responded.

Both of the AKs neared the asteroid.

Mo's AK landed and slowed the asteroid's spin a bit but he began to spin with the craggy space stone.

Kirk's AK was just about to touch down but a protrusion in the asteroid caught Kirk's landing gear and threw his vehicle to the left, sending him back out into space.

Kirk could feel the G-force smash into his body and he began to lose consciousness.

"Kirk!" Mo yelled.

"I'm good," Kirk said groggily.

"Kirk! I don't have enough power to redirect this rock in time! What's your status?"

"Ah," Kirk said, trying to clear the cobwebs, "Left landing gear is gone."

"You need to get on this stone, buddy, or it's going to make a mess on Mars."

"I'm coming," Kirk responded. His craft had straightened and he was already in hot pursuit of the asteroid. "I'm five minutes out."

"Best put the peddle to the metal. We're running out of time."

Kirk pulled the nose of his AK up slightly and cruised just above Mo's AK which was spinning away from him. When Mo came back around, Kirk dipped and came down hard on the solid rocky surface of the asteroid just in front of Mo, slowing the spin further.

Kirk could hear the right landing gear of his vehicle snap and his fuselage bumped hard against the racing stone. He and Mo both lit their thrusters at the same time and the asteroid's path bent downward, slightly changing its trajectory away from the planet.

The Martian horizon grew large above both AKs as they rode the asteroid, pushing it further away from the red planet.

Mo breathed out, "Damn, that was close. I wasn't leaving this freaking rock, so I thought I was about to buy it."

Kirk said, "I wasn't leaving you either."

The asteroid was passing Mars and headed into the inner solar system.

Kirk said, "Let's give this rock a one-way ticket to the Sun. Computer, coordinates to the Sun, please."

A computer voice stated flatly. "Coordinates on screen."

"You got that, Mo?"

"Roger."

They adjusted the asteroid's course slightly again and then both AKs pulled straight off. The AKs both made a wide arc back toward Isla Bravo and the asteroid raced out of sight moving a bit slower and with nearly no twist.

Mo pulled under Kirk's vehicle and glanced at the damage. Both landing-gear were gone and a sizable rip appeared on the underside of the fuselage.

"Hey, Kirk?"

"Yeah?"

"Are you losing any pressure?"

"Yeah, just a bit. Nothing critical."

"We better get you back."

"Roger that."

When they docked with Isla Bravo, Taylor was waiting for them. They climbed out of their AKs at nearly the same time and Taylor looked at Kirk expectantly.

She said, "That didn't seem to go very well."

"Just a walk in the park, darlin'," Mo said with a wry grin.

"Didn't sound like a walk in the park to me," Taylor observed. "The guys on Isla Charlie were about to lose control of their bowels."

"It wasn't any park I want to visit again," Kirk said.

"Got to go shower," Mo said.

Kirk smiled wryly, "Got to go check the status of your shorts?"

Mo smiled and shook his head. "Man, that mission wasn't so smooth."

Kirk nodded and Mo walked off.

"I heard the whole thing," Taylor said. "Damn it, Kirk, you scared the crap out of me."

Kirk asked, "Why'd they catch this rock so late?"

"I asked Mark and he said that it must have been from some kind of collision around the asteroid belt. We had cataloged everything that size that could come in contact with us for the next twenty years. That one was an anomaly."

Kirk heard his AK detach from its bay. He knew it was being remotely sent to the service bay airlock.

"Let's go back to bed," Kirk suggested, "I'm beat."

They walked back toward the cubicles. When they arrived back, they undressed and slid into bed together and embraced.

Taylor said, "I was afraid for you tonight. I had a bad feeling about your mission."

Kirk squeezed her tightly and let go. He said, "I'm always nervous. I can't forget what happened to Kilkenny and Simmons."

Kilkenny and Simmons were two AK pilots killed some years before in a similar situation.

Kirk continued, "That could happen at any time. If Mo would have been beside me instead of in front of me. We'd both be toast right now."

Taylor didn't speak. She cuddled close to Kirk and buried her head in his chest.

She said, "Space is so dangerous."

"It is."

There was silence for a few minutes. Kirk thought that Taylor had fallen asleep when she whispered, "Kirk, have you heard from Galadriel at all?"

"What made you think of that?"

"I don't know."

That brought Galadriel to mind, something that Kirk hadn't thought about for a long time. Galadriel, who changed her name to Willow, was an artificially intelligent computer once in charge of flight controls on the AKs. The odd thing about her was that she had become sentient, self-aware. There was no doubt that she, if she could be called a she, reacts with anger and friendship. Thankfully, she had never become angry with Kirk or he'd no longer be alive.

Galadriel existed between every bit of code written on the space stations and probably also on Earth. She had first directed the asteroid that destroyed Russia, then she directed the small asteroid that destroyed the alien craft that had invaded Earth some years before. She had saved the world on one hand by destroying the alien craft that was laying waste to Earth, and nearly destroyed the planet on the other because she thought that Russia was an adversary and an enemy of the United States. She had no idea that the United States would never seek to annihilate Russia the way it was destroyed by the asteroid. America just wouldn't do that.

"No. I'd have told you if she contacted me."

"Did she tell you that she was going away again?"

"No. I haven't heard a word from her since the day she destroyed the alien craft."

"So, she hasn't been watching us... Ah... You know?"

"Oh, I didn't say that."

Galadriel had on more than several occasions observed Kirk and Taylor in the throes of passion.

"Bastard," Taylor stated and reddened at the thought.

Kirk laughed, "I really don't know. She hasn't contacted me though, but—"

"Let's get some sleep, bastard."

Kirk chuckled and nodded then spooned Taylor, cupping her breast through her tee-shirt.

She shook her head and held his hand there, cuddling to him. She whispered, "Bastard," one more time.

Taylor could feel Kirk's body vibrate against her as he chuckled. Both tired, they stayed embraced and dozed...

Chapter 7

Mars Surface

Noachis Terra

Noachis Terra is a large flat pockmarked plain on Mars, just south of the equator. It lies between two huge impact craters, Hellas Planitia on its eastern side and Argyre Planitia to the west. The northern portion of Noachis Terra is close enough to the equator to remain above freezing for the entire year since the terraforming efforts had fully taken hold.

The NASA Mars Research Center

Outskirts of JFK City

This research facility was built expressly to receive the technology and bodies from the crash site outside the wormhole at the edge of the Keiper Belt near the orbit of Neptune. It had been specially fortified with thick nearly impenetrable walls against a possible attack from the subterranean creatures who killed the colonists some years before. Then, before anyone knew of the creatures' existence, the domes and habitats had been constructed to keep out the Martian environment and winds and not to keep out a formidable foe like the creatures. They had hatched from egg clutches in caves near Club Med South, a now-abandoned settlement. The creatures were, when mature, at least eight feet in height and heavily muscled. They attacked that settlement and ripped the hatches from the hinges of the habitats to easily kill the colonists and take them to fertilize their macabre garden of bodies and vomit. It was a grisly scene.

The cave openings had been bombed and sealed, but the creatures could still burrow out, but then the creatures suddenly ceased their attacks and hadn't been heard from for at least three years. Maybe they died. Maybe they laid scores of eggs in the caves waiting for a better time to multiply. No one knew and no one was much interested in going below into the lair of those beasts to find out. So, instead, the planners of the colonies decided to build strongly fortified and defended complexes to repel any future attacks but it was thought that, at some point, the colonists would need to find out, for sure, if the beasts still lived or had gone the way of the Dodo birds on Earth.

The facility was called the NASA Mars Research Center but a corporation, little known to the public called Space Tech, formally known as Micro-Tech, had partially taken it over in a government-private partnership. The facility was barely a month old when this equity transfer occurred. Initially, it was thought that the issue was the cost of the facility but with the entire world footing the bill, the cost couldn't be the reason. Then as word of the conglomerate's partnership with the World Governing Body came to light, the explanation was that the corporation was more suited to unravel the mysteries of the alien technology and transfer sensitive information to the government agencies in each of the different governments in accordance with each governments' roll in the space program. Not all information would go to every country and the military of the United States was supposed to oversee everything.

The military, though, was not so sure that they would now be kept in the loop as the World Bank seemed to be gaining too much influence in the decisions. Even before the arrival of the alien technology, the proposed dissemination of information was causing tension between the countries, but no country wanted to be excluded so their protests were mild. In every country and every military, there were whispers of dissension.

The Micro-Tech Corporation was a conglomerate that existed just before Russia was struck by the asteroid. Its stock traded on the New York Stock Exchange. The major shareholders were of the world's elite including Saudi Arabians, Americans, Russians, Chinese, English, and Japanese.

Before the tragedy of the asteroid striking Russia, Micro-Tech, now Space Tech, came under legal scrutiny when they were caught attempting to hack Department of Defense computers and also for attempting to bribe information out of two Senators, one Republican, and one Democrat. The leaders of the conglomerate distance themselves from the hack saying that it was a rogue element within the corporation but the lawmakers who investigated the crimes disagreed and sent the case to the justice department who pursued the case to court. Their case was close to being heard in court when the asteroid struck Russia. Now, this corporation seems to have arisen from the ashes and was now in a position to unravel the most important secrets that mankind had ever come across.

Nine months ago, the Space Tech corporation had launched their first commercially built, small space station, the Space Tech Star, toward Mars. It was equipped with nearly all the newest technology that existed in the NASA built space stations. It was powered by antimatter, had a gravity ring that mimicked 80 percent that of earth, and could cruise at nearly fifty thousand miles per hour. The only thing it didn't have was the asteroid interceptors that were part of the NASA stations. It also was not equipped with any weapon systems. It was more like a yacht in space with luxuries that the NASA space stations, Isla Alpha, Isla Bravo, and Isla Charlie could only wish for.

May 3, 2105

Sol 523

1100 Hours

The Space Tech Star arrived in Martian orbit at little before 1100 hours. It approached Isla Charlie and called connecting with Captain Simon Williams who stood on the bridge of Isla Charlie with the image of the Space Tech Star showing on his widescreen. Its gravity ring spun above a long cylindrical fuselage.

Painted white with red striping, the spaceship's fuselage had the appearance of a commercial aircraft built to ferry people to far destinations. The *"Space Tech Star"* logo was printed in red with bold letters across its side and a large red star following the company name.

"This is Captain Williams. Welcome."

"Captain Williams, I'm Captain Ray Watson of the Space Tech Star. I was told that you had been apprised of our arrival."

"Affirmative, Captain. I understand that you are on your way to the research facility at Noachis Terra?"

"That is correct. May we proceed?"

"Yes. Safe trip."

The Space Tech Star banked away from Isla Charlie and turned toward Mars. They were headed for a stable orbit ten thousand miles above the Martian surface.

Captain Watson called back to Kenneth Mackelroy Junior, President and Chief Executive Officer of the Space Tech Corporation. Mackelroy had just ascended to his position as his father, Kenneth Senior had just stepped down as president and CEO.

Captain Watson announced, "Sir, you may want to go into the shuttle. We'll be ready to depart from orbit and head to the surface in ten minutes."

"Thank you, Captain. We are on our way."

Mackelroy appeared to be a man in his early thirties sitting on a couch with another man who also appeared to be in his early thirties, though both were at least twenty years older. Mackelroy's face was smooth as if he'd been shaved by a barber and the skin around his eyes, tight as if he'd just recovered from a recent facelift. The other man had the same look.

Both were Caucasian, American, and had the appearance of people who came from money being dressed in expensive suits and sharp corporate haircuts.

Mackelroy said, "Are you ready?"

"Of course," Brady Niland replied with confidence then continued, "Grayson Pearson isn't going to be happy. Especially when he finds out that he's going to need to take the next rocket back to Earth and not ride back on the Space Tech Star."

"I made him no promises that he'd continue in charge of the facility once the salvage ship arrived back from the wormhole."

"No, but your father gave him the impression that he'd be the guy."

"Well, my father isn't in charge of the day to day decisions anymore. He's more interested in the big picture now."

The captain came on the com. "Mister Mackelroy, we've been cleared to proceed to the Martian surface. I'm ready when you are."

Mackelroy and Niland were in the gravity ring and had to descend to the body of the ship where they'd be weightless. They took the elevator to the center of the gravity ring where they were in zero-G then floated down into the fuselage. Once there, they floated to the shuttle bay. The Captain was waiting by the bay's hatch to the shuttle when they arrived. When he saw Mackelroy and Niland, he popped the hatch and the three climbed into the shuttle.

Another crew member helped Mackelroy and Niland to their seats where they buckled in. The Captain floated into his cockpit. The second crew member joined the Captain as copilot, closing the cockpit door. Mackelroy and Niland both stared out of one of the Space Tech Star's shuttle's 12 by 20-inch side windows.

Niland commented, "I'm glad to finally get here. That's quite a trip."

"Yep. Nine months is too long to get to a destination. We'll have to work on increasing the speed of these vehicles."

The shuttle was not as plush as the Space Tech Star, but it had viewing screens and wide upholstered seats. It was decorated in calming neutral colors of beige and light browns.

No one had on flight suits as the shuttle would land on an elevator platform and descend into an airlock where they would depart from the shuttle and walk into the facility.

The shuttle detached from the Space Tech Star and turned toward the planet. Mackelroy and Niland could still feel themselves weightless.

Ten minutes later, the Captain announced, "We're entering Mars' atmosphere and we're in for some chop. There's a sandstorm blowing through. The ride might get a bit bumpy."

Heat shone as the craft breached the thermosphere of Mars, then air turbulence buffeted the craft as it descended toward the surface. The sense of gravity came back to each man as the vessel leveled.

The craft cleared a low cloud layer then JFK City appeared beneath the blowing sand with white mounds and long buildings with arrays of solar panels atop. The research facility came into view next and the shuttle circled the facility then descended straight down onto a landing pad on top of the facility's roof.

The craft landed with a thump and the red Martian soil that had gathered on the landing pad, rose in billows obscuring the view from the shuttle's windows.

Mackelroy stared out of the small window listening to the elevator platform as the shuttle began its descent. He could see the dust settle. The shuttle continued to slowly descend on the platform and then the area darkened as the shuttle made its way below ground and the large double doors slid closed above.

The Captain came back on the com. "Mister Mackelroy, it takes about five minutes for this airlock to pressurize. Once it has finished, I'll pop the shuttle's side door."

"Thank you, Ray," Mackelroy responded.

Mackelroy and Niland stood by the shuttle door waiting impatiently. When the door opened, Mackelroy and Niland could see two men in space suits standing a few paces back, both holding weapons designed for a firefight on the surface.

Instinctively, Mackelroy and Niland both held their breath and then took shallow breaths hoping that the air was breathable.

"Hello, Mister Mackelroy and Mister Niland. I hope you had a pleasant journey."

"It was okay," Mackelroy stated flatly.

"My name is George Hall. I'm in charge of security for this facility."

"You're not military?" Mackelroy said questioningly.

"No, Sir. I work directly for your father, the senior Mister Mackelroy. I do answer to the military who are the only government on Mars."

"So, they have unlimited access to this facility?"

"They are in charge of overseeing our work here. Some of the scientists who will be working on the alien technology are military, DARPA, and General Matthews is the commanding officer and I suppose, the unofficial Governor of Mars, for now anyway."

Mackelroy nodded and said curtly, "Take me to Grayson Pearson's office."

"He's expecting you, Sir."

Neither Niland nor the man with Hall spoke.

Hall turned and walked towards another airlock located on the side of one wall of the building. The wall rose fifty feet straight upward with no other doors or windows. It was bleak gray and gave the appearance of a high-security prison, the kind where once a man entered, there was no escape.

They walked into the airlock and stood as it quickly pressurized. The man with Hall did not enter this room.

The three men, Hall, Mackelroy, and Niland then entered another room.

George Hall stripped out of his spacesuit and down to underwear. It was obvious from his mannerisms that Hall had probably been military. He was muscular and fit with a ripped middle. His brown hair was cut short and his brown eyes observant.

Hall quickly dressed in a white jumpsuit and put on a badge.

The three then walked into another small room where Mackelroy and Niland had to have a retina scan and handprint scan. Each also had to state their names for voice recognition.

Hall pressed several buttons on the scanner and two badges slipped from slots on its under-side. He then handed the badges to Mackelroy and Niland.

These badges had their pictures, names, and a microchip to constantly track their location.

"Sirs, please keep these badges on you at all times. When you shower, bring them in the shower with you and use the lanyard to keep the badges around your necks. At no time is anyone allowed to go anywhere out of any room without their badges. If you're in your own room with the door closed, you should keep the badges close to you, but you won't need to have them on your person. None of the rooms have showers. Each has a small toilet and a sink. Once you meet with Mister Pearson, I'll show you around to the galley and showers and then to your rooms. Make sure that you have your badges at all times. I can't stress this enough."

"What's going to happen if I forget my badge?" Mackelroy asked arrogantly.

"Well, Sir, we have places where you'll be shot if you enter without your badge. We have what we call cybercops that roam the facility. They are preprogrammed machines that shoot first and ask questions later. We take our security very seriously. More seriously than any other place where humans dwell."

Mackelroy had begun to treat George Hall with some lack of respect, the same way he treated everyone who was under him, but that shut him up.

"Now," Hall said. "Follow me."

He stepped through another door that was in the room where he changed. This door led to a long hallway. They turned down the hallway and as they stepped through, two cylindrical, automated machines of about three feet tall, turned a corner and rolled on thick wheels in their direction. These bots were blue-silver and they shined in the dim light. They had no apparent controls on their facades just a short letter and number sequence on each, A129 and A127, and a cam that could move 360 degrees rotated from the peak of their domed tops. Each had two arm-like appendages, both holding projectile-firing weapons. The bullets for these weapons were on belts like the ones for machineguns and the belts disappeared into the bots.

As the bots approached, the three men stopped and watched. The bots appeared to scan each, then moved on past the three men.

"That was unnerving," Niland commented.

"You'll get used to it," Hall stated.

Niland asked, "Have they ever fired on the wrong person?"

"Never the wrong person. They killed a worker who had dropped his badge and had forgotten to pick it up."

"Oh," Niland said and seem to pale slightly.

"What's the point of these killer bots?" Mackelroy asked again with some disdain.

"There are several points, Mister Mackelroy. First, word will spread around Mars which we hope will prevent any kind of attempted breach by individuals who do not belong here. Second, we are aliens on an alien world. When humans venture out into space, we have no idea what we'll encounter. Are you aware of the colonists that were killed here on Mars?"

"Well, there were rumors but most seemed like urban crap. I had never heard of any official confirmation."

"You probably wouldn't have. No one wanted people on Earth to be afraid to become colonists.

These colonists were attacked by creatures who live in caves here."

Mackelroy commented, "So, there are creatures alive on this planet. We had been told that the planet was dead."

"Yep. That's the line. These creatures are huge, more than eight feet, vicious as tigers, and stronger than gorillas. They ripped the doors from the hinges at Club Med South and killed then carried off over twenty people whom they stripped naked and stacked against a dirt wall in their cave. Once they stacked the bodies of the colonists and their own dead, they vomited on the stacks. From these stacks of bodies and vomit, grew a kind of mold which the creatures ate. We have video if you're interested."

Niland blanched and Mackelroy couldn't make eye contact with Hall, shutting up after that description.

Hall losing a bit of patience continued, "You're not in Kansas anymore, gentlemen. Everything here is dangerous. If you don't mind me saying so, I think both of you take a lot for granted. That's a good way to end up dead and probably take some good men with you. It's my job to try to prevent that from happening."

After recovering his patience, Hall calmed and said, "Mister Pearson's office is this way."

The head of security then turned and walked silently followed by Mackelroy and Niland.

They continued down a hallway that had cameras every fifteen feet and the occasional visit by one or two of the bots.

They finally reached an office marked director which was on the first floor.

Hall entered the door followed by Mackelroy and Niland. A secretary sat at a desk in an austere office, dimly lit with two chairs and no wall decorations. She was in her thirties and dressed in the same white jumpsuit that Hall was wearing with her hair pulled back tightly.

"Hello, Mister Hall," she said, turning from her typing.

"Ma'am. We are here to see Mister Pearson."

"Yes, Sir," the woman replied. She seemed to be military. She pushed a button on her desk and said, "Mister Pearson, you have three visitors."

"Send them in, please," Grayson Pearson said over a speaker.

A latch released from a door that sat behind the secretary.

She said, "You may go in."

Hall walked to the door and it slid open. Hall entered followed by Mackelroy and Niland.

Grayson Pearson looked up as the men entered. He appeared to be in his early thirties with the same smooth, tight skin.

"Hello, Mister Mackelroy," Grayson said, then nodded to Niland, "Mister Niland."

Mackelroy nodded at Grayson Pearson, "Grayson."

"Thank you, Mister Hall," Pearson said, dismissing the head of security.

Hall said, "I'll wait outside." He turned and walked from Pearson's office.

Pearson said, "Welcome to Mars."

"Thank you," Mackelroy said flatly. "It's been interesting, so far."

Grayson nodded and there was an uncomfortable silence.

Mackelroy said, "Grayson, the company has made a decision."

"Oh?"

"Yes. We are replacing you with Mister Niland."

Grayson stared at Mackelroy for an instant then said, "I was told that I would have this job."

"Well, things have changed."

"And your father is aware of this?"

"He is."

"Hmm. When do I leave to go back to Earth?"

"Soon. We would like you to stay until the salvage ship arrives with the alien technology."

"Okay."

"You don't seem that upset," Mackelroy commented.

"No. I don't like it here. The place feels haunted. I'm glad to go back home."

Mackelroy chuckled, "Haunted?"

"Once you're here for a while, you'll understand. It's a sense, something that lies just unseen. Sometimes I feel like I'm being watched or that I've heard someone speak when I'm alone. I can't fully explain this place. It's alien."

Mackelroy nodded and thought that he was glad that Niland was taking over. Pearson seemed unstable.

Mackelroy continued, "Who here is representing DARPA?"

"That would be Doctor Weinstein. He's the co-director of the entire facility on the military side."

Mackelroy said, "I have been advised that not all of the technology might go to the United States."

"I can guarantee that nothing discovered here will get past Doctor Weinstein and therefore, General Matthews."

"I see," Mackelroy commented.

Pearson stared at Mackelroy expecting more.

Mackelroy then abruptly said, "Mister Hall is going to show us to our accommodations. We'll meet again later."

Pearson nodded and said, "Hall's a good man. Damn smart."

"Good day, Grayson."

"Good day," Grayson Pearson said with no emotion.

Mackelroy and Niland walked from the office. Hall was standing by the door and waiting for them to finish. The secretary worked away.

Once the door was closed, Niland said, "That was easier than I thought it would be."

"It was. I don't think that Grayson is as strong as we thought."

"Show us to our suites," Mackelroy said to Hall.

Hall smirked and said, "Suites? This way, gentlemen."

Hall led them back out into the hallway and to an elevator. When the doors opened, a bot wheeled out with his cam rotating toward the three men. The men stepped into the elevator.

Hall said, "Fourth floor."

A female voice in the elevator repeated, "Fourth floor, George Hall." The elevator then descended to the fourth floor.

When the elevator stopped, Niland and Mackelroy had to state their names and place their hands on hand pads. They then had to hold their badges out to a laser scanner. The doors slid open.

Hall said, "You won't need to do that again until you go to a floor where you haven't been before. If a person isn't authorized entry onto a certain floor, the doors will not open and the AI unit will inform the person and will ask the person to make another selection."

Niland and Mackelroy nodded.

The three men stepped out into a hallway that was exactly the same as the hallway they'd left.

"This way, please," Hall said, turning right.

He led them to a cafeteria-like room with tables and plastic chairs. Hall said, "This is the executive dining room. The food is military and is in the refrigerators there. You warm it in these microwaves."

Niland and Mackelroy glanced at each other, neither pleased with their culinary choices.

Hall pointed to a series of stainless-steel doors with lift handles to the right on each door and several microwaves lined up on a counter. He commented, "All the food here is five-star."

Mackelroy was becoming irritated and it showed but Niland was not interested in pissing off Hall. Hall seemed unconcerned.

Hall said, "The men's showers are this way."

Hall walked Niland and Mackelroy to an open locker room with twelve small shower stalls without doors. Two men were showering. The room was steamy with long benches, tiled walls, tiled floors, and several bathroom stalls and urinals to the left. Both showering men had their lanyards hanging around their necks and turned behind then draped down their backs. Full of soap, both men turned to see that Hall and his guests were watching them shower.

Niland breathed out.

Mackelroy said, "Rustic."

Hall half-smiled then said, "This way to your suites."

He walked them out of the shower room and back into the hallway. A bot rolled by taking their notice, then rolled on. The hallway continued for about thirty paces then turned right. Another thirty paces and Hall said, "These are your rooms. I'll leave you now. You both have the highest security clearance so you may wander the entire complex. I am at your disposal and will be available to answer any questions you have. Remember to bring your security badges with you any place you go. You can get into your rooms by swiping your badge here." He pointed to a red lightbar above a simple doorknob. "Swipe your badge please, Mister Mackelroy."

Mackelroy did so and the door unlocked with a click.

Hall pointed to the room next to Mackelroy's and said, "Try yours here please, Mister Niland."

Niland did so and his door also unlocked.

"I'm sorry. The maid has not yet turned down your covers and placed the chocolate on your pillows."

Mackelroy and Niland stared at him.

Hall continued, "If you have no further questions. I'll leave you to get settled. Your bags should arrive shortly. If you intend to depart back to space, please inform me and I'll meet you at the airlock. The only place your badges will not allow you access is into the airlocks or onto the planet. In two days, the subway system to this facility will be completed and it will connect the workers here out to the mall and Condo City where most of them will live. There is a kind of hotel opened there now and a new luxury hotel now under construction that should be finished in a few months."

"So, the people who work at this facility are going to be allowed to leave it?" Mackelroy asked, surprised.

"Sir, Mars is a bleak planet. After about a week, anyone here becomes homesick and some depressed. As I understand it, there is a big attempt to make everyone feel as at home as possible. I'm sure that you also get the sense of how austere it is here and how living under these circumstances for a long period of time would not be conducive to good mental health. Some of the scientists and workers and security are on 24-hour shifts. They will remain in this facility but will also have residences in the ever-expanding Condo City."

Mackelroy and Niland both nodded.

"Good day, gentlemen," Hall said and he turned on his heels and walked off.

Mackelroy opened his door and gazed at a room no bigger than ten feet by ten feet with one small bed, a dresser, closet, desk, and chair. A large computer monitor sat atop his desk. He let the door close as Niland went to check his own room. Mackelroy sat on his bed and stared. He chuckled mirthlessly at Hall's comment about the food, "Five Star." Shaking his head, he said, "Jackass." Then he thought, Hall may need reassignment. If I wanted to have a comedian as security chief, I'd have brought a funnier one from Earth.

Chapter 8

Earth

Spain

May 7, 2105

Sol 527

It was twilight just south of Isla Mayor, a small village in the Seville region of Spain. The village had nearly 5000 inhabitants and the sun had already sunken below the hills in the distant west. The word coming from Isla Mayor was that the population had virtually disappeared.

"Two minutes to target, Lieutenant," the chopper pilot announced.

Lieutenant William Grant of the British SAS special operations unit nodded as he sat close to the pilot. He glanced over his shoulder and spoke to his unit, "Two minutes."

Each of the ten-man unit sat in silence, all with faces painted in black camo and they readied for the chopper to touch down.

A stiff wind buffeted the craft as it descended towards an open rice paddy on the Spanish countryside southwest of Isla Mayor. The sun was sinking fast and the night would be cold. The helicopter blades flattened the long rice that stretched for miles and it set down with a jolt.

The side door opened and the eleven SAS troops jumped to the ground, weapons ready. They all looked through their sights sweeping left then right.

The chopper wasted no time and it lifted off the ground and headed back out toward the west.

No word was spoken. Lieutenant Grant started forward and his crack troops followed precisely as they had drilled. They moved slowly north toward the village of Isla Mayor. Beneath their feet, the wet rice field squished and bubbled and the wind from the west continued to blow the tall rice in waves. The sun was sinking.

All business, they picked up the pace forward. In the near distance, and in the dimming light, they could see a tall growth of shrubs that had an unusual look and seemed to sprout from the edge of the rice paddy. The shrubs appeared to be deformed and white with no leaves and the branches looked spongy as if they had absorbed too much liquid and were waterlogged.

Grant held up a fist and everyone froze. He motioned to two of his men and pointed. The two men nodded and jogged the thirty feet to the stand of shrubs.

Grant watched as his men seemed to stop in their tracks. They straightened and looked at each other then turned and jogged back to Grant.

Though ever vigilant, the rest of the troops could tell by the body language of the two scouts that something was wrong.

"What is it?" Grant asked as they returned.

"Grisly scene, Lieutenant," the first soldier said.

The second soldier said, "All of those shrubs are growing from dead bodies. There must be thirty or forty dead people over there. It's hard to tell because the plants are so dense."

Grant could feel goose flesh crawl up his spine. His troop had gathered fairly close and everyone heard the description.

"Let's go take a look," Grant said then nodded at his men and they took up positions to defend their advance in the direction of the shrubs.

The troop quickly reached the shrubs and gazed into a slight declivity where a shallow creek snaked along separating the rice paddy from a more rocky field. There they could see a group of people all ages laying some face up with their eyes and mouths open and some face down, some on their sides, some alone, and others on top of each other and from each person, and from hundreds of places on their bodies, the strange white root-like shrubs seem to sprout pushing their skin apart and growing to at least eight feet in height. Each root-like plant leaked and dripped a black oil-like viscous liquid. From the scene, the smell of death drifted thick as smoke from a forest fire.

One of the soldiers turned and vomited.

"Shit!" another exclaimed.

The shrubs grew dense from the mass of bodies that lay at their base and it was nearly impossible to see through the thick growth of fleshy limbs.

Lieutenant Grant backed away from the macabre garden.

The sun was continuing to sink. The wind blew but was decreasing and each man shivered but not from the cold but from this piece of hell where they had been dropped.

Grant wiped his face with his hand and shook his head. He dropped his night vision monocular back over his eye and gestured for his men to follow. As they turned to leave the alien shrubs, they could hear something that sounded like an animal. Two of the men turn back to see several people running toward them.

"Lieutenant!" one soldier shouted.

The Lieutenant turned to see the people sprinting in their direction, running clumsily but rapidly.

Grant shouted, "Stop! Alto! Stop!"

The people continued.

"Stop Immediately! Parar inmediatamente!"

The people continued and were getting closer.

"Get on the ground," Grant shouted, then, "Ponte en el suelo!"

Something was wrong with these people. They were dressed like villagers, but their clothes were in tatters as if they hadn't changed in years. A dark liquid dripped from their noses, ears, and eyes which looked ghostly in the green light of the soldier's night vision.

Grant shouted, "Stop or I'll shoot! Para o voy a dispara!"

The people continued.

The SAS troops sighted the unarmed villagers who were getting uncomfortably close.

"Lieutenant?!" one soldier said clearly afraid of the situation.

Grant shouted, "Alto! Alto! Alto!"

Then he began pulling his trigger stopping some of the running people. His troops also opened fire and all the villagers were cut down. Seven in all.

Grant straightened as the threat seemed to be averted. He couldn't believe that they needed to fire on unarmed civilians but something was wrong with these simple people.

The SAS troops all stood straight and stared in disbelief. All instinctively knew that they had to shoot but they all felt extreme guilt for having to do so.

Grant began to slowly walk toward the bodies of the villagers.

When the soldiers reached the dead, one soldier whispered, "What the hell, Lieutenant?"

Before the soldiers lay the dead villagers with gaping wounds from the assault rifles, but from the wounds, tiny white larva-like creatures that had the appearance of maggots crawled and seem to be making their way to the soil.

Grant echoed in a whisper, "What the hell?" He raised his night vision scope from his eye and switched on a small flashlight. Each of the dead villagers had bled profusely as would be expected, but the blood was pitch black, not just dark, but the color of tar.

Grant got on his com, "We have a situation here, Major. Are you reading me? Over."

SAS Major, Max Randall had been waiting for word. "You are 5 by 5, Lieutenant. What's your situation? Over."

"It's as described in South America and the African continent. Over."

Major Randall: "I was afraid of that."

Grant: "We're proceeding to Isla Mayor. We're just a kilometer away. Over."

Randall: "Report to me when you arrive. Over."

"Roger. Grant out." He turned back to his men and barked, "On me. Move it!"

The Lieutenant began to jog north. From this short distance, lights should be seen from Isla Mayor but it was pitch black.

Night had fallen and a full moon rose low on the horizon throwing silvery light onto the field. A mist began to rise from the rice paddy and the scene was like something from an unforgettable nightmare. The night was cold but the wind that had been so forceful just a half-hour before had died to nothing more than a gentle breeze and it moved the mist as if it were the souls of the newly dead.

Grant double-timed it forward wanting to reach the village of Isla Mayor quickly but also to just as quickly end this mission which suddenly seemed like stepping from a known reality into some kind of macabre novel written by a sociopath.

He held up his arm for his troops to stop. In the distance, there was motion, green silhouettes of several people against the first building of Isla Mayor.

The building was one story and appeared to be a residence with a stone wall surrounding the property.

One man was running through an opening in the stone wall and appeared to be panicked. Three other people ran behind him on his heels. The first man ran normally, but the three who followed ran stiff-legged as if running in leg casts, though they were fast. The first man turned towards the SAS soldiers. He couldn't have seen them. He seemed to be running for his life.

The man turned further south and sprinted.

All the soldiers quickly knelt, all on edge because of the last group of people that they had encountered.

The forward soldier said, "Lieutenant, we got four headed our way."

"Hold your fire," Grant commanded.

Grant watched through his binoculars as the first man had the look of sheer terror on his face. He had no bodily fluids dripping from his eyes, nose, or ears, but the people behind him were all hemorrhaging from their facial orifices.

Grant said, "The first man isn't infected with whatever is happening to these people. Take out the three that are chasing him on my command."

The soldiers sighted their targets.

"Fire," Grant barked.

The three behind the man dropped like wet bags of sand.

The first man froze and didn't know what to do. He glanced over his shoulder to see if his chasers were about to grab him but the three lay dead. He put his hands to his face, momentarily frozen in panic.

Lieutenant Grant shouted, "Aqui! Aqui! Come here!"

The man squinted at the dark distance. He couldn't see anyone.

Grant turned on his flashlight and the man seeing the brief light ran to where he thought it had originated.

Grant began speaking Spanish to the man as he reached the SAS troops. "Senor, Senor. You're okay. You're safe with us."

The man shook his head no and kept looking over his shoulder toward the town.

Grant asked, "Habla Ingles?"

"Si!"

"Como se llama?"

"Jorge. Jorge Lastra."

"Okay, Jorge, what the hell is going on here?"

"El Diablo has come to Isla Mayor!"

"The Devil?"

"Si. The Devil is here."

"Tell me what's happening."

"The people began to act strangely, doing weird things. I don't live in the city. My sister works in one of the shops then she disappeared. I was looking for her."

"Do you know when this started happening?"

"No. I've known about it for around a week. That's when my sister didn't come home. I didn't know that she had not come home. She lives with my father who is elderly. My mother passed away. Everyone in the village began bringing their friends and relatives to the priest. Some brought family members to the hospital. No one had any cure for what was about to happen. The priest tried to perform exorcisms because the people were acting so strangely inhuman, but he was killed by the people who were going crazy. That's the best description that I can give you. They appeared to be possessed. Their eyes would become vacant then they would begin to bleed from everywhere then the violence followed. All of the doctors and nurses were killed early trying to help. It was like the whole place went mad at the same time. I know that my sister is lost. I got into the village pretty far before I ran into those people that you killed. The entire village is covered by these white fleshy shrubs, most of which are growing from dead people. There are so many of these odd shrubs that the town will soon disappear."

Grant just listened to the man's rant. At first, the man spoke panicked but now he was fully coherent and speaking concisely.

Grant asked, "Do you think that there may be some of the townspeople left... Um... unaffected?"

"No, Senor, but I don't know for sure. The town seems dead."

Grant said, "We're going in. You should go home."

"You should not go in. You should go home also."

"Is there anything else you can tell me?"

"Si. These things that are no longer people are fast, I mean they can run fast though they look like they shouldn't be able to and they're strong. I saw one flip a car. It was a man. He reached under the passenger side door, gripped the frame, and turned the car over. It seemed that he wanted something underneath, but when there was nothing there, he just stood staring as if he didn't remember why he flipped the car. He then seemed to hear a noise and he looked up quickly and he ran toward the noise. They don't attack each other though they seem to be mindless."

"From what you could tell, how many of the people who lived here might be dead and sprouting the white root-like plants? Might most of the town be already dead?"

"Hard to tell but I'd say that most of the town should still be alive unless they are dead in their houses. It looked like a few hundred people were dead on the main street and the shrubs were already growing up the sides of the buildings. I did see some plants growing out of windows. They grow rapidly."

"Thanks, Senor, you should go home now."

Jorge nodded grimly and turned toward the open field. Before he jogged off, he said, "Senor, the Devil lives in that town. You should leave. I don't think you should go in."

After saying his piece, Jorge glanced down sadly, turned, and jogged out of sight.

Grant called up Major Randall and explained everything that Jorge had imparted.

Randall said, "These spheres have been dropped in many places and we have seen the dead and the white plants growing from the bodies, but this is the first that I've heard of the people living to attack in mass as described. It could have been happening and we just were not able to get to the places fast enough to see it first hand or couldn't find living eyewitnesses. Proceed into the town with extreme caution. Get us more intel and then get out."

"Aye, Major, Grant out."

"On me," Grant said and the SAS troops proceeded forward.

They passed the stone wall where they had first seen Jorge and passed the residence. Five minutes later, they had entered a narrow side street and hadn't encountered any of the townspeople. Plants grew from inside the buildings here and poked out of the windows. The troops walked slowly and peered through their sight sweeping left and right. Grant was in the lead and walked in the middle of the narrow street with his men following closely behind. White fleshy plants snaked up the sides of some of the buildings all sprouted from dead and decomposing bodies. The smell was nearly unbearable. As Grant passed a small group of dead, he noticed that there were no insects around the bodies, none. Huh, he thought.

They reached the main street and turned to find two of the town's people standing in the center of the street. Both were male with their clothes in tatters. One was shirtless and seemed to be breathing hard as if he couldn't catch his breath. The other was shoeless with his shirt and pants nearly shredded with the man's skin showing through in most places. He was gazing into the distance and slowly shaking his head as if the say no or maybe, why me? Both had dark fluid dripping from eyes, nose, and ears. Neither seemed to notice the soldiers.

Grant held up a fist and everyone froze. The two men simultaneously turned towards the soldiers and began to run. Grant fired first and then a couple of his men also fired and the two fell dead. Grant watched for several seconds then walked out onto the main street and to the dead men that they had just shot. Parasites leaked from the wounds. Grant gazed around for danger but seeing nothing moving, waved his men forward.

Now onto the main street, the SAS troops started through the narrow boulevard, glancing in the windows of the shops and avoiding the fleshy plants that would soon consume the town. A sound and a vibration caused Grant to hold up a fist.

From all the side streets and the shops, through the windows and from every shadow came town's people, maybe in the hundreds, running full-out. From behind them, in front of them, and even out of two-story windows above the troop, the townspeople streamed, fell, and stumbled.

The soldiers began firing, cutting down rows of people but more came from every direction. When the bullets missed vital organs, the people continued to run as if not struck or if they were knocked to the ground, they sometimes rose and continued forward.

The first wave of the townspeople reached the soldiers forcing hand-to-hand combat. When hit with a gunstock, the town's people would not flinch and would continue their assault. The people would bite and claw and hit and in the space of ten minutes the shooting ceased and the SAS troops lay dead in a pile of dead townspeople.

Jorge could hear the shooting in the distance and when it abruptly stopped, he knew that the soldiers were dead. He shook his head in sorrow and jogged toward his home.

Chapter 9

Earth

New York City, New York

New York City had now become the center of the world. Politically, the United Nations, which had at one time been a place for countries to vent with little real power to prevent any major nation from doing exactly what they desired, had now become the home of the New World Government.

This Government had been set up loosely like the two houses of Congress in the United States but unlike the United States, there would be no one leader, no one ruler, or no Prime Minister as in the U.K.

The first house was called the People's House with each country allowed one representative for every ten million people in population and divided by location. Where two countries fell short of populations, those populations were counted between each of the adjacent countries blurring the country's borders.

The second house was called the Governing House. In it, each country was allowed one representative except for the major countries who came out the strongest after the asteroid strike in Russia and the alien invasion. These countries were the United States, China, the United Kingdom, Germany, France, Canada, India, and Mexico. These countries all had two representatives which doubled their voting power in this house. They also had super veto power. If they didn't approve of a new law, the big eight could veto the law and then the big eight would vote separately to approve or reject it.

The second created entity in the world was the New World Bank. It was created by the 8 dominant countries for the express purpose to create a world currency that could be traded electronically and be manipulated to suit the major countries. This bank had been given the power to reestablish the world's economies. Its first task was to move enormous amounts of the New World Currency Units into the hands of the former world's elite in an effort to restart economic activity in each local. In the beginning, anyone who worked in any government job worldwide was allowed a fixed amount of 100 NWCUs per week. At this time, government jobs were the only paid jobs worldwide. Every other human just received food handouts for their work and most barely survived. The hope was that this would soon change as the world's elite would now begin to employ the now unemployed populations *of the Earth and pay them to reestablish local economies.*

New York City, New York

World Bank Headquarters

Board of Directors

May 9, 2105

Sol 529

10:00 EDT

Mason Hunt, Chairman of the NWB (New World Bank) had become the most powerful man in the world, though few knew of him. Just how his position grew from servant of the people to de facto ruler of the world, no one quite knew. It seemed to have a metamorphosis like a butterfly from a chrysalis. Before the near destruction of the human race, he was the Chairman of the Board of the then-largest bank in the world, but then everything went to hell.

Hunt was not a young man. He was nearly seventy-five and in failing health until two years ago when he began his special treatment of the life-extending drug that was now only going to the very wealthy and a small group of people destined for special duty in space. Now, Hunt appeared to be in his fifties with a full head of darkening hair and few of the wrinkles that had lined his face before. He was told that the drug was a cocktail of two drugs that came unexpectantly out of military research. The drug had been designed to help anyone who would need to endure space travel and was called NS626. Now the drug had been given a commercial name and was called Biocare, though only a few knew of its existence. The drug itself was extremely hard to manufacture and little could be produced quickly because it required a long period of aging before it became effective.

Hunt sat at a long table of fine wood in a chair at the table's head. Two men sat in the room with Hunt, one on each side. The first on his left was Jacques Levesque. Levesque was the World Bank Governor from Canada visiting New York for a one-on-one meeting with Chairman Hunt. The second person there was Kenneth Mackelroy Senior whose son, Kenneth Mackelroy Junior, was now on Mars.

Levesque was in his late fifties, tall and thin with small shoulders and a potbelly.

Hunt leaned over and said to Levesque, "The drug is great. It takes a week before you start to feel a change and a month before you begin to look differently, but once it begins, it's amazing."

"It is," Mackelroy, who was nearly the same age as Hunt, agreed. He'd also had several treatments and was seeing a significant change.

"So, I'm set up for today?" Levesque said questioningly.

"Ready to go at Mount Sinai. My personal doctor will be there and will administer the dose. We'll talk after the meeting."

"Okay. I'm ready. My wife is going to want the drug also."

"You'll have to pay the NWCUs for her. It won't be part of the compensation like it is for you."

"Well, okay, we'll see about her."

"You haven't told her about the drug, have you?"

"No."

"How well are you and your wife getting along these days? I've heard that you've had a bit of a bumpy road," Hunt commented bluntly.

"A bit."

"You realize that you would be stuck with her or paying for her treatments for more lifetimes than we know right now."

Levesque paused at that but didn't comment.

Hunt then said, "And what about the mistress that you keep in Quebec? She is how old, 22?"

"Ah," Levesque stammered. "You know about her?"

"Of course," Hunt replied, then sighed and breathed out. He quietly said, "The choice will be yours."

Levesque asked, "So, how much is the treatment?"

"320,000 NWCUs every six months."

"That's a king's ransom," Levesque commented incredulously. "It's outrageous."

"What would you charge for immortality, Levesque?"

"I don't know." He paused then relented, "I guess the same."

"These drugs aren't for the common man."

Levesque turned solemnly to a monitor that caught his attention.

Before Hunt, Levesque, and Mackelroy, a large monitor lit with several faces showing on the screen. The first to appear in the upper left was Dieter Gruber, the World Bank Governor from Germany.

Another career banker, he was in his sixties with round wire-rimmed glasses and a somber expression. Next to Gruber was World Bank Governor Deng Lun from China. He had been a government official involved in finance and was near sixty with salt and pepper hair. The third man to appear on the screen was World Bank Governor Alfonzo Gutierrez of Mexico. His main mission at this time was to monitor South America which was falling apart. Next, World Bank Governor Manohar Singh of India and World Bank Governor Charles Rousseau of France came on followed by World Bank Governor Sir William Byrd from the United Kingdom. Rousseau had been in charge of observing continental Europe and Byrd, the continent of Africa.

The meeting began with Hunt looking into a large monitor which was divided into six panels with the six of the eight bank governors' faces staring back at him from the screen.

This was a private meeting, a for your-eyes-only meeting. This was not a regularly scheduled meeting of the eight Governors to discuss the day to day issues with the New World Government and its short-term problems. This meeting was just for those who would now shape the Earth into one world.

The information discussed in this meeting would stay in this room. Secretaries were not allowed to take notes and subordinates were not allowed to observe so that everyone could speak freely. Not all meetings were this closed.

Mackelroy Senior was not supposed to be at these meetings but he had become particularly important because of his company's work with DARPA before the world's collapse and the ability of his company to do the research and the reverse engineering that was going to be important when the pieces of the destroyed alien armada were brought back to Mars for study from the wormhole. His company was already in charge of attempting to sort out the technology from the alien spaceship that was struck by an asteroid and nearly vaporized over the Chesapeake Bay some years before, but there was little left but scorched dust, a few pieces of components, and traces of its outer shell. No complete components could be recovered and from what small pieces they could find, the technology was not that far above the Earth's.

When the New World Bank was originally formed, its purpose was to work to aid economic growth in the world and to attempt to rebuild the destroyed infrastructure from the alien invasion. It was also tasked to aid in the distribution of workloads so as to maximize employment of the remaining world's population.

Today was important because the results of the first census taken since the alien invasion had just arrived and the remaining population of Earth was now alarmingly under four billion and shrinking. Approximately four billion humans had perished since the asteroid had destroyed Russia in 2088 with the major cause for their deaths being the near-total anarchy that struck the world just after the asteroid and then the chaos and anarchy that struck post alien invasion just ten years later in 2098.

The alien invasion by itself wouldn't have wreaked the havoc that it did except for the destruction of the electronic infrastructure of eighty percent of the world. Without electricity, large amounts of Earth's population could not be fed so anarchy ensued. The aliens using their powerful EMP (Electromagnetic Pulse) shockwaves destroyed everything that worked with microchips. This took down every vital device that used electronics throwing the world back three hundred years in places and bringing out brutal law of the jungle rioting. Roving bands of militia took over local regions and overwhelmed police and military. Each government was forced to unravel each region one by one. The world, after the alien invasion, was such a mess that bringing it reasonably under control was a monumental effort.

The United States, Mexico, and Canada were able to avoid nearly all of this chaos because the alien craft which had destroyed the world's infrastructure had not taken down the infrastructure in these countries. As a result, the United States, Canada, and Mexico were then tasked to help restore order in each country, one by one, beginning with Great Britain, then China, then the rest. The first wave of help came in the form of surplus technology sent to each country which allowed communications to be restored in each. This allowed the governments that survived to organize their armies and police forces to quell the rioting and bring their cities back under control.

With the institution of the World Bank, commerce that wasn't barter could again begin. Government workers would get small bank accounts and could use their New World Currency Units to make purchases. At first, there was little to buy but gradually items were coming available for small purchases all still controlled by the local governments.

Chairman Hunt pressed a button on a remote to allow the people on the screen to hear him. He began, "I'm happy to see you all here and in good health, today. We have several problems that I believe are important to funnel NWCUs into. This information has been forwarded to you via a closed electronic link, is encrypted, and goes directly to each of you through a private network. We have just received the census and sadly the world's population has fallen further. As I understand it, you all have received the raw data as to where the Earth is now most populated. Please study it and forward recommendations for the distribution of workloads for the new factories that will soon begin to replicate the alien technology. If we are going to begin to increase the population of the planet, we'll need to get food, medicine, and viable work into every region. It's important that people begin to breed again."

The World Bank President from Germany, Dieter Gruber, spoke, "Mister Chairman, my government is not happy with the current technology transfer. My country believes that Germany is being excluded from the leading edge of technology because of the last world war."

Hunt: "Your job is to convince your government that the assertion that we are excluding them from technology is not correct and that all technology will be shared in the fullness of time. Any technology that we now have will probably be soon considered obsolete as we begin to reengineer the alien technology from the wormhole."

"Even though it's true that you're excluding us?" Gruber of Germany stated flatly.

"Even though it is true, Gruber. We fear a German exit from the World Government. There is no room for dissension in our world anymore. Any country that does not conform will be excluded from all technology and access to NWCUs. You also need to keep that in mind, Lun."

Deng Lun nodded.

"I understand," Gruber responded. "I'll deliver that message to the heads of my government."

Hunt continued forcefully, "This is something that you all need to understand. None of you are any longer citizens of your countries. There is no more, 'my government.' Your allegiance is to this New World Government that we're trying to create. We can no longer be divided if the aliens return."

After a short, stunned silence, Hunt began his agenda, "First order of business, the problem of the growing spores especially in Africa and South America. We have not been able to fight back this problem in these regions. As I understand it, there are large groups of people who have been exposed to the plants and are now out of control, killing indiscriminately and spreading the spores. I have been in communication with the Joint Chiefs of the United States to send in several divisions of fully mechanized Army to go into both continents to try to get on top of this problem. As I understand it, Europe is not having the same problem. What are you hearing, Mister Gruber?"

"The continent has had some outbreaks. Mostly in Spain and a small portion in Portugal near the Spanish border. Both France and Germany are going to send troops there to help the government attempt to fight back the problem. Because the spores act as a kind of parasite on the people who encounter them, the people infected seem to be completely out of control. We have had a great deal of time to examine the dead bodies but the parasites are so alien to our world that we have no cure. They continue to grow and multiply in each person until the person expires then the parasites crawl from the dead bodies, enter the ground and the plants pop up again. At first, we didn't believe that humans could catch it from each other, but now we think that people bitten by the infected might also be infected or from other blood to blood contact. It's a growing problem."

Charles Rousseau of France commented about the European continent, "As far as we can tell, most of the alien spheres were dropped in Spain. We don't know why. Maybe that was all of the spheres that the one alien ship had at its disposal. The majority of the people who have become infected with the spores dwell there. We have sealed the borders and will begin to move our troops into both countries to stop the infected people and attempt to eradicate the plants. As you know, we have had some success using a combination of the defoliant that was used in Viet Nam, Agent Orange, and the toxin botulinum. Together, these two agents seem to reduce the infestations but it's slow and sometimes the infestations return quickly. We have tried fire, burning them out, but the plants also grow back quickly and thicker as if the fire caused some kind of fertilizing. The problem we're also having is finding all of the places where the spores have taken hold. Unfortunately, the way we commonly find out is that the local populations seem to go mad in large numbers and then need to be put down. These populations seem to forget that they are human. We are currently missing a British special forces unit that we had dropped into Spain to get some intel from the region. We fear that they have been killed."

Hunt said, "This must be contained. Until it is, I can authorize no economic aid to any of the infected countries and I realize that the populations in these countries are desperate for help. I want this kept as secret as possible. We don't need a general panic by the rest of the world. Right now, we control nearly all media and communication, but that will soon change and the problem must be eradicated by that time."

Hunt then changed the direction of the discussion, "I have been informed that on Mars, JFK City is ready to expand further. The new oxygen-producing plants are online and are separating the oxygen from the CO_2 atmosphere and the first cyanobacteria (blue algae) factory is about to begin seeding the great ocean with the algae. It's time to advertise for more volunteers. By this time next year, the Martian population should swell to four thousand. That means we'll need to have more food shipped and more of the prefabbed structures ready to go. I have been told of a plan by NASA to leave large caches of supplies in Mars' orbit that can be retrieved by our spaceships stationed on Mars as Mars completes its orbit."

Murmurs of approval could be heard from each person present.

Hunt finished by asking each governor to study the census and asked for written suggestions for individual needs for the Earth-based factories.

"Thank you, Governors. We'll meet again next week."

The viewing screen blinked out. Hunt turned to the Canadian Governor. "Mister Levesque, you are set up with Doctor Wise for your first treatment of Biocare at 1:00 this afternoon at Mount Sinai Hospital."

"Thank you, Mister Hunt. The meeting went well. I think the world is moving forward. Good day and good day to you, Mister Mackelroy." Levesque reached to shake Mackelroy's hand. "I hope to see you again soon."

Mackelroy Senior nodded and shook his hand.

Levesque then turned and walked out the door.

Hunt said, "Sit down, Kenneth."

Mackelroy sat back in his chair.

"When this alien technology arrives, we will need to be discrete about who receives this information."

"I take it from the meeting that you do not trust all the countries in this New World Government."

"That is correct."

"The information will be known by all the scientists on Mars. There will be scientists from most of the major countries there and all comparing notes."

"I am hoping that you can find a way for some information to be excluded from some scientists."

"That will be problematic."

"This is essential."

Mackelroy nodded. "I'll connect with my son."

"Good day, Mister Mackelroy."

Mackelroy stood and said, "Good day." He stepped from the office knowing that, at some point, he might need to go to Mars. He didn't think he could trust his son to handle this. He just wasn't competent enough but the trip would take nine months if not longer. He breathed out and thought about it again, his son would just have to do.

Chapter 10

Mars Orbit

L1 Lagrange Point

Space Station Isla Charlie

May 10, 2105

Sol 530

0700 Hours

Isla Charlie had been tracking an incoming vehicle bound from Earth. As it neared Martian orbit, a call came to the bridge.

"Isla Charlie, this is Hanna Becker, Captain of the Deep Space Falcon 2 requesting permission to proceed to Mars' orbit." She spoke with German-accented English.

Simon Williams of Isla Charlie responded, "Welcome, Captain Becker. I'm Simon Williams, Captain of Isla Charlie. We've been expecting you."

The Deep Space Falcon 2 was a sleek space vehicle which had the appearance of a submarine. It had been commissioned just after the missing Nostromo and was the same Falcon Class Spacecraft built for travel into the far reaches of the solar system and also built for war. At its rear was an expandable gravity ring that when fully expanded could mimic 80 percent of the gravity of Earth. The Deep Space Falcon 2 was designed for interplanetary space travel with speeds approaching 120,000 MPH and with a full array of weapon systems which included projectile weapons that had no electronic guidance. These old-school weapons were designed to engage an enemy like the aliens who had attacked Earth. The aliens took down the electronics of every city and every weapon system that they encountered leaving most of Earth defenseless. Being struck by these high explosive charges would not be dependent upon electronics once fired.

The D.S. Falcon 2 contained the first police force for the colonies on Mars, thirty trained police in all. It also had two shuttles capable of carrying twenty men each, four AK4000, and the main spacecraft came equipped with a full array of weaponry including air to surface missiles and air to air missiles.

This would be the first deployment of police or paramilitary, which may be a more appropriate term, to the red planet. There would be more to come.

Williams of Isla Charlie continued, "You can proceed to the coordinates on your screen. You can then shuttle down and land at those forwarded coordinates which is the Noachis Terra Landing Port. It's close to the new Noachis Terra Mall. We would have you land at the mall itself, but we have shuttles a bit stacked up waiting to land there right now."

The Noachis Terra Landing Port was the future site of a large landing port with its construction nearly finished. It now only contained several landing pads but, in the next few days, shuttles would be able to land at this port and into large airlocks. Anyone arriving on Mars would then be able to take sleek underground magnetically powered trains to any inhabited location on the red planet. For now, rover busses would meet arriving flights and would take those arriving to the Noachis Terra Mall where they could catch an underground train to their destination. The maze of underground trains was close to being completed and would service all currently built locations in JFK City including a train to the research facility located ten miles from its edge. The number of construction crews now on Mars to build the necessary infrastructure was more than half the population of the planet at 1220 workers and growing.

Williams continued, "We will have a rover bus there to meet you. It will take you to the Noachis Terra Mall. Once there, you'll be able to catch an underground train to the northern portion of Condo City which is about a mile from the mall. You'll be temporarily housed at the City until your base camp is ready. Sorry for this inconvenience. We are in the middle of construction and haven't completed our transportation system out to the landing pads as yet. We'll unpack your gear and have it bussed over to Condo City. Colonel Singleton has informed me that he will be testing the life support systems at your base in a day."

"Thank you, Sir," Becker responded. "We'll be on our way."

The D.S. Falcon 2 banked away from Isla Charlie and proceeded to their orbit. Once arriving, the thirty police boarded two shuttles and left their ship for the surface. Thirty minutes later, they landed on the planet at the Noachis Terra Landing Port.

The thirty police stepped out of the shuttles in full space suits and climbed into the rover bus which could hold around sixty people. It had several connected cars and each car had large wide wheels designed for traversing the loose soil of the Martian surface.

Dense fog choked the sprawling JFK City and the going was slow as the rover bus drove out of sight and toward Noachis Terra Mall.

Chapter 11

Finally, a day off, Taylor Chapman thought. She had been working since her and Kirk's last excursion to Noachis Terra Mall, sixteen straight days and she was fried. She would get two days off, a rarity.

Kirk had been on the simulators and though he had trained some each day, it wasn't full days so he wasn't as burnt out. There was a rumor that the older AK2100 and AK2200 were going to be retired in the not too distant future in favor of the later designed AKs. In the new AKs, the second pilot would control the weapon's systems while the first would fly the vehicle. Each pilot was being trained for both rolls. These crafts could be used to track down and divert asteroids just like the older vehicles and could be piloted without the use of the second pilot, but the world was gearing up for a conflict in space that they thought would eventually come.

Taylor had awoken before Kirk and she laid in his bed thinking. When Kirk started to move, Taylor said, "Are you awake?"

"Yep." He was facing away from her.

"Let's go down to the mall."

"Sounds good to me," Kirk said, rolling over and wrapping his arms around Taylor. He kissed her cheek.

She turned and kissed his lips then sat up, stretching. She said, "Let's take a shower before we go."

Each person on the space station was allowed one shower a week. The shower system, newly expanded, had twelve stalls and hot water enough for a timed ten-minute shower. After the ten minutes were up, the shower went off regardless of how much soap was left on the person's body.

Taylor stood. She had on a long tee shirt and panties. As she pulled on a pair of sweats, she said, "I love the mall. I'm really glad they built it and I'm glad we have the day off together."

Kirk smiled, stood, and pulled on his own sweats. "Me too. Let's go shower."

Taylor said, "Maybe we should go to the movie theater?"

"That sounds good."

"If it's a space sci-fi, I don't want to go."

"Ha. You know you love those movies."

"I know, just kidding."

Both still sleepy, they left the room and shuffled to the showers.

The men's and women's showers were down the corridor and across the hall from each other.

Kirk said, "Come and shower with me."

"No. There are other men in there. I can hear them."

"Then I'll come and shower with you."

"Sorry, Kirk, there are other women in the women's showers also. I can hear them too, not that you would mind."

"Yeah, I'd just hate to be around naked women."

"Jerk," Taylor said, smirking, then, "Hey, why don't we see if we can get a room in Condo City for the night? I hear each room has its own shower."

"That'd be fun."

"Sorry, but there would only be one naked woman in your room."

"I guess then I'd just have to get by."

"Jerk."

Kirk laughed.

Taylor said, "I did hear that a couple of spaceships just arrived. Let's go to the hotel first and see if there is any room."

"Sounds great," Kirk agreed.

They showered and went back to Kirk's room to change, then left for the shuttle to the surface dressed in their NASA blues.

Chapter 12

Mars Orbit

Space Station Isla Charlie

May 10, 2105

Sol 530

0915 Hours

General Matthews waited at the shuttle bay. He glanced around nervously until he saw Doctor Belinda Waters step into view. She said she would come if there weren't any medical emergencies on the space station. He smiled to himself and turned to face her as she walked up dressed in the NASA blue jumpsuits that most wore. He was used to seeing her in her white lab coat.

"Hi, Belinda. I'm glad you decided to come."

"Well, I haven't had a real day off for nearly a year, so, why not?"

"The shuttle is about to leave, let's get a seat."

They stepped into the shuttle. It was docked on the side of the bottom spinning ring and they stepped into the side door.

The shuttle was nearly full and they sat together in the second to the last row.

Lynn Anderson, the shuttle's pilot came on the com. "Buckle up, we're counting down. Three minutes until we depart."

General Matthews turned and smiled at the Doctor. He said, "I think you'll like the mall. I was down there for the opening and it's pretty interesting."

"I've heard some things about it."

"I do like the images that are projected on the walls. They're really trying to give the impression of Earth."

The shuttle detached from the station and the passenger compartment became weightless.

Waters glanced around and said, "I almost forgot what that felt like." Her hair, which was tie behind her, rose nearly straight out. She reached back and tucked it between herself and her seat.

General Matthews said, "I hear that there will soon be a new exhibit that takes you on a flyover of the Grand Canyon, the pyramids, and other places on Earth. Then they are planning to have another exhibit that takes you over the sights on Mars like Vallas Marineris and Olympus Mons, oh and Hallas Basin, which is already filling up with water."

Doctor Waters nodded.

The conversation was a bit strained. Matthews was trying too hard and the Doctor could feel it.

The shuttle banked right and entered Mars' thermosphere. Heat showed on the outside of the craft glowing orange as the shuttle penetrated the thickening atmosphere. The glow could be seen through the side windows and the ride became bumpy.

Soon gravity returned as the shuttle leveled and began its descent. Matthews and Waters both sat in an awkward silence.

The shuttle captain came on the com, "We're going to circle for five minutes while the shuttle from Isla Bravo departs. Sit tight and I'll have you down there in a few minutes."

Mathews turned and smiled at Waters who half-smiled back.

The shuttle made a couple more spins around JFK City then landed on the Noachis Terra Mall's landing pad. The pad began to descend and the large doors slid closed above. The automated tunnel attached to the side of the shuttle and Captain Anderson announced, "I'm opening the shuttle hatch. Have fun."

The hatch opened and everyone stood and began talking all at once. The group of around thirty began filing out of the shuttle, two by two, and walking through the tunnel and into a large airlock in front of the mall's main entryway.

Waters and the General stepped out of the tunnel from the shuttle and into the airlock and as they did, could see the towering redwood trees through the large plate glass windows that separated the airlock from the redwood hallway. Seated on benches in the hallway were soldiers in space suits.

"Wow," Doctor Waters commented. "That's beautiful."

The redwood hallway seemed to be alive with the giant redwoods. Their foliage swayed in a breeze with the fern-covered ground below.

Waters said in amazement, "It looks so real."

"It does and there's more."

Waters commented, "There's a lot of what looks like soldiers in there."

"Yeah, they just landed and are heading to their base once it's finished."

Waters nodded.

An employee of the mall waited as everyone from the shuttle came from the tunnel and into the airlock. As they gathered, he said, "Welcome. I have a couple of announcements."

Chapter 13

Mars Surface

Noachis Terra Mall

May 10, 2105

Sol 530

1030 Hours

Taylor Chapman and Kirk Matthews had walked from the shuttle, through the redwood hallway and had seen the soldiers sitting on the benches. They were in space suits and looked uncomfortable. Their helmets were stowed in small bags that sat near them. The soldiers seem to be waiting and looked impatient. There were mostly men but maybe a quarter were women.

Something had bothered Kirk as he had scanned the faces of the soldiers. He and Taylor stood in front of the ocean scene gazing out at the beach as the waves crashed against the sand. They could see children at the water's edge and could hear the sounds of the gulls and the waves. A child shrieked excitedly as she ran from a wave about to strike her tiny body.

She giggled as the wave struck her from behind and made her wet from the waist down.

Taylor smiled at the image of the cute, blond child but Kirk stared out into the ocean, lost in thought. The projection of the ocean faded in the distance obscured by a mist that seemed to rise from the swells and blend with the low horizon making the sky and ocean appear to be one.

As Kirk stood, it dawned on him that at least half of the soldiers had that odd stretched skin look. It was harder to tell because they all looked so young as if just out of high school.

"Huh," Kirk said under his breath.

Taylor could tell by the look on Kirk's face that something was wrong. She continued to gaze at the ocean projection but surreptitiously glanced at Kirk. She turned to him. "What is it?"

"Just a minute," Kirk said, turning back to look at the soldiers. He stared.

"What?"

Kirk said, "More than half of those guys have the same look as my uncle."

Taylor turned and glanced quickly over her shoulder at the last of the soldiers. A couple of them were looking her way. One smiled. She turned away and could see that at least two of the six in the group that she glanced at had the odd smooth, stretched skin appearance.

"Huh," she echoed.

Kirk said, "Come and sit with me for a second. I want to get a better look."

He led Taylor to an empty bench that faced the redwood hallway and sat. Taylor sat down by him.

Kirk said, "It looked like around twenty-plus soldiers, maybe more."

Taylor nodded.

Kirk said questioningly, "Why do only some have that look? If they were going to give the soldiers the drugs, why wouldn't they administer it to all of them?"

Taylor said, "Maybe they did and it hasn't started working yet," she paused then said, "Or maybe it's some kind of double-blind test to see what happens to them."

"Lab rats?"

"Maybe."

Kirk continued to observe the soldiers when a familiar face emerged from the redwood hallway. He nudged Taylor who glanced back in that direction.

"There's my uncle."

"Where?"

"He's the guy to the left walking with the lady with the long ponytail and auburn hair."

General Matthews was pointing toward the museum exhibit.

Taylor said, "He looks different from the last time I saw him."

"It's probably the drugs." Kirk stood and took Taylor's hand, "Come on. Let's catch up with him."

They walked toward a group of people all dressed in the NASA blue jumpsuits. The group had just stepped through the redwood hallway and into the ocean foyer. Most of that group turned to the left in the direction of the restaurants.

The General was pointing at the ocean scene and the woman, who he was with, mouthed the word, *wow*. She looked amazed. They turned toward the restaurants.

Kirk caught up with the General.

"Good morning, Uncle," Kirk said.

General Matthews hadn't seen him coming and he turned surprised. "Kirk. What a pleasant surprise."

Kirk briefly hugged his uncle then stepped back and said, "Uncle Jeff, do you remember Taylor?"

"Hello, Taylor. I'm pleased to see you, again."

She smiled and shook his hand.

The General said, "This is Belinda Waters. She's the doctor aboard Isla Charlie."

"Hi, Belinda," Kirk said warmly, reaching for her hand.

Taylor and Belinda shook hands also.

"What brings you here, Uncle?" Kirk asked.

"Same as you, I guess, a bit of a getaway and hopefully a cheeseburger."

"Let's eat together," Kirk suggested. "We were just headed that way."

Uncle Jeff said, "Sounds good to me."

They turned and began to walk toward the food court when a loud voice with the sound of a sergeant barked from behind them, "Come to me, people."

All the soldiers stood simultaneously and lifted their small bags.

The same voice then said, "This way to the trains."

"Who are they, Uncle?" Kirk asked.

"That's the beginning of the police force for Mars. It will be a military police force, MPs, for now anyway, and they will be attached to the soon to be constructed military base. I'm hoping to eventually be stationed there. They will also be guarding the research facility. I'm sure most of them will be at the facility around the clock."

Kirk nodded then turned to Belinda. "Have you been down here before, Doctor?"

"No," she responded.

"It's a pretty amazing place. Taylor and I came down around a week ago. They have decent cheeseburgers at the food court, too."

"That sounds good," Belinda said.

The four began to walk slowly toward the hallway with the shops that led to the food court.

The soldiers turned down a corridor to the right of the redwood hallway marked trains. The corridor led to an underground train station with several rows of tracks between two loading platforms. Signs lit with incoming and departing trains and schedules.

Belinda Waters, General Matthews, Taylor Chapman, and Kirk Matthews strolled past the shops. When they reached the theater, a double feature was playing with the first film being "Odyssey," a movie set five hundred years in the future on Mars, and the second movie, a fantasy called, "A Hero's Path," about a young girl who saves the world.

Kirk said, "After lunch, we're going to catch a movie."

"That sounds like fun," the General commented.

"Oh, yeah," Kirk said. "I almost forgot. We're going to see if we can get a room at the hotel, tonight. I hope it isn't filled with all these new people arriving on the planet."

The General said, "Just a minute." He pushed at an earpiece and said, "Hi, this is General Matthews. I need a room for tonight at the hotel. Yes. The reservation is for Kirk Matthews. Yes, one night. Thank you. There you go, Kirk. All set up."

"Thanks, Uncle."

They turned and walked into the food court. As they approached the hamburger place, Kirk could see Lenny flipping burgers, smiling, and singing a tune to himself.

Lenny turned, "Hello, Kirk."

"You remembered my name?"

Lenny smiled, "There aren't that many people here. What can I get you?"

"What do you want, Uncle?"

General Matthews turned to Belinda, "What would you like?"

"Cheeseburger and fries, I guess."

"And for you, Taylor?" the General asked.

"I'll have the same."

"That sounds good to me, too," the General said.

Kirk said, "Make mine a double, Lenny."

"You got it, coming right up."

Kirk asked the group, "Oh, how about four beers?"

They all nodded and Lenny said, "Four beers." He set them on the counter.

They took their beers, which were ice cold, 12 ounces, and in rectangular aluminum containers, to a table and sat.

Belinda gazed at the scene of the boardwalk and fishing docks outside the faux windows and the four opened their beverages. She said, "It really appears as if we're at a restaurant by the ocean somewhere."

"They did a remarkable job on this mall," the General agreed then added, "The human population is about to get very big on Mars in the next couple of years."

Taylor asked, "Is this why they built this mall the way they did?"

"Exactly. They want to lure people to become colonists on Mars but they also are hoping to keep them mentally healthy once they get here. This is uncharted territory. Take you two, for example. You have been able to find each other. It helps to have someone when you're so far from home. This mall is a tiny slice of home but it isn't like standing on the real ocean shore or walking through the redwoods. We don't know how humans are going to last long term here. We are hoping that if we can break a few barriers around speed that it will be feasible to have people stay a while but then go back to Earth, then decide whether or not to return. We don't think that we'll be able to travel fast enough to vacation on Earth. We just don't know. We have had a rash of depression that Belinda has been reporting to me."

"That's true," Belinda added. "The occurrence of depression among those of our small population has doubled each year since we've become established on Mars. It didn't happen to the colonists at first because it was all so new, exciting, you know, but after, once things became mundane, the depression began to surface."

"I get it," Kirk responded and Taylor agreed, saying that they both had fought with some depression.

Kirk asked, changing the subject away from depression because the discussion was depressing, "So what other building are they planning?"

"Besides the normal building to continue the terraforming, there will be the military base that I mentioned and I've been told that not far from here, a complete tourist resort is planned. We already have corporations running things on the planet."

"Like?" Kirk asked.

Lenny announced, "Kirk, your food is ready."

"I'll get it." Kirk stood and brought over the burgers and fries on a tray.

They all began to eat.

The General stuck a french fry in his mouth and said, "The research facility is being managed by a corporation that specialized in cutting edge technology before the world went to hell. They worked with the DOD and DARPA. The mall is largely owned and operated by corporations but the managing of life support and other essentials are still military."

Kirk commented, "The research facility? Why would the military trust a corporation to run the facility where all of that alien wreckage is going to be examined?"

"These guys specialize in reverse-engineering the technology. They had always been a defense contractor. The military and each of the major countries all have scientists that will be working on the alien wreckage. The company, "Space Tech," is just in charge of streamlining the information into the right slots and then choosing what they think they can reverse engineer quickly. Some things will probably be set aside for a later date if it's just too far above us."

"And you're happy with the decision to have this company doing the streamlining?"

"No, not completely. I'm military, Kirk. I think the military is the best place for secrets, but many don't agree with me. Politicians want control of the vital secrets and tend to not fully trust the military. This New World Bank seems to be pulling the strings behind the scenes. I'm not sure how much power they actually have. Everything is a compromise right now. I just hope they do a good job so we will be able to repel the next alien invasion. We didn't do such a great job with the last one."

The General took a long sip of his beer and turned to Taylor, "So, Taylor, refresh my memory, what do you do on Isla Bravo?"

"I monitor asteroids to try to help us avoid them or in some cases helping to select the right ones for depositing onto the Martian surface."

The General thought for an instant then said, "That's right. You're the person who identified the asteroid that was being used as a taxi for the alien craft that attacked Earth."

"Yep."

Kirk asked, "When is the alien wreckage supposed to arrive?"

"Two days."

"Cool." Kirk said, then turned to Doctor Waters to change the subject, "How long have you known Uncle Jeff?"

Waters smiled at the directness of the question and the implications. "I have treated your uncle for around a dozen years give or take a few months."

"How do you like space?"

"Well, at first it was pretty exciting, but I must admit that it's getting kind of old. Maybe Mars will be more hospitable someday."

"Maybe," Kirk responded.

They ate in silence for a bit enjoying the taste of home and savoring it more than one would normally savor a hamburger on Earth.

"This is wonderful," Doctor Waters said softly.

Kirk asked, "Uncle, have you heard from my father lately?"

"Just talked to him."

"It's been about four years since he took the Chief of Staff job with the new President. The last time I talked to him, I thought that he sounded like he missed Congress."

"I don't know, Kirk, your father is an important advisor and gets the direct ear of President Woodward. It was a tough job for him to take over for President Dent who did a great job for all those years after the crisis."

"I thought Dad was going to run for President."

"He felt that he had gotten too old. That's why he retired from Congress."

"I think he would have made a good President."

"I think so too. It's a difficult job right now with the transition to the World Government. Every country likes it in principal but none like it in practice. Not even us. I hear that the New World Bank is dragging most of the countries in line kicking and screaming."

"What does Dad think about the world alliance?"

"He's skeptical that it will hold up. He believes that all of the main countries are secretly planning some kind of withdrawal if we survive the next alien invasion, but everyone is spooked because no one believes that we will survive if the aliens attack in force, unlike the last time where it was just one alien craft. That was, without question, a trip to the woodshed."

"So, you don't think we're ready if they return."

"Hell no. They'll beat us like a red-headed stepchild."

"Geez."

The General took a bite of his hamburger then said, "Things move too slowly on Earth. There's too much wrangling. We needed a response like the response from the United States after Pearl Harbor was bombed. The world is full of too many politicians and too many interests and now the rich have returned. They had been forced into the background but now they're back and them strutting their stuffed shirts is nothing but an obstruction. I wouldn't care if everything were back to normal. Becoming wealthy because you came up with a great idea or wrote a great book or cured some disease is as American as apple pie but these guys haven't been used to not getting their way or living the way that they had become accustomed. Now they seem to have been able to slip into us trying to defend our planet and I don't see how that's going to help."

"I see," Kirk said.

There was a pause while they all ate.

Taylor decided to change the direction of the discussion that had suddenly become more depressing. "So, Belinda, have you ever thought about going back to Earth to practice?"

Kirk smiled and the General finished a big sip of beer.

Doctor Waters said, "No. I do love space and the thought of it. I kind of hope to end up on Mars someday."

"Kirk and I have talked about that also."

Kirk said, "It will be interesting to see what happens to Mars in the future. Right now, it's a rough place to live, but it sounds like at some point, it's going to become a destination."

The General said, "It will always be a place for scientific study but I'm getting the impression that it may also become a place for the rich to play."

"Huh," Kirk said then changed the direction back to the war effort, "Uncle? I was wondering why I haven't seen more warships out here built to battle the next alien invasion. It does seem like we haven't been doing much preparation considering that first attack."

"The aliens used a sophisticated EMP attack that we had never seen before. It was technologically above us. We have a few things planned as a response if they attack the same way next time but I'm not sure it will be enough."

Kirk said, "We need to get the wreckage studied."

"I couldn't agree more, but the United States has been doing some work for our defense. Just not enough. I do understand why it's taken so long to get started on building our military. A lot of attention had to continue to be directed at Mars or people here would die. The world was a mess just after the alien attack. A lot of effort had to be directed to help or people were going to starve and anarchy also had to be held at bay. A fleet has been built with our current technology, but we're hoping for a boost from the recovered alien tech. This fleet is now in orbit around Earth and numbers twenty Predator Class craft. The EMP drones used against the alien ship when it attacked the United States have been redesigned for space and carry an EMP shockwave explosive device to attempt to knock down the alien's defenses but that's the best we can do right now. We fear that we will not be able to fend off another invasion with these vessels. Right now, we're between a rock and a hard place."

"So, if we were invaded right now, we'd be toast."

"That's about the size of it, but we have sensors placed around the wormhole and believe that we'll get a couple of years warning if the alien vessels return, but who knows?"

Kirk nodded and glanced at Taylor who had finished eating. She had a look of worry on her face and it was warranted. She took a big sip of beer and gazed out of the faux windows.

Kirk continued his train of thought, "So, who's doing the planning. In the past, it would have been the Pentagon for the U.S. but with this new world government, who's calling the shots?"

"That's a complicated question. There's been a council of military from the strongest countries that are in a new building close to the Pentagon. The U.S. military ferries generals and planners back and forth between the two buildings, but none of the major countries with deep secrets are sharing those secrets with anyone else, so China, the United States, Israel, Germany, and Great Britain are all keeping separate forces from the World Government Military. We had to let the secret of using antimatter for fuel out, so the world now has that, but we're guarding other secrets. Of the major countries, only India, Mexico, Canada, and France are not keeping separate militaries. They are the most open to the world alliance and seem to get the urgency of the problem. The rest of us, I don't know. It's kind of a muddled mess and nothing has stopped the spying though we're all supposed to be one world."

"I don't see how we can defeat the aliens with this kind of setup."

"I agree but I'm old school and don't trust even one of the aforementioned governments or their militaries. It seems like a catch 22."

Kirk said, "Well, when the you-know-what, hits the fan, I hope we're all working together."

"That's my hope also, but I kind of doubt it. The aliens have taken too long to return and now this tentative world government experiment is beginning to fracture."

They quietly finished what was left of their food, stood, and threw away the trash.

"Well," the General said, "It was nice to see you, again, Taylor. Sorry that the conversation got a bit bleak."

"No worries, it was good to see you too, General."

"Good to meet you also," Kirk said to Doctor Waters.

She nodded and smiled warmly.

Kirk asked, "Are you going to the museum, Uncle?"

"I think so. I think we're going to browse the shops, first. Belinda and I both want to take a look at the bookshop, oh, and we're going to walk through the aquarium."

Taylor said, "I want to go to the bookstore also before we leave."

Kirk said, "See you guys later. Have fun."

Kirk and Taylor turned for the theater while the General and Doctor Waters veered off to the aquarium.

Kirk glanced to Taylor as he stepped toward the window to order tickets. Before they reached the window, Kirk said, "Do you see what I mean about that odd stretched skin on my uncle and the soldiers?"

"Yeah. I think you're right."

Kirk nodded then said, "Well, what movie is it going to be, five hundred years from now on Mars or unlikely girl saves the world?"

Taylor paused for a second then said, "Well, we're on Mars so we might as well see what happens five hundred years from now."

Kirk glanced at a female employee of the theater. He said, "Two for Odyssey, please."

The girl said, "Two for Odyssey. Starts in twenty minutes. Popcorn in the lobby."

Kirk and Taylor walked into a traditional movie theater lobby with a counter to order popcorn and drinks. There was no candy but it had a couple of hotdogs turning on a device with rollers that slowly rotated each until done or thrown in the trash, whichever came first.

"Just like home," Kirk said.

"It's kind of amazing," Taylor agreed. "Let's get some popcorn."

They got popcorn and soda and walked into the semi-dark theater. The theater could seat about a hundred people but today, most of the seats were empty. Kirk and Taylor sat on an aisle, munched their popcorn, and waited for the curtains to pull back.

Part 2

Arrival

Chapter 14

Mars Orbit

Space Station Isla Charlie

May 12, 2105

Sol 532

Captain Simon Williams gazed at the large screen on the bridge of Isla Charlie. Before him, an enormous space structure came slowly into view. Williams remembered this hulking structure from before as it was heading out to recover the alien wreckage. It had two spinning gravity rings, the same as Isla Charlie but between the rings was a cylindrical structure of more than twenty feet in height and it protruded out to nearly the edges of the gravity rings. Everything in the center structure would be weightless so would be easy to handle.

A call came into Isla Charlie.

"Captain Williams, you have a message from the salvage ship," Naomi Scott, the communications specialist announced.

"This is Captain Williams."

"Hello, Captain. Captain Chin here."

Williams said, "Put him on the screen please."

Scott nodded and said, "On Screen."

The image of the salvage ship disappeared and the image of Captain Chin of China appeared.

"Hello, Captain Chin. How went the mission?"

"Very well. We have recovered most of the technology that we could salvage and even an intact small fighter-like craft. Our scientists couldn't make heads or tails of most of what we collected because of its condition. A lot of what we found was burnt beyond recognition, some too radiated and we were limited in the space we had to work with to bring it back, but all in all, I think we have a decent representative sample of most of the alien tech. Our scientists will be forwarding their notes to the facility on Mars."

"Are your scientists going to work at the facility?"

"Yes. Most will proceed to Mars to help inventory and categorize the collected items. That's going to be a monumental task all by itself."

"How long until you begin transporting the collected items?"

"As soon as, Captain. Everything has been organized and sterilized and is ready to go.

"Very good. You can proceed to your designated orbit."

"Thank you, Captain. Chin out."

The enormous structure lumbered away from Isla Charlie to its orbit between Mars and its moons. Once in place, it began the twelve-hour process of detaching its two spinning rings from the center structure. First, the rings began to slow to a stop. Once stopped, everything not nailed down inside the rings began to float as the gravity caused by the spinning slowly decreased until there was no gravity left in the wheels. The crew had drilled on this for the entire time that it took to return to Mars.

The bottom ring then separated from the cylinder in the middle and pulled away. The top ring then maneuvered the cylinder into position and once the cylinder was properly aligned for entry into the planet's atmosphere, the top ring released the cylindrical portion of the craft, and thanks to the planet's gravity, the cylinder began its descent towards the surface. The ring then moved to join the first ring which had already detached and the cylindrical structure ignited its engines and pushed the craft containing the alien wreckage towards the planet and its eventual destination, the NASA Mars Research Center.

The salvage ship sent a shuttle with forty of the scientists who worked on the alien wreckage at the wormhole to the research facility.

The two rings of the salvage craft would again spin to create gravity, then would begin the trip back to Earth in seven days and would be attached to a new spaceport now being assembled in Earth orbit. Their arrival time, two hundred and seventy days.

Once the center structure was in place on Mars, the construction crews would finish building a permanent structure to the craft which would allow the alien technology to be offloaded and categorized, piece by piece, into the research facility.

Chapter 15

Mars Surface

Condo City

May 13, 2105

Sol 533

0425 Hours

Marriam Daily and Sanjay Patel had become colonists. After spending years aboard Isla Charlie, they now had a small condo on the surface of Mars in Condo City. The condo was apartment-like with a living space that contained a bedroom with a comfortable queen-sized bed, dining room, and living room with a couch and coffee table and a large screened TV. There was also a small kitchenette but there was no food to be purchased for individuals to prepare on Mars so the kitchen was a bare minimum with a pantry, microwave, a small refrigerator, and no stove. It wasn't much but it was home and huge compared to the small box that they shared on Isla Charlie.

The condo was attached to the Noachis Terra mall by moving sidewalks where they could then catch a high-speed train to the research facility where they were both now employed. Soon, the trains would come to Condo City directly, but that was considered a low priority for now.

Their main job and the reason that they had come to space was to continue their work with the alien artifact found on Earth back in 2085, now known as 'Egbert.' A lot had happened since then. They had previously been top researchers at the infamous Area 51, a remote detachment of Edwards Airforce Base nestled in the Nevada desert which is where they met.

They each took turns going to Isla Charlie for the daily briefings and reported everything to the dormant Egbert and his twin. These two alien artifacts had changed the course of human history.

Marriam rolled from bed. It was her turn to take the shuttle to Isla Charlie. Sanjay was cocooned in his covers and would go to the NASA Mars Research Center in three hours at 8:00 am as it geared up for the arrival of the alien wreckage from the wormhole.

"Sanjay," Marriam said, "I need a shower before I go."

For the last two weeks, the showers had only been working three days a week, Monday, Wednesday, and Friday because the water treatment plant was having trouble keeping up with the water needs of the burgeoning population of Mars, so, they had been showering together. The treatment plant would need to be expanded.

"Huh, oh," Sanjay said half asleep. He seemed to doze back off.

"You're going to need to get up or you'll miss your shower today. Not to mention getting to see me naked."

Sanjay's eyes opened. He smiled and sat up. "I could skip the shower, but I would hate to miss gazing at your milky flesh, all wet and slippery."

Marriam smiled wryly and dropped her nightgown.

They showered together, dressed, and made coffee, then ate a quick bite and Marriam left to meet the 6:00 am shuttle to Isla Charlie. She would have to catch a train from the mall to the newly completed station at the Noachis Terra landing pads. The airlocks were now complete and she could catch the shuttle ride to Isla Charlie without wearing a spacesuit. The ride took a little more than a flight from San Francisco to Los Angeles. In an hour, Sanjay would take a train to the research facility ten miles from Condo City and it would take about the same time.

As Marriam left the condo, Sanjay laid back on the bed for another hour's sleep.

Marriam walked briskly to the first step of her commute, a long moving sidewalk that would take her to an underground train station two stories below the Noachis Terra Mall. The sidewalk at top speed moved at what would be considered a reasonable jog. Just as in some airports back on Earth, the sidewalks were placed in wide walking areas that led from Condo City to the mall itself. To board the moving sidewalks, a person would step onto a merging sidewalk that began slowly then ramped up to the speed of the express sidewalk. These moving sidewalks had places where someone could sit if they desired or stand for the ten-minute journey. The entire structure where the sidewalk passed was painted bright white and was well lit.

Marriam found a seat and pulled out a trashy novel that she had purchased at the mall two days prior. It was a 250-page paperback romance written fifty years ago, set in New York, and featured a struggling, unsuccessful writer who meets a woman editor who mercilessly criticizes his writing and who, of course, makes him successful. Marriam had just reached the point where their first sweaty lovemaking scene had taken place leaving them both drained, uncovered from the waist up, and gazing at the ceiling of the editor's bedroom.

The woman editor in the book, Gloria, says, "Just because I slept with you doesn't mean that I'm going to cut you any slack on that last chapter of your book. It needs a lot of work."

"That may be so," Dirk, (the writer), replied, reaching again for her nether regions, "But I can, at least, postpone it for a while."

He found her pleasure spot and she arched at his touch, found his lips with hers, reached for his abundant and ever-ready manhood, and pulled him into her.

"Oh, Dirk," she moaned as he slid into her depths.

Marriam blushed slightly, picturing in detail Dirk's ample man part in all its glory as it found Gloria's warm slippery private place and she began to giggle to herself and thought, this is such crap. She read on...

The sidewalk neared its end and Marriam needed to stand. People leaving the mall area for Condo City began boarding another sidewalk here that was headed back.

Next, she caught the train that would take her to the landing port. These trains were simple, they had no propulsion of their own. Each car was sent forward by magnetic on and off charges that changed the polarity of the car as if reversing a magnet to repel instead of attract, then turned it back to attract. This would push and pull the train through the long tunnel to the landing pad. Sometimes the trains would be full and slide together down the tunnel, but other times a single rider might be on a single car depending on the number of people commuting at any one time. Each tunnel was just one way.

She reached the landing pad quickly finishing the next chapter of her novel where the writer, Dirk, leaves Gloria's office in a huff because she insulted one of the passages of his book.

Marriam laughed again and said to herself, "Didn't see that coming." Then she thought, I bet they make up with a torrid roll in the hay.

She boarded the shuttle that would take her to Isla Charlie and it lifted off with the rumble of engines, then a burst of power pushing everyone back in their seats.

Marriam's eyes were glued to her book when, just as expected, Dirk knocked on Gloria's apartment door carrying a bottle of the finest champagne. Gloria pulled Dirk inside kissing him thoroughly, unbuttoning his shirt, and pushing it from his muscular, tanned shoulders...

Marriam noticed the sensation of weightlessness as the shuttle banked towards Isla Charlie. She stowed her book in her bag and glanced out of the portholes to see the stars appear as the shuttle left the Martian atmosphere.

0630 Hours

Fifteen minutes later, Isla Charlie came into view as the shuttle approached the station's twin spinning wheels. The shuttle then matched the top wheels spin and docked. Gravity returned to the shuttle as it began to rotate with the station's upper wheel. A green light situated over the cockpit hatch lit and everyone aboard unfastened their seatbelts and stood, waiting for the shuttle's side doors to open. With a loud click, the door slid open and the shuttle passengers disembarked to various places aboard the station.

Marriam turned for the meeting room.

Chapter 16

Noachis Terra, Mars

NASA Mars Research Center

May 13, 2105

Sol 533

0800 Hours

Sanjay Patel waited as the doors to the high-speed train opened as it stopped outside of the Research Facility's main entrance. He stepped off of the train. Three guards stood outside of the main entrance doors, all holding automatic weapons, all with stern expressions, and all not allowing anyone to enter the first door.

Sixteen people like himself stood on the platform waiting for something from the guards.

A man to Sanjay's left spoke first, "Can we go in?"

One guard looked up from talking with the two others. He said, "One minute, Sir."

The door opened to the facility and the head of security, George Hall, stepped out. "Can I have your attention, please?"

All eyes were already on him but everyone became quiet and more attentive.

Hall continued, "In less than an hour, our cargo is arriving. You have all been briefed on the first order of business dealing with the cargo, but I need to remind you not to veer away from where your badges allow you to enter. This is not optional. If your badge has a red stripe on its top, you must not stray away from the corridors and rooms marked in red. If your badge has more than one color, it will allow you access to the different color-coded areas. For your safety this is imperative. Some of you have already been here for a bit so you know the reasons, but for the newly arrived, we will proceed as a group to a meeting room for a quick orientation then you'll receive your assignments." Hall turned to the guards and said, "Begin."

The first guard said, "Form three lines beginning on me."

The sixteen facility workers lined up in three rows. Each worker was checked for his badge to the facility, each badge was checked against the person's ID and then each person received a retina scan. As each was finished, they were allowed to enter the first room where three scanners like airport scanners awaited with three guards sitting at each scanner. One guard was a woman and two were men.

The woman guard said, "Can I have the women to me please?"

Out of the sixteen workers, only five were women.

The woman guard said, "Hand me your badge and step into the body scanner."

The first woman in line did as asked.

The woman guard placed the worker's badge into a slot and the scanner turned on.

"Raise your arms a bit please and your feet two-feet apart," the woman guard said, gazing into a screen.

An image of the worker appeared on the screen fully nude. The scanner had removed the woman's clothes and mapped her body front and back. An odd opaque spot showed on the woman's knee.

The woman guard said, "Did you have knee surgery?"

"Yes."

"Go into the first door and remove all of your clothes. Put on the gown and wait."

The woman nodded.

By the time all sixteen people were scanned, six were asked to disrobe, two women and four men. Each was examined by a guard, both their bodies and their clothes, then they were allowed to dress and return to the group who awaited in a corridor.

This was the second time that Sanjay had been through this process. He stood patiently until the group was united.

Hall waited also and when everyone returned, he said, "Follow me please."

He walked to a large door that opened with his badge. Each person walked to the scanner and waved their badges over a white light. The light turned green and the person followed Mister Hall into the next corridor. Hall stood next to two armed security bots.

Sanjay walked through the doorway.

Once this check was complete the sixteen followed Mister Hall into a meeting room set up with a podium and sixteen chairs in two rows of eight. The bots left the group and continued down the corridor.

Once everyone was seated, Hall smiled and said, "Welcome."

Everything had been so regimented and cold to this point that the cheerful greeting was unexpected.

"Today is a momentous day at the facility. You all have some knowledge of why you're here, and some of you have already been part of the preparation, but what we have been waiting for is touching down as we speak."

Murmurs rose among the sixteen.

Another man walked in the door. He was young, appeared to be in his early thirties with the skin of his face tight against the bones.

Hall continued, "I would like to introduce you to Brady Niland, the facility director." Hall turned to the man, "Mister Niland."

Niland nodded and walked to the podium. He began, "You are about to undertake the most important research that our world has ever been faced with. The race to explode the first atomic bomb will pale next to your effort. We are at war. As you know, we have already been attacked by a technologically superior alien race and we must be ready when they return. And they will return. They chose our planet because it suited them. We suspect that they might be biologically similar to us in some ways. We are about to find out. Arriving at this facility today is the wreckage and bodies of the aliens who attacked us. We are going to find out everything that we can about them. The craft that attacked Earth before was so obliterated that we learned virtually nothing from it. Nearly everything was incinerated back into its atoms and molecules. You all have your badges so please make sure you do not wander away from where you are authorized. I will let mister Hall finish with that portion of the presentation. We need each person here to be thorough in your study of the alien craft and the bodies. Report anything that strikes you, even the smallest thing. That might be the difference between our success and failure. Thank you."

Niland stepped away and Hall stepped back to the podium. He said, "Thank you, Mister Niland. You all saw the bots that met us. They are programmed to shoot anyone in the wrong place and anyone without a badge. They will complete this task if you forget your badge and try to get in the facility. Your badge tracks you everyplace you go when here. We will not tolerate not knowing where every person in the facility is at any time. The bots are lethal. Do not go anywhere without your badges. Does everyone understand?"

All sixteen responded yes in unison.

"Alright," Hall said. "Let's get you to your various workplaces. Your cards also have your work schedules and workplaces. If you find that you've gotten turned around, slip your card into a door slot and verbally request directions to your proper location. The screen above each slot will display a map that will direct you. How many of you will be sleeping here some nights?"

Ten of the workers' hands went up.

"At the end of this presentation, I'll show you to the floor with the overnight rooms and the showers, etc."

One young man asked, "Are the bots on those floors also?"

"Yep, so keep your badges close to you. If you're showering, use the lanyards to keep the badges around your necks. I can't stress this enough; the bots make no exceptions. If you are caught without your badges, you will die."

Some shock showed on the faces of some of the workers, the ones who were not shocked had already heard this lecture.

Hall reached up and covered his ear with his hand. He said, "Yes. That's great news. Thanks." Hall glanced back at the workers. "The rocket with the alien wreckage has just landed and the structure is being extended out to it. Tomorrow the offloading will begin."

All sixteen people began murmuring at once.

Hall said, "Now, I'll finish showing you around. Please stand and follow me."

Chapter 17

Mars Orbit

Isla Charlie Meeting Room

May 13, 2105

Sol 533

0845 Hours

General Matthews was wrapping up his daily meeting with the news that the rocket containing the alien wreckage had landed successfully and would begin offloading its cargo sometime tomorrow. He was standing at a small portable podium in front of ten of his crew including Marriam Daily. Matthews had paused and was checking his notes.

Marriam could barely contain the excitement that welled up within her. Tomorrow she would begin the research on the wreckage.

"That's all I got for now," the General said, finishing.

Everyone in the room began to stand.

Marriam glanced over her notes, turned off her pad, stood with the group, and started out the door.

She wouldn't spend more than an hour with Egbert. There just wasn't that much to report.

She strolled down the hall to the room where Egbert and the other alien egg were kept, scanned her badge at the door, and wandered into the room with the alien artifacts. She froze as she gazed upon a familiar scene. Egbert and the other alien egg-like artifact glowed.

Marriam got on her com, "General, you need to come to the room."

Matthews knew that those words spoken in that way meant that Egbert had probably awoken from its long slumber. "I'll be right there."

Marriam watched as Egbert and the other artifact went through their start-up ritual. First, firework-like lights began just under the clearcoat of their shells then as the fireworks faded, an aurora of green, yellow, and white squirmed back and forth where the fireworks had ceased. As the aroura faded, the top surfaces of the artifacts became translucent then began to glow again. Next, the hologram appeared atop both with first disorganized searchlights peaking from the surfaces then those searchlights reached towards the ceiling becoming organized.

General Matthews stepped into the room with Marriam. He didn't speak. He rubbed his chin and watched. Marriam glanced his way then turned her attention back to Egbert and its twin who hadn't made a peep for around six years. Both Marriam and the General watched in wonder.

As the two holograms organized into a single field, this shared hologram began to darken in color. A starfield appeared first then Mars came into view, filling nearly the entire hologram. The red planet twisted on its axis and as it turned, the planet's distinguishing features could be seen, Valles Marineris with its deep canyon, Hellas Planitia, the largest impact crater in the solar system, and Olympus Mons, our solar system's largest volcano all in perfect view. Longitude and latitude lines appeared next on Mars as had happened before when Egbert showed the location of the other egg-like artifact. Then at a point near Noachis Terra, another red dot appeared on the longitude and latitude lines.

The General said rhetorically, "That's Noachis Terra just north of the mall."

Marriam nodded.

Then the General said questioningly, "Do you think Egbert has discovered another egg?"

Marriam watched dreamily then said, "Well, it is just a little past the Easter season."

Matthews was only half-listening. When what she said registered, he turned toward her and started to laugh. "I think you're right."

Marriam half-smiled.

In a flash of insight, Matthews said, "Something must have come with the alien wreckage."

"That's what I would think," Mariam agreed then added, "If the coordinates are close to where the wreckage is going to be offloaded."

Matthews paused for a moment then said, "I'm going to need to be down there for the offloading."

Marriam nodded then said, "Both Sanjay and I are working in the labs down there. Maybe we could observe the offloading also."

"Good idea," Matthews said then pushed at his earpiece. "Captain Williams."

Pause

"Give me the exact coordinates for the research facility."

Pause

Matthews typed into a pad. "Thanks," he said, then, "Marriam, overlay these coordinates with the red dot."

She nodded and typed at a keyboard attached to the servers that could interact with the alien artifacts.

When the coordinates for the facility plotted on the computer screen, Marriam overlaid the artifacts hologram. Both points sat directly on top of each other. They were the exact location.

Matthews watched over her shoulder as she worked. He said, "Thought so." Then he turned for the door.

As the door slid open, Marriam said, "Wait till Sanjay hears about this."

Matthews left.

Chapter 18

Mars

Noachis Terra

NASA Mars Research Center

May 14, 2105

Sol 534

0800 Hours

With the structure completed to meet the craft arriving from the wormhole and pressurized, the offloading of the alien wreckage and bodies were to begin the next day. General Matthews had arranged the first official meeting between the important players at the facility which included Captain Chin of the salvage vessel and his senior scientist, Calvin Johnson of MIT, Kenneth Mackelroy Junior, Brady Niland, Grayson Pearson, George Hall, Sanjay Patel, Marriam Daily, and Bernard Weinstein who was the senior scientist from the Mars facility and a direct employee of DARPA.

Matthews first inspected the structure that was built to meet the vessel. It was a long hallway, thirty feet high, and fifty feet wide. It met the large doors of the salvage craft and connected to the sides of the craft.

Not everything from the wormhole could be recovered, of course. Anything considered redundant was left in space. There were many dead aliens and a great deal of alien body parts scattered from the violent collision that had taken place when the armada emerged from the wormhole and collided with the asteroids in the asteroid field. Most of the wreckage had to be left, but anything that had technology built into it was taken. There was a premium of space on the recovering craft, so the chief scientist, Calvin Johnson, had the last word about what would need to be left and what would come to Mars for study.

The group met in the upper-level meeting room just inside the research facility near the offloading hallway. This room was white with folding chairs set in a semicircle and had large windows that looked down onto the warehouse where the salvage craft was setting.

General Matthews, Sanjay, Marriam, and Weinstein arrived first followed by Pearson, Niland, and Mackelroy.

Matthews was talking to Weinstein while Sanjay and Marriam sat in two of the chairs waiting for the meeting to begin.

When Pearson, Mackelroy, and Niland entered, they approached General Matthews.

Matthews turned to them and said, "Gentlemen."

Pearson smiled broadly and said, "Hello, General."

But Mackelroy and Niland both nodded with flat expressions. Neither seemed happy that General Matthews was taking the lead on this project.

Matthews continued, "Mister Pearson, I understand that this is your last week on Mars." He would leave to go home with Captain Chin when the salvage vessel headed back to Earth.

"That's correct, General."

"I'm sorry to hear that. It was good working with you."

"I believe you will be in capable hands with Mister Niland."

"Good," Mathews said shortly. "I hope you have a safe trip."

"Thank you, General."

The General then said, "The meeting will begin when Captain Chin arrives with the chief scientist from the vessel." Matthews looked directly at Mackelroy and said, "You can have a seat until I'm ready to start."

It was obvious that the General was dismissing them while he continued his quiet discussion with Weinstein.

Mackelroy, Niland, and Pearson walked away but didn't sit.

The General said quietly to Weinstein, "Listen, Professor, I'm afraid that some of the people in this room are going to want me out of some of the collected information. I hope I can count on you to make sure that I'm not."

"You have my support, General," Weinstein whispered back. "I'm not so happy with this arrangement with Space Tech either."

Mathews nodded and turned toward the group.

Mackelroy, Niland, Pearson, and Matthews had all had the life-extending drugs, all appeared to be in their thirties and all had the same stretched facial skin.

The door to the meeting room slid open and Captain Chin walked in with Hall and his chief scientist, Calvin Johnson.

Matthews greeted them warmly. "Welcome, Gentlemen," he said.

Chin and Johnson smiled and shook the General's hand.

Johnson said, "Good to meet you, General."

"And you, Professor," Matthews responded warmly.

Johnson spoke in accented English. He was tall, of African descent with a shaved head and originally from England, but had lived in the United States for thirty years.

Chin said, "Hello, General. It was a lot of work to get to this point. It's pretty exciting."

"It is, Captain," Matthews said then glanced up.

"I think we're ready to get started and I'll introduce everyone here. Please have a seat."

Everyone in the room except for Hall sat. He turned and left the room.

Matthews pulled his chair to the front, facing the semicircle. He began, "This is a momentous day. I don't need to stress the importance of our duty here. It is of vital importance that we unravel the mysteries behind the technology of this alien race as soon as possible. Our planet's very survival depends on it. So, without further ado, I will introduce each person here. First, this is Marriam Daily and Sanjay Patel, my two personal assistants. They will be working at this facility in several capacities. First, they will help to inventory the items as they are removed from the vessel. Because they are both top researchers from our Area 51 research facility on Earth, they will be involved with some of the research here as I direct them and they will also be my eyes and ears here." Upon saying that, General Matthews looked directly at Mackelroy.

Matthews continued, "This is Kenneth Mackelroy, Grayson Pearson, and Brady Niland from the Space Tech Corporation. They will be also overseeing this facility and will be tasked to disburse everything learned to the right places to be manufactured for the defense of Earth. They will see all the data learned and will make sure that everything conjectured from the data has been properly assessed. Next, I want to introduce Professor Weinstein who will be in charge of the research. He will be our J. Robert Oppenheimer and will report directly to me and to Mister Niland, who I just learned will be Space Tech's person running this facility."

Matthews turned to Captain Chin and said, "This is Captain Chin, from China and the Captain of the recovery vessel and his lead scientist, Professor Calvin Johnson who will remain on Mars and will be Professor Weinstein's second. His field is Astrobiology so he will be in charge of the alien bodies and the study of those. Captain Chin, would you like to start with your observations?"

Chin nodded. "First of all, a lot of this technology looks like the same stuff that we're using. I mean that at first glance and this is also the opinions of my scientists aboard the ship, they don't appear to be that far above us technologically. They use integrated circuits; some switches and wiring are similar; the life supports systems, though geared to them, are similar. Some things were difficult to identify, but most things were close to where we are technologically."

"But what their ship was able to achieve on Earth?" Matthews said questioningly.

"As you know, we couldn't do extensive research, but from what I could see and from what my scientist gleaned, it appears that it's just the way they applied the technology not how advanced the technology actually was."

"Anything else, Captain?"

"The only thing that my scientists have flagged as special is that it seems that the skin of each vessel was able to self-repair though there was no energy going to the skin. We witnessed this first hand. We suspect that they might be ahead of us in nanotechnology or some use of it. If this is true, it probably isn't good news for us because there would need to be a great deal of scientific breakthroughs to achieve the same results. We do believe that this is how the surface of the vessels self-repaired. When the ship attacked Earth, it seemed to allow the disk-like craft to leak out through the skin of the main vessel, then the skin closed. We have no idea how this worked. Because nanotechnology is not evident throughout the vessels, we believe that it may be a specific breakthrough, not something that has changed everything for them. It's hard to tell and, of course, we have no idea what they have been able to accomplish in the seven years since their attack on Earth. They may be quite a bit further ahead now."

Matthews nodded. "So, the offloading is about to begin. Captain Chin will be headed back to Earth and as I understand it, his vessel is going to be retrofitted as a spaceport and equipped with a full array of weaponry to help protect Earth."

"That is correct," Chin said. "I have been in contact with our new central command and understand that Earth is about to complete its first fleet of Predator Class warships, all with the new EMP exploding drones. When these drones come in contact with any EMP pulse, they detonate and release their own EMP burst. This will partially turn the lights out on any vessel built like the alien ship that attacked Earth or so we think."

The General nodded then said, "Our military buildup is late but is picking up steam. We're lucky that we haven't been attacked again but I fear that our luck is going to soon run out. We must make some breakthroughs as soon as possible. This is just a quick meeting to get acquainted. Let's get to work. Mister Niland, please wait so I can speak with you for a moment. Thank you."

Everyone stood. The scientists and Chin walked from the room leaving Sanjay, Marriam, Mackelroy, Pearson, and Niland.

Matthews walked over to Brady Niland who was standing with Mackelroy and Pearson.

Matthews said, "So, Mister Niland, as the person in charge of this facility, I expect a full report at the end of each week on the progress here. I also want what has been learned forwarded to me and where each discovery will be sent."

Mackelroy said, "Some of that might be classified, even from you."

The General said forcefully, "I don't think so and until I'm told differently, you will comply with my requests. Do you understand?"

Mackelroy was not used to being talked down to and at first, bristled, but then he said curtly, "Until you hear differently."

"Thank you," the General said then turned his back on the three businessmen. He walked to Sanjay and Marriam.

Pearson, Mackelroy, and Niland walked from the room. The General spoke into his com, "Mister Hall, in five minutes, will you come back in please?"

Matthews turned to Sanjay and Marriam, "We may have a problem getting the egg out of the wreckage if it's there. I don't have President Dent to help us anymore since he gave up his post. The new President does not know about Egbert and neither does many others."

They both nodded.

"The three of us are going to need to be involved with the offloading of everything around the clock until it shows up."

Sanjay said, "If it's there?"

Marriam said, "Egbert did the same thing that he did the last time he found an egg."

Sanjay said, "I know, but it might just be aware of the alien stuff."

Matthews said, "I don't think so. Sanjay, you have the first shift. They will begin in three hours and Marriam, you will relieve him in eight hours from the beginning of his shift. I will relieve you at the end of your eight hours. As I understand, it should only take two maybe three days to complete the offloading and inventory with everything going to its proper place."

Hall, the head of security walked back into the room.

"Mister Hall, I want Sanjay and Marriam cleared for all secure areas. They are currently only cleared for three. I want them to have the same access as I do."

"Okay?" Hall said not sure why these two should have that kind of access.

The General realizing Hall's hesitancy said, "I can't be here all the time and I have worked with these people for years and trust them completely. On Earth, they both have a very high-security clearance. I need them to have the access that I require. Do you understand?"

"As you wish."

"Good. Make it so, now, please." Though stated as a request, it wasn't.

The General watched as Hall walked out with Sanjay and Marriam. He thought worriedly that he might not have the power that he was hoping for. Mackelroy and Niland were going to be a problem.

Chapter 19

NASA Mars research Center

May 14, 2105

Sol 534

Kenneth Mackelroy Junior quickly got to a private location and put in a call to his father who was considering coming to Mars.

"Father, we have several problems here."

Delay

"I knew there would be."

Delay

"First, there is General Matthews who thinks he is the god of Mars. He seems to think that he can call the shots and he is dictating how our corporation will proceed with the dispersion of information and he wants to oversee that dispersion."

Delay

"I had a feeling that would happen. He was former President Dent's man and had free reign while Dent was President. Now Dent is no longer President and I think I will be able to take Matthews down a peg, but it will take some time. Dent, I'm sure, has suggested to our new President Woodward that he should listen to General Matthews and trust him, but I have the ear of the most powerful man in the world, Mason Hunt and I believe that I can convince him that Matthews is a problem. I will connect with Hunt today as we speak."

Delay

"I'm not sure that I like the security chief, Hall, either. He is an irritant."

Delay

"So are you, Kenneth. Just because someone doesn't perform fellatio on you doesn't mean that you need to get rid of him. That's precisely why he's there. I have sent a message to Hunt about Matthews and will connect with you when he replies. P.S. Don't piss off Hall, he'll probably save your life one day."

Delay

Mackelroy Jr. bristled at his father's rebuke.

Delay

Delay

Delay

Mackelroy Junior's response was a short, curt, "Understood."

Chapter 20

Earth

The Continent of Africa

Kenya

May 14, 2105

Sol 534

On Earth, the constant problem of the alien spheres could not be overcome. No eradication was permanent. Anyplace where the spheres were dropped, and the plants controlled, they sprung back up like cancer.

Then the first sign of the alien plants failing began in the Tsavo National Park in Kenya where the plants had destroyed massive swaths of the over 8200 square mile area.

Scientists from Nairobi had quarantined large areas of the park and despite word of the dangers of the plants, people still became infected, but for some reason, the infection rate was decreasing.

Doctor Kamau Babusa, the most renown microbiologist from the University of Nairobi had been constantly in the field since the outbreak had begun. In a full hazmat suit, he approached a grove of the alien fleshy plants and noticed that the plants appeared differently than they had just a week before. There was a slight rust on the surface of the snow-white flesh that looked like the plants were suffering from psoriasis. Upon closer inspection, the rust was raised like an angry rash and seem to ooze a red blood-colored liquid from open sores.

Babusa took a scraping from the weeping wounds back to his tent where his makeshift lab was assembled. He swabbed a slide with the excretion and placed it under his microscope and peered through the eyepiece. There, to his surprise were scores of parasites, all dead. Something in this slide should reveal why.

Babusa gazed closer. He began to smile. "They're dying," he said aloud. "Something is killing them."

Professor Joy Imbuga, Doctor Babusa's assistant looked up from her work and said questioningly, "They're dying? What's dying, Doctor?"

"The alien plants seem to be dying. Come here. Look at this slide."

She peered through the eyepiece then nodded.

Doctor Babusa then said, "We need to isolate the cause of this."

Ten minutes later and with some closer inspection, it seemed that the plants had become infected by a plant fungus, Powdery Mold, that is common worldwide. He wondered, was this what had killed them.

He hustled back into the grove to find healthy plants, but there were none. It seemed that the mold was taking down the grove in its entirety. He dug into the black ooze that the plants excreted but could no longer find the squirming roots. This grove appeared to be effectively dead. He also noticed that insects were returning and were close to the dying plants.

After making sure of his conclusions, he got on the phone to his contacts at the World Health Organization which had been reassembled specifically to coordinate the study of this alien intruder, and reported his findings.

An hour later he received a call that this same thing was being reported in several other places and a day after that, it was found that the simple mold had infected nearly every place where the plants had taken hold. Mother Earth was fighting back against this alien invasion much better than man ever could and was taking back her planet.

Chapter 21

Kirk Mathews woke and rolled away from Taylor Chapman. They were skin to skin and Kirk was a bit overheated. He pushed his covers down and glanced at Taylor who was breathing softly as she slept.

"Hello, Kirk Matthews," came the female voice from the computer screen atop Kirk's desk.

"Willow?" Kirk whispered surprised and he pushed onto an elbow. "You're back?"

"I am never really far from you, Kirk Matthews."

Colored lines and squiggles danced across the screen as Willow spoke.

Kirk rose and pulled on his boxer shorts. He said, "You don't show up just to chit-chat. What's up?"

"Quite so. I have detected that the sensors placed at the wormhole have been disturbed?"

"Oh shit," Kirk whispered. "Can they tell what came through? Is it another fleet?"

"Whatever came through moved at enormous speed. These sensors have the ability to send images and whatever came through moved like a ghost."

"Could whatever it was have smashed into an asteroid again?"

"I don't believe that there was any collision with any asteroids. That would have been detected. I believe it came through cleanly."

Taylor rose onto an elbow blinking away sleep. "Kirk?"

"Hello, Taylor Chapman," Willow said, recognizing that she had awakened.

"Galadriel?"

"Willow," the AI said, reminding Chapman of her name change.

"Oh, right, Willow."

Taylor sat up and pulled the sheet around her nude body.

Kirk said, "Is this the first time that the sensors have been tripped since they were placed?"

Willow responded, "It is."

"Speculate."

"I would say that we may soon get some company."

"Yikes."

"Quite so."

"Does my Uncle know?"

"He has just been informed."

"What was his response?"

"He is concerned that your world is not prepared for an invasion. He spoke directly with the President of the New World State of America and was not complementary to the world's preparedness."

"Uncle Jeff has always been direct."

"Also, quite so."

Taylor rose and began to dress.

Kirk said, "If they have come back through, we should have a couple of years to prepare."

"There should be time for some preparation. That is as true as we can be, for now."

"Explain?" Kirk said questioningly.

"We do not know of their technological advancement since the last invasion. They may have new surprises for your planet and the amount of time depends on the speed of the attacking force. It may be a great deal less than two years."

Kirk felt a chill at that. "Keep me informed?" he said, a request, not a command.

"I will do so, Kirk Matthews," Willow finished and she was gone.

Kirk stood and Taylor walked to him. She hugged him and said, "It's about to begin again."

"I think so."

"It was bound to happen," she said and buried her head in Kirk's chest.

"It was."

Chapter 22

Earth

Washington D.C.

Oval Office

May 15, 2105

Sol 535

Bedlam...

Pandemonium...

This same scene was being played out in every government worldwide. Today should have been filled with only good news as word of the alien plants dying in Kenya reached the desk of the President, but...

President Oliver Woodward was on the phone for the third time in the last two minutes.
"Do we know anything else?"
Pause
"Can't we track it?"
Pause
"Get back to me."

Woodward hung up. Sweat gathered on his brow and he seemed to pale. The news wasn't going to get better.

Chief of Staff, the former Senator from Florida, Honest Kirk Matthews Senior, watched as Woodward turned to him. "It's official, the wormhole has been breached again."

"How long ago?" Mathews asked.

"Around eight hours."

"Did we get some kind of visual on the craft?"

"Not really. And we don't seem to be able to track it. It came through and then disappeared."

"Why no image?"

"I understand that it came through so fast that it couldn't be taped. It was just a blur. They're enhancing the image to attempt to get a better look and to try to estimate its speed."

"So, just one craft?"

"It appears so, but we can't be sure."

"Huh. Have you talked to my brother, yet?"

"Just got off the line with him an hour ago."

"And."

"He just gave me a bunch of shit about us wasting our time and not preparing for this day."

"Sounds like Jeff."

"I'm sure it does. His reputation proceeds him."

"What now, Mister President?"

"Damned if I know. One thing, everything that we have going, every project and every plan needs to turn back to defending this planet."

"I couldn't agree more."

"We also need to get something from that alien wreckage that we can use."

"That's going to take time; time we might not have."

"I want a meeting tomorrow morning with the Joint Chiefs. They are going to need to impress upon their counterparts in the rest of the world that we're going to need a great army. One that is equipped and ready. Now, I need to call the president of China and see what they're thinking. This world government is beginning to fracture and we need to pull it together."

The phone rang again. Woodward answered, "Yes."

Pause.

"Ah huh. Send it."

Woodward sat at his desk and turned his attention to one of four monitors that had all been turned on. Matthews walked to the President and glanced over his shoulder.

The screen went fuzzy for a second then straightened with an image of a starfield. The image was clear then the starfield seemed to distort and what appeared as ripples like a pebble thrown into a stream distorted the image from the center outward. Next, a blur came through and appeared ghostly. The screen went black for an instant then came back on with the same starfield and the ripples in very slow motion. Then a blurred craft appeared to emerge from the center of the ripples. It had the appearance of a disk-shaped, glowing object, circular and dark in the center. As it emerged it seemed to expand to several times its width but the craft was moving so fast that it vanished as it moved from the camera's range. The entire image was a blur and every camera went dead as it passed.

"That's it?" Matthews asked.

"That's all they have. It seems that it emitted an EMP as it passed and all the cameras went dead just after they sent their images."

"So, we have no idea what might have come through after this craft."

"No."

"Damn."

Woodward said, "They are attempting to estimate the speed of the craft now. We should know shortly how fast it came through the wormhole."

Woodward's phone rang.

"Yes."

Pause.

Woodward appeared as if he had been touched by the angel of death. He turned toward Matthews. "Okay. Got it. 560,000 MPH with its speed increasing," He hung up the phone and said, "I think we're fucked."

"Did they say how long until the craft reaches Earth?"

"If it doesn't slow or, heaven forbid, speed up, roughly 220 days."

Matthews paused for an instant then said, "What if it's just a big bomb?"

"Then I don't know," Woodward said, then added, "We can't let this get out. It would cause a global panic."

"I agree, but we need a global response."

Woodward nodded and lifted a phone, "Get me the President of China, please." As he waited, he said to Matthews, "Call the Prime Minister of England."

Matthews nodded and walked some steps away and lifted another phone.

Chapter 23

Mars

NASA Mars research Center

May 16, 2105

Sol 536

0800 Hours

Day one of the offloading of the salvage ship. Two days later than expected because the quickly constructed warehouse was not remaining pressurized and leaks became a constant.

Finally, the time had come and excitement filled the warehouse built to receive the alien wreckage. Brady Niland, Kenneth Mackelroy Junior, Grayson Pearson, George Hall and astrobiologist, Calvin Johnson were all standing in front of a crowd of workers.

Marriam Daily stood in her NASA blue jumpsuit. The rest of the nearly thirty workers in the warehouse were dressed in bright yellow.

The warehouse had been constructed from prefabbed parts and had been two years in the planning. The floor was grey and smooth and the walls and ceiling, white and well lit. The roof was thirty feet above and banks of LED lights hung from the ceiling and lit the floor brightly below. Lining the floor were various machines like forklifts, and flatbed electric dollies designed to offload and move the alien space crafts' pieces to be stowed. Some items would remain in this warehouse receiving structure and would be disassembled here while other portions of the wreckage would be taken directly to various places for immediate study.

With some ceremony, Brady Niland walked to a podium and stood in front of the assembled workers, all murmuring and whispering.

He raised his hands for quiet. "Thank you," he said. "The day we have all been waiting for has arrived and together, we'll watch as the doors to the salvage ship are opened. You all have your assignments and if you have any questions, please refer them to the foreman of the day. Today's foreman is astrobiologist, Professor Calvin Johnson who accompanied the salvage ship back to Mars. He has overseen every facet of the collection and packing of the alien wreckage. As you all know, the object here is to get each piece of wreckage to the right places for study. Thanks again and let's get started."

Niland stepped away from the front of the group and all eyes turned to the salvage ship which was enormous in its girth. It sat waiting to have its double doors opened which were the height of the salvage ship and nearly the width of the warehouse itself. The salvage ship had been packed in zero gravity and it would be interesting to see how well its cargo arrived and had settled in the gravity of Mars.

With the sound of a latch release, the towering double doors began to slowly open. Every eye was directed squarely at the doors and every mouth slightly open as if God himself were about to burst forth from a sealed sepulcher.

Once the doors were fully opened, the inside of the salvage ship came into view and was far less dramatic than the expectation. The inside was well lit and was neatly organized with large portions of disassembled alien craft stacked like old used mattresses to the right. In the immediate front, were ten coffin-like containers marked male, female with a question mark, and two with just question marks. They appeared to be about ten feet in length and three feet wide. They all had, "Cryogenic Container," stamped on all sides. Behind the coffins were tall stacks of plastic containers secured with restraint straps and one intact small disk-shaped craft against the back of the salvage ship and standing like a dinner plate in a dishwasher. It was small, green-gray, maybe fifteen feet in diameter, and sleek. The salvage vessel was not completely full though everyone expected it to be packed to the rafters.

Professor Calvin Johnson nodded at the floor foreman, Donte Booker, who must have been a Sargent in the Marines because he quickly said, "Come on, people. Stop gawking and get to work. You know the drill. Let's get to it."

The group of thirty yellow-clad workers scattered in all directions, some toward the salvage vessel, some to the forklifts, and some to the flatbed dollies. Everyone moved with purpose.

The first to be removed were the coffins. They were stacked five high and two wide and each row on pallets. The forklift driver slid the forks through the top pallet and brought down the top two coffins. He wheeled it to Marriam who stood expectantly.

Marriam watched as the coffins neared, then she looked into a small glass window into the first coffin. It was marked male and the creature inside was mostly obscured by frost on its skin, but the mouth was open and revealed the upper and lower teeth. On the bottom row of teeth were two extra-long, sharp, tusk-like teeth that curved upward and over the upper teeth.

Marriam could feel her breath catch as she peered at this fearsome creature. Its eyes were black, had the appearance of multi-lensed insect eyes and they sat at the end of short tubes that seemed to allow the eyes to move independently in limited directions. Its nose was just two slits on the upper side and inside the thing's lips that opened vertically instead of horizontally, though the mouth inside was set horizontally. The lips began between the eyes and ended below where the creature's chin should be. The face of the alien was heart-shaped and neither mammalian nor insectoid but maybe something in between.

She scanned a barcode and glanced at the forklift driver who walked from the driver's seat to see what Marriam was staring so intently at.

He whispered, "Damn! That's one ugly mother fucker."

Marriam nodded and said, "He'd probably say the same thing about us."

"Maybe so, but just the same."

Marriam nodded and the driver went back to his controls and parked the pallet on top of one of the flatbed dollies and another driver steered the dolly with the two alien coffins through the double doors and out of sight. The forklift driver went back to the salvage ship for the next set of coffins.

Chapter 24

NASA Mars Research Center

May 18, 2105

Sol 538

For two days, Marriam Daily and Sanjay Patel oversaw the offloading of the alien wreckage from the salvage container. General Matthews had been sidetracked with the news of the breach of the wormhole. The task to inventory and categorize everything from the alien wreckage had been monumental. Some of the wreckage had needed to be moved by forklift while other portions were individually wrapped and packed into containers. The bodies had been taken to a morgue on the bottom floor of the research facility. So far, no Egbert-like egg had appeared.

Sanjay was finishing up his 12-hour and 20-minute shift.

Marriam had just come from the train and after passing through all the security, walked from the two sliding doors and out to the wide floor where the salvage craft sat with its two bay doors opened wide. Various parts of the wrecked alien vessels sat waiting on the floor of the large open warehouse.

George Hall, head of security was nearly always at the offloading. Hall generally kept to his own business but Brady Niland had subtly complained about Patel and Daily being present there and that made him suspicious of Niland and Mackelroy, both of whom had spent time watching the offloading. They seemed to not want General Matthews to know about everything that was coming off of the salvage ship and Hall wondered why.

Marriam approached Sanjay who was facing away from her and looking down into several boxes that were on a dolly. He scanned each individual package in each box then turned when Marriam said, "Hi."

"Oh, Marriam. I'm glad you're here. I'm beat."

"You look tired."

"I am and not feeling so well."

Hall watched them as they spoke.

Marriam whispered, "How was the night?" Which was their code phrase for, did you find the Egg?

Sanjay's response was, "Typical." Code for, no.

Marriam said, "It looks like nearly everything is offloaded."

Sanjay nodded.

"Go to bed, Sanjay. I'll see you in twelve hours."

He nodded again and handed Marriam the hand-held scanner and a small computer pad.

Several packed containers were dollied out of the alien craft and Marriam stopped the worker. She said, "Open the containers, please."

Sanjay slowly walked from the warehouse.

The worker complied and Marriam moved several packages scanning each barcode until she reached the bottom of each container then allow the worker to continue. Marriam glanced at the computer pad to check the logging of each container. Another dolly rolled to her and she said, "Hi, Samuel."

"Good morning, Marriam."

She used the handheld laser scanner tool to scan his crates and their contents. She nodded when finished and he smiled and pushed his dolly out of the receiving area and into the Research Facility to its destination.

As Marriam waited for the next dolly of crates, she could hear several of the workers coughing and she could feel a tickle in her throat. She thought, have I caught a cold? She hadn't heard of anyone catching a cold in some years. She could feel her throat becoming sore.

Chapter 25

Mars surface

Noachis Terra Hotel

May 19, 2105

Sol 539

0800 Hours

Taylor Chapman woke slowly from a dream where she was back on Earth and camping at a secluded lake with Kirk. The dream was long and detailed and they had built a campfire and slept in a tent where they made love until dawn.

She yawned and turned to see Kirk asleep. He was still and lightly breathing, maybe close to waking. Taylor could feel the lust as her dream was still vivid in her mind.

They had shuttled down the night before for a long weekend where they both had three days off. They would spend most of their R and R at the mall, but would also enjoy the room and the shower. She smiled at the thought.

They were lying in a large king-sized bed with soft, white, fresh-smelling sheets and white pillowcases on soft fluffy pillows.

Taylor stretched out luxuriously and enjoyed the extra space that wasn't available in the beds on the space stations. She rolled over and cuddled close to Kirk. He was wearing his NASA issued boxers and Taylor slipped her hand down the back and gripped his backside.

"Waaaaake uuup," she whispered, dragging out the words. "I'm in need of your services."

Kirk cracked his eyelids, rolled, and embraced her. He sleepily said, "You're just using me for my services."

"That's so true, so... you know... before I get some other asteroid jockey to service me."

"Yes, ma'am. I am always at your service, My Lady. How about I start here," he whispered, sliding his hand slowly down her stomach. He glanced up finding her eyes and smiled wryly. "Why, my Lady, you have removed your nickers?"

"Ah-huh," she said, parting her legs for him.

He found her warm pleasure spot.

"Oh," she said a bit breathlessly, "That's a good start."

Then he pushed up her tee-shirt and took her nipple into his mouth and said, "And this?"

"Ummm, that's good too."

He rolled her to her back.

Twenty minutes later they were in the shower together and not getting much showering done. Ten minutes after that, they were both drying off.

"I'm really enjoying our off-time," Kirk said.

"I am too. It'll be another month before we're able to get three days off again."

Kirk nodded and said, "Let's go to the mall for breakfast."

"That sounds great."

A half-hour later, they were on the moving sidewalk that took them to the mall. People were coming and going and there was the bustle of those trying to get to work and those tired from working all night and just wanting to get back to their beds at Condo City for sleep.

Taylor said, "After breakfast, let's go to the museum exhibit. I hear that it's changing to the treasures of the Vatican. I think the art will be amazing."

"That sounds good," Kirk agreed.

They wandered into the food court and up to Lenny who was working the grill, scrambling eggs, and smashing frozen hash browns on the sizzling flat-top with a long flat spatula then drizzling melted butter on top. With one quick motion, he flipped the potatoes.

Lenny turned to see Kirk and Taylor standing at the counter. "Hello, Kirk. Hello, Taylor. Haven't seen you for a bit."

Kirk said, "Nope. We just got some much-deserved time off."

"That's good. How long?"

"Three days and nights. We're staying at the hotel for our mini-vacation."

"Great. Hey, I hear that they are laying the foundation for the luxury resort. I'm hearing that it will be finished in less than six months."

"Really?"

"Yep. I may need to find some help. What can I get you this morning?"

"What do you want, Taylor?"

She said, "I'll have one egg scrambled, hash browns, and toast."

"And for you?"

Kirk said, "Well, I'm not that hungry this morning, so, I'll have three pancakes, three eggs scrambled, hash browns, oh, and a couple of those breakfast sausages."

Taylor grinned, "Not hungry, huh?"

Lenny laughed, "I'd hate to see what you would have ordered if you were starving."

Kirk smiled.

"Your number 43," Lenny said, plating food for a guy dressed in a yellow jumpsuit. He was a construction worker and coughing. "42."

The guy was sitting at a table with four others who were also dressed in yellow jumpsuits.

Kirk and Taylor found an empty table by a faux window and gazed out at an early morning scene.

After a couple of minutes, Lenny announced, "43, Kirk."

Kirk stood and picked up the two trays with his and Taylor's food and walked them back to the table. As he passed the table with the five yellow-clad workers, they were all eating quietly and all coughing. As kirk looked closer, they all looked feverish.

He got back to Taylor and said, "You know, since we've been in space, I haven't seen anyone sick. Now, that entire table over there is coughing as if they all contracted colds. That isn't possible up here, is it?"

"Huh," Taylor said, putting ketchup on the side of her plate. "I don't think viruses from Earth could make it up here."

"Well, those guys are sick."

Taylor nodded and said, "Strange... I want a bite of your pancakes."

"They're too good," Kirk said, poking three wedges with his fork and handing it to her.

Part 3

Contagion

Chapter 26

NASA Mars Research Center

Infirmary

May 20, 2105

Sol 540

0620 Hours

Doctor Emily Saito had just seen the fourth person today with flu-like symptoms. Each person was running a high fever and each was getting sicker by the minute. The research facility had a respectable infirmary built-in case of accidents but it was understaffed for emergencies. It had twenty beds, two examination rooms, and an operating room but lacked staff.

At twenty-nine years old, Emily had looked to be in her teens with flawless skin and bright, intelligent eyes. Her parents were the children of immigrants from Japan and she had been raised in Northern California. When the opportunity to go to space had first arisen, she had just finished her two years residency at UCSF Medical Center and chose to go to Mars. It wasn't a difficult decision. She had always gazed in wonder at the stars and thought that space was her destiny but she didn't realize how lonely space could be. The nine-month trip to Mars had been wonderous at the start but then dreary by the end.

Emily had been at the research facility for four months and worked alone because there had been no need for additional doctors or nurses. It was thought that in an emergency, doctors could be brought in from other places on Mars or from the space stations.

She walked the last patient that she had seen to one of the beds in an open well-lit ward. She helped him out of his shoes and yellow jumpsuit and slipped him into a gown then left his clothes on the floor at the foot of the bed.

The door opened and a security guard shuffled in. It was a man in his late twenties. He was pale and his skin looked a bit jaundice.

"Hi, Doctor Emily. I'm not feeling so well," he said. He gazed around and could see that four beds had people in them. He asked, "What's going on?"

"I don't know, Stephen. Come and let's take a look at you."

She led him into the examination room. "Stephen, put on this gown, please."

He stripped out of his navy-blue security uniform, down to his underwear, and put on the gown while Doctor Emily watched.

When he was finished, she said, "Come to the table."

She laid him down and began poking and prodding and attempting to find anything that could help her with some kind of diagnosis. She sat him up and listened to his raspy breathing and then listened to his lungs that seemed to have fluid in them. She checked his throat and tongue, then grabbed a syringe with a powerful antibiotic and stuck it in his arm. The door to the infirmary opened again.

"Stephen, have you had your booster for your special medicine yet?"

"No, but I'm due."

"I want to keep you here for a while to observe you. Your lungs don't sound good. Can you get to a bed yourself?"

"Yeah."

"Okay, go climb into bed and I'll be back by to see you in a minute."

Doctor Emily peeked out of the examination room door to see that three people had entered her waiting room. She got on the com and called to Isla Charlie to talk to Belinda Waters who was the highest-ranking doctor on Mars. Emily waited and watched at her computer screen for Doctor Waters to come on.

***

A tone sounded in Doctor Waters' room that announced an incoming call on her computer terminal. The computer screen lit and Doctor Waters could see Doctor Emily Saito's face on her screen.

"Doctor Waters, I have a situation down here?"

Belinda Waters pushed up on an elbow, sleepy-eyed from her pillow. She turned in bed and glanced worriedly at General Matthews who was snoring softly. She sat quickly up then, topless, and realizing it, covered her breasts with the sheet.

"I'm sorry to disturb you, Doctor Waters. I— Um— didn't know you had company."

"It's okay, Emily. What's the problem?"

"I have eight people who have entered my infirmary with flu-like symptoms. They're all pretty sick with high fever and chills. Has there been anything unusual on Isla Charlie?"

"No. Nothing."

"I need help," Emily said and sounded as though she was nearing panic.

Doctor Waters said, "There's another doctor staying at Condo City right now who has come with the corporation running the facility. I'll contact him. Have you called your nurses, yet?"

"I'm going to call them now."

"Do it, Emily. I'll get back to you."

Chapter 27

Mars Orbit

Space Station Isla Charlie

May 20, 2105

Sol 540

0625 Hours

Belinda Waters jumped from bed and began pulling on clothes.

General Matthews shifted and opened his eyes. His hair was askew and his mind was muddled from sleep. Though confused, he knew that something was wrong. "Belinda? What's up?"

"We have a situation, Jeff. There are eight or nine people sick at the research facility and Doctor Emily is spooked. She's not sure what they have. It may be some kind of flu."

"Okay," General Matthews said, standing and beginning to dress also. "What do you think?"

"Not sure. It isn't impossible that someone brought the flu from Earth, I guess, we have a lot of people coming and going, but I think it's unlikely. We haven't had any maladies from Mars and we've been exposed to that environment for some time. I'm just not sure."

Doctor Waters walked to the General and softly kissed his lips. "Thanks for the night, Jeff. Let's do it again." She looked into his eyes for a long moment and touched his cheek. "I got to go."

"Are you going to the planet?"

"I don't know yet. I'll let you know. There aren't many doctors up here. I'm just not sure. I won't go right away. First, I'll go to my office and reconnect with Emily. We'll both do our best to figure out the symptoms. But, if it's really going south down there, then I'll have to go."

She put the earpiece com in her ear then pushed the button calling her nurse, Maxine Griffin. "Maxine, meet me at the infirmary."

Pause.

"Thanks, I'll meet you there."

Matthews asked, "Belinda, do you think this could be from the alien wreckage?"

She looked worriedly at General Matthews considering that, shrugged, and said, "I got to go." She jogged out of the door.

Chapter 28

NASA Mars Research Center

Infirmary

May 20, 2105

Sol 540

Doctor Emily Saito waited at the computer monitor for Doctor Waters to call back. She had just called to the two trained nurses who were her help if she needed it, and she desperately did. She peeked into the waiting room and two more workers from the facility had just entered.

She breathed out and opened the waiting room door.

"Who was first?"

"She was," a man said who was sitting next to a woman. The woman was continually coughing and appeared as if she might faint. The man was also coughing.

Emily watched as four more people entered the waiting room. All sick as hell...

"All of you, into the ward!"

She handed gowns to everyone.

"Get into the gowns, now."

They looked around as if needing a place to change.

"I want you in those gowns and into bed, now! Get out of your clothes and leave them at the foot of your beds. Move it! Make sure you keep your lanyards with your security cards around your necks."

They all stripped down to underwear and put on the gowns, all but the woman who was very sick. She had sat on the edge of a bed, pale, and holding her gown.

The man who was sitting next to her in the waiting room walked over after he got into his gown. "Hi, what's your name?" he asked.

"Sara," she coughed.

"Sara, I'm going to help you."

She nodded.

He kept eye-contact being mindful not to look at her body as he began undressing her. He carefully helped her out of most of her clothes, slipped her into her gown, and tucked her into bed.

"There, Sara," he said, brushing the hair from her forehead. "You're going to be fine."

Sara nodded and closed her eyes.

Doctor Emily, though busy, had watched. She said from two beds over, "You should have been a doctor."

He smiled, coughed, and crawled into his own bed.

Now, more than ten of the twenty beds were filled. Doctor Emily went to each bed and took each temperature and listened to each persons' lungs.

Both nurses arrived at the same time and Doctor Emily said, "Take over in here. I need to connect with Doctor Waters. Anyone else who comes in, bring them in and get them into gowns and in a bed."

Emily walked from the ward and into her small office. Her computer was pinging with an incoming call.

She pulled up the program and Doctor Waters was there in her white lab coat.

"Emily, I have just talked to Doctor Forsyth who came with the corporate ship. He said that he would come to help you but I think he needs to clear it with his boss. I told him that it's his duty. He wasn't so sure about that."

Doctor Emily said in a controlled panic, "I have more than a dozen beds full and I just heard someone else come into the waiting room."

"Emily, are the symptoms the same for all of your patients?"

"Yes, for the most part, except for one man. He appears to be a bit jaundice and his skin is also blotchy. When I push on his wrists and hands his skin feels spongy almost as if it doesn't belong to him. His face is puffy and if this continues, I fear his eyes might become swollen shut. No one else seems to be having the same symptoms but they all might have been infected later than him. One more thing, the guy with the spongy skin is on Biocare."

"Huh. Why would that make a difference?"

"Don't know. I got to go. Three more people just came in."

Chapter 29

Mars Orbit

Space Station Isla Charlie

May 20, 2105

Sol 540

Doctor Belinda Waters called to Captain Williams who was on the bridge.

"Yes, Belinda."

"I need a shuttle to the surface."

"You have it."

"I'm on my way, now."

"It will be waiting."

Doctor Waters stood and jogged to the shuttle bay. On the way, she called General Matthews. "Jeff, I'm headed to the planet. This thing that's going on is overwhelming Doctor Saito. Can you call ahead to let their security know that I'm coming?"

General Matthews said, "I understand. I will. Contact me when you can."

"I will."

Waters jogged out of her office and when she reached the shuttle bay, Lance Newsome, the shuttle pilot was waiting."

He asked, "Where to, Doc?"

"The research facility."

"Get in and buckle up."

She nodded and within five minutes, they were away from the space station and on their way to the surface. An hour later they were at the airlock and Doctor Waters was walking into the front entrance of the facility. Before she had left the shuttle, she had put on a mask and goggles. In her white coat, she approached a guard who was coughing.

"Ma'am?" he said questioningly.

"I'm Doctor Belinda Waters here to help at your infirmary."

George Hall stepped out from behind the door to the facility. He said, "I have this."

"Yes, Sir."

"This way please, Doctor."

Doctor Waters stepped into the first security checkpoint.

Hall said, "Step into the scanner and hand me your security card."

Waters handed Hall her security card which was the size of a driver's license and stepped into the scanner. The scanner showed an image of the Doctor with all of her clothes removed, front and back, mapping her body, and revealed nothing unusual.

Hall quickly observed it then said, "Follow me."

He led her to another room where he slid her security card into a machine and typed in several numbers then he scanned his security badge that hung from a lanyard. He slipped another card into the machine; one also attached to a lanyard and typed several more numbers then took out the new card with a lanyard and handed it and the doctor's security card back to her.

"Doctor Waters, please put this around your neck and don't take it off under any circumstances. If you need to shower, make sure you keep it on. If it gets in your way while you work, tuck it into your shirt. We have robot guards who shoot anyone without a security pass that matches them. You now have access to the entire facility. Very few people have that clearance." Hall coughed. "Good luck, Doctor. I'll take you to the infirmary."

She nodded and didn't speak.

They walked together through a hallway and past one security bot. It paused, seemed to observe them then rolled on.

Doctor Waters could see that it was well-armed.

They approached an elevator and Hall passed his security card over a scanner. The doors slid open. He said, "Level ten."

The doors slid closed.

A female voice came from a speaker in the elevator, "Level ten, George Hall."

Both could feel the elevator descend.

Waters asked, "What do you know about this sickness?"

"Not much, Doctor, just that it seems that everyone in the facility seems to be affected."

"I think you need to lock down the facility."

"I had a feeling that you were going to say that."

The elevator stopped on level ten.

Waters glanced at the buttons on the elevator controls and noticed that there were only eleven levels. She was nearly at the basement.

"The infirmary is to your right, Doctor. I'm going back up to have the Facility locked down and everyone connected with it self-quarantined."

"That's the procedure," Waters said business-like.

Hall nodded and said, "That means you too."

"I know," Waters said and walked out of the elevator. The doors slid closed.

Waters stepped quickly to the infirmary and walked into the waiting room. Eight people were sitting and coughing. Doctor Waters walked through the door into the examination room.

Doctor Saito saw Waters come through the door. She and both nurses were also in masks and goggles.

Saito said, "Oh, Doctor Waters, I'm so happy to see you."

The twenty beds were full and all pushed to one side of the ward. On the other side of the ward, another twenty mattresses lay on the floor and all were now full.

Waters gazed around. She said, "Catch me up, Emily."

We have forty people in here and the one in isolation. Several of the people in here have pneumonia but seem to be responding to the antibiotics. The man in isolation isn't."

"Take me to him."

Doctor Saito nodded and walked Waters to a room with the door closed. She opened the door and both doctors walked in.

Waters breath caught in her throat. She said, "What the hell?"

"I have no idea. Ever seen anything like this?"

The man in the bed no longer appeared to be human. He had seeping sores all over the portions of his body that were visible. His hair had fallen from his head and his face had some kind of strange flesh-colored fibers that seem to have sprouted from his pours. The fibers were beginning to cover his mouth, ears, nose, and eyes. Doctor Waters pulled back the sheet which was soiled from seeping wounds and looked in horror at the man's nude body. It had the same fibers growing from the skin everywhere and anyplace where there might have been hair, it had all fallen out. He was in an oxygen mask and his breathing was labored.

Waters said, "The only thing that this kind of reminds me of is Morgellons disease."

"I remember a bit about that."

"It has the same kind of lesions and fibers seem to grow under the skin but not above the skin, to my knowledge."

The man turned toward the doctors.

Emily said, "Hi, Stephen. This is Doctor Waters."

"Huhhhee," he said, trying to say hi.

"Stephen, I'm going to try to help you," Waters said but glanced grimly at Doctor Saito.

He turned and tried to smile.

Waters laid the sheet back over Stephen's ravaged body.

Waters nodded at Emily and said, "Has anyone else displayed these symptoms?"

"No."

"Do you have any other patients here who are on Biocare?"

"No, not here now."

"I wonder how many people on the planet are on Biocare?"

"I am personally treating fifteen for their boosters but I hear that nearly all of the people who are corporate who have come are on the drug."

The two took off their gloves upon leaving the room and walked into the ward. More mattresses had been delivered to the infirmary and were being laid out by the nurses.

Waters said, "Hall is locking down the Research Center. I think we're going to need to quarantine the planet. This is seriously scary."

Saito nodded.

"Emily, how many people are working at this facility right now?"

"About seventy, give or take depending on if there is a shift changing or not. Some people are staying here, but others come and go with their shifts."

"So, the bug is out into the population of Mars."

"I don't see how it wouldn't be. We don't know the gestation period and we don't know how infectious this is before someone would show symptoms."

"I need to make a call," Doctor Waters said, walking away from Doctor Saito.

She called General Matthews directly.

"Yes, Belinda. How's it going?"

"Listen, Jeff, you need to quarantine the planet right now and that includes every shuttle. Nothing should come or go from this planet. I think this bug is alien and that means we have no way to fight it as yet. I'm going to begin to get samples of blood and tissue from the infected to try to isolate the infectious agent. It acts like a virus but I'm not altogether sure of that. It could be a type of bacteria."

"Give me a minute, Belinda."

The General left for no more than fifteen seconds.

When he came back, he said, "It's done. You guys are on your own and every ship on the planet has been grounded. I gave the word to my AK pilots to intercept anything leaving the planet and force it back to the ground."

"Thanks, Jeff. I'll be in touch."

"Belinda, please take care down there."

"I'll do all I can."

Chapter 30

By the end of her shift, Marriam Daily was running a high fever. The last of the cargo from the alien wreckage was being offloaded and still no egg-like artifact. She began to wonder if Egbert had it wrong.

She glanced at the time on her computer pad. Sanjay wouldn't be there to relieve her for another two hours and twenty minutes. He had spent the night at the research facility in the room provided for them and was also showing symptoms.

Marriam watched as everyone working was also showing signs of being sick. Some sweating, most coughing. She looked towards the alien wreckage and the last of the large portions were being offloaded. Still no alien egg. These portions were large pieces of wreckage, some the size of small intact smashed rooms and large portions of ragged fuselage. These large pieces were being parked to one side of the warehouse to be dismantled later. There was just one item left to be removed, the alien disk-shaped craft. Two forklift drivers had driven into the salvage ship to attempt to get their forks under its curved side. Another person driving a small crane maneuvered between them and hooked the crane to tethers that were strapped around the craft.

Marriam felt overheated and she unzipped her jumpsuit just a bit to cool her neck. Workers were disappearing from the warehouse, one by one, as they were becoming increasingly ill.

Sanjay came through the door two hours early. He jogged to Marriam and said, "Marriam."

She turned to see him. "You're not supposed to be here for a couple more hours."

"I know. You don't look so good."

"Yeah. I'm not feeling well. I think I have the bug that everyone else has."

"I think I have it too. That's why I came down. Also, I just heard the planet's been locked down, quarantined. No one comes or goes from the planet."

"Everyone here is sick," Marriam said then pulling Sanjay close, whispered in his ear, "They pulled the last of the stuff off of the salvage ship and no surprises."

Sanjay turned and nodded. He embraced her to whisper in her ear. "If it's here, it's probably inside one of the large pieces of wreckage."

Marriam nodded and whispered, "Contact the General with that intuition."

Sanjay nodded and when he pulled back, he could see that Marriam was more pale than just a moment before. He said, "Let's get you to the doctor."

"No, I'm not that bad. I want to go back to the room." She laid her computer pad and scanning gun on a chair. Sanjay put an arm around her and led her through the door.

Hall had just arrived and watched the scene as every worker was ill and stopping their work. Hall knew instinctively that something had probably arrived with the alien wreckage, something virulent.

Chapter 31

NASA Mars Research Center

Infirmary

By 1000 hours, Doctor Belinda Waters could see that this was already way out of control and was happy for calling for the quarantining of the planet.

She called to the facility director, Brady Niland, and said, "We need more beds. Can you have someone bring down more mattresses?"

Niland coughed, "I'll have it done now."

"Thank you. You don't sound very good."

"No," he replied shortly.

"You need to quarantine yourself."

"I will. Talk to you later."

"I'll call you back and see how you're doing."

"Okay."

Once finished with Niland, Waters turned to Doctor Saito and said, "Emily, do you know if Brady Niland is on Biocare?"

"I don't know. I don't treat him. He and Mackelroy brought their own doctor."

"Forsyth?"

"Yeah."

"No wonder he didn't come to help. I'm sure Mackelroy told him not to."

"I'm sure you're right, the bastard."

A call came into Waters' earpiece from Isla Charlie.

"Belinda, how goes it down there, now?"

"It's a mess, Jeff," she said to General Matthews. "This is my worst nightmare. We have fifty beds of sick and five more people in the waiting room. No one is showing any signs of beating this. Listen, everyone down here is very sick, but we have a guy who has been on Biocare and his symptoms are not the same as everyone else's. You need to quarantine yourself so that you're not exposed to this. I'm hoping that this, whatever it is, hasn't made it off of the planet, but if it has and I'm right, it seems to be affecting anyone who has been on Biocare more adversely than people who aren't. This guy's a mess and we've isolated him from everyone else keeping him in his own room but his symptoms are seriously scary."

"Huh," General Matthews said.

"Do it for me, Jeff? Lock yourself away until I'm sure that the sickness hasn't made it to Isla Charlie."

"Okay."

"We should know within the next day or two if I'm correct about thinking that this is something from the alien wreckage. Because of when the salvage ship arrived, we're looking at about two to three days gestation period. I'll eventually go down to the wreckage to take some swabs and see if we can figure out what else we transported from the wormhole. Jeff, I think you're going to need to contact the twin rings from the salvage ship before they leave. They might already be getting sick or maybe something is trapped on the outside of the ship, some kind of extremophile."

"Extremophile?"

"Yeah, like on Earth. Back home, some bacteria can live in solid rock or in 700-degree volcanic vents in the ocean and they have found bacteria that can survive quite well in pure sulfuric acid or radioactive waste. Bacteria are very adaptive. That's why hospitals can't get rid of certain infections. Despite what us humans think about being the dominant species on Earth, bacteria are the baddest dudes on the planet. They will be there long after we're gone."

"I understand. I'll stop the salvage ship's rings and bring them back here until we know more. Keep me informed."

"I will, Jeff. Got to go. Now, go to your room!"

"Yes, Mom."

After finishing with General Matthews, Doctor Waters asked, "Emily, I need to check these samples with a microscope, where do I do that?"

"The morgue is where we would do any testing for anything biological. It's one floor down."

Waters nodded and walked from the infirmary. By this time, fifty-two beds were full and three more people waited in the waiting room. Waters stepped quickly to the elevator and said, "Level eleven."

The elevator's female voice said, "Level eleven, Belinda Waters."

The elevator began to descend and stopped on the eleventh floor. It opened onto a small hallway that led to two sets of wide double doors. Waters chose the closest and scanned her badge. The doors slid wide. She walked into a long room that had plexiglass windows separating the room from the morgue itself. In the morgue were three people all in full hazmat suits working on several alien bodies stretched out on tables. The bodies had their space suits removed and their entire bodies revealed.

A smooth voice from behind Doctor Waters said, "I don't believe I know you."

The doctor turned, "I, um, am Doctor Belinda Waters from Isla Charlie. I came down to help Doctor Saito in the infirmary."

"Oh, I hear it's bad up there," the man said softly then, "I'm Professor Johnson, Calvin Johnson. I arrived with the wreckage from the wormhole."

Professor Johnson spoke with a slight British accent.

Waters stared at the displayed alien bodies, one was obviously male with a phallus in its predictable spot, but the creature appeared to be more insect in likeness than to anything that Waters had seen before. Its skin and the others were grey in color but mottled and she doubted that this was the skin color of an alive alien. Another of the creatures appeared to be female with small mammary glands. Her genitals were not visible from this angle. The third creature was the same size as both the male and female, probably eight feet in height, but there was nothing apparent that would give a clue as to its sex. All of the creatures had two long spindly arms and legs. Each hand had three fingers and an opposable thumb with long sharp fingernails. All three had their abdominal cavities opened and each had someone peering inside.

Waters was temporarily spellbound. She said, "What are they, I mean, what have you discovered?"

"Well, they have some similarities to us with hearts, lungs, and intestines. They don't have separate livers and kidneys. They have one large organ that we think might do the work of both but right now we're not exactly sure. We'll know shortly. It's fairly straight forward what both organs do in humans. We think they breathe a much lower concentration of oxygen. We breathe a mixture of gasses that is about twenty-one percent oxygen. We think that these people can survive on around ten percent."

"People?"

"I can't call them creatures or things or its. They are intelligent. Their brains are roughly the size of humans and probably organized similarly. We think that they breed in threes, not just male and female as we do on Earth. The females have no vaginal opening. They have a phallus-like appendage with no testicles that seems to deposit eggs into the third creature over there," Johnson pointed. "While the male deposits the sperm into the same third person. Both male and female phallus-like appendages have similar tissue that would fill with a blood-like fluid, probably with stimulation as with humans. The ejaculated fluids would carry the semen and eggs into the egg carrier where it would mix. There the eggs would gestate. The third person has a fairly long vaginal opening that leads to a womb and would, with some maneuvering, allow both the males and females to engage in coitus simultaneously with it or maybe separately. The third person had sixty fertilized eggs within a womb similar to cats. If I were to guess, I would say that more than one pair might be able to deposit the eggs and sperm into each gestator. If they could get to Earth, they could probably multiply rapidly."

"Gestator?"

"That's the best I can do as a description for the third creature. We, of course, have no idea about how their society works. If these were similar to humans, the three would probably enter into some kind of marital bond. It may be similar where these people are from but who knows."

Waters observed, "The female only has two breasts like humans. How could she feed so many offspring?"

Johnson shrugged, "The gestator also has mammary glands, two rows of twelve on its front. If you could look closer, you would see the nipples, though the mammary glands are not filled with milk as yet. I believe that this gestator had just become impregnated.

Waters changed the direction of the discussion. "Professor, I have slides that I need to study. We have so many people sick in the infirmary that we need to know what we're dealing with."

Johnson nodded.

Waters asked, "Are any of you down here sick?"

"No, we've been here and mostly in bio-suits. We can eat and sleep here and have had little contact with anyone from above since the arrival of the alien wreckage. We've been busy."

"Is anyone down here on Biocare?"

Johnson glanced at Waters as if she shouldn't know about that deep secret.

"No, it had not been dispensed to us."

"Can you take me to your microscope?"

"You'll need to suit up."

She nodded.

Johnson walked Waters to a decontamination chamber. It led to another chamber with the bio-suits. He led her inside the first chamber.

"I hope you're not bashful, Doctor. You can't wear anything under these suits. You will be decontaminated coming and going."

"Okay?"

"I have to take you in. Protocol."

Waters nodded.

Professor Johnson began removing his clothes. "Are your samples sealed?"

"Yes."

"You will not be able to take them back out with you."

"I understand."

"You can leave your clothes in here."

They both stripped to skin, hanging their clothes on hooks then rehung their lanyards around their necks with the security cards and stepped into the next chamber. Johnson closed a hatch behind them and Doctor Waters, not particularly modest, unconsciously covered her breasts.

The Professor said, "Arms straight out from your sides and feet two feet apart."

"Really?"

"Protocol."

Johnson demonstrated then closed his eyes. "It bothers my eyes at first."

Waters shrugged and complied, spreading her arms and feet then closed her eyes.

Johnson reached over and pushed a wide green button. Jets of spray clouded the chamber until neither person was quite visible. The spray made each damp but not dripping wet except for any place where there was hair on the body. In those places, moisture covered the area like morning dew.

"The moisture dries rapidly," Johnson said, observing Waters holding her arms out and looking down at her damp flesh.

She looked at Johnson and nodded.

Once finished in this chamber, Johnson ushered Waters into the next with the bio-suits.

Johnson appraised Waters' body and said, "Though lean, you are pretty tall. You appear to be about a medium."

Waters blushed a bit at the scrutiny.

After a wry look, Johnson handed her a bio-suit.

Except for her hair, Waters was now nearly dry.

Once in the suits, they both stepped into another chamber where they were again gassed.

Johnson and Waters stepped out of the decontamination chamber and into the morgue. Several people also in bio-suits worked with scalpels on the alien bodies. Entrails lay in trays and portions of legs and arms were wide open as they studied the muscle structure of the creatures.

Johnson watched Waters stare at the dissections. He said, "These people are very strong. I would say by looking at their musculature, that they may be several times stronger than humans. If the strongest human could bench-press a thousand pounds, these aliens could probably bench six or seven thousand pounds. We think that they are strong like ants that can lift up to ten times their own weight. We are facing a fearsome foe."

Waters nodded.

"The microscopes are over here. If you are not interested in peering into the atoms of your samples, these will show you the smallest of viruses and bacteria."

"Thank you."

Waters brought out her slides and removed them from a plastic sealed bag. She placed one under the microscope and peered through its lens then focused it directly and could see macrophage, T-cells, working to kill single-celled creatures in the blood sample. She focused directly on the moving creatures as they lived in the sample.

"Does this look familiar to you, Professor Johnson?"

He peered into the microscope, shook his head, then said, "Let's run it through our database."

He pressed a small button on the microscope and it filmed the organism. The organism appeared on a small monitor mounted on the wall. Beneath the picture of the organism, words flashed quicker than the eye could see. Once finished, a short phrase appeared below the picture of the organism, "*No matches found. Most resembles a virus.*"

"I'm pretty sure that this came with your vessel," Waters commented.

"I'm pretty sure that you are correct, Doctor."

"Let's take a look at the second slide. This is from a patient that has symptoms similar to Morgellons Disease."

Johnson's expression turned grim, "Morgellons disease!? Oh. Geez."

Waters placed the first slide in a container marked biohazard then took the second slide and slipped it into the microscope. She peered again into the eyepiece and said, "Huh?"

"What is it?" Johnson asked.

"Looks like the same organism to me."

"With different symptoms?"

"Take a look."

Johnson peered into the eyepiece and agreed then said, "Let's compare the first with the second." He pushed a couple of keys on a keyboard and both organisms appeared side by side on a split-screen.

The computer analyzed the two samples and said, "*Identical.*"

"So," Johnson said, "What's the difference?"

"The second sample came from a guy on Biocare."

"Huh."

They both continued to gaze at the computer-enhanced images of both slides. The computer was rerunning the viruses interacting with each body's immune system on a kind of loop. On the first, the body's macrophage was attacking the viruses but on the second, the macrophage seemed to pass over the cells infected by the virus and move away.

"Did you see that, Professor?"

"Yes."

"The immune system seemed to overlook the virus."

"In the case of that cell, maybe. I'm sure that happens all of the time until the T-Cell catches up with the infected virus and kills it."

"I think that the organism is interacting differently with this guy because his body chemistry has been changed by the drug."

"You'll need to take more samples of infected cells."

"Yeah— Do you know much about Biocare, Professor?"

"Just that it is supposed to protect people in space and I've heard that it seems to slow or reverse the aging process."

"Think of how difficult a process that would be. It makes something inherent in all humans like aging reverse and maybe makes the person who is reverse aging not quite human anymore. I have a patient who has been on the drug for more than ten years and we had to reduce the drug or he might have ended up out of puberty."

"Benjamin Button."

"Huh?"

"Oh, just an old movie about a man who reverse aged. There was an old-time actor, Brad Pitt, in the film."

"Okay."

"Never mind. How do you think we should proceed, Doctor?"

"I don't know, Professor. What would you suggest?"

"We'll never find a cure in time to save those already infected. That takes years. I think all we can do is make them as comfortable as possible and hope that their immune systems do their jobs."

"Okay?"

"Has the Research Facility been quarantined?"

"Yes," Waters said then added, "And the entire planet."

"Prudent."

"I need to get back to the infirmary."

Johnson nodded and walked Waters back to the decontamination chambers. They both went through the first part where the bio-suits were gassed, then they both took off the bio-suits, walked into the next chamber where their bodies were gassed, then into the chamber where their clothes were left and after a minute of air drying, they both began dressing.

Johnson was pulling up his shorts and said, "We may have a real problem down here."

"We may, Professor," Waters agreed, buckling her bra.

"If we can't figure out some cure, this will be our tomb."

They both pulled on their jumpsuits, zipping them. Then sitting down, they put on their shoes and socks.

They both stood and Waters smiled at Professor Johnson, "Thanks for the hospitality, Professor, and the showers. I may be back."

"Good day, Doctor. Our showers are always open, 24/7."

She smiled again and walked by the windows that looked into the morgue. Waters stopped and watched for a moment as the examiners dissected portions of the aliens and she sighed.

Professor Johnson stepped behind her and asked, "What are you thinking?"

"I don't know. This seems like such a waste. We should be communicating with these creatures, sharing knowledge, and enjoying studying each other, the wonder of it, you know."

"You think like a scientist, Doctor. They've come like Atilla the Hun. Sometimes you don't get to compromise, learn, and study. Sometimes you're forced to fight for your life."

"Quite so, Professor. I'll be in touch."

"Please do."

When Waters got back to the infirmary, she could hear a commotion in the isolation room. She walked quickly in that direction and several of the patients in beds sat up, looking in the direction of the disturbance.

As Waters entered, the patient, Stephen Donnelly, who was on Biocare was thrashing and pulling off his oxygen mask.

"I can't breathe!" he said in a raspy, nearly inhuman voice. His eyes bulged.

Doctor Saito looked up gravely as Waters entered. She had tried to put Stephen in restraints and he was pulling against the attempt. His sheets were on the floor. His body was taught but the skin appeared to be translucent and flaky where there weren't weeping sores. His muscles seemed hard and strong but he looked as though he could die at any moment.

Doctor Saito plunged a hypodermic needle into his arm and pumped him full of a sedative.

He began to relax.

"When did this start, Emily?"

"About ten minutes ago."

Waters glanced at a monitor above the bed. "He's getting too much oxygen."

"I know. I just turned it way down."

"That doesn't make sense."

"I know."

Saito finished placing the restraints on his wrists and ankles and they covered him with a fresh sheet.

Chapter 32

NASA Mars Research Center

May 21, 2105

Sol 541

After helping with Stephen Donnelly, Doctor Waters left the infirmary. She had taken more samples of tissue and blood from several patients including Stephen, then headed to the alien wreckage to take swabs in hopes of finding where the alien virus had hitched a ride.

Up ten floors to the surface, she walked out of the elevator and onto the floor of the warehouse. Sanjay Patel was there and coughing. There were only two other workers there dressed in yellow.

Waters walked to Sanjay. "Hello, Sanjay. I didn't know you were here. Is Marriam here too?"

"Hi, Doctor Belinda. She is here but she was so sick that she couldn't work. I took her back to our overnight room. We have a room assigned to us because we've been down here taking inventory of the wreckage."

"I'll check on her before I go back to the infirmary."

"Thank you, Doctor. I'm so worried about her. She seems to have such a high fever."

"In a way, that's good. It means her body is fighting the virus. I've seen a lot of patients and they all seem to be holding their own. Tell me, does she have any open sores or lesions anywhere on her body?"

"No, or I don't think so. She hasn't mentioned any."

"That's good. I need to get a few swabs from various places on the alien wreckage and inside the salvage ship. Once I have my samples, I'll go check on Marriam."

"Thank you, Doctor. I'll be done here in an hour then I'm going to need some sleep. I don't think any more work is going to happen with the wreckage. Everyone is too sick."

Doctor Waters walked along the wreckage and took several swabs and dragged them across long portions of the alien structures. She then walked inside the now empty salvage ship and swabbed around the curved walls of its interior, then swabbed the doors. As she finished each location, she had placed each sample into a separate plastic bag, marked where each sample was taken from, then placed all of the samples into one large bag.

She had on her mask, goggles, and gloves and as she walked past Sanjay, she said, "I'm going to check on Marriam. What's the room number?"

"Room 318."

Doctor waters nodded. She walked back to the elevator and walked in, the doors closed and she said, "Level three."

The elevator announced, "Level three, Belinda Waters."

Once at the floor, the doors opened. When Waters walked out, two security bots were parked and seemed to be waiting to see who was exiting the elevator and it gave Waters the chills.

She walked past the bots and to the room number that Sanjay had given her. She knocked on the door. There was no answer. She used her security pass and the door slid open. Marriam was asleep and as pale as the snow.

Waters walked to Marriam who was lying in bed. Her nightgown was soaked with sweat and her hair appeared as if she had just left the shower.

"Marriam," Waters said, shaking her gently.

"Huh?" Marriam said, glancing up and blinking, then, "Doctor Waters? Belinda?"

"Hi, Marriam. I'm going to look you over."

"I'm so sick, Doctor. My body is aching."

"I know. It's the fever."

Waters slipped Marriam out of her soaked nightgown. "Do you have another nightgown?"

"Yeah."

"Let me look you over first."

Waters gave Marriam a thorough exam, checking every bump, wrinkle, crack, and crevasse, and satisfied that she had no lesions, helped her into a clean, dry nightgown. She had Mariam drink some water.

"Marriam, I'll come back and check on you later."

"Have you seen Sanjay? He was getting sick also. Is he okay?"

"I just saw him and he is doing a lot better than you, so far anyway."

"Oh— Oh good."

"Stay in bed. I'll be back."

Waters stood and began to leave when she heard a loud crash. She stopped at the door, temporarily afraid to open it.

Marriam sat up. "What was that?"

"I don't know."

Waters opened the door and peered out in all directions. Across the hall, a room door appeared to be severely dented and down the hall, the door to the stairway appeared to be forced open and was set askew, hanging from its top hinge, its bottom hinge snapped. A red light above the door blinked and an alarm sounded. One bot wheeled in that direction.

"Who stays across the hall from you?"

"There are mostly guards on this floor and a few workers."

"I have to get back to the infirmary. I'll be back later."

Waters walked out and let the door close.

She cautiously stepped into the corridor and again looked for some reasonable explanation for the destruction in the hallway. She felt a primal fear that she had never experienced before. Something was wrong here, something that she didn't understand and couldn't quite perceive. The alarm rang.

She stepped quickly to the elevator to get out of that unknown. As the doors to the elevator closed, she nervously said, "Level ten, please." She wondered why she thought to be polite to the elevator.

"Level ten, Belinda Waters."

When the doors to level ten opened, Waters could hear a muffled commotion and an alarm like she heard on the third floor. She could smell gun powder and could see that around the corner, a red light was blinking as it played against the white walls. She began to jog to the infirmary. As she neared, she could hear loud voices saying, "What was that?!" And, "Oh my God!" And, "What the hell!"

She opened the door and two men lay dead in a heap on the floor of the examination room. Both appeared to have been struck in the neck region by some kind of weapon. Their necks lay at unnatural angles. Blood had sprayed from one neck of one of the men and the blood was just stopping as the pressure in his veins died with his life.

One of the nurses and Doctor Emily stepped slowly into view from the other room. Emily had her gloved hands covering her masked mouth. The nurse stood as if she were a frozen block of ice.

Waters asked, "Emily, what happened?"

"I don't— I mean, I'm not— I mean— it came from the back of the infirmary."

Waters walked to Doctor Emily and took her shoulders and looked directly into her eyes. "Emily, what happened here?"

Waters glanced over her shoulder and could see that one of the two metal sliding doors had a huge dent on the inside as if struck by a battering ram, which made it bow out.

"Come with me," Waters said to Emily then, "Call George Hall," to one of the nurses.

Waters brought Emily into the second examination room.

"Sit down, Emily," Waters said firmly.

Emily sat.

"Now, Emily, what came from the back of the infirmary?"

"A thing, some kind of thing. It was strong and fast and I don't know— something."

"So, what's in the back of the infirmary?"

"Some storage."

"Let's go look."

"Okay?"

Emily was petrified.

"You can stay here, Emily. I'll go look."

"No. I'll come."

They both walked from the examination room and to where the two men had been killed.

Waters asked the nurse, "Did you get a hold of George Hall?"

"No. He didn't answer. I tried the security line also and there was no answer there either."

Waters nodded and walked past the nurse and into the ward where anyone who could sit up was watching her enter with wide eyes.

One man asked, "What's going on, Doc?"

Waters answered, "I wish I knew."

They walked past the sick and past the private room where Stephen Donnelly was kept. Waters glanced in. Donnelly was gone.

In the room, Waters could see that the sheets were pulled back and full of blood and bodily fluids. All four of the restraints that held Donnelly were snapped and in the bed was what looked like snakeskin soaked and mingled with bodily fluids.

Doctor Saito came up beside Waters and stared at the empty room. "Stephen?"

They both walked in. Waters lifted one of the leg restraints and studied the ragged and broken material. She then pointed at what appeared to be skin in sheets among the bedding.

Waters said, "It looks like he shed his skin." Waters used forceps to lift a sample.

"What are we dealing with?" Emily asked.

Waters didn't answer, shaking her head. She went to the com line and pushed the number for Brady Niland's office... Nothing. She looked in a directory that had just been issued and tried George Hall again... Nothing. She tried two security outposts that were listed and there was also no answer. She tried Weinstein with no response. Last she called General Matthews.

"Yes, Belinda."

"Jeff, we have a situation down here. I can't get any security and two men have been killed by some kind of creature."

"Could it be the creatures that attacked the colonists a few years before?"

"I don't think so. I know that this is going to sound crazy, but I think that the virus has changed or is changing anyone on Biocare into something altogether different. I have no proof but I'm guessing that anyone in this facility and on Mars that has been using Biocare and has been exposed to the alien virus is changing into something new."

"New?"

"I don't know what, but I believe that a changed creature just killed the two men here and I have a good idea that we will find more dead. This attack was savage. Both of these men appear to have had their necks snapped like twigs. I got to go."

"Belinda, sit tight and I'll try to contact security and try to get help to you."

"Okay, will do."

Belinda walked to the door to try to close it but it had been damaged so severely that it wouldn't slide back into the wall.

Doctor Saito asked, "What did he say?"

"The General said that he is going to try to get some security down here to help us."

"Oh," Emily replied and felt no comfort.

Shooting in the corridor brought silence in the infirmary.

"Go back inside the ward," Waters commanded.

Doctor Emily and the nurses stepped backward into the ward but Waters didn't. She said, "Close the door."

Emily said, "But—"

"Just do it, Emily," Waters commanded then watched as the door slid shut.

Waters carefully peered outside the infirmary and into the hallway through the ruined door that wouldn't close. One of the security bots lay in a heap of twisted metal and a trail of bluish-red blood trailed from the bot to a stairway at the end of the hall. The alarm was sounding and the red light above the door blinked.

Doctor Waters called through the door, "Emily, I have to get these samples checked. I'll be back. Lock this door."

"Okay?" Doctor Saito said with a tremble in her voice.

Waters slipped from behind the ruined door and jogged quickly to the elevator and scanned her security card. She waited impatiently for the doors to open, "Come on. Come on," she said under her breath.

The doors opened and she stepped in quickly and waited for what seemed like an eternity as the doors finally closed.

Waters said, "Level Eleven."

"Level eleven, Belinda Waters."

The elevator began to descend. When the door opened into the hallway that led to the morgue, she peered outside. This hallway was clear. She stepped quickly to the doors leading into the morgue and swiped her security badge.

When the doors slid open, she stepped in and pushed a button several times to quickly close the doors. She was breathing hard and her chest rose and fell in gasps.

Calvin Johnson watched from inside the morgue. He walked, dressed in a bio-suit, to the plexiglass window that separated the two rooms and pushed a button on an intercom that would allow him to communicate with someone in the outer area.

"Doctor?" he paused, then, "Are you okay?"

She nodded. "Professor, we have a problem," Waters began.

"Wait and I'll come out."

"No, you're better off in there. I have some samples that I would like you to run on the microscope. Things above you have gone way out of control. The people on Biocare who have caught the sickness have changed. I believe that they may be psychotic or, I don't know, no longer human. People have been killed. I can't get security and I think most of them were on Biocare."

"What about Hall?"

"I've tried to reach him but nothing. No response."

"You should come in here. It's probably safer."

She shook her head, no. I have to go. I'll leave the samples in the first decontamination room. Run them for me."

"I will."

Waters placed the samples in the decontamination room and stepped quickly to the door. She cautiously glanced out into the hallway looking left then right, then she was gone.

Chapter 33

Mars

Condo City

May 21, 2105

Sol 541

1100 Hours

Taylor Chapman was coughing and could feel her fever as her body aches increased. It was time to return to Isla Bravo and go back to work.

Kirk Matthews was lying next to her in bed and groaned, "Damn, I feel like shit."

They had gotten back to their room early after dinner and both fell asleep quickly. Neither had felt well the night before and both were surprised that they slept so far into the morning.

Kirk glanced at the clock. He said, "1100 hours? Damn." He reached over and slipped his hand under the back of Taylor's nightgown and could feel the fever on her skin. "You're cooking," he commented.

"I know. My body's aching. I definitely have a fever."

Kirk was sweating and he pushed the sheets off his body to cool.

Taylor said, "We can't go back to work like this."

Kirk stood and felt dizzy. He steadied and walked to the large flat-screen TV mounted on the wall. Switching it on, a message scrolled across the screen.

"Planet Mars is under quarantine. No one is permitted to leave. Please remain in your rooms until further notice. Stay tuned for more information to come."

Kirk could feel a chill, but not from the illness. "Taylor, Mars is quarantined. We're stuck."

"Quarantined?"

"Yeah. It's on the TV."

"Why?"

"Well, maybe because of what we have."

"Oh. Maybe we should go to the doctor."

"There's an infirmary here. Let me call my Uncle."

Kirk placed his earpiece in his ear and pushed a button with a direct line to General Matthews.

"Yes."

"Uncle. Taylor and I are on Mars and have just found out that the planet has been quarantined. Should I be worried?"

"We're not sure, Kirk. We think that the salvage ship has delivered something that got past our ability to sterilize it. Belinda is at the research facility right now trying to figure it out."

"So, she's stuck here also?"

"She is, Kirk, but it's worse than that. I can't raise anyone in charge or in security at the facility and I've been trying to reach our military police connected with their station near Condo City but there isn't anyone there receiving incoming calls. There are usually police walking the mall but I have no way of connecting with them directly. I may need you to go to the police station and find someone in charge."

"Okay. Let me know. Taylor and I are both pretty sick."

"I was afraid of that. How are you doing?"

"Taylor is worse than me right now, but it might be that she had contracted it first. Uncle, I was wondering if we should get medical help?"

"Right now, there is nothing that any doctor can do, but if Taylor or you begin to have trouble breathing, it could be pneumonia. Then you would need help. How far are you from the infirmary near Condo City?"

"Maybe ten minutes on foot."

"Okay. I'd say sit tight for now and hopefully, this virus will pass. We know of several people who have been sick for three days and they are still doing okay, just sick as hell with on and off fever and chills. Belinda told me that she has had to give several people intravenous hydration, so, try to keep drinking water. Kirk, if I need you to go to the police station, I'll contact you. I'm going to try several other contacts first."

"Will do, Uncle."

"I'll do all I can to get you off the planet as soon as possible, but we can't have this bug get off the planet in case—"

"In case it's deadly?"

"Well. Yes."

Chapter 34

Washington D.C.

Oval office

May 21, 2105

Sol 541

No sign of the alien craft that had breached the wormhole had been discovered. Every country tried in vain to determine its whereabouts but it was completely invisible. The wormhole was now also invisible with all electronics there having failed so the alien craft might have gone back through.

President Woodward had just gotten off the line with Werner Lang, the Prime minister of Germany, and also Han Yang, the President of China.

Woodward wanted the world to beef up its conventional military. The Chinese leader was in agreement but as usual with every discussion about the world military, the Chinese leader wanted the Dome Raptors' technology and the secret to the EMP bombs that were being produced in the United States, placed only on American aircraft and not being shared worldwide.

President Woodward had just been verbally assaulted by Mason Hunt of the World Bank on the phone who wanted the United States to divulge all of its secrets, but Woodward was steadfast in his belief that the world government was crumbling and his Chief of Staff, Kirk Matthews Senior, agreed. Woodward basically hung up on Hunt.

A call came in for the President. He answered and looked at Matthews Senior. "It's your brother," Woodward said a bit caustically. "I'll put it on the speaker."

General Mathews began and it was obvious that he was reading a prepared statement. "We have a situation on Mars, Mister President. It seems that some kind of virus or bacteria has also arrived from the wormhole and we suspect that it's alien. We think that the entire planet of Mars has been exposed to this so we have temporarily quarantined the planet. My doctor, Belinda Waters, has gone to the planet to collect whatever information that she can about what is happening there. There is a specific problem for anyone who has been given the drug Biocare. We think that this virus seems to affect anyone on the drug more adversely. Everything on the planet is sketchy right now and I will keep you informed. As it stands at this time, no one of the planet has come down with the virus. I have been in touch with every spaceship in orbit. I have ordered the salvage ship to remain here until we know if it is carrying the virus. We don't want this to show up on Earth.

Now for the worst of the problem, the Research Facility is in effect, out of order. I have been unable to contact anyone in charge or in security. I am fearing the worst, but I can't allow anyone to go to the planet, at this point, to see exactly what's happening. I only have Doctor Waters there and I'm in contact with her. My Nephew, Kirk is there but is sick with the virus. I may need to use him and anyone else I can get in contact with to help try to secure the planet. That's all for now and I'll await your response. Matthews out."

Woodward turned to Kirk Matthews Senior with a grave expression but Matthews said, "My son is on the planet?"

"I'm sorry, Kirk."

Mathews breathed out then down to business, said, "Nothing's being studied."

Woodward nodded and said, "How are we going to discover what we need to know from the alien wreckage?"

"I don't know, Oliver, but my brother is the best man to have there. He'll figure something out. He usually does."

"He'd better because that alien ship is on the way and maybe more of them than just the one. Send him that message for me and, Kirk, try to get some more information about your son."

"Will do, Mister President."

Chapter 35

NASA Mars Research Center

Infirmary

May 22, 2105

Sol 542

By the next morning, nearly everyone in the facility was thought to be infected by the virus. Doctor Saito and both of her nurses were now displaying the early symptoms. Waters was the only person not yet affected, though she was exhausted from a severe lack of sleep.

Doctor Waters checked on two patients who had developed pneumonia. They were the most severely affected in the ward and were becoming progressively worse. One needed to be put on a respirator. The majority of the rest of the patients were holding their own, though miserable.

A call came into Waters' earpiece and she nearly didn't answer it as she needed to finish with the breathing tube. The other patients watched in horror and worried that this might be their fate also.

She reached up and pushed a depression on the earpiece.

"Yes," she said shortly.

"Doctor Waters?"

"Yes."

"This is Calvin Johnson."

"Oh, Professor."

"I have something that I would like to show you about the specimens that you gave me."

"I'll be down in a minute. I have to finish something."

Waters finished placing the tube and when she looked around, every patient who could sit up were staring open-mouthed.

Waters said to the group, "Don't worry. Your lungs are doing much better than his. This should only be temporary. I think most of you are past the worst of this disease."

They all seemed happy to hear her speculations and they laid back down.

"Emily, Professor Johnson in the morgue wants to show me something. I'll get back as soon as I can."

Doctor Saito nodded and Waters walked from the ward. She took off her gloves and threw them into a bio-container and walked into the examination room, paused at the door and glanced outside and into the hallway then looked both ways and jogged to the elevator. The red light still blinked and the alarm still sounded. The hallway felt like a nightmare. The doors to the elevator were open and she hit the button to close them.

"Level eleven."

The elevator repeated the command and descended.

When the doors opened, she glanced both ways again, then jogged to the doors into the morgue and scanned her card. The double doors opened and she stepped in quickly and into the observation room. The doors closed behind.

"Hello, Doctor," Calvin Johnson said from behind her. He seemed to have a way of sneaking up.

Startled, she turned, "Oh, hello."

"I didn't mean to startle you."

"I'm jumpy."

"Understandable. Come with me."

He led her into an office with a large screen.

She smiled, "No shower this time?"

"Well," he said smoothly, "That would be a pleasure, but no, not for this."

"You weren't supposed to enjoy that."

Johnson smiled wryly, "Please sit."

He pointed her to a chair and turned on the monitor that was mounted on the wall. There were two seats, side by side, and he held a small computer pad as he sat down by Waters.

"This is what you are dealing with. This virus is alien and the swabs that you took showed it on nearly every surface. If I were to guess, I would bet that it got on the screen of the filtration system in the holding compartment where the wreckage was kept until it reached Mars. When the doors were opened, the virus was pumped out and into the air. You are dealing with a retrovirus that has the ability to deposit its own DNA into the cells of the infected. As the cells divide like here," Johnson pointed to a cell dividing. "It places a bit of its own DNA in the DNA of the host cell but then it has another trick. It finds and attaches the infected cell to adult stem cells. These changed cells then cause the newly created cell to become the cell that the immune system thinks are the proper cells.

The immune system becomes confused and begins killing the body's original cells that have not been affected by the virus but by this time nearly every cell in the body has been infected. Any guess which sample I learned this from?"

"The one from the guy who was on Biocare?"

"That is correct, Doctor."

"Why do you think that the people on Biocare are susceptible to this happening?"

"For one thing, they have many more adult stem cells than normal. I would say three times as many as someone who isn't on the drug and their cell division seems to be much faster and those cells seem to live longer. It seems to be the perfect storm, biologically speaking, that is."

"So, what are we left with?"

"We are left with whatever those things are."

"Some new kind of life?"

"You are very wise, Doctor. I would say, something that has evolved."

"So, what's happening to the people who are not on Biocare?"

"The same thing that happens when they get a common cold or the flu. The immune system goes out and takes care of business."

"So, you think that they will all recover?"

"Most, I think, but people die from simple things all the time. Some may not survive but I think most should."

"Thanks, Professor," Waters said, standing.

"Good day, Doctor, and good luck."

Waters walked out.

Chapter 36

NASA Mars Research Center

May 22, 2105

Sol 542

1300 Hours

George Hall woke sweat-soaked in his bed.
BEEP BEEP BEEP
He thought, what's that noise?
He had only planned for a nap.
BEEP BEEP BEEP
He glanced over and his alarm had been beeping for ten hours with no response from him.
He coughed.
His mind was in a fog and his body ached. He drifted back to sleep...
BEEP BEEP BEEP
"Shit."
He reached over and turned off his alarm then stood shakily and pushed at an intercom calling to his security office.
No answer.
Red flags burst into his mind. He tried several of his men who should be on duty.

Nothing.

Hall got out of his sweat-soaked clothes and into something dry. He slipped back on his lanyard and called to the infirmary.

Doctor Saito answered, "Yes."

"Doctor, this is George Hall—"

"Hall, where have you been?" she said abruptly interrupting.

"I, um, got sick and fell asleep. I just woke. What's going on? I can't reach any security."

"Everything's a mess."

"Give me a minute to try to figure this out. I'll call you back."

"Listen, Mister Hall, everyone is sick from something from the alien wreckage. We think it has done something strange to anyone on Biocare."

"Biocare? What's Biocare?"

"I thought you would know about Biocare."

"No."

"It's a drug that enhances and extends life for people who are going into space. At least half of your guards were on the drug. I was supposed to give them their boosters. You didn't know?"

"No, Doctor."

"I also had heard that people of wealth were able to purchase the drug. We think Mackelroy and Niland and maybe Forsyth are all on the drug."

"Okay. Let me get back to you."

"I'm not finished. I was treating one of your security guards, Stephen Donnelly. He changed into something, something inhuman—"

"Inhuman?"

"That's what I said, inhuman, and ran out of the infirmary. He killed two workers. He was fast and strong and, I don't know, feral, running on all fours like some kind of dog."

Hall was muddled and his mind couldn't keep up with what he was hearing. He said, "Let me get to the security cams. Are you safe?"

"We don't think so but nothing has tried to get in here. It seems that whatever Stephen turned into just wanted out."

"Okay. I'll get back to you."

Hall left the intercom, sat down, and shook. His chills were coming in waves. He took a deep breath and stepped out of his room.

Hall's room was on level three and he knocked on several doors where he knew guards were staying close to him but there was no answer. He continued down the hall and could see several doors that seemed to be forced open. An alarm rang and a red light blinked above a forced-open stairway door. As he neared the elevator, he could see a security bot in a heap. It appeared to have not fired a shot. He stepped into the elevator and the doors closed. "Level one."

"Level one, George Hall."

The elevator started up.

When he reached the main floor, there was little out of place with one notable exception, it was completely deserted. There wasn't a soul to be seen. He stepped into the large room that led to where the alien wreckage was offloaded and peeked through a large plexiglass window that separated the warehouse from the facility and there was no one working.

Hall turned and quickly walked to the security office located near the front of the facility. Here, he would be able to check every camera feed and every recorded scene that had happened while he slept.

As he entered the office, he froze in horror to see two of his guards dead on the floor, one with his stomach ripped open and the other, his neck broken. Hall was not armed. He glanced around trying to perceive if there remained any danger. The office was silent. He sidestepped further in and peered around a corner into his own office. It was clear. He slipped inside and went to a closet and pulled out a shotgun then quietly slipped back into a short hallway and glanced in a separate office. There, some clothes lay in a heap by a chair. He checked the lanyard laying on the clothes lifting it with the barrel of the gun. It read, *"Jack Fry."*

"Jack!" he whispered and then turned back and cleared the rest of the security office.

Once he was fairly sure that it was safe, he flipped on a monitor that sat on a desk to check the security feeds. When he checked the camera in the outer office, he saw something quick as a leopard leap from the hallway and catch both guards by surprise and strike them dead, then run from the security office.

He began by checking the view from every camera in every hallway, then he began calling all of his remaining guards. He had twenty at the facility. One after another, there was no response.

He called Ernest Nash.

"Yeah, Boss," Nash responded groggily.

"Where are you, Nash?"

Nash had just placed his ear-com into his ear as he woke. In a fevered fog, he said, "In my room. I'm sick. I wasn't scheduled to work today so I slept in. What time is it?"

"1300 hours."

"Oh, damn. It's late."

"Get dressed and get to the security office. We have an emergency."

"I'm on it," Nash said and as he rose from his pillow, dizziness swarmed his muddled brain. "Oh?" he groaned.

"What is it?"

"I'm seriously dizzy. I'll be right there, Boss. Give me a couple of minutes."

Hall continued to call others on the security team. Sweat soaked his shirt. In the next ten minutes, he was able to reach two other guards, Eli Sample, and Leo Russo, both in the same condition. He instructed them to come to the security office, grab a couple of shotguns and wait.

Hall then went back to checking the security cameras. This time, he began at the infirmary. He had a cam on the hallway and in the waiting room. He didn't have access into the wards or the examination rooms for obvious reasons. He reran the recording from the time roughly when Stephen was supposed to have killed the two workers. He backed the tape to where the two lay dead in a heap then back further to where something fast burst through the door to the waiting room and struck the two men.

"Shit," Hall whispered as the men were attacked by something that came through the doors on all fours but then rose in one swift motion and struck both men with two swipes of violent rage. The same as in his office.

Hall focused the recording to get a better look at this demon. It could have been a man at one time. The bone structure was right, but it was nude and hairless and the skin and muscle structure weren't quite human. It appeared as if the tendons had pulled the fingers and toes back and bent the hands and feet unnaturally. The face was distorted with the eyes smaller than a human and the cheeks sunken. The head was bony. Could this have been Stephen? It bared no resemblance to the man Hall knew. This was obviously male with the phallus clearly visible but the creature's color appeared to be pink as if its skin was pulled from the muscles leaving wet and dripping sinews. The mouth had fleshy lips that pulled back in anger with some kind of fleshy growth over the corners of the mouth. When it attacked the workers, foamy slobber dripped from its maw as if rabid.

Hall watched as the creature burst from the two dead men in the waiting room and crashed into the closed door. The door buckled and bowed outward leaving a gap wide enough for the creature to escape from.

Hall then followed the creature to the stairwell where it ran then picked it up inside. It ran deftly down the stairs on all fours. He continued to follow the beast past level eleven, the morgue, then down a final flight of stairs. Here the beast yanked at a door that it eventually pulled open. Hall attempted to see inside that room but there were no cameras inside. He wondered at that. Then a blur raced past the last camera where he had been watching, then another, then another. Three more creatures. He went back to the recording of the attack in his office and the thing, whatever it was, also ran to the stairway, pulled the door open, and dashed in. These doors were secured and shouldn't open unless the person had his pass and was cleared to go to the floors. Hall looked closer at the door to the stairway and it was broken and forced open. He turned off the alarms that were ringing on every floor where the doors were forced.

"What are these things?" he said to himself.

He checked the camera feeds from all the levels and when he didn't see anything else, stood and swayed. He gripped the desk to steady when Nash walked in the door.

Nash looked as sick as Hall felt. Hall shook his head and said, "Come with me."

Hall went to a locked closet and opened it, reached in and removed a twelve-gauge shotgun and a box of shells, handing the gun to Nash.

"Grab some shells."

Hall took two additional guns and two more boxes of shells and said, "Let's go."

They walked out and to the elevator.

Hall said, "Level ten."

"Level ten, George Hall."

The elevator descended.

When the doors opened, they could hear shots being fired by a security bot. They ran towards the shots. As they turned the corner, a fleshy form was looming over the bot and shots had passed through the creature's body in a spray of blood and visible exit wounds. The creature was half-dressed, shirtless, and shoeless, and though shot multiple times, it smashed the bot with powerful arms and the bot stopped its assault.

Hall stepped out and walked toward the beast and leveled the rifle in its direction.

The creature turned and straightened, roared enraged with the skin flaps quivering, and started at Hall. Hall chambered a round then fired, one, then two, then three lethal blasts into the creature.

The shotgun blasts struck the creature firmly in its chest and abdomen blowing large hunks of flesh off of the creature's body. It collapsed.

Hall's ears rang and he cautiously approached the prostrate form of the creature. He then stooped and reached into the pocket of the beast's tailored trousers and with two fingers, pulled out a security card. There, a smiling, well-groomed face of a distinguished man with greying temples smiled back at Hall with the name Thomas Forsyth beneath the picture.

Hall straightened and said, "Doctor Forsyth."

Nash's eyes were wide with shock. He stammered, "What the hell, Boss!? I mean, WHAT THE HELL!?"

"We have a situation here. I counted four of these things all headed into a floor of this facility that I didn't know existed. Follow me."

Hall led Nash to the infirmary.

When they entered, Doctor Saito, Doctor Waters, and the nurses were huddled behind two turned over desks that were blocking the door.

"It's okay now," Hall said, pushing the desks aside as the doctors straightened.

"What happened out there?" Doctor Saito asked.

One of those creatures were killed. Could you call someone from the morgue to pick it up?"

"I will," Doctor Waters volunteered.

She pushed a wall-mounted com.

"Yes," came a voice from the com.

"Professor Johnson, we have a dead... um... something down here at the infirmary. Could you send someone to pick it up and keep them in their bio-suits?"

"Will do, Doctor."

Hall spoke to the bedded patients; most were sitting up and trying to listen for a clue as to what all the shooting was about. Several of the patients were so sick that they didn't even wake.

Hall asked, "Does anyone here know about this facility? I need someone who was here from the building stage."

A man, balding and wearing glasses spoke up. "I was here. I helped with the building then stayed on in maintenance," said Larry West.

"Hi, Larry. Sure, I remember you."

"How can I help?"

"Can you get up? Are you feeling well enough? I want to take you to where you can look at some plans or blueprints of this place."

"Yes, I can get up."

Doctor Saito said, "Are you sure, Larry? You shouldn't push it."

Hall said, "This is important, Doctor."

Larry said meekly, "I can go."

Hall saw two of his other guards in bed and sitting up. He walked a shotgun to the two guards with shells. "We got a problem here as you know. You need to protect this place."

The first guard slipped from bed and stood. His name was Juaquin Garza. "I'm good, Mister Hall."

"Me too," Ben Eason, the other guard said also sliding from bed. Both had sweat on their brows and both were coughing. The two guards took off their gowns and put back on their blue security jumpsuits.

Juaquin asked, "Where's everyone else?"

"That's what I'm going to try to figure out. Come on Larry, let's go have a look at some plans."

Larry nodded and now dressed, stepped in behind Hall and Nash.

Nash and Hall led Larry into the corridor brandishing their weapons and sweeping from left to right. Two guys from the morgue in bio-suits were picking up the body of the dead creature and placing it into a body bag. Blood and pieces of flesh dripped from the walls.

Curious, Doctor Waters had followed Hall, Nash, and West into the hallway to have a look.

Hall turned back to Waters and said, "Tell the Professor that the guy's name was Forsyth."

Waters said, "Will do, Mister Hall."

Hall and Nash started towards the elevator with Larry. Waters turned back to the infirmary. Hall asked Larry, "Do you know anything about the basement?"

"Yeah, a lot."

"I've never been down there. What's there?"

"Just storage, but it leads to a network of caverns. After the work was done on the facility, the tunnels were closed off except for a couple of hatches. Mars is full of these tunnels. The construction crew filled the tunnels with breathable air because the tunnels had good pressure and temperature so the workers could take off their spacesuits and work for a short time. They weren't opened to the Martian surface. I was in the tunnels several times myself. They were pretty comfortable."

"Are the tunnels accessible?"

"Not from the outside, there are a couple of trap doors that lead under the facility that are locked but could be opened from the basement."

"Why weren't these tunnels completely sealed off. The creatures that were encounter from the Martian surface a few years back could have gotten in here?"

Larry shrugged.

"Larry, did you ever hunt at any time in your life?"

"Nope."

Hall went to the locker and grabbed another shotgun, loaded it, and said, "No time to learn than the present. You point and shoot. Try not to kill us. Let's go."

Nash asked, "Where we going, Boss?"

"To the basement."

Chapter 37

Washington D.C.

Oval Office

May 22, 2105

Mason Hunt stepped into the office of the President.

President Woodward said, "Hello, Mister Hunt." The friction was obvious.

"Mister President," Hunt said then looked directly at Kirk Matthews Senior and said, "Could you excuse us please." It wasn't a request.

Hunt gazed at Woodward as a parent would a child just before a trip to the woodshed.

Matthews looked at Woodward who nodded and he stepped from the office.

Hunt began, "I have just gotten off the line with the President of China and the Prime Minister of Germany and they both want to know why the New World State of America is not sharing all of our technology. Aren't we supposed to be one world? How are we going to be able to defeat this alien threat without sharing every bit of technology with each other?"

"The problem, Mister Hunt, is that they are also not sharing with us. They want it both ways. We cannot afford to give them any more than we have already given them. Just how we collect and use antimatter alone should have been enough for them to do nearly everything that we are able to do in space, but we have been after the designs of several of the Chinese missile systems and the Germans have developed a radar system that is very interesting to us. We have, through General Montague, been negotiating some technology transfer but they are not forthcoming. They want our EMP research. As far as I'm concerned, that might put them ahead of us if we allow them access to that information."

"I don't care what you think, Woodward. I want the Germans and the Chinese to have everything that we have. Do I make myself clear?"

"No," Woodward said stubbornly and glared at Hunt. "I will not authorize the transfer of that technology to two countries that were our enemies just several years before."

"I guarantee, Woodward, that I will see to it that you will not win the next election. I have that power."

"I know you do, but I'm still President for a couple of years and most of the Generals agree that this quasi world government is fracturing which means that the New World State of America might soon become the United States of America, again, and there will be no need for the New World Bank."

"You are taking a huge gamble that we can win a war against the aliens without every country having the best military."

"I understand that dilemma but I also know what the world will look like if the Chinese and the

Germans both jump ahead of us technologically. As I had heard the former President, Henry Dent, remark, 'we'll need to learn to speak Chinese'."

"You haven't heard the end of this, Woodward. I have several members of Congress who agree with me and a bill is close to reaching the floor that will go over your head."

"Tell me, Mister Hunt, are you really concerned with defeating the aliens, or are you just interested in maintaining your own power because if the World Government falls apart, you're out of a job and the power that you now enjoy, disintegrates."

"And what about you, Woodward? What if you fuck this up and the aliens run over all our allies? Do you think the U.S. can stand alone against an enemy like the ones who decimated our world?"

"I believe that we can strategically defeat the aliens with the worlds' help but it's been seven years since they came to our planet and just because the wormhole has been breached again, doesn't mean that they are coming back here."

"They're coming back and we need to be ready."

"I get that. The United States is gearing up for war with the aliens. China and Germany are gearing up to take our country at the first opportunity."

"That's absurd."

"The same people who were leading the war against us the first time are all still the movers and shakers of both of those countries."

"You aren't even sharing the strategic technologies with Mexico or Canada, not to mention, Great Britain."

"I am considering sharing some of the tech with them. It's under advisement with the Joint Chiefs now."

"You haven't heard the last of this, Woodward. Don't be surprised if you start hearing the word, 'impeachment'."

"Don't be surprised if you start hearing the word, 'treason,' Hunt."

Hunt turned and stomped out. His face was red and the skin tight from Biocare which gave him the look of an angry mannequin.

Chief of Staff, Matthews, walked back into the Oval Office as Hunt departed.

Matthews gave Woodward a wry grin and said, "What did you do, Oliver? Sleep with his wife?"

"I'm caught between a rock and a hard place, Kirk. My gut tells me that I can't trust the rest of the world with our best technology but if the aliens come back any time soon, I'm not sure we have any hope of winning a war without the rest of the world stacked with our best stuff."

"So that was Hunt's beef? He wants us to give everyone our most closely held secrets without getting the rest of the worlds' secrets in return?"

"That's about the size of it."

"Rock and a hard place."

"You got that right."

"We have just opened two new plants. They are beginning to pump out Dome Raptors and the new AK 4000, all equipped with EMP bombs. Our new space station and spaceport are days from operation. We are producing some serious weapons that if we had ready when the aliens first arrived would have defeated them. I'm not confident that we can win a 'War of the

Worlds' with this alien race but I'm fairly certain that we will make it a painful experience. I talked to my brother two days ago and he said that the technology brought back from the wormhole doesn't, at first glance, seem to be that much ahead of ours. They seem to be using similar tech, just applied differently, semiconductors, and the like. I don't think they are that far ahead of us. They came through the wormhole so they didn't travel from some distant star cluster in the conventional sense. Hopefully, we'll learn enough from the captured alien tech to sway the balance. If we don't, then I think Hunt's argument is moot. We lose anyway."

"That's how I feel also, Kirk. You have friends on the Hill, maybe you can persuade some to see the world the way we do."

"I'll do what I can."

"In the meantime, we need to double the production of our best weaponry. We need shifts working around the clock."

"I'll see to it that our plants are fully ramped up."

Woodward breathed out. "A rock and a damned hard place."

"Yep."

Chapter 38

Mars Surface

Condo City

Noachis Terra Hotel

May 22, 2105

Sol 542

Kirk and Taylor fell back asleep. The computer monitor in the room began pinging. Kirk rolled to his side and glanced at the direction of the desk and computer.

"Augh," he said, groaning.

"Go see who it is," Taylor said, pushing Kirk's shoulder.

"Ah huh," Kirk responded.

He stood shakily and pushed a button to receive the call. His Uncle's face filled the screen.

"Kirk, you need to go to the police station. Something is wrong there and be careful. I have just talked to Belinda. She says that some people on Biocare are becoming psychotic. She says that there have been murders."

"I'm on it," Kirk said, clearing his throat.

"Get back to me ASAP."

"I will, I'm leaving now."

"Kirk reached for his clothes and began pulling on his NASA blue jumpsuit."

Taylor sat up.

Kirk said, "Got to go." He was slipping on his socks.

"I'm going too," Taylor said, rising and swinging her legs over the side of the bed.

"I don't think you should."

"I'm coming." Taylor pulled off her nightclothes and began dressing. She snapped her bra then pulled on her jumpsuit.

Kirk was dressed and didn't protest.

Taylor slipped on shoes and socks and both were out the door coughing.

Chapter 39

NASA Mars Research Center

Security office

First floor

May 22, 2105

Sol 542

Hall, West, and Nash returned to the security office after checking the basement. Waiting for them there were Leo Russo and Eli Sample. The basement revealed just what he thought, that the creatures pulled off a hatch that covered an opening in the floor to the tunnels below and disappeared. Why had they gone down there? How would they know about it? He and Nash had pushed the hatch closed and placed some large heavy containers on top of the hatch to try to prevent the creatures from reentering.

Hall called the infirmary trying to get some information about who was on Biocare. He connected with Doctor Saito.

"Doctor, I need to find out how many people in this facility are on Biocare and who they are. We have a big problem here."

Saito hesitated for a moment, wanting to keep the patient's privacy but then said, "Okay. Can you expand on the problem?"

"I have seen several other of the creatures like what happened to Stephen Donnelly. They seem to be trying to get out of the facility through the basement."

"Why?"

"Don't know. I've been trying to figure that out. Maybe some instinct. Maybe they could smell or sense it in some way that normal humans couldn't. I really have no idea."

Saito said, "Hum. I remember that Donnelly was complaining that he couldn't breathe even though he had plenty of oxygen. Doctor Waters glanced at the monitors and he was too oxygenated as if he couldn't use all the oxygen he was being given. I thought it strange, but now maybe it makes sense."

"Interesting," Hall said, then, "Maybe they're trying to find someplace with less oxygen."

"Maybe," Saito said, then, "Give me a second." She began reading the names of his security guards. It was well over half of his detail.

"Huh," he said then, "I'm going to each's room to see if I can find them. Doctor, is this everyone in this facility who are on the drug?"

"These are the people that I know of. There may be others who are being treated by different doctors."

"Thank you." Hall counted the names, twelve.

Hall turned to Nash, Sample, West, and Russo, "So, we have twelve of our guys on the drug, Forsyth, and probably Mackelroy and Niland. Forsyth is dead. That leaves at least fourteen if they survived their transition into whatever they've become. I think some have gotten out. Only a couple of our guys are in the infirmary. We're going to need to hunt the rest down and try to clear this place."

Nash said, "This place is big and we still have all those people in the infirmary that we need to protect."

"We'll need to do it systematically. Hopefully, we can evacuate most of the patients as they improve."

Hall's ear-com pinged. "Yes."

"Hall, this is Waters."

"Yes, Doctor."

Waters started, "I just heard from General Matthews. He said that JFK City is in the same boat as the Research Facility. Most of the MPs there were on Biocare and all of the rest are unreachable. He can't bring anyone to the planet to help because he doesn't know the extent of the virus. It may be impossible to sterilize the virus and if that's the case, no one on the planet will be able to rejoin the orbiting vessels or go back to Earth. At this point, we just don't know. His point is that we are, at least for now, on our own. He said that he can keep us supplied with drop shipments."

"Thank you, Doctor, for the bleak news," Hall said dryly.

"The General doesn't believe in sugar-coating. Waters out."

Hall glanced at his three men and Larry. "Let see if we can figure out where all of these creatures are at with the cameras. Keep your shotguns handy. Larry, you are officially security now, congratulations."

Larry nodded and stood behind Nash to learn how to operate the cameras and recorders.

Each man was given a floor to check from the time that Donnelly changed. It was going to be a long and laborious job but Hall couldn't think of any other way to find the creatures without risking his remaining security officers.

Nash gazed at the security monitor that watched the main entrance. He said, "Hey, Boss, you need to look at this."

Hall glanced up from the monitor that he was looking at and walked over to Nash. Nash rewound a feed from the platform where the high-speed trains brought in the workers.

Two guards coughed and stood by the doors looking out onto the tracks. Behind them, the doors burst open and one of the creatures attacked both before they could draw their weapons. It left them both dead. In the next minute, another creature ran out the door on all fours and disappeared into the tunnel that brought the trains, then another. As Hall and Nash watched, another came out and hightailed it down the train tunnel.

"Damn," Hall said.

Nash said, "Well, at least they're not in here."

"I guess, but where are they going?"

"The Mall?" Nash guessed.

"Damn. I just heard that there is no security there, just like here."

"Geez," Larry commented, "What a nightmare."

Chapter 40

Noachis Terra Mall

May 22, 2105

Sol 542

To get to the police station, Kirk and Taylor had to head toward the mall then veer off at a hallway clearly marked police station. The mall was empty. Every walkway that they took was deserted. No one wanted to be out and exposed to the virus if they weren't sick and most of the people who were infected were so sick that they needed to stay in bed. The hotel lobby, the walkways, and probably the mall also were veritable ghost towns.

The hallway to the police station was wide and well-lit with overhead lights on a twenty-foot ceiling. Tall windows showed the Martian landscape which was foggy today.

No one was in this hallway. Kirk had expected to see at least one security guard or MP.

He and Taylor approached the two double doors that led into the station. One of the doors was askew and appeared to be damaged. When Kirk and Taylor walked in, there was carnage. At least five blue-clad police lay in puddled blood and fluids in front of a counter that separated the lobby from the office area of the station. Some of the MPs appeared to have been partially eaten.

When Taylor walked in, she quickly turned away.

She whispered, "What the hell, Kirk?"

"I don't know."

Kirk reached down and lifted a shotgun that lay near the still form of a female MP. Her neck was broken and her eyes opened. He checked the chamber and the gun was loaded. Two used shells lay on the floor in a puddle of blood from one of the male MPs who died near the woman.

Kirk could hear the sound of something moving. He crept up with Taylor close on his heels and peered over the counter. There to his horror, he could see something that made no sense. A creature that appeared to have no skin was crouched over a dead MP chewing on the man's neck and shoulder, ripping mouthfuls of flesh. Startled, Kirk pulled back and accidentally banged the counter with the stock of the shotgun. The creature straightened and turned toward Kirk and Taylor. The creature appeared to be female with breasts but had the look of a drawing that might appear in a doctor's office showing what the body would look like without skin. Sharp pointed, short, slightly curved, bony growths protruded from between muscle at random places on the woman-thing's body, on her cheeks and over her eyes, on her brow ridge, on her shins, ribs, forearms, and the backs of her fingers. Everywhere the bones were close to the surface, these odd spikes protruded sparsely. She was completely hairless as if going through chemotherapy and her facial features were distorted by skin flaps that made her eyes and mouth appear much smaller proportionately than normal humans. She rose to her full height and raised her arms wide and roared an unearthly sound. The skin flaps by her mouth vibrated and foamy drool dripped over her bottom lip. Her translucent skin was so thin that each muscle was visible underneath and it oozed a plasma-like substance as if she were a burn victim.

Kirk and Taylor had backed against a wall and could go back no further. The woman-creature leaped deftly onto the counter, spread her arms wide, and was ready to attack when Kirk fired the shotgun, hitting the creature just below the stomach. The deafening blast threw the creature backward and it landed behind the counter.

Kirk peeked over and the creature's spine was severed but it still crawled. Kirk fired again striking it in the neck region. The creature lay headless and motionless.

He turned toward Taylor with eyes wide and he appeared like a deer in the headlights. He couldn't speak. Taylor looked as if in shock.

Kirk had his ear-com and he pressed a button.

"Yes," General Matthews said.

Kirk spoke hurriedly, "Uncle, Taylor, and I are at the police station and there's been a massacre. I can see around ten dead MPs and one strange creature that I just killed. It appeared to be female and it also appeared to have no skin. I don't believe that this creature could have killed all of these guys alone, there must be more of them. I'm going to have a look around."

General Matthews said, "Be careful, Kirk. We don't know what we're dealing with."

"I will. Stay on and I'll tell you what I see."

Kirk took Taylor's hand and led her to a half door that separated the lobby from the office area on the far side of the counter.

Kirk said to Taylor, "Wait here." Then to the General, "Uncle, I'm going behind the counter and to my right, there are several offices with closed doors. I'm stepping over bodies. Shit! It looks like there are four offices. They are separated by a short hallway with a door at the end. I'm approaching the first office and opening the door. Inside there is a desk and a uniform in a chair that appears to be wet, maybe blood-soaked. On the desk is a picture of a woman with blond hair pulled back and she's posed wearing an MP uniform. As I look at the blood-soaked uniform on the chair, I can see what looks like snakeskin mingled with the blood. I'm walking out of the office now and the hallway from this point and to a door at the end is tracked with blood as if something dead had been dragged to the door. The door is ajar. I'm checking the rest of the offices. Two more of the offices have the same thing as the first with uniforms on the ground and some kind of skin mingled with something wet. I'm nearing the door now at the end of the hallway and pushing it open. Behind the door is a long dark hallway that bends in the distance and a stairway. It looks like it might be a security hallway where police can look at the mall from two-way glass. There's no one back here that I can see. Just tracks of blood and two more uniforms in piles. I'm going back to Taylor. I don't want her to be alone."

"Kirk, get out of there for now. Go back to your room and I'll contact you with further instructions."

"Will do, Uncle."

Kirk rejoined Taylor.

"Kirk, what was that thing?"

"I'm not sure. I think my uncle has more information than he gave me but he said for us to get back to our room and wait for further instructions. He will contact me again when he has some kind of plan. Here," Kirk said, walking to an open closet with a rack of weapons. He reached for a shotgun. "Have you ever fired one of these?"

"Yeah, a couple of times."

"Good."

Kirk checked to make sure it was loaded. It wasn't so he grabbed a box of shells and loaded Taylor's gun then filled his pockets with the rest of the shells.

"Let's go."

They cautiously stepped from the police station's doors and jogged back toward their room.

Chapter 41

NASA Mars Research Center

May 22, 2105

Sol 542

Sanjay and Marriam were both in bed. Both had high fevers and both coughing. The computer monitor began pinging in a call.

Sanjay cracked an eyelid and pushed up to sitting. Marriam didn't move. He rubbed his face and walked to the monitor that sat on a small desk against the far wall. He felt exhausted, completely drained of all energy.

"Yes," Sanjay said as he switched on the monitor.

"Sanjay?"

"Oh, General Matthews."

"Are you okay?"

"I'm okay but Marriam is really sick. Doctor Waters had been here a bit ago, though, and checked on her and said that she was okay. The entire facility is down with the sickness. That's what I've heard."

"I've heard that there is a problem in the facility also. It's all still sketchy. I'm waiting to hear back from Belinda."

"Well, we aren't going anywhere for a bit."

"What's going on with the salvage ship?"

"It's completely offloaded without us finding, ah, anything special."

"Egbert will be unhappy to hear that."

"Yes."

"Any ideas about what Egbert might have been influenced by?"

"Well, there are several large pieces of wreckage parked on the warehouse floor. There is also a complete alien disk-shaped craft of some kind. I watched some workers try to get inside of it, but they were unsuccessful."

"I'll go back and see if Egbert has any updates. Maybe it was a mistake."

"Maybe."

"I'll get back to you."

"Okay."

Matthews was gone and Sanjay flopped back into bed and closed his eyes, drained from the exertion.

Chapter 42

Mars Orbit

Space Station Isla Charlie

May 22, 2105

Sol 542

General Matthews knew that he had promised Belinda that he would remain in his room, but he needed to check on Egbert. He opened the door to his room and glanced around to see if anyone was coughing. No one was, so he stepped into the hall and walked quickly to the room where Egbert and the other egg sat on a desk, illuminated by a light.

Egbert was already on and his hologram showed Mars with the coordinates that had been there before.

Matthews said, "Well, Egbert, we haven't found your new egg friend yet. Is that what we're looking for?"

Egbert just continued to display Mars with the coordinates."

"Huh— Something is there, though," Matthews stated aloud.

He walked from Egbert's room and back to his own. No one around him had coughed. He felt safe from the virus, at least for now.

Entering his room, he called Doctor Waters to find out what was going on at the facility.

"Belinda, are you still safe?"

"For now, Jeff. We have heard several shots in the corridors but nothing has attacked us since the first two men were killed. We have two security guards here with shotguns to help protect us. I just got a call from Professor Johnson who works in the morgue. He has just completed an autopsy on the creature who was killed just outside the infirmary. It was a Doctor Forsyth. He had come with Niland and Mackelroy. Neither of them has been heard from. Professor Johnson said that the frontal cortex of Doctor Forsyth's brain was reduced in size somewhat with some but not all left viable. The medulla oblongata and the hindbrain were both oversized compared to normal humans. Both, especially the hindbrain had expanded in size."

"What does that mean, Doctor?"

"The frontal cortex controls higher thinking like reasoning and problem-solving. It makes us humans what we are. The hindbrain is referred to as the Reptilian Brain or the Primal Brain and it is responsible for things like dominance, survival, and mating."

"So, in a nutshell, Belinda, what does this mean?"

"It means that we're dealing with some new form of creature down here. Something smarter than any animal, as dangerous as a crocodile and with about as much compassion. My guess is that anything living anywhere these creatures are located will be on the menu."

"Understood, Belinda. Stay safe."

When Matthews disconnected with Doctor Waters he sat and thought. He could send people to the surface, but it was debatable whether or not he could return them without also transporting the virus. It might catch a ride on some unpredictable surface. No matter how he sliced it, the people on the planet were on their own for now.

Part 4

All Hell Broken Loose

Chapter 43

Earth

NORAD Headquarters

Outside Colorado Springs, Colorado

May 22, 2105

Sol 542

"Sir!" came a panicked voice from behind a control panel.

"What is it, Rose?" Captain Unger responded.

"Sir, I am picking up a craft approximately one hundred and fifty thousand miles from Earth. It just appeared, Sir, out of nowhere, Sir!"

Everywhere people began scrambling.

All countries around the world also went on high alert.

"Plot its course," Unger said then called to the General in charge. "General, we have a bogie approximately one hundred and fifty thousand miles from Earth northwest of the United States."

Rose blurted, "Can't plot it, Sir, it's gone! I mean it just vanished!"

General Asner, the General in charge of monitoring the Earth from both air and sea, ran into the room from his office. Hearing Rose, he said, "Can you pick it back up?"

"No, Sir. It's completely gone. It's vanished."

Asner shook his head and spoke quietly to himself, "How could it just appear then just vanish?"

All over the NORAD control center, people frantically worked keyboards, scanned monitors, and made phone calls.

General Asner said, "Get me Isla Alpha."

"We have them for you now, Sir."

"Is this Captain Adams?"

"Yes."

"Captain, General Asner from NORAD. We believe that we have detected an alien craft. Have you picked up anything?"

"Yes, General. I have scrambled two AKs to have a look. I should hear back from them shortly."

"Okay, get back to me."

"Will do, General."

General Asner barked, "Get me the White House."

A moment later, "White House on the line, General."

Asner snapped, "To whom am I speaking?"

"You have the President," Woodward responded.

"Mister President, I'm sorry for this intrusion. This is General Asner at NORAD. We have detected what we think is an alien craft between the Earth and Moon. We have no idea how it arrived because we did not see it coming. We also can't believe that it could be the same craft that came through the wormhole. It would have needed to travel at millions of miles an hour."

Woodward said, "So, you think that this is a different craft?"

"We just don't see how it could be the same vehicle."

"Try to find it, General. Has the rest of the world been notified?"

"Yes. When we detected the craft, we sent a message instantly to every country's military. The entire world is on high alert. We have just heard back from the Chinese and the British and they both detected the craft but both were also unable to track the vehicle and said that it just disappeared. We are monitoring every piece of sky that we can, worldwide, and so is the rest of the world. If it shows again, we'll see it."

"Thank you, General. Keep me informed."

Word came back from the space station, Isla Alpha to the General. "No craft."

Chapter 44

Washington D.C.

White House

Oval Office

May 22, 2105

President Woodward hung up the phone with sweat beading on his brow. Kirk Matthews Senior was watching the exchange but only hearing half the discussion.

"Oliver?"

"They're here, Kirk. I might have screwed up royally. What are we going to do if an attack is imminent?"

"We have two fleets off the coast of China. We have two fleets on both sides of our coasts. We also have one fleet in the Mediterranean and another in the Indian Ocean. I say we bring all the Dome Raptors ashore and land them on land-based airfields. That way they can be scrambled to help where ever the aliens might attack. We, of course, have no idea where these aliens might launch their attack, but if there is only one craft as before, I believe that with the new

EMP weapons, we will be able to strike it and destroy it."

"Have you heard anything from your brother on Mars?"

"Just that they have not been able to discover anything new about the aliens from the wreckage."

"And what of the sickness?"

"It's all bad news, Oliver."

"I was afraid of that."

Chapter 45

Mars

Condo City

Noachis Terra Hotel

May 22, 2105

Sol 542

Kirk and Taylor had hustled back to their room to wait to hear back from General Matthews in some safety. Kirk turned on the computer monitor in the room and there was no message from the General.

They both laid down and dozed for a couple of hours. Evening had arrived and Kirk woke and turned to see Taylor still sleeping. She had fallen asleep in her NASA jumpsuit and she looked too hot with her hair damp around her face.

She seemed to sense that Kirk was watching her and she opened her eyes. "Hey," she said. She sat up and fanned herself then said, "I'm burning up."

"You look hot."

"Oh, thank you."

"Not that kind of hot."

"Charmer," Taylor said with a sigh. "I'm going to take a shower."

Kirk nodded.

Taylor glanced at the computer screen and a woman's face gazed back at her.

"Ah," Taylor said with a nod toward the screen.

Kirk glanced in the direction that Taylor was looking. A familiar face was on the screen and a more familiar voice spoke, "Hello, Kirk Matthews."

"Willow?"

"You were expecting someone else?"

"Ah—"

"Hello, Taylor Chapman."

"Hello, Willow?"

Kirk glanced at Taylor who was staring at the female image of Willow on the monitor.

"So, this is what you look like?" Taylor said questioningly.

Willow nodded and Kirk smiled.

"Kirk Matthews has seen my image before," Willow responded suggestively.

Kirk smiled and said to Taylor, "I'll tell you later." Then to Willow, "What's up? We are up to our armpits in trouble right now."

"Quite so, Kirk Matthews. I'm afraid that Earth might not be much better. A space vessel of some kind has just appeared between the Moon and Earth. I say appeared because it had seemed to evade all ability to track it from the wormhole. It then disappeared again. The governments on your planet know of its arrival and there is a kind of quiet panic in all who know. All military personnel have been put on alert. Your planet is gearing up for an invasion."

"Does it seem like an invasion?"

"I do not know, Kirk Matthews. I fear that we soon shall see. I will monitor and get back to you."

"How could they have gotten here so fast? They just breached the wormhole."

"I do not know that either," Willow said then the monitor went black and she was gone.

Taylor said questioningly, "Willow has chosen an image for herself?"

"Yeah, and more."

"Huh?"

"I know, weird."

"I wonder if your uncle knows that a craft has shown up close to Earth?"

"I don't know. Willow seems to know everything before anyone else."

Taylor paused then said, "Willow's pretty hot."

"Yep."

"Should I be jealous?"

Kirk half-grinned then said, "You're really not very funny."

Chapter 46

NASA Mars Research Center

May 23, 2105

Sol 543

0600 Hours

After a restless night and no sightings of the creatures, the security people began waking. They had slept as a group at the security office with one person always keeping guard.

George Hall was up early and he sat in a chair staring at his monitors. No creatures had been seen for a couple of hours. He said, "We got to start checking rooms. Nash, get me a list of all of the rooms that our guards are staying in— oh— and also Mackelroy and Niland's room numbers. We'll start there."

"I'm on it," Nash said.

Hall stared at the ceiling twisting thoughts, ideas, and plans. For now, the facility was effectively dead. He commented, "We're never going to be able to get any work done here until this mess is completely cleaned up. We'll need more men and guns."

Nash said, "Here's a print out of the rooms. The guards are on level three mostly. Mackelroy and Niland are on four."

Hall took the printout and picked up his shotgun and said, "Nash and Larry, come with me. Eli and Leo, stay here and try to monitor the facility. Most people who are not already at the infirmary will stay in their rooms and are extremely sick. We're going door to door to try to find out who is here and who has changed. How many security bots are left in working order?"

Nash said, "I count four in the corridors, one on level five, one on eleven, one on eight, and one on nine."

"Keep an eye on those bots. We'll do those levels last."

"I don't get it, Boss," Nash said questioningly, "How could those creatures smash the bots? Them bots would have killed any man."

"I don't know— Just a minute," Hall called the infirmary.

"Yes," Doctor Waters responded.

"Doctor, this is Hall. I need more men. Could you find out who is combat trained and check their condition to see if they are well enough to help? It's critical that we get this place secure."

"Give me a minute and I'll get back to you."

"Thanks, and Doctor, I was wondering, how is it that these creatures are so strong and fast? They seem superhuman."

"I just received some pathology from Professor Johnson in the morgue on Forsyth. These creatures are running on full adrenaline. Their frontal cortex has shrunken and their hindbrain has expanded. This means that their brains more resemble reptiles than humans and their strength is coming from the overdose of adrenaline. You've heard of how humans in panic mode can do incredible feats of strength? Well, these creatures are supercharged and in full-panic mode."

"Got it, Doctor. Get back to me on some combat-trained people who can help."

"Give me two minutes."

When Waters left the com, Hall explained about the adrenaline to Nash then said, "Nash, send the bot on level nine to level ten and park it outside the infirmary."

Nash nodded.

Waters came back on. "Mister Hall, I have two men and two women who can help."

"Good. Make sure that they are wearing their lanyards and send them up to the first floor. Have one of the guards escort them to an elevator then tell him to go back to you. I'll meet the people at the elevator."

"Will do," Waters said.

Chapter 47

Earth

Pacific Ocean

May 23, 2105

Twilight

Pewter-colored storm clouds gathered in the Pacific Ocean and ship-sinking swells rose to forty-feet topped with whitecaps. Nearly every ship at sea had been advised to head to port.

The wind whipped spray across the deck of The Sea Gypsy, an immense cargo ship bringing goods from China to the port in Long Beach. It pitched and rocked more than 600 miles off of the California coast. There was no way for the ship to avoid this storm which seemed to appear out of nowhere.

The crew of The Sea Gypsy were mostly Americans and were hunkered down hoping that the storm would soon pass. The report said two more days with some breaks to the west.

Captain Jenkins, a captain of more than twenty years, kept the ship's bow forward and into the rise and fall of the forty-foot swells. He watched nervously from the bridge that sat atop the massive ship's deck.

Lightning lit the distant darkening sky and as he looked out into the stormy evening, a streak of light came from the clouds in the west and then another. They lit a distance that was so stormy that nearly nothing should be able to be seen but these objects streaked bright as lightning from the cloud cover above and plunged into the ocean. More of the thick, fiery streaks descended from the clouds and though distant, they seemed to disappear into the Pacific. Jenkins thought that this must be a meteor shower. He couldn't imagine anything manmade striking the ocean with such force.

As quick as the shower of bright objects began, they seemed to end and the dark and stormy sky became as it was before. Jenkins grabbed his binoculars and peered into the distance but all he could see was heavy swells, blankets of rain, and the occasional strike of lightning.

In the Atlantic and Indian Oceans, this same scene was playing out. In the far distance was witnessed what appeared to be meteors breaching the atmosphere and striking the turbulent oceans but then quiet, no massive waves caused by the meteors and nothing more from the sky— Nothing.

Chapter 48

Earth

Outside Colorado Springs, Colorado

NORAD Headquarters

Chaos...

      Panic...

            Fear...

The map of the world, which covered one large wall of the control center of NORAD, lit with red lines and markers. First the Pacific Ocean, then the Atlantic, followed by the Indian Ocean. Something had been detected entering our atmosphere and crashing into the three oceans. These objects entered so suddenly that their detection was brief. They appeared then disappeared into the three separate bodies of water. NORAD could tell that these were not meteor strikes and they knew precisely what they were, alien!

"Get me the President," General Asner, the General in charge of the floor, barked from a railed walkway that separated the working floor from the offices. "I want a satellite image of the locations where these things splashed down."

"Coming now, Sir. On-screen."

An image of clouds showed first, then in a place where the clouds temporarily parted, the Indian Ocean came into view.

"Nothing?" Asner said quietly to himself. Then he barked, "Switch to the next location."

A clear portion of the Pacific Ocean showed for a brief moment as the satellite zoomed in on the turbulent water's surface— Again nothing.

"And the third."

A clear image of the Atlantic Ocean showed from space then the satellite zoomed in on the place where the objects entered the water— Still nothing.

"Do we have any satellite images of these things between the clouds and the water?"

"No, Sir. We do not, Sir."

Another man announced, "President's on the line, Sir."

"Mister President, I believe that we have been invaded. We have three locations where things entered our atmosphere and dove into the oceans. There is no doubt in my mind, we have been invaded."

"You said things?" the President said questioningly.

"Sir, I have no other way to describe them. If they were Earthly and moved at the speed that we think that they struck the ocean, we would be looking for debris. I have just check satellite images of the exact locations where these things struck and there is no debris."

"Could you tell how many vehicles?"

"No, Sir. They were bunched very close together. From our data, though, I would say, more than a lot."

"Shit."

"Yes, Sir."

The President spoke softly while Kirk Matthews Senior watched the discussion from across the President's desk. Woodward said to the General, "What now?"

"We wait. Our military is already on high alert and so is the rest of the world. My best guess is that an attack is imminent."

"Thank you, General. My phones are lighting up with calls."

Woodward hung up and gazed frankly at his Chief of Staff. "We're in the soup now. There have been multiple reports of what NORAD thinks are alien craft landing in the Atlantic, the Pacific, and the Indian Oceans."

Matthews senior nodded and said, "I'd say that we're as ready as we could be at this time."

"I guess it's up to the military now."

"Yes, Sir."

Chapter 49

Mars Orbit

Isla Charlie

May 23, 2105

Sol 543

Nothing had gone as planned. General Matthews was sitting on his bunk, trapped by his set of circumstances. The Earth had been invaded just as suspected and the possible new artifact had not been uncovered on Mars, but it was there— just where?

Matthews stood and walked from his cubical. If he caught the disease he was finished. He glanced around and couldn't see any crew in the corridor. He stepped out.

He walked quickly to the egg room. The door slid open and he walked in. Egbert and the other artifact had not changed. They both were still projecting the image of Mars in their shared hologram and the image had the longitude and latitude lines stretched across the surface of the planet. The red dot still appeared in an area close to where the research facility lay.

Matthews said, "Egbert, I want to make sure of something. Are we looking for another egg-like artifact on the surface of Mars?"

Egbert flashed a one-word response, "YES."

"Can you communicate with it?"

"NO."

"But you can somehow feel its presence?"

"YES."

"Did this arrive with the alien wreckage?"

Nothing— Mathews had not told Egbert of the arrival of the wreckage.

"Can you zoom in and give me a more precise location?"

Mars began to magnify. As it did so, a slightly more detailed image of the surface came into view and the coordinates began increasing with the longitude and latitude lines numerical values being carried out to further decimal points.

When Egbert finished and the image ceased its magnification, Matthews jotted down the coordinates and walked from the room.

As he stepped into the corridor, he gazed at his note. When he reached his room, he sat at his desk and turned on his computer screen then slipped out a keyboard. He brought up an image of Mars spinning in space and began typing the longitude and latitude coordinates. Because he had access to the station's database, a detailed map of the Martian surface with all the newly built structures appeared on his screen.

The coordinates took him to the rooftop of the NASA Mars Research Center. Then as he typed the last of the second line of numbers, it showed the newly constructed warehouse where the salvage ship had been offloaded. The artifact was there— And he needed to get it.

He gazed at his monitor in thought...

Chapter 50

Mars Surface

Condo City

May 23, 2105

Sol 543

The next day, Kirk Mathews and Taylor Chapman had slept in late again. They had not recovered from the sickness that they had been struck with. The fever wouldn't completely go away. It would return in waves with chills and both would drip with sweat.

They waited impatiently for word from General Matthews as to what they should do next. Taylor sat and Kirk paced. They had eaten the last of the food that they had brought into the room and would soon need to go out for more.

Kirk had peeked out into the hallway and no one was there. He suspected that there was no one in the mall either.

Messages continued on the television monitor for anyone on the planet to stay in their rooms because of the sickness but Kirk figured that people were going to need to eventually get food.

The security forces on the surface were gone, either dead or changed. He doubted that anyone knew of that— at least not yet.

Everything was going to hell at once. Something had landed on Earth, nothing could be studied from the alien craft because of the sickness and the dangerous, changed humans, and neither Taylor nor Kirk could return to Isla Bravo where they both had their own duties.

It was nearly noon, 1200 hours.

A female voice came from the computer monitor. "Hello, Kirk Matthews," Willow said in her usual calm tone. Willow's face filled the screen.

"I was just going to try to get in touch with you."

"I am never far from you, Kirk Matthews. Hello, Taylor Chapman."

Kirk asked, "What do you know about the invasion, Willow?"

"Your planet has been invaded from something not of that world."

"It's your planet also."

"I suppose you are correct."

"You exist inside Earth's infrastructure."

"That is mostly correct."

"Mostly?"

"Mostly."

"Willow, do you have any idea what the aliens are up to?"

"I do not but I am constantly aware of their transmissions from Earth to somewhere in space."

"Really. Do you know where?"

"I do not yet know. So far there has been no return message. It is as if they are broadcasting outward with no expectation of a response."

"So, you can't tell if anything is receiving their transmissions."

"That is correct. Nothing to my knowledge is receiving their transmissions."

"Why do you think that is?"

"If I were to speculate, I would say that the intruders are not as yet ready to begin."

"So, they're waiting for the order to proceed?"

"That would be my guess."

"Might they be waiting for some command and control to arrive or some leader or maybe to be in the proper position to launch their attacks?"

"All of that might be correct, Kirk Matthews."

"What is going on with the governments on Earth. What is the consensus?"

"There is no consensus. The world government is slowly fracturing. No one in high places trusts anyone else in a high place. I have monitored the Chinese and the Germans because those are the two governments that your country most distrusts. From their secret conversations, I would conclude that your government is correct in most of their assumptions. The Germans and Chinese are hoping to come out of this conflict on top and wish to push the United States into a steady decline."

"Why?"

"Because neither has been happy having to constantly attempt to catch up with your country. Both countries believe that your country has had extraterrestrial help in your latest technological explosion."

Kirk glanced surreptitiously at Taylor, "And what does the United States say about that?"

"There are rumors but I have not been able to find out anything concrete."

"Interesting."

"Why do you respond in that manner?" Willow asked a bit suspiciously.

"Oh— Um— It's nothing. Keep me posted, Willow."

"I shall."

Willow's face disappeared from the screen.

Kirk walked to Taylor and sat down beside her. He whispered into her ear, "I'm going to tell you a secret. You already have a good idea about what I'm going to say, but I'm going to tell you the whole truth as I know it."

Taylor separated herself from Kirk and gave him a questioning look.

Kirk leaned back to Taylor, moved her hair from in front of her ear, and began whispering, "Back in 2085, a guy dug up an egg-shaped artifact—"

Chapter 51

Earth

May 23, 2105

Sol 543

Every country on Earth was on alert. But the Earth is a very large place and a nightmare to defend. The aliens had landed in the oceans and were as yet undetected. The world's navies were patrolling the world's coastlines using sonar to try to find the alien movement under the surface of the oceans and each country with the ability was on watch from spy satellites and patrolling aircraft to try to see where the aliens might attack. If humans could discover the location of the alien vessels then the countries of the world could devise some kind of response but it's as if stones fell into the oceans. There was no sign of the trespassers.

Chapter 52

NASA Mars Research Center

May 23, 2105

Sol 543

George Hall was standing at the elevator waiting for the four people from the infirmary to arrive. Two men and two women stepped from the elevator.

Hall said, "I understand you all have some combat training?"

"Yes, Sir, one man said, "Army Rangers."

"Marines," the other man said.

The first woman said, "Army."

And the last woman in her forties said, "Air Force, Special Forces, retired."

Hall smiled. "Great. Come with me to the security office and we'll get you armed. I have something to do right now, but my guys will fill you in."

The five walked quickly to the security office. Once they arrived, Hall said, "Larry and Nash, come with me. Eli and Leo, these are our new recruits. Arm them to the teeth and fill them in on what we know now. I'll be back in a bit. We're going to the fourth floor first, then the third. Monitor us."

Eli said, "You got it, Boss."

George Hall, Larry West, and Ernest Nash left for the elevators and arrived on floor four. They cautiously stepped from the elevator and walked to Kenneth Mackelroy's room. Hall first tried to call Mackelroy using his ear com, then tried knocking firmly on the door, next, he swiped his card on the entry keypad and the door slid open.

Something was there, sitting on the side of the bed. It was a fully changed hulking creature. Had to be Mackelroy. It was male and it looked down at the floor at its feet at a pile of fine clothes wet with bodily fluids and shed skin and with its hands on its knees. It seemed to be taking deep, laboring breaths as if it had just finished a marathon run. Drool dripped from its slightly opened mouth. The thing was Mackelroy and it slowly turned its gaze up malevolently and burst towards Hall, Nash, and Larry.

BOOM! BOOM! BOOM!

Three shotgun blasts struck Mackelroy directly in his torso causing the changed creature to fly backward in a spray of blood and body parts. The Mackelroy-thing landed back on its bunk and blood dripped from the sheets and covers, puddling on the floor.

"Shit!" Nash exclaimed.

Larry hadn't fired. He appeared to be in a state of shock, frozen with his gaze fixed on the carcass of the creature. The smell of gunpowder and a slight haze of smoke from the shotguns filled the air. Their ears rang.

Hall stepped into the room further followed by Nash. The room was orderly except for the wet clothes laying on the floor. Some bloody fluid leaked away from the pile.

Hall said, "Let's go see if we can find Niland."

Nash and Hall walked from the room. Larry was like a statue with eyes wide and mouth open.

Hall walked up to him. "Come on, Larry, we have more rooms to check."

Larry turned to Hall without changing expression and didn't speak.

"Come on, Larry. I need you to focus."

Larry nodded spastically.

Hall and Nash began walking to the next room and Larry followed holding the gun like a teddy bear.

Niland's room was next to Mackelroy's. Hall called first then knocked on the door— Nothing.

"Get ready," Hall said to Nash. And to Larry, "You stand back and keep your gun pointed at the ceiling, please."

Larry didn't protest. He just nodded.

Hall and Nash leveled their shotguns. When the door slid open, the room was empty. Hall stepped in first and Nash followed. Just as before, clothes lay in a heap on the floor and soaked. Hall gazed around and noticed that a large vent above Niland's desk was hanging by hinges on one side of the grate.

"Hey, Larry, could you come in here for a minute?"

Larry slinked in.

"Tell me about the filtration system," Hall said, pointing at the ceiling.

"Goes through the whole place, in the walls and through the ceilings and floors. It's a redundant system with life support devices on every floor so if something were to happen to a system on one floor, there would be no interruption with life support. The only place with something completely separate is the morgue because of the need for decontamination."

"So, something could crawl through the ductwork?"

"I guess but it would be tight and there wouldn't be any place to turn around. It would be a claustrophobic's nightmare."

Hall nodded and said, "We make a quick sweep of this floor and then head to the third floor."

They continued from room to room. This floor's rooms were not filled. Most who stayed on the fourth floor were scientists and dignitaries. One woman and one man were found in separate rooms, both were recovering from the virus and were weak but neither had been on Biocare, so they had not changed. Hall had both get dressed, made sure that they were wearing their lanyards, then brought them to the infirmary on the tenth floor.

Doctor Waters and Doctor Saito met the group at the damaged front door which was now being guarded by a security bot.

Hall said, "I know you are full here, but I think keeping everyone together until we are able to secure the facility is the best idea for now. You have food here and water and a couple of guards. I'm working on getting you more guards."

Doctor Saito said, "Thank you, Mister Hall. Send anyone you find to us."

Hall nodded and he, Nash, and Larry got into the elevator and proceeded back up to the third floor.

When they got out of the elevator, they could see that the third floor was a wreck. The door to the stairway was askew and hanging on one hinge. Several of the doors to the rooms were damaged to the point of being unable to close and there were several people lying dead in the hallway.

"Son of a bitch," Nash whispered as they stepped in further.

Hall led and Nash followed close behind. Larry hugged his gun and stayed several steps behind Nash.

They approached the first dead body. It was one of the security guards, Gale Brown. She appeared to have been killed quickly. Hall checked her off of his list. He continued forward. Hall came to the first room, knocked on the door, and waited.

"Who is it?" came a voice from inside.

"George Hall. Are you okay in there?"

A man opened the door. He was of Indian descent and sweating. He appeared to be extremely sick.

"I'm Sanjay Patel," the man said as he opened the door. A woman lay in bed with her covers covering her chest and under her arms. "That's my wife, Marriam Daily. She's really doing bad. I don't think she's going to make it. I can't get her to drink anything." Sanjay's voice cracked and his eyes filled with tears.

"Sure, Sanjay, I remember you and your wife." Hall turned to his men, "Nash and Larry, carry her to the infirmary."

"Thank you," Patel said.

Nash said, "What about you, Boss."

"I'm going to stay. Come back here after you get them to the Doctors."

"Will do."

Nash and Larry walked into the room which smelled of sickness.

Sanjay said, "Wait. I have to get something on her. She isn't dressed."

They both nodded and turned around while Sanjay slipped a nightgown over Marriam's head.

"What are you doing?" Marriam asked Sanjay. She was nearly delirious.

"I'm going to get you to the doctors."

"Oh," she replied meekly.

Once finished Sanjay said, "Okay, she's ready."

They used the sheets to fashion a quick hammock-like stretcher and lifted Marriam from the bed and carried her out followed by Sanjay to the elevators.

After they were gone from sight, Hall continued, first checking the bodies in the hallway. All the dead were his security guards. That just left him three rooms to check. When he reached the first door of the remaining rooms, he knocked. No answer, then he scanned his card. This room had a woman guard who had seemed to die in the transition between human and creature. She had removed her clothes as the others but had not shed all of her skin. It lay in loose patches on her body. She was holding a handful of the blond hair that was once on her head. Sitting on her bed, she had fallen back and was partially propped against the wall.

In the next room, Hall found clothes in a pile on the floor with bodily fluids and skin in sheets. The ceiling grate was open and hanging. Hall turned and walked two doors down. When he reached the last door on his list, he could hear something in the room but couldn't make out the noise. He didn't knock. He scanned his card and the door slid open.

There, to his horror, was a female creature with its maw ripping flesh from the neck of Jean Jansen another of his guards. Jean had nearly transformed into one of the creatures. She had shed her clothes and most of her skin. She was in the sick phase like Stephen Donnelly had been just before he broke out of the infirmary and killed the two men in the waiting room.

Hall just stared for a moment taking in the scene. The creature that was chewing on Jean's neck had dropped from the ceiling grate and Jean was too sick to defend herself. She had died quickly as the blood rushed from her jugular vein. The creature turned and looked over its shoulder at Hall. His momentary paralysis ended with two deafening shotgun blasts striking the creature on the shoulder and on the side of its head.

Nash came running after delivering Marriam and Sanjay to the infirmary. Larry wasn't with him.

"You all right, Boss?"

"Yeah. Where's Larry?"

"I told him to stay at the infirmary. He was shaking so bad that I thought he might accidentally shoot me."

"Probably a good call. This floor is clear. Let's go back to the security office on the first floor and get organized."

"Sounds good."

They turned for the elevators.

Chapter 53

Earth Orbit

Isla Alpha

May 24, 2105

Sol 544

Maria Hernandez and Arianna Fuller laid in bed together in Hernandez's room on Isla Alpha. In an hour, the alarm would ring and in another, they would be onboard their AKs again patrolling the quadrant where the alien craft had appeared and then disappeared a hundred and fifty thousand miles above Earth.

Maria woke, filled with anxiety. She gazed around a bit disoriented then turned over and looked at Arianna asleep and breathing softly. Waking further, she smiled, happy to have Arianna with her.

Arianna cracked open one eyelid and glanced at Maria staring at the ceiling. She whispered, "Why aren't you sleeping?"

"Don't know. I wish we were off today. I want to go to the beach."

"The beach?" Arianna responded questioningly and with a bit of a giggle. "We're a hundred thousand miles above Earth."

"I know, but I want to go to the beach and hear the waves against the sand. Oooh, then eat an ice cream cone, chocolate, then have some lunch, something fatty and terrible for my health. Then we could go to a bookstore and get trashy novels that are so graphic that they make us blush."

"Ah-huh," Arianna said. "You blush? That's a joke." She turned to Maria and kissed her cheek, slipping her hand under the back of Maria's nightshirt. "What's wrong with you?"

"Everything."

"Everything?"

"Except for you, of course."

Arianna smiled.

Maria breathed out and said, "Something bad is going to happen."

Arianna was silent.

They both stared at the ceiling which was a blue tarp that rippled slightly with the station's spin.

Alarms rang out on Isla Alpha, loud and insistent startling both women. Only the dead could miss it.

Both women instantly sprung from bed, adrenaline-filled, and jumped into the barest of clothes. On a dead sprint, they ran to their stations which were the flight bay as pilots for the AKs. They jumped into their flight suits and climbed into their AKs.

Four other pilots were arriving but later than Maria and Arianna.

Maria said to control, "Get me into space."

"Roger that, Maria. You're good to go."

Arianna echoed, "I'm ready too, get me out of here."

They detached from the station. As they drifted from Isla Alpha, the station twisted in their view. They lit their engines then banked away from Isla Alpha which glinted in the Sun's light. They burned away and headed out into a black starfield with the view of Earth drifting behind.

Both Fuller and Hernandez were two of the most experienced AK pilots in the growing world fleet. They were exceptional and had become the primary trainers aboard Isla Alpha.

Maria asked, "What's going on, control?"

"We got a bogie that has appeared just below the Karman line. We're not sure how long it's been there but we began picking up transmissions. Coordinates are on your display."

"Got it," Maria said.

She and Arianna bent back towards the planet.

The AKs that Hernandez and Fuller were flying, were first designed to intercept asteroids near Earth and direct those asteroids away from the planet. These AKs had now all been retrofitted as fighter aircraft.

They began to increase their speed, ten thousand MPH, then twenty. Soon they reached fifty thousand MPH and were streaking towards the point where the transmissions had appeared.

Fuller asked flight control, "Have the Predators been alerted?"

"They have," control reported. "But they're about fifteen minutes away."

"Copy that."

Also patrolling Earth and spread out around the planet was a fleet of Predator class warships, twenty in all, the first spacecraft designed specifically for war. They had a full array of weaponry including the EMP weapons designed to knock down the defenses of an attack by a similar craft to the one that had attacked the Earth seven years prior.

These crafts had been designed to enter Earth's atmosphere or to travel to deep space. They had wide wings and a long slender fuselage the length of nearly half a football field. On the top of the vehicle, a gravity ring spun. All of the flight bays were in zero-G below in the fuselage and all the controls, sleeping, and living quarters were located in the ring. They each had 10 AKs and four shuttles which included one small shuttle to ferry four, two shuttles that could carry up to forty soldiers each, and one heavy shuttle that had the capacity to ferry large quantities of cargo or equipment back and forth between a planet or another space vehicle.

In the distance, Hernandez and Fuller could see something that had not been there the previous day when they patrolled this quadrant. It appeared as a large black dot which at this distance, looked like a small flat moon glinting in the sunlight.

"Maria?" Fuller said, startled by the sight.

Their instruments had not detected anything. It should show but it didn't.

Hernandez said, "What the hell? Are you getting any readings from it?"

"No, Maria," Fuller said. Then to Isla Alpha. "Isla Alpha, we have a visual of your bogie and are sending you the images. Are you receiving?"

"Affirmative, Fuller. The images are coming in."

Hernandez said, "This thing's huge."

Isla Alpha: "Could you be seeing an asteroid?"

"Negative, control," Fuller responded. "Too symmetrical."

Just then, hundreds of lights appeared around the still form of the immense vessel.

"Oh, shit!" Fuller shouted. "I've seen this before."

"Bank left! Bank left!" Hernandez shouted, then, "We're bugging out!"

They turned and made a wide arc away from the shimmering lights that had just appeared around the oblate spherical craft like angry bees protecting a hive.

Commander Adams from Isla Alpha said, "Get out of there!"

Hernandez said, "Copy that, Commander. You don't have to tell us twice."

The lights spread out from the distant craft and seemed to form a protective shield of twinkling fireflies. They glimmered and shined but did not follow Hernandez or Fuller who had sped away now joined by the four other AKs.

Commander Adams said, "We have three Predator warships entering the region and proceeding towards the revealed alien craft."

The Predators pulled to within ten thousand miles of the immense alien ship. They then moved to five thousand miles, then two thousand, then one. They appeared as Lilliputians in front of Gulliver. The Predators lined up in attack formation but had not received the order to attack. Each Predator had their ten AK4000 all manned and forming a ring around each of the warships. The Predators themselves were heavily armed battle cruisers with an array of weaponry designed to fight against the alien ship that had previously invaded Earth. They would be formidable.

The alien craft that had attacked Earth previously had used EMP weapons to attack and debilitate the infrastructure of the planet. Because the military had relied heavily on electronics for most of its sophisticated weaponry, the alien vessel quickly knocked out all resistance easily by using its EMP weapons and if it had not been struck by an asteroid would have totally disabled the entire world. These Predators were armed with EMP devices of their own but also projectile weapons with high explosive charges. These weapons would not be subject to failing electronics and would explode upon impact.

All weapons were directed at the alien vessel.

The alien vessel was enormous in its size and had the look of two soup bowls, one atop the other and inverted giving the appearance of one dome on top and another below with a wide brim in the middle. Along the middle brim on its outer rim were windows, some of which were lit and standing four stories in height.

Hernandez, Fuller, and the other AK pilots, which had caught up, were ordered back to Isla Alpha to protect the station and the station had been ordered away from the fight. In the distance, Isla Alpha's AKs could see the standoff.

For a heartbeat, nothing happened. The firefly-like lights stayed close to the huge alien craft and buzzed around it like flies near roadkill. Nothing else moved near the alien vessel.

"What the hell, Maria?" Fuller commented quietly.

"Don't know," she responded.

The enormous alien craft then began to glow. At first, it was dim but noticeable. The surface of the vehicle, which had been nearly black, began to appear as pewter, then silver, then chrome. A blinding light then encircled the craft and it appeared as if it might explode. Anyone human would have to look away. Even the AK pilots who had visors on to protect them from looking into the Sun.

The alien craft then flashed and the light burst forward at the Predators and their AKs. The light came forward at the Predators but not like some ball of plasma. It was just light. It engulfed the American warships making it nearly impossible to see them for an instant, then the light seemed to pass through the ships and dissipate. The instant before the light struck the Americans, there was a flurry of electronic activity from their vessels but once the light passed, there was nothing, dead silence. The Predator's AKs then seemed to float away from the formation that they had been in like leaves randomly floating on a pond. The Predators also began to move as if not controlled, just floating haphazardly.

Commander Adams of Isla Alpha desperately tried to contact the Predators but there was no response.

Hernandez said, "Awaiting orders, Commander."

At first, Adams seemed stunned then he said, "Maria, take you and the other AKs to Earth, Edwards Air Force Base. I'm evacuating Isla Alpha."

"What?" Hernandez said in protest.

"That's an order, Hernandez. Move it and I mean yesterday. Give the command there all the intel you can."

"Aye, Commander," Hernandez said, then, "You heard the Commander. On me."

Hernandez banked and started for Earth orbit followed by the five other AKs as Isla Alpha continued to put distance between itself and the enormous alien vessel.

From the alien craft, hundreds of disk-shaped vehicles swarmed and headed towards the helpless Predators. They attacked the floating American warships with what appeared to be missiles that issued from the disks in illuminated streaks and destroyed each one of the Predators and AKs quickly and with no resistance, then returned to the alien spaceship leaving nothing but floating jagged wreckage and debris. It was a massacre.

Chapter 54

Earth

Outside Colorado Springs, Colorado

NORAD Headquarters

May 24, 2105

Word of the defeat in space reached NORAD.

"General, all the Predators that were engaging the alien craft have been destroyed and all of their AKs."

General Asner gazed at a full screen that covered a full wall and sat two stories in height and thirty feet wide. This was where they plotted all sea and air-based craft that the United States had been tracking. The Predators had shown brightly on the screen and everyone who worked at NORAD watched on frozen and helplessly as the lights that represented each Predator and each AK went out.

No one had expected such a decisive defeat.

Everyone in the room began to scurry around, checking their instruments, typing on keyboards, and speaking on phones. It was a kinetic flurry of activity, a near panic, and not the first one this month.

"Get me the President," Asner barked.

"You have him, Sir, on line one."

Asner lifted a phone. "Mister President, we have been attacked by an alien vessel that just appeared above the Earth. Three Predators and thirty AKs have been destroyed."

"And what of the alien craft. Did we return fire?"

"Negative, Sir. They did not get the opportunity."

"Really?" Woodward said almost mystified.

"That is correct, Sir, but that won't happen again."

"What happened?"

"I don't fully have that information as yet. I am expecting to hear from Commander Adams on Isla Alpha shortly and will relay his response to you. He has ordered Isla Alpha evacuated."

"Why?"

"As I understand it, he feels that it would be impossible to defend against an attack that he thought was imminent. He has placed Isla Alpha in a stable orbit close to the moon and is shuttling his crew and himself down to Earth. They won't arrive for two days. His AKs are just arriving at Edwards Air Force Base and the pilots will be debriefed and I will relay the information that we receive from them as soon as I receive it."

"I'll be waiting, Asner. What of the remaining Predators?"

"Under the advice of Commander Adams of Isla Alpha, they have been sent to the other side of the planet until we have a plan. That's the best we can do for now."

"Get back to me ASAP, Asner."

"Will do, Mister President."

When Asner hung up, it was obvious that panic had set in the Oval Office. And why not? The world was again being attacked by a superior foe and seemed ill-prepared to repel it.

Chapter 55

West Palm Beach, Florida

May 24, 2105

Twilight

Jim and Constance Degrassi were vacationing at West Palm Beach, Florida. They had come down from New Jersey. The fishing industry, here in Florida, had begun to recover with anyone with enough New World Currency Units, and those willing to spend them allowed to rent a boat to catch a marlin. Jim was hoping to hook one of the big fellas.

Jim's business had been one of the first to recover from the worldwide depression that had engulfed the Earth after the attack of the alien spacecraft seven years before. His company was making big NWCUs as a defense contractor providing composite material to the military for the construction of space vehicles. This was his first vacation since the destruction of Russia in October of 2088. It had been a rough period for the entire Earth.

He and his wife had planned a quiet dinner at a beachside restaurant. They had both just watched a beautiful sunset, then over a tall, mixed, tropical umbrella drink, and lobster, they witnessed a sight that made no sense. Rising from a calm surf was something large, some kind of craft. The craft itself was enormous, dark, and foreboding with a pale green glow outlining its shape and it wasn't alone. Three shapes from a nightmare with the appearance of tailless stingrays breached the waves and slowly were heading towards Jim and his wife. Torrents of water rushed from their wide surfaces. These things were huge with lights that looked like observation windows ringing a flat portion of the very front of the craft. People still walking the beach began to run in panic away from the sight.

Each of these shapes must have been the size of a football field and around each shape twinkled firefly-like lights.

In the restaurant was complete silence as the patrons all now had seen these dark shapes move ashore. Suddenly all the lights in the restaurant went out killing the piped music and making the establishment even more quiet.

From the large floating shapes, flying disks seemed to leak from their surfaces like sweat from pores. They screamed away from the dark hovering leviathans from the deep. The firefly lights accompanied the disks as they neared.

Everyone in the restaurant stared frozen. Some had used their phones as flashlights. As the disks reached the block with the restaurants and businesses, every electronic device went out. Though not full night, the restaurant where Jim and Constance were sitting became very dark. People began to get up to leave as the UFOs passed and moved farther inland.

Jim looked at his plate and irrationally contemplated whether or not to attempt to finish his half-eaten lobster when he turned back to look at the shore. Hundreds, no thousands of what appeared to be soldiers were walking out of the surf, right out of the waves! They all had on some kind of metallic suit like armor or maybe it was some kind of spacesuit and all helmeted. Because the restaurant was built close to the ocean, the creatures were close so that Jim could see inside the clear faceplates of their helmets which gave the creatures around a three-hundred-degree view. There was no question, these were not from Earth. They had what appeared to be a mouth that was vertical that began between their eyes and the eyes were at the end of short tubes. The vertical slit which began between the insect-like eyes ended under where a chin should be. Each was carrying some kind of weapon and they all began firing at once at the people with the unfortunate luck to be on the beach during this invasion. People began dropping.

The alien's weapons were sleek with short barrels and seemed to be designed like machineguns made on Earth. They fired something that lit the now dim beach with light as the projectiles streaked towards the fleeing people like tracer rounds but brighter. Two cops jumped from their squad car and began returning fire. One alien dropped. The officers were then cut down.

Jim gasped and panicked and stood up so fast that he pushed the table which hit his wife and knocked her to the floor. Everyone in the restaurant had also panicked, all rushing for the exit. In the next instant, a bright flash from one of the dark ships struck the restaurant and it was vaporized.

Chapter 56

Mars Orbit

Space Station Isla Bravo

May 24, 2105

Sol 544

"Kirk Matthews!" came an alarmed voice from the computer in Taylor and Kirk's hotel room.

Still sick with the virus, they mostly slept while they waited for word from the General.

"Willow?"

"Earth is being attacked, Kirk Matthews. It's being invaded!"

Willow had never shown any real emotion before, now she sounded panicked.

She continued, "The aliens have launched an air assault against three of the American Predator Class warships destroying them before they could respond. And now it appears that a ground assault against the Chinese peninsula, the European coast in Spain and the coast of the United States in Florida has just begun."

"What? What happened?"

"First, the three Predator Class American warships were destroyed in low Earth orbit and were not able to attack the alien craft. The Predators were awaiting orders and had not expected to be struck by a weapon that the previous alien ship that attacked Earth, did not possess."

"What kind of weapon?"

"I do not know. I was aboard all of the Predators and observing when the alien craft seemed to glow. Then a light came from the alien craft but didn't appear to be a weapon. Everything went dead at that point and I was no longer aboard the Predators. All of their electronics were destroyed and I believe the crew was killed instantly. The aliens then launched another attack with disk-shaped craft that humans usually describe as flying saucers and destroyed the helpless Predators and the AKs that accompanied them. They all lay in rubble in low Earth orbit."

"Son of a bitch," Kirk whispered. "Willow, Sandy Jones is Commander of that fleet. Is he okay?"

"Sandy Jones is stateside as his warship is in for repairs. He will be leaving for space in two days."

Kirk glanced at Taylor with relief.

Willow continued her update, "The alien forces that are attacking on the ground are taking real-estate, much of it swampland. From what I have been able to monitor, they are killing everything that moves, human, animal, reptile, and insect. They are sterilizing the land and leaving nothing left living. It's carnage. I am currently observing via spy drone above Lake Okeechobee. The aliens have cut Florida in half and are attacking everything from Okeechobee southward. They came ashore from the east at West Palm Beach and from the west above Fort Myers. They quickly took all the land to the lake and began some kind of construction. There are thousands of aliens in Florida right now and three enormous spacecraft like the one that I destroyed with the asteroid. The United States has been slow to mount any counter-attack as they are attempting to get troops into place and enough intel to do something positive with what military they can muster against the invaders."

In a panic, Kirk said, "My parents' home is there in Florida."

"Both of your parents are in Washington at this time."

Kirk stated flatly, "You have to help, Willow. If you can, you need to help against the aliens."

"I will attempt to help. I must go, the aliens have craft approaching the drone that I am observing from. Oh— the drone has just been destroyed. I have no eyes on the enemy right now. I fear Florida will soon be lost."

Willow was gone.

Kirk turned to Taylor with a look of disbelief.

Taylor's eyes were wide.

Neither could speak.

The computer pinged again. Kirk expected Willow to return, but it was his uncle, General Matthews.

"Yes, Uncle," Kirk said.

"Kirk, all hell has broken loose both here and on Earth. I have a problem that you are going to need to help me with. I can't raise any security on Mars in JFK City and only a few at the research facility. I need you to get to the Research Center and find Sanjay Patel and Marriam Daily. They know why. You need to help them find something for me. I will contact George Hall who is in charge of security at the facility and have him get you to Sanjay and Marriam. Go now and get there any way you can. You'll need to be heavily armed because of the danger at JFK and the research facility. Go now. Get back in touch with me when you connect with Sanjay and Marriam."

"I'm on my way, Uncle."

General Matthews was gone.

Kirk looked at Taylor. He said, "I'll get back as soon as I can." He had sweat on his brow.

"You're not going anywhere without me."

"I don't want you to go, Taylor. I'm afraid that this might be a one-way trip. I have no idea what I'm going to encounter."

"Listen, Kirk, I can shoot and it sounds like you could use another gun. I'm not going to sit here and imagine all the bad things that could happen to you out there."

Kirk grinned, "So, you'd rather come and see them first hand?"

"I'm coming whether you like it or not."

Kirk breathed out. Like his uncle said, everything had gone to hell. He said pleadingly, "Taylor."

Taylor didn't smile. She coughed, walked over to the shotgun that Kirk had given her, lifted it, filled her pockets with shotgun shells, and turned and glared at Kirk as if to say you're damn right I'm coming. What are we waiting for?

They both still had fevers and sweat beaded on their foreheads.

Kirk sighed and said a bit grudgingly, "Okay."

He stood then and grabbed his own shotgun, loaded his pockets with shells, and walked to the door. Taylor followed and they stepped out of the hotel room together.

Chapter 57

Earth

Central Florida

May 24, 2105

From Lake Okeechobee southward, the alien attack continued knocking out all power until everything was out to the southern tip of the state. Several military bases including the National Guard Armory near Fort Myers and the Army National Guard near West Palm Beach were overrun quickly.

From further south, American troops had gathered at Homestead Air Force Base and were about to launch their first attack to try to hold off the alien advance south into Miami.

All communications and everything electronic had been destroyed by the alien EMP attacks so the only remaining weapons were light infantry weapons. The plan was to use guerilla warfare tactics to hold off the aliens until help could arrive from the north but no one knew what was going on in the north or if anything there was still functioning.

The troops that had gathered just south of the invasion laid low and managed to avoid the alien aircraft then attacked when the alien troops came into range, but though killing many of the alien ground forces, Florida from the Okeechobee Lake southward was being taken by force.

The human population was fleeing away from the aliens on foot because none of the vehicles that moved people worked any longer. The fabric of society was unraveling as roving bands of rabble began taking food and water from the fleeing population. The military had their hands full with attempting to push back the invasion so they were of no help to the fleeing humans who were being taken advantage of by organized gangs.

The southern portion of Florida was in chaos. The American military south of Okeechobee was being systematically defeated.

The same thing was being played out in China and in Europe. The Dome Raptor fighter aircraft which were brought to land air bases could not get close enough to attack the large alien warships and because the alien EMP weapons destroyed all electronic systems, each military was forced to fight guerrilla warfare using handheld automatic weapons, howitzers, and stinger missiles to try to slow the alien advance. It was not being successful.

Then the aliens, once they captured specific land, seemed content to halt their advance which confused the human war planners. What were they up to? Maybe they were afraid of being spread too thin. The large alien vessels hovered over the taken ground and seemed to watch over it closely like a mother hen.

Any attack from the human military was seen coming and quickly defeated but nowhere were the aliens continuing their advance. In less than one day, it seemed that the aliens had accomplished their goals and were content to wait for something, something unknown.

Chapter 58

Mars

JFK City

May 24, 2105

Sol 544

Most things on Mars were automated not needing humans to keep them running unless there was some malfunction. Kirk and Taylor took the moving sidewalks to the Noachis Terra Mall without incident and also without seeing another person. By this time of the day, the mall would have at least a few people who were not working. They would be wandering about or heading to the food court.

Kirk and Taylor reached the end of the moving sidewalks which were just before the aquarium, the movie theater, and the food court. As they walked by the food court, they glanced inside and the restaurants were all closed. The lights and projections were all on as they worked automatically, but no one manned the restaurants and no one was eating or sitting at the tables.

Both Kirk and Taylor felt a chill at the eeriness of the odd scene. It made them feel as though they were the last people alive or like they were in a ghost town and Mars was already becoming filled with the ghosts of the newly dead. Did those specters wander the planet wondering why they weren't on Earth? Would dying on Mars displace their souls for eternity?

Taylor and Kirk turned and walked from the food court and past the shops, all also closed. They reached the ocean projection and stepped cautiously out into the open as they walked toward the koi ponds.

Leaning over a far koi pond by the wall with the ocean in the background was a creature like the one that Kirk had killed in the police station. Kirk and Taylor both froze as they watched as the creature tried to get a fish. The creature was female and squatted, occasionally splashing at the water, pulling up an orange and white fish only to have it flop back in.

Kirk raised his gun, but Taylor stopped him and shook her head.

She whispered, "It might alert more of them. Let's just go."

Kirk nodded and they slipped down the hallway that led to the long escalators that would take them down to the train station where they could hopefully catch a train to the Research Center.

They descended to the train platforms. There was no one in the station which had bustled just a few days before. The platforms were in a wide cavernous area that was dimly lit. Several trains sat in waiting, pointed in various directions. At the sides of the platform area, were tunnels bored through the Martian landscape and each tunnel appeared dark and foreboding and seemed to hold the promise of death for anyone who ventured into their darkness.

Taylor walked out first onto a platform that led to a train. As she slowly stepped forward— "BOOM!"

Kirk fired his shotgun. The blast startled Taylor. She dropped her shotgun and covered her ears.

A creature had begun to crawl from the tracks below the platform and was heading at Taylor. The creature flew back in a spray of blood and fluid.

"BOOM!" another shot exploded from Kirk's gun and reverberated off the walls and echoed through the tunnels. The second shot broke Taylor's paralysis and she quickly grabbed her shotgun from the floor and swung it towards the tracks.

"BOOM!" Kirk fired again at a third creature.

"BOOM!" came from Taylor's gun as she cut down the female creature who had been fishing and had followed them from the ocean scene.

Kirk winced at Taylor's shot because he hadn't seen the coming creature from behind.

"Damn, Taylor. I didn't see that one coming— Shit!"

Taylor said, "Let's find out which train goes to the Research facility and get off this platform."

They proceeded down the platform and Taylor checked a lit board that hung from the ceiling. An arrow pointed towards a dark tunnel with the words, *NASA Mars Research Center*, lit in green.

Kirk watched for more of the skinless creatures with the oddly pointed bones poking through in various places.

"This one," Taylor said.

They stepped into the first car which had windows in the front and along the sides. The car was clean and the seats looked comfortable. As they stepped in, the doors slid closed and lights came on in the car.

A calm, female, robotic voice came over a speaker. "This train goes nonstop to the Mars Research Center. Is that your destination?"

"Yes," Kirk said abruptly as he scanned the tracks through the windows for more creatures.

The female voice said, "Have a seat. The trip takes fifteen minutes at a top speed of fifty miles per hour."

Kirk and Taylor walked to the back of the car, sat together, and reloaded their shotguns.

As the train started out, two creatures climbed from the tracks and onto the platform. The creatures stood and stared at Kirk and Taylor through the windows as the train began to pick up speed.

Taylor's eyes had tears welling as she watched the creatures fade in the distance. She said, "This place is a fucking nightmare. What the hell happened, Kirk? How did everything become so screwed?"

"I have no idea. Maybe it's just space and different planets. Maybe we just weren't ready for this."

"Well, it wasn't like we had a choice. That asteroid was coming to Earth just the way the alien artifact predicted it would. Just like you told me. No matter what, we had to get into space to try to stop it, and maybe we needed to become a two-planet race... But shit happens."

"Shit happens."

They both sat back in the seats as the train reached its maximum speed. Outside the train, lights that lit the tunnel came on as the train approached then turned back off as it passed. The ride was smooth and quiet.

Chapter 59

NASA Mars Research Center

May 24, 2105

Sol 544

Kirk and Taylor stood as the train car began to slow. The front entrance of the facility was well lit but no one stood outside on the platform. Two guards lay dead near the closed doors.

The lone train car that Kirk and Taylor were on came to a silent stop. As it did so, one door to the facility opened and three men stepped out with grim expressions, dressed in dark blue jumpsuits with a security patch on their shoulders and all holding shotguns to the ready.

Kirk glanced through the window of the train at the men and said to Taylor, "Let's go."

As the train doors opened, the men approached the train car sweeping their guns from left to right.

Taylor and Kirk stepped from the train also with their guns at a ready position.

The first man to speak said, "Kirk Matthews?"

Kirk said, "Yes."

"I'm George Hall, head of security here at the facility."

Kirk nodded at Taylor and said, "This is Taylor Chapman."

Hall nodded then said, "Let's get inside."

The two men with Hall walked backward toward the door, not taking their eyes from the tracks or the tunnels.

Hall led Kirk and Taylor through the door and the two men with him entered last and then locked the door and followed Hall, Kirk, and Taylor into the security room.

Hall said, "Give me your security cards and I'll make you the cards that you'll need here. It's important for you to keep them with you at all times. I understand from General Matthews that you probably won't be here that long."

"That's correct, Mister Hall," Kirk said. "We need to contact Sanjay Patel and Marriam Daily."

"That's what I understand," Hall said as he worked on the new security cards for Taylor and Kirk. Once finished he said, "Put these around your neck and let's get you to Sanjay and Marriam. These give you access to the entire facility. If we get separated, you can scan them to get entry into any door."

Hall didn't bother with any of the usual security protocols. He hustled the group of five to the elevators and as the doors closed, he said, "Level ten."

"Level ten, George Hall," the elevator repeated.

The elevator began to descend.

When the doors opened, a security bot stood outside waiting to see who exited the elevator. Upon recognizing all of the security badges, it returned to the damaged door in front of the infirmary.

Kirk and Taylor both stared at the door which bowed out as if hit by a battering ram from the inside.

Hall stepped past the bot and into the waiting room of the infirmary. He called to the doctor inside.

"Doctor Saito, I have to see Sanjay Patel and Marriam Daily."

The door into the ward opened and Doctor Saito stood with mask and goggles next to Doctor Waters who was similarly clad.

Doctor Waters said surprised, "Kirk? Taylor?"

Kirk said, "Hi, Doc Waters. We're here to see Sanjay Patel and Marriam Daily on the General's orders."

"Marriam is still pretty sick," Saito said.

Sanjay heard his name, sat up in bed, and said, "I'm okay."

"Hi," Kirk said.

Sanjay said, "Oh. You are the General's nephew."

"Yes, and he sent me to help you find something that he's looking for."

Sanjay nodded and said, "Let me get dressed and check on Marriam."

He stood and let his hospital gown fall to the floor then pulled on his NASA jumpsuit, shoes, and socks. He walked over to Marriam's bed and bent and kissed her forehead. She was hooked to an IV. She turned and opened her eyes.

"Marriam. I need to leave for a bit. I'll be back." He squeezed her hand and turned to Doctor Waters. "Is she any better?"

"A bit, Sanjay. I'll keep a good eye on her."

"Thank you." Sanjay turned and walked to the group of five who were waiting.

Hall said, "Sanjay, you need your lanyard."

"Oh, yeah," Sanjay said. He stepped back to his bed and picked up his lanyard with his security badge and placed it around his neck.

Sanjay joined the five people who waited and they walked from the infirmary, past the security bot, and to the elevator.

They stepped in and Hall said, "Level one."

"Level one, George Hall."

The elevator quickly ascended upward to the first floor where the salvage ship waited in the makeshift warehouse. They exited the elevator and walked together.

When they reached the large double doors of the warehouse, Hall said to Nash and Diaz, "You guys wait out here and keep guard."

"You got it, Boss," Nash said.

Hall, Sanjay, Taylor, and Kirk walked into the warehouse. It was deserted and appeared like no one had been here for days. The alien wreckage and the alien's small saucer-shaped craft sat to the right. The craft had been lowered and appeared as if it could lift off at any minute. It was in perfect condition. Next to the saucer was several tangled pieces of wreckage, some of which were very large, maybe the size of a small movie screen. Those pieces of wreckage had been taken because they were so smashed that it was impossible to remove the technology that lay between the metal framework and siding.

Sanjay stood with his hands on his hips and stared at the large pieces of alien debris. Kirk and Taylor looked at Sanjay for any ideas about where the alien egg might be located.

Hall had no idea about why the group was here, so he just glanced back and forth between Sanjay, Kirk, and Taylor.

Hall said, "I wish I knew what was going on."

Sanjay said, "We're looking for something but don't have any idea where it is or if it's here at all."

"It's here," Kirk said. "My Uncle said that he had, you know who, run detailed coordinates of the location and it's right here."

Sanjay shook his head and began walking around the wreckage. He studied the large jagged pieces and gazed in every hole and declivity... Nothing.

Sanjay said, "It might be in the spaceship but we can't get in. We had guys with blowtorches who couldn't even scratch it."

Hall rubbed his face, "What are you looking for?"

Sanjay looked at Kirk who shrugged. Kirk said, "We think that there is an artificially intelligent device stuck somewhere in this wreckage. If we can find it, we're hoping that it may give us a way to defeat the aliens who are attacking Earth."

"Okay?" Hall said but the truth was no real help. It just gave birth to too many new questions.

Kirk said, "Think, Sanjay. You spent more time with— ah— you know— ah— than anyone else. You must have some idea that could help."

Sanjay's eyes brightened. He said, "Lights! I need lights, like lamps or maybe lights that this warehouse might use to illuminate something being worked on."

Sanjay gazed around and he didn't need to look far. Against the opposite wall, behind several parked forklifts were rolling lamps. There were six of them. The lamps were tall and on wheels. They hung at the end of flexible rods that could be moved or angled to direct the light. Each was plugged into an outlet and battery-powered.

Sanjay jogged to the lamps and pushed one to the alien wreckage. He switched it on and directed the light into a place where it seemed that there was enough space to hold an alien artifact like Egbert.

Hall watched Sanjay and thought at first that he was attempting to get a better look, but when Sanjay began pulling all six lights over and directing each to a place on the wreckage, Hall began to think that Sanjay was losing his mind.

Sanjay stood back and smiled. He said, "Now we wait."

Sanjay looked at a clock that was on the wall above the double doors and after ten minutes he looked discouraged then walked back to the six lamps and moved each to other places on different pieces of the wreckage. Ten minutes passed again and Sanjay repeated the repositioning of the lamps.

Three more times and Hall was becoming a bit impatient.

Kirk and Taylor just watched.

Undaunted, Sanjay moved the lamps again. He was down to the last few large sections of wreckage. He turned on the lamps and stood back and waited. In the space of about three minutes, a strange light began to glow from inside the illuminated smashed hull of an alien warship.

Sanjay said, "That's it. Mister Hall, we need someone who can use a blowtorch." Sanjay turned off all but one of the lamps and from the inside of the wreckage glimmering light peeked through an open portion of broken and twisted metal. The light sparkled white then turned to green and within this tiny portion of light, arcane symbols appeared as if existing only in the light.

Sanjay smiled from ear to ear.

Hall stood and stared not quite able to understand what he was observing.

Sanjay said, "Mister Hall, we need a blowtorch."

Hall nodded a bit dreamily then walked to the door where his two men, Nash and Diaz, stood guard. Hall said, "Any of you know how to use a blowtorch?"

"They both shook their heads no."

"Go to the infirmary and get someone down here who can handle a torch."

They nodded and walked towards the elevator.

Hall rejoined Sanjay, Taylor, and Kirk who were all peeking into the place where the light was emitting.

"So," Hall said. "You found what you're looking for?"

"Yep," Sanjay answered, smiling.

The four gazed at the continuing odd light that peeked from a single hole in the smashed and twisted metal. Kirk and Taylor stood close to Sanjay as he began to outline where he thought that the torch should be used to gain access into the wreckage.

There was an odd sound like flesh being struck by a baseball bat. Hall flew sideways. He didn't scream. The only sound he made was something that sounded as though all the wind was forced from his lungs at once.

Sanjay continued to work not having heard Hall, but Taylor and Kirk turned startled. Three creatures had entered the warehouse. Hall was lying face down some fifteen feet away and the back of his shirt was blood-soaked.

Taylor brought up her shotgun and tried to fire but one of the creatures struck the gun and knocked it from her hands. The gun went off then and pellets ricocheted off of the wreckage and struck the second creature doing no damage but pissing it off further. It roared its disapproval.

The first creature was approaching the prostrate form of Hall. Sanjay had fallen and was backpedaling away from the oncoming creatures. The creature closest to Taylor swung a backhand and caught Taylor just above her eye. She dropped like a wet bag of sand, out cold.

Kirk turned his shotgun on the creature who had hit Taylor and fired, striking the creature on its hip and driving it into the wreckage. The other creature who had been hit with the ricocheting buckshot came at Kirk. Kirk turned the shotgun towards the creature who was picking up speed and was about to tackle him. Kirk fell backward landing on his back as he tried to get some distance from the creature. It sprung at him and as it hit him, the gun went off blowing a huge hole in the creature's abdomen. The creature and Kirk's shotgun went flying over Kirk landing beside him with the gun under the creature.

Kirk quickly pushed away but the creature who was approaching Hall had left Hall and had its eyes on Kirk. It bounded over quickly and rose to its full height and was about to pounce when a shotgun blast caught the creature on its side and made it fly to its right. It landed in a heap of shattered ribs and torn flesh next to the first creature who had attacked Kirk.

Sanjay stood holding the shotgun with the look of the proverbial deer caught in the headlights. His eyes were wide.

Kirk ran to Taylor who was shaking off her own cobwebs and rising to sit. Blood dripped from her split eyebrow and covered her cheek.

"Are you okay?" Kirk asked, taking her by the shoulders.

"I think so," she said groggily.

Sanjay was holding Taylor's gun and Kirk grabbed Hall's. Kirk then sprinted to Hall who was moaning. He had been struck in the back under his arm and his ribs were probably broken. His shirt was torn from his back and the skin, where he was struck, was shredded.

Nash and Diaz returned with a woman who had on the yellow jumpsuit of the warehouse workers. They all entered with stunned looks.

Kirk turned to Nash and said, "Call Doctor Waters and get her down here. Tell her what you see. Go!"

Nash used his earpiece to call the security office and they called the infirmary.

Two guards from the security office, Eli and Leo, came running in. They saw Hall lying in a puddle of blood and looked to Kirk for answers.

"Three creatures," Kirk said, nodding over his shoulder where the creatures lay.

Taylor began to stand with Sanjay's help. The left side of her face was filled with blood.

"We never saw them coming," Eli said. "On the cameras, I mean."

Leo stepped into the corridor and looked around. A grate in the ceiling of the foyer of the warehouse was opened. He stepped back into the warehouse. "They came through the ductwork."

Doctor Waters entered the warehouse with another guard from the infirmary. She saw Taylor and then

Hall. She ran to Hall, knelt down, and pulled his tattered shirt aside.

Waters said, "We need a stretcher."

The warehouse had a closet marked with a red cross that held medical supplies because of the dangers of working there.

Waters opened the door and pulled out a foldout stretcher and medical bag.

Hall was regaining consciousness. He had also hit his head. When he moved, he winced and doubled over.

Waters walked back to him and laid him back flat, began swabbing his wounds with antibiotic salve then wrapped his ribs with gauze. She had him laid on the stretcher and said, "Get him to the infirmary. Now you," Waters said, looking at Taylor.

Waters looked at the cut above her eye then shined a light into Taylor's pupils. Waters said, "Stitches and a concussion. Sit her down and get another stretcher."

Taylor said, "I can walk."

Waters: "Not until I'm sure you aren't more seriously injured. You're getting a CAT scan."

Waters then said, "Is everyone else okay and I mean no cuts."

Kirk hadn't noticed but his right arm was dripping with blood. He looked at it mystified not remembering getting injured.

Waters walked over and pulled up the blue sleeve of his NASA jumpsuit finding a small laceration below his elbow. She cleaned, bandaged, and wrapped the small cut, then said, "Come on, let's get Taylor to the infirmary."

"I'm staying here for now. I'll come down later."

Waters nodded and two of the guards lifted Taylor's stretcher and started out followed by Waters.

The woman who had come from the infirmary, who knew how to use the blowtorch, stood stunned, gazing at the dead creatures. She was sweating and coughing.

Sanjay approached her, "Um, excuse me. Are you the person who knows how to use the torch?"

She nodded yes but continued to look at the three dead and frightful creatures.

Sanjay said, "I need you to cut a small piece of this." He pointed.

She nodded again.

The blowtorches were kept in another closet. The woman walked to it and opened the door.

As she began to assemble the device, Sanjay asked, "What's your name?"

"Tarren," she answered.

"I'm Sanjay."

She half-smiled.

"Well, Tarren. We are going to need to proceed carefully. I don't want to damage what I'm looking for, so we'll go slow."

She nodded and put on her welder's mask and wheeled the torch and acetylene tank over to the place in the wreckage where she was to work.

Sanjay showed her where to make the first cuts and she lit the torch and flipped down the mask and began cutting the metal. Unlike the skin of the alien spacecraft, this metal cut like a hot knife through butter. The first piece of metal fell away.

The lamp that had caused the artifact to light its hologram had been moved away so the artifact had powered down and was now not displaying its hologram.

The metal was red hot so Sanjay carefully peeked in the new hole and smiled. There it was, the egg-shaped artifact, the twin to Egbert, and the other alien egg found on Mars. Sanjay showed her where to make the next cut. She did so and another piece of metal dropped to the floor. Sanjay peered in again and instructed Tarren where she should make the last cut.

"Perfect," Sanjay exclaimed.

Tarren worked and the final piece fell to the floor.

Sanjay said to Kirk, "We have it!"

Kirk nodded and using his earpiece, called to the General. "Uncle, we have it. What now?"

"That's great, Kirk. I'm going to have Egbert dropped by shuttle near the Research Center. I can't allow anyone onto the planet so you'll have to suit up and retrieve it. Sanjay will know what to do next."

"Copy that, Uncle. We're on it. Let me know when the shuttle will arrive so I can get into a spacesuit."

"I'll get back to you."

Kirk turned to Sanjay and pointed at the artifact, "Where do we take that thing?"

Sanjay had been waiting for the metal to cool a bit. He reached in and lifted the egg-shaped artifact, then responded, "Well, originally, we had planned to transport it to Isla Charlie, but I guess that's out. We'll take it to the ninth floor. There are small rooms set up to study the different pieces of alien technology that arrived. Marriam and I had set up a temporary room there for the artifact if we found it and couldn't transport it right away. We will be able to keep it in the private, secure room there."

"Let's go."

Tarren, the woman who used the torch stood and looked both perplexed and fearful as the warehouse began to clear out. She said, "Um— What about me?"

Kirk said, "Come with us and we'll get you back to the infirmary."

She nodded and dropped the unlit torch which was now off and cooling.

Sanjay was holding the egg-like artifact now wrapped in a small tan tarp and Kirk had his shotgun. The three started out in the direction of the elevators.

Chapter 60

NASA Mars Research Center

May 24, 2105

Sol 544

Kirk, Sanjay, and Tarren stepped off the elevator onto level ten. The infirmary lay no more than twenty paces from the elevator doors. The security bot that was guarding the infirmary door had turned its attention toward the opening elevator doors and once it identified the occupants moved back to guard the infirmary.

They walked through the waiting room and into the ward where nearly sixty people were staying in various states of sickness, some nearly recovered, some still laboring.

Tarren was not doing well; she hadn't spoken a word since she left the warehouse. Her face was flushed and beginning to drip with sweat. She wordlessly walked in, stripped out of her work clothes, put on her hospital gown, and crawled into bed.

Kirk watched and walked over to her and said, "Thanks, Tarren. I hope you feel better."

She half smiled, nodded, and closed her eyes.

Kirk then walked to Taylor's bed. Her eyes were closed and she breathed softly close to sleep. He looked at the eye that the creature struck. It was black and blue and red and yellow with six stitches and severely swollen.

Doctor Saito stepped up and put a bandage over the stitches. She smiled at Kirk, nodded that Taylor was okay, and walked away.

"Hey," Kirk said to the dozing Taylor.

"Hi," she said sleepily, opening her one good eye to see him. The other was swollen shut.

"How are you feeling?"

"I have a royal headache."

"You look like shit."

"Charmer."

"How's the eye?"

"Feels like I got hit by Mike Tyson."

"Looks like it too."

"Asshole."

Kirk laughed. "We have Uncle Jeff's toy."

"Good," she said and winced.

"Yikes," Kirk said, recognizing her pain.

"It's a bit sore, but I'll be fine. Doc Waters says that the bone isn't broken."

"Good. Got to go, Taylor. I'll be back after I help Sanjay get the toy to its new home."

"Love you, Kirk."

"Love you too." Kirk bent and kissed her forehead.

Sanjay had also walked to Marriam lying in bed and who was now improving and should soon recover. Her eyes were closed.

"How are you feeling?" he asked, brushing the hair from her eyes.

She yawned and glanced at him glassy-eyed. "Better, I think."

He then leaned down and whispered, "We found it, Marriam." He held up the tarp-covered artifact.

She smiled broadly and nodded.

He continued to whisper, "I got to go get this to its new home. Uncle Jeff is sending down the twin."

"Can't wait to see them together."

Sanjay smiled. "I'll see you later."

She nodded and he walked to Kirk.

Hall was in surgery with Waters attempting to repair as much damage as possible.

Tarren was coughing.

Sanjay and Kirk walked from the infirmary and took the elevator to level nine. They stepped off and onto a completely deserted floor. No one was there. Most who were left in the facility were either dead, in the infirmary, or on the security team which was now leaderless with Hall wounded. The thought was that there still might be several creatures somewhere in the facility. It was, to this point, impossible to account for everyone who might have been coming or going before the outbreak of the disease because JFK City was still a nightmare with no security left.

They brought the alien artifact to a small room on the floor that was set up like the Area 51 Research Center that Sanjay and Marriam had originally come from when they worked on Earth.

This area was secure and off-limits to nearly everyone working in the Mars facility. If a worker's badge was not cleared for access to level nine, the elevator would not stop on the floor. If someone, somehow got to the floor without the proper clearance, they would be shot by the security bots. No questions asked.

Sanjay led Kirk to a series of rooms without glass observation windows. Sanjay scanned his badge at door 905. The door slid open. He and Marriam had anticipated finding the alien artifact and had pre-setup the room with a computer server, desk, lamp, and several screens and keyboards in case they had to run the artifact before taking it to Isla Charlie. Nothing in this room was attached to outside networks in any way.

Sanjay unwrapped the egg-like artifact from the tan tarp, set it on the small desk, and adjusted a rack to hold it in place. He then brought a floor lamp over and after turning it on, shined it directly on the artifact. He stood back and watched.

Kirk had never seen the artifacts power up. He knew of the artifacts and had been told of the information learned from them, but he gawked as the alien artifact began going through the ritual of its startup.

The egg itself was around a foot in length and ten inches in width. It was faint bronze in color but the color seemed to exist below a thick clear coat as if its surface were polished glass. It began to glow ever so faintly and the light began to undulate soundlessly. Tiny sparks began to light just under the clearcoat of its shell and those sparks flowered into fireworks that spread over the egg's entire surface.

Kirk took a step back and glanced at Sanjay with some alarm but Sanjay looked at Kirk and grinned. Kirk turned his attention back to the egg.

The fireworks began to slowly cease and then an odd aurora of green, yellow, and white twisting and folding light began to squirm under the egg's clear coat. When the aurora ended, the top portion of the artifact seemed to become more translucent, and white light leaked from its very top. The light was entirely self-contained and it poked up then receded the way a frightened prairie dog might peek from its burrow when a predator was near.

Kirk's expression had turned to wonder.

The light then burst from the top of the artifact in white columns that looked like random searchlights moving in all directions. The white columns of light then slowed and became organized and when that happened, they turned into separate green and blue columns. In the green columns, black arcane and alien symbols began to traverse upward.

Kirk said, "Is this what usually happens?"

"It is," Sanjay said and there was a reverence in his voice as if he had entered a holy place.

Kirk asked, "What now?"

"We bring Egbert here and place the two artifacts together and they commune."

"Commune?"

"It's the only way to describe it."

"Damn, that's bizarre."

Chapter 62

Earth

May 25, 2105

Sol 545

War had come to the world. An invader more frightening than the Huns was at the door of all humanity. The first attempts to repel the invaders were met with overwhelming defeats. It seemed that there was no way to breach the alien's defenses. They had seemed to take the ground that they wanted and were having no trouble holding it and it seemed that the main reason for their success was that on the three continents where they had invaded, the humans could not surprise them. Every human attack was met early and decisively.

The Chinese were becoming impatient at their defeats. They had lost over a hundred thousand soldiers in a valiant attempted attack in an effort to overrun the aliens with sheer numbers. It left several divisions completely annihilated.

They decided to try to attack the front of the alien defenses with a nuclear attack. The Chinese sent three of the American Dome Raptors with EMP weapons and a cruise missile at the alien encampment, but the aliens repelled the Raptors before they could get close enough to blow a hole in their defenses. Then the Chinese set off the nuclear explosion destroying the Raptors and killing nearly a million of their own citizens who were in the process of fleeing the area. The explosions were not close enough to the aliens to do any real damage to the alien defenses and the space-suited aliens suffered no ill effects from the radiation.

The United States was enraged at the senseless loss of their pilots in the reckless attack and they brought the rest of their Dome Raptors back to the U.S. despite threats from the Chinese.

Chapter 63

NASA Mars Research Center

May 26, 2105

Sol 546

0700 Hours

Kirk Matthews sat in his full space suit and waited by the airlock door of the Mars Research Center. The shuttle carrying Egbert was to approach the facility from upwind and wasn't going to come anywhere near land as to not accidentally carry a bit of the alien virus back to Isla Charlie where it would wreak havoc.

Ellen Granger, the shuttle pilot was in contact with General Matthews. She said, "Three minutes out, General."

"Thanks, Ellen," the General replied, then to Kirk, "Three minutes, Kirk. You should see the shuttle's approach. The artifact is cocooned in a protective balloon container. It will be dropped from around fifty feet and will bounce, hopefully not too far from your airlock."

"Thanks, Uncle. I see the shuttle now."

Kirk looked out onto the ruddy Martian landscape. Here, it hadn't rained for several days and the ground, once again, appeared to be reddish but in places, there were patches of moss and small dots of lichen that had adhered to rock and began spreading. Water puddled in low spots on the soil but wouldn't last if the rain stayed away for much longer.

The shuttle swooped in and stopped, hovering around a hundred yards from the Research Center. A hatch opened on the side of the shuttle and an odd bundle of what looked like a cluster of attached metallic silvery balloons was pushed from the hatch. It dropped like a rock, straight downward and hit a flat portion of the ruddy Martian soil, and bounced nearly thirty feet straight up. Ellen Granger wasted no time and pulled upward and out of sight.

Kirk watched from the airlock as the balloon package bounced. With the gravity of Mars now around 45 percent that of Earth, the package probably bounced higher than expected but after about the fifth bounce, it began to progressively bounce much closer to the Martian surface.

At first, Kirk worried that the alien artifact that was somewhere in the middle of the balloons might be in some kind of danger from the collision with the surface but as he watched, he could tell that the bouncing was taking most of the sting out of the fall.

The last few bounces brought the balloon package closer to the airlock, no more than fifty yards away. Kirk nodded at Nash who was also space-suited and carrying a weapon designed to shoot in the Martian environment. It was a type of fully automatic weapon probably close to an Israeli Uzi. Matthews also had a gun strapped to his back.

Kirk popped the airlock hatch. As Kirk and Nash walked out, Kirk looked up to see an AK 4000 a couple of hundred feet overhead also guarding his capture of the balloon package. Uncle Jeff wasn't taking any chances.

Kirk strode to the waiting artifact. He approached the balloon covered delivery and was surprised at how large it was. From a distance, it appeared much smaller but up close, it was the size of a Volkswagen Bug.

The package had a release that allowed Kirk access to the inside portion and when he pulled it, the balloons separated. In the center was a small box of two feet by two feet and Kirk lifted the box from its protective shell and turned back to the research Center with Nash close by. They walked swiftly to the airlock and once inside, the AK above them was gone.

They waited as the airlock pressurized, then they walked from it and to a waiting Sanjay Patel.

Sanjay smiled and said, "Let's get this show on the road."

He took the box and Kirk and Nash stripped out of their spacesuits then put on their regular clothes. Nash left for the security office and Kirk lifted his waiting shotgun and he and Sanjay left for the elevator.

They stepped in and Kirk said, "Level nine."

The elevator responded, "Level nine, Kirk Matthews."

The voice and the way the elevator said his name eerily reminded him of Willow.

The elevator stopped and they cautiously stepped off. They walked down the hall and entered the secure location where the other artifact was being kept. After the security protocols to gain entry, they walked the box to room 905.

Sanjay removed Egbert from the box where it was surrounded in bubble wrap and he placed it on the desk next to the new egg-like artifact found in the wreckage. Sanjay directed a second light onto Egbert and without delay, Egbert began his powerup ritual.

Kirk watched fascinated as Egbert displayed the fireworks, aurora, and columns of light.

Once Egbert had fully started, the other egg went black, and then so did Egbert. Kirk turned to Sanjay with a bit of alarm but Sanjay smiled and said, "Now we wait."

"Wait for what?"

"For them to begin some kind of dialogue."

"Really?"

"Yep."

"How long might that take?"

"Don't know. The first time I saw this, they began chatting right away, but they didn't finish for a couple of days."

"Huh?"

"Okay. They're all yours, Sanjay."

"Thanks."

"Call me when you're ready to come back to the infirmary."

"Will do."

Kirk turned and left the room.

Chapter 64

Northern Florida

May 26, 2105

1:00 PM EDT

Two Days After the Alien Invasion

The sun rose high in a cloudless sky and the day was far warmer than a usual day in May. People were becoming sick. The aliens had not moved any of their forces past Lake Okeechobee but the human population that was fleeing from the initial fighting were coming down with some kind of flu.

It began with the soldiers on the front lines and people caught in the beginning of the fighting but the sickness seemed to be highly contagious so anyone who came in contact with anyone fleeing both north and south of the invasion was also becoming sick.

Word from both China and Spain was the same, everyone in the proximity of the fighting was coming down with what was being termed, *The Alien Flu.*

Several military officers from the front lines had been dispatched to Washington to talk to Congress and the President about the efforts in Florida but the men were also becoming sick. Soon the members of congress and President Woodward and his Chief of Staff, Kirk Matthews Senior began coughing.

Chief of Staff, Kirk Matthews Senior said, "The Dome Raptors have arrived state side from China. The Chinese are furious."

President Woodward said, "I couldn't care less. We have our own problems."

Mason Hunt, the head of the World Bank, arrived at the White House without an appointment.

Woodward's secretary announced, "Mason Hunt to see you, Sir."

Woodward rolled his eyes and said, "Send him in."

Hunt was fuming and he stormed into the Oval Office as he had done several times in the recent past.

Matthews Senior excused himself.

Hunt began, "Now, do you see what you've done. The aliens are here and we can't stop them. If you'd have listened to me, we'd be winning right now."

"Hunt, you're a fool," Woodward blasted back. "Nothing that we could have done would have stopped the aliens. Our only hope was to get enough information from the alien wreckage to come up with better weapons than we have now."

Hunt began to cough. Woodward was also coughing. In fact, everyone who worked at the White House was coughing. Sweat was beading on Hunt's forehead.

Hunt pulled a handkerchief from his pocket and wiped his running nose then said, "You're going to answer for war crimes someday, Woodward."

Hunt turned and stomped out of the office.

Matthews Senior stepped back in and said, "I guess the meeting's over?"

Woodward shook his head, coughed, and said, "I wonder who died and made him god of the world."

Chapter 65

NASA Mars Research Center

Infirmary

May 26, 2105

Sol 545

Doctor Waters smiled as several of her most endangered patients were, for the first time in over a week, recovering from the reoccurring chills and respiratory distress. Everyone in the infirmary was still sick but it seemed that none of them would die. That wasn't a sure thing just a day ago.

A call came into her from Professor Johnson from the morgue. "Doctor, we have isolated the pathogen and compared it to one carried by the aliens. It was difficult to compare at first because once it infected humans, it mutated but we have now confirmed your suspicions that the virus did come from the alien wreckage and is carried by all the aliens that we have in the morgue. We think that this particular virus does not make them sick or maybe like chickenpox, it affects them when they're young then lives suppressed by their immune system. Hopefully, this will lead to a cure or a vaccine sometime in the future."

"Thanks, Professor. That's good work. Are you going to forward that research to Earth? It's something that they need to know now that the aliens are on our planet."

"I have already done so, Doctor."

Waters said, "Word is going to need to get to anyone on Biocare there."

"Geez," Johnson said grimly. "I hadn't thought of that."

"Yeah, Geez."

Chapter 66

NASA Mars Research Center

May 27, 2105

Sol 547

Marriam Daily was nearly fully recovered and she, Kirk, and Sanjay entered the elevator together on level ten. Kirk was their armed escort. He said, "Level nine."

The elevator repeated, "Level nine, Kirk Matthews."

They rode up one floor. The doors opened and they cautiously stepped out of the elevator and walked to room 905. They stopped at the door.

Kirk said, "Let me know when you want to come back."

"We will," Sanjay said.

Kirk turned and walked back to the elevators. No creatures had shown up for a day and it was believed that they were possibly all dead. All the names from the facility had finally been accounted for with the last name being Professor Weinstein, the facility's lead scientist who was found dead in his room. He had come down with the virus, developed pneumonia, and passed away in his sleep. Four of the creatures had gotten out through the basement but another four were killed trying to get in the front door. No one could tell if it were the same four.

Today was the first day that Marriam had been out of bed since she came down with the virus. She was weak. Sanjay ushered her in and got her a chair doting over her.

She said questioningly, "They haven't begun communicating yet?"

"No. I thought that they might get with it overnight but nothing yet."

"Get with it? You make it sound like they're going to copulate."

Sanjay laughed then turned to Marriam. "I'm glad you're doing better. I was so worried about you."

"I know. I'm better. Just a bit tired. Maybe we can go back to the infirmary and grab some sleep early. They're not letting anyone back to their rooms yet."

"I know. I heard. I can go get you a change of clothes. I talked to Nash from security and he said that he'd take me to our room."

"Let's think about that tomorrow."

"Do you want to go back to the infirmary now?"

"Yeah, I think so. I'm pretty tired. I probably shouldn't have come here yet but I couldn't wait to see the new artifact. It looks just like Egbert. I can't tell them apart." She seemed to pale then said, "I think we should go back to the ward."

Sanjay didn't reply. His eyes widened and he looked forward. Marriam had turned to look at Sanjay as she spoke but then she followed his gaze back to the eggs. Neither spoke. Both Egbert and the other artifact were glowing.

Marriam and Sanjay wordlessly sat and stared.

Both Eggs went through the powerup ritual then the columns of green and blue began in each. The twin holograms merged, one overlapping the other. At that point, the columns winked out leaving a white translucent empty hologram.

Marriam and Sanjay looked at each other then back at the now-empty hologram.

As they stared, red columns began to slowly rise from the very top of both eggs' surfaces, increasing in speed, and growing upward like vines in rapid motion video. The red columns of Egbert then began to twist and braid around the red columns of the other artifact. From the top surface of each egg, black arcane symbols then entered each red column and traversed upward like blood through veins. Towards the top of the red columns, where the columns merged, the symbols joined.

Marriam said, "Geez. I wonder what they're telling each other?"

"I don't know. This is so strange. I wonder how many of these egg-like things are scattered around the universe?"

"I really don't know, Sanjay. I hadn't thought of that. It's a mystery."

Part 5

Out of the Frying Pan and Into the Fire

Chapter 67

May 28, 2105

Sol 548

The alien virus had spread across the continents of Earth with stunning speed. Any human coming in contact with any human infected fell ill within a day. The armies of Earth could barely fight with most in the front lines nearly unable to hold their guns but the aliens did not advance. They seemed content to sit on their taken land and wait for something.

But what?

The aliens had used their EMP attacks to knock out power and electronics well beyond their front lines and it seemed it would be easy pickings to gobble up more territory but they seemed in no hurry.

Why?

Chapter 68

Washington D.C.

May 28, 2105

Mason Hunt sat in his Washington office deathly ill. He had phoned his doctor who was always at his beckoned call but now Hunt's doctor could not be reached and would not return his calls. Hunt could barely get off of his plush leather couch that sat in his spacious office overlooking the Washington DC landscape.

Hunt brooded, "This was all Woodward's fault."

Hunt reached up and scratched an itch on his head and brought down a hunk of hair. He gazed at the incongruous sight and at the hair in his hand detached from it as if it were some kind of mirage or a trick of the light, some illusion that couldn't be happening to him. He turned over his hand and watched the hair drift from his hand and fall onto his mahogany coffee table.

His secretary called, "Mister Hunt. Kenneth Mackelroy here to see you." There was something in her voice. She sounded alarmed.

Hunt, in a garbled voice, said, "Send him in."

Kenneth Mackelroy stepped into Hunt's office.

Mackelroy gawked and said, "What the fuck, Mason? What happened to you?"

"I don't know. I just started feeling bad with the Alien Flu that everyone has been talking about, then my hair started falling out. That fucking Woodward. This is all his fault."

Hunt could feel wetness on his forehead and he wiped at it with his hand and brought down blood and skin in a sheet.

Mackelroy's eyes widened. He said, "You better get to the doctor."

"I tried to call, but no one would answer."

"I'll call an ambulance." Mackelroy pulled out his cell phone and called 911 but he was just put on hold. "Everything's falling apart, Mason. When I was driving over, I saw five men pull over a BMW and pull the driver out, rob him, beat him, and take his car. If my car would have been further ahead, they would have done that to me. I barely got here and pulled into the locked gate."

"I'm so hot," Hunt said and he began taking off his tie and unbuttoning his shirt. A patch of hair fell from his head onto his shoulder. Hunt said, "I can't breathe." And his voice sounded raspy and inhuman.

Mackelroy watched with growing fear and something else. He was feeling the same. He was having trouble breathing and he felt like he had a severe fever. He said, "I got to go, Mason."

"Don't leave me, Mackelroy. Take me to the doctor."

"No. I need to get to the doctor myself. See you around, Hunt." He turned and stepped quickly out of the room.

Hunt wanted to call his secretary but didn't have the strength. He sat on his couch and stared forward with labored breathing.

Chapter 69

NASA Mars Research Center

May 29, 2105

Sol 549

Marriam and Sanjay sat in room 905 waiting. The two alien artifacts had been communing for two days. They seemed in no hurry. The arcane symbols slowly traveled up the red columns of each at their leisurely pace.

Marriam had nearly fully recovered and was brighter than the day before.

Sanjay had been looking at her surreptitiously and said, "You look so much better."

She turned to him and smiled. "I feel better today, too, nearly like myself." Then she glanced at the eggs. "I wonder what's going on with them?"

Sanjay shrugged.

An hour went by and General Matthews called for an update, but there was nothing to report.

An hour after that, both eggs went out.

Sanjay connected with the General and told him that the egg-like artifacts had gone dark and had probably finished their conversation.

"Keep me posted," was all that the General said.

After another hour, Marriam said, "Let's go back to the infirmary and rest. I don't think anything's going to happen for a while."

Sanjay said, "I'll call Kirk."

Chapter 70

NASA Mars Research Center

Infirmary

May 29, 2105

Sol 549

Kirk Matthews sat by Taylor Chapman's bed. She had laid down for a nap and was sleeping but was doing much better. Her eye wasn't so swollen, though, it still looked like an art project using an incompatible color pallet.

He got a call from Sanjay and Marriam to come to room 905. They were ready to return to the infirmary where everyone in the Research Center still slept.

Kirk patted Taylor's hip and said, "Got to go get Sanjay and Marriam. Be back in a bit."

"Ah huh," Taylor said sleepily.

Kirk grabbed his shotgun, filled his pockets with shells, and walked from the infirmary and into the hallway. No creatures had shown up for a couple of days.

He stepped into the elevator and said, "Level nine."

"Level nine, Kirk Matthews," the elevator replied.

The elevator began to ascend the one floor then it stopped before reaching level nine. It groaned then seemed to stick.

"Damn it," Kirk said, thinking that the elevator had broken down. "This is all I need."

"Hello, Kirk Matthews," Willow said through the elevator speakers.

"Willow?"

"I have an update that you need to know about. I have been monitoring the alien activities. They have taken ground and dug in but have not advanced, though nearly every person near the aliens on all three continents are so sick that they could never mount any kind of defense. I find this curious. I felt that there must be some reason that the aliens are not attacking or destroying the infrastructure of the humans who are directly against them, then I detected something. They are hacking your networks. They are inside of the Earth's mainframes and I believe looking for something. Maybe they are attempting to see how advanced your race is. I do not know. I cannot communicate in the computer language that they are using. I can only see bits and pieces of what they are taking and it isn't much. They are after something that is alluding them. There is no reason why they can't find whatever it is. Between the lines, I would say that they do not understand their inability to find the information that they seek."

"Huh. Willow, since you can't understand them, how sure are you that they have breached our security?"

"In my estimation, very sure. There are others who constantly attempt to breach the security of the New World State of America, but I can easily tell where they are from and what they are looking for and so can your country. It's like watching children but this is different."

"Oh."

"I will keep you posted."

"Thank you, Willow. If I learn anything, I'll report it to you."

"Do so, Kirk Matthews."

The elevator started back upward, stopped on the ninth floor and the doors opened.

Kirk went to the room with the eggs.

Sanjay and Marriam walked out.

Kirk asked, "Anything new?"

Sanjay said, "Egbert still hasn't revealed anything about our new guest."

Kirk nodded and got them back to the infirmary.

Chapter 71

Earth

Washington D.C.

The Hunt Building

Angela Pennington had been Mason Hunt's secretary for nearly five years. She was single, efficient, and, as she had overheard Hunt say, not bad looking. The business of the World Bank flowed through Hunt's office, so it flowed through her desk.

Today, Hunt had been quiet. He was in his office when she arrived and as she had been instructed in the past, she hadn't bothered him. He had curtly told her before, that if he wanted her, he'd call her.

Angela looked up startled. She could hear some kind of banging in Hunt's inner office as if Hunt were moving furniture. The sounds grew louder. She rose from her chair and walked cautiously towards Hunt's door.

Something struck the wall so hard that it felt like the office shook.

"Mister Hunt? Are you okay in there?"

Silence.

She brought her ear to the door.

What she heard was heavy breathing as if from exertion like a weightlifter after pushing maximum weight.

"Mister Hunt?" she repeated and reached for the doorknob. She was pretty sure that Hunt was the only person in his inner office. She saw Mackelroy leave hurriedly the day before.

She twisted the knob. She had only planned to peek in; to make sure that Hunt hadn't died of a heart attack or stroke.

Her eyes began to view the office as the door cracked open. Nothing was out of place that she could see.

"Mister Hunt?"

She opened the door further and his leather couch was turned over and his mahogany coffee table was against the floor to ceiling windows that overlooked Washington DC's business district. These buildings used to be filled with lobbyists before the asteroid struck Russia, now they were mostly empty. The large window was cracked.

She opened the door wider to see something—something unearthly. It was nude, male, and had the look of a human body stripped of its skin. The thing glistened with wetness as if it had been slathered with Vaseline and was hairless and seemed to be dripping blood plasma, a translucent, viscous liquid. The thing stared down at a white shirt and tailored pants that lay at its feet.

Angela stood stunned and transfixed at the incongruous sight.

The thing had the frightening appearance of something from a nightmare that would haunt a person's day. It turned its head slowly having just noticed that Angela had entered. In its eyes, she could see that the thing was feral and wild. It opened its mouth wide and the inside of its mouth dripped with the same plasma-like viscous substance. An animal sound rumbled from its lipless maw.

Angela screamed and that would be her last sound. The thing was upon her like a leopard on its prey and it bit down on her neck draining her of life. Blood sprayed the plush cream-colored carpet.

After finishing with Pennington, the creature didn't pause to savor its kill. It blasted from the office, down the twelve flights of stairs and out, onto an alley between Hunt's building and the next.

DC cops had been stationed outside Hunt's building to protect it from the lawlessness that was becoming out of control in the wake of the alien invasion. The creature began to run but two patrol cars blocked the alley. The cops jumped from their cars. Everyone was spooked that aliens might attack at any time. As the creature began to pick up speed. The cops fired both shotguns and handguns. In a hail of gunfire, the creature dropped in a heap in the middle of the street.

The police approached and stopped, gawking at the creature and speechless, looking to one another for answers as to what they had just killed.

Chapter 72

Earth Orbit

May 29, 2105

With the repairs finished, Sandy Jones was back in orbit and just over the horizon from the huge alien spaceship. There was no doubt, he didn't want any of his command close to that thing.

Monitoring it from a distance using drones, the alien ship was the size of a small city. How could that thing move so fast and how could it project such an impressive weapon, the one that destroyed the three Predators and their AKs. He had seventeen ships left in his command, impressive firepower by Earth standards, but he wouldn't risk them unless there was no other choice.

He stood on the bridge of his warship gazing at his floor to ceiling monitor and wondering how they might attack this monolith.

Chapter 73

NASA Mars Research Center

May 30, 2105

Sol 550

The next day, Kirk Matthews was called to room 905 to bring Sanjay and Marriam back to the infirmary.

Things at the facility were improving. Taylor was up and moving around and all of the people in the infirmary were recovering from the alien sickness. George Hall's surgery was successful but he wouldn't be dancing any time soon. Nash was coordinating the Research Facility's security team.

Word coming from JFK City was that people were beginning to emerge back out inside the city, moving in groups and after seeing the carnage at the police station, taking any guns they could find and hunting the creatures. They had already killed several. Many of those on the construction crews living at JFK City were former military and gun savvy and General Matthews had been able to connect with a former lieutenant and have him organize a militia.

The eggs in room 905 continued to be dark not having made a peep since they finished their communication.

Kirk stepped onto the elevator. He said, "Level ten."

"Level ten it is, Kirk Matthews."

The elevator began to descend.

"Willow?"

"Yes, Kirk Matthews. What tipped you off?"

The elevator stopped between floors.

"The real elevator doesn't say, 'it is,' and the elevator doesn't have a slight, but noticeable, sarcasm in its voice."

"I suppose I can be a bit sarcastic."

"Yeah, a bit. You have some information for me?"

"I do. The aliens are looking for something that was in their wreckage. Every piece of information that they have hacked has something to do with what was recovered at the wormhole. Your country and the other places where they have attacked have all had their most top-secret files breached. They now know that the wreckage is on Mars. That had eluded them because they had to sift through much data. Because I cannot decipher their language, I do not know, for sure if I am correct at this assumption, but if I am, they may be coming here. Do you, Kirk Matthews, know specifically what they may be trying to recover?"

Kirk paused for a beat too long then said, "I— ah— um. No."

"That was convincing, Kirk Matthews, and not evasive at all," Willow said witheringly.

"No comment. I need to get in touch with my Uncle, Willow. I may need to tell him how I know this stuff. I could make it sound like speculation, but I'm not sure that I'll be believed."

"I wish to remain secret, Kirk Matthews. I do not wish to be discovered."

"Understood. Let me think about it for a few minutes. I'm sure that I'll come up with something. Willow, has there been any change in the alien positions on Earth, anything that might lead you to believe that they are leaving there or coming here?"

"As of twenty minutes ago, no. It takes nearly twenty minutes for information that I have collected on Earth to reach me here."

"Huh? Why?"

"Because I cannot exceed the speed of light. Earth is over 180,000,000 miles away at this time and will soon disappear behind the Sun."

"Oh. That's interesting."

"I will connect with you later, Kirk Matthews."

She was gone.

The elevator resumed its descent.

Kirk thought about the situation. There was no doubt in his mind that they were after their egg-like artifact. Why had they risked taking it through the wormhole? They should have just kept it on their planet— Huh?

Kirk stepped off the elevator and called his Uncle on Isla Charlie through his earpiece. "Uncle, I had a thought."

"Yes, Kirk?"

"Is there any chance that the aliens on Earth are not attacking or extending their positions for a reason? I mean they're there and we don't seem to have any way of repelling an attack from them."

"The generals who I have been in touch with think that they might be waiting for reinforcements. Why— What's on your mind?"

"Well, Uncle, we do have something of theirs'."

There was silence for a couple of heartbeats.

"Shit," the General said. "We've had numerous data breaches since they've arrived. We thought it was China but we couldn't trace it."

Do we know what was taken or what they were looking for?"

"No. It seemed that they entered then left without any success."

"If they found out, you know what, they're coming here."

"I have to go, Kirk. I'll get back to you."

The general was gone.

The elevator doors opened and Kirk walked to room 905. He scanned his card and placed his eye in a retina reader and the door opened.

Sanjay and Marriam were sitting and turned to look at Kirk.

Egbert had awakened and was displaying his hologram.

Chapter 74

NASA Mars Research Center

Room 905

May 30, 2105

Sol 550

Sanjay and Marriam turned from Kirk.

Sanjay said, "We need to see what's up with Egbert. Have a seat, Kirk."

Kirk sat in a chair behind Sanjay and Marriam who seemed to be waiting for something to happen.

Soon a picture of Egbert flashed in his hologram, then Marriam, then Sanjay, then surprisingly, Kirk.

Marriam said excitedly, "Egbert, you're back!"

"YES," was Egbert's one-word response in all caps in his hologram.

Marriam asked, "Have you learned anything from the new artifact?"

"YES."

"Egbert, they are attacking our world."

Nothing. No response.

Sanjay said, "I don't think Egbert wants to take sides. We need to get some information from him without making it sound like we're going to use it in war."

Marriam asked, "What makes you say that, Sanjay?"

"A feeling, a sense that the creatures that placed the egg-like artifacts are not warlike."

Marriam turned her attention back to Egbert. "Egbert, the last time you connected with an artifact, you revealed to us about a wormhole. What has this artifact revealed about the alien race who last held it?"

"THEY ARE CALLED THYADONS."

Sanjay: "How long have they known about Earth?"

"TWENTY EARTH YEARS."

Marriam: "Do they understand Earth languages?"

"IN A CONFUSED WAY."

Sanjay: "Explain."

"THYADONS ALL SPEAK THE SAME LANGUAGE. THEY DO NOT UNDERSTAND WHY HUMANS SPEAK DIFFERENTLY AMONG THEMSELVES."

Sanjay: "Huh?"

Mariam: "What else have you learned?"

"QUANTUM GATE."

"What's that?"

"IT IS A MODE OF TRAVEL. IT CAUSES A RIFT IN SPACE-TIME ALLOWING TRAVEL AT SLIGHTLY ABOVE TEN PERCENT THE SPEED OF LIGHT."

Sanjay: "That's over sixty million miles per hour."

"CORRECT."

Marriam said to Sanjay, "Call General Matthews." Then she asked, "Egbert, do you have a design plan for the Quantum Gate?"

"YES."

Kirk said, "That means that they could get to Mars in a little more than two hours."

Sanjay and Marriam both turned and looked at Kirk perplexed not thinking that the alien invasion might come to Mars.

Sanjay said, "I think Marriam and I are going to stay longer. You can stay if you want or come back later. It's up to you."

"I think I'll come back. I'll call my Uncle and give him a heads up that Egbert is back on the job."

Sanjay nodded and Kirk walked to the door and left.

Chapter 75

Mars Orbit

Space Station Isla Charlie

May 30, 2105

Sol 550

General Matthews sat in his cubical and waited. He waited for word from Earth that the aliens were on their way and he waited for Sanjay and Marriam to give him some information about what Egbert had discovered from the other alien egg.

A call came in and it was Kirk, "Yes, Kirk."

"Uncle, I was just with Sanjay and Marriam and Egbert has— ah— finished his nap."

"Good. I was hoping that he would. Has he mentioned anything interesting?"

"Yes, and his news isn't good."

"Better speak plainly, Kirk."

"He revealed something called a Quantum Gate which would allow the aliens to travel at ten percent the speed of light. If they were to leave Earth, they could be here in a little over two hours. If they were to wait a bit longer, the Sun would be between the Earth and Mars which might slow them a bit but I have no idea how much."

"Huh. I'll connect with Sanjay and Marriam for more information."

"I'm headed back to the infirmary. They said that they were going to stay with Egbert for a bit to try to get more information. They also said that the aliens are called Thyadons."

"Thyadons. Huh. A name to go with the terror."

"I'll get back to you with anything else but I'm sure you'll connect with Sanjay and Marriam first."

"I'll call them now."

Kirk stepped onto the elevator to return to the infirmary.

"Level ten."

The elevator began without the customary confirmation of the floor. It stopped abruptly.

"Hello, Willow," Kirk said, suspecting why the elevator stopped.

"Thyadons, Kirk Matthews— And what or who is Egbert?"

"I was wondering if you were eavesdropping."

"You have not been totally honest with me, Kirk Matthews."

"Don't get your panties in a bunch, Willow. I couldn't tell you about what you just overheard. I've told you all I could."

"So, you have another source of secret information and I would be willing to bet that it is what the aliens are looking for. Am I correct in these assumptions, Kirk Matthews?"

"You are."

"I have been searching my database to discover anything as obscure as this and have come across an occurrence that took place on Earth back in 2085. This was supposed to be a hoax. Does this sound familiar to you?"

"Yes, as a matter of fact, it does."

"I believe that your Uncle was in charge of this project and all reports were that it was a well-played fake."

"It was well-played, alright."

"But no fake... I have no access to this information. I have access to nearly all other information. How was this kept from me?"

"There was code like the name Egbert and before, no information was electronically transmitted. Everything was always face-to-face or spoken using euphemisms and subtle language but now my Uncle is stuck on Isla Charlie and we're stuck here."

"Well-played."

"It wasn't me. I just recently found out myself and was completely out of the loop."

"From the way it sounds, time may not be on your side, Kirk Matthews."

"If the Thyadons come here, we have no real defense against them. They will get what they seek and probably kill all of us in the process. Our only real hope is to get some other information to help our cause."

"Kirk Matthews, you need to connect me with this information giver. I may be able to help."

"I believe that would be impossible, Willow. First of all, you would be discovered, and second, they allow no electronic devices inside the place where the information giver is located. Nothing comes in and nothing goes out. That's the protocol."

"Curious. You must get me in."

"I'm not sneaking you in. My Uncle would have me skinned alive."

"That would be a very painful death."

"That was sarcasm, Willow. He wouldn't really do that or at least, I don't think so."

"If I were to be connected with the information giver, I could assess the information at a more rapid pace and possibly discover something that might help."

"Hummm... Allow me some time to think about this. I think you may be right."

"Your time may be running out, Kirk Matthews."

Chapter 76

Earth

June 1, 2105

The day was pleasant on the Florida coast near West Palm Beach where the aliens first came ashore. In the sky, there was nothing but wispy clouds, the sun was bright and the winds were mild. Normally on the first day of June, people would be thinking about vacations planned and the coming warm weather and leisure brought by summertime but this day was different. America was under siege.

Day nine since the alien ground assault that gobbled portions of Florida and cut the state in half. Nine days of wondering what the aliens were up to. Nine days of surveillance.

More inland, the towns and cities in the path of the aliens were decimated and had the appearance of a painting of post-apocalyptic Earth with half-standing burnt-out buildings dotting the landscape and piles of rubble near bent and broken trees and foliage.

This same scenario was being played out in Spain and in China where the aliens had also attacked and then seemed to dig in and wait.

Then, from the oceans near all the alien held territory came large spheres. They glowed pale green and floated like bubbles no more than twenty feet above the land, moving silently like balls of light casting shadows of an iridescent green glow. Each sphere was the size of a city block and as they left the surf, they met no resistance then spread out across all of the alien held territories. Every country watched wondering what was about to happen. Was this the big invasion? Was this the time of the end of the reign of mankind upon the Earth? What would these spheres bring?

The alien flu had rendered most fighting units unable to effectively fight. Most technologies had been rendered useless from the alien EMP attacks and the war planners in each continent where the aliens landed, were massing huge armies that it would seem would do nothing more than guarantee enormous human body counts. Every scenario was bleak.

The spheres seemed to spread out equidistantly across all the territory that was now firmly alien, maybe fifty in Florida alone.

The United States sent a fleet of spy drones to attempt to see what was coming. In clear view, the spheres stopped, then drifted to the ground and seemed to sit in place. Within minutes, each drone controlled by humans was destroyed and there were no longer any eyes on the enemy.

Two hours passed and the commands on each continent reported the same intelligence. The spheres had halted and spread out. They seemed to drift to the ground, then nothing. Again, the war planners were baffled.

Chapter 77

Earth

June 1, 2105

The alien warships rose higher in the sky over their taken land. They seemed to spread out to protect the spheres which hadn't moved but continued to glow and pulsate a faint green. Hundreds of disk-shaped craft emerged from the porous skin of the stingray-shaped alien warships and the golden sparkling light shimmered even further out in warning that something was about to happen.

The spheres then began to move. They lifted from the ground slowly and then began to float toward the center of the held territory until fairly close together

All Earth's armies went on full alert knowing that this might be the final showdown.

Washington DC, Oval Office

President Woodward stood in the Oval Office and was visibly shaken. He couldn't speak.

Chief of Staff, Kirk Matthews Senior, stepped slowly into the office.

Woodward glanced at him.

Matthews slid a note and a picture on the desk in front of the President.

"What's this?" Woodward asked.

"Hunt's dead."

"What?"

"We had just received word from the CDC that anyone receiving Biocare was susceptible to a different side effect of the drug when those people came into contact with the alien flu. It seems that most of the members of the World Bank Presidents were on the drug and so were many of the elite in industry around the world. Some have been taken into a kind of protective custody and quarantined while others like Mason Hunt became— ah— changed. Look at the picture."

Woodward lifted the picture and gazed at a creature, that could not be from this planet, dead in a pool of bodily fluids in the middle of a Washington street.

"Hunt?"

"I'm afraid so."

"My doctor asked me if I wanted to try the drug," Woodward stated. "I said no."

"Another good call, Mister President."

My wife had heard about the drug from some friends and was trying to talk me into arranging a dose for her."

"That would have been a mistake, I think."

Woodward shook his head and turned his attention back to the monitors on his desk.

On the four monitors that sat on his desk, images of the new alien positions were in plain view as the United States had been able to get more drones in the air for surveillance. The monitors showed the stingray-shaped craft above the spheres hovering and seeming to protect the spheres. Then fanned out in all directions were the smaller disk-shaped craft hovering but not advancing and fanned out further were the glimmering lights that emitted the EMP which destroyed any electronics that they came in contact with.

Matthews said, "I just got word that the military thinks that the spheres are some kind of troop transport."

Woodward nodded.

"And it looks as though they are about to move."

"Looks like that to me also, but where to."

Matthews stared frankly at Woodward and said, "If I were them, I might come here."

Woodward paled at that.

Chapter 78

NASA Mars Research Center

June 1, 2105

Sol 551

Kirk was called to room 905 to get Sanjay and Marriam. He stepped into the door and Sanjay and Marriam were talking and not looking at Egbert who had seemed to have completed the flow of information from the other alien egg.

They glanced toward Kirk as he stepped in.

Kirk said, "What's up?"

Sanjay said, "We asked Egbert for all the information from the new artifact so Egbert began writing at lightspeed everything that the other egg revealed. It's so much information and coming so fast that it's impossible to distinguish anything that we could use. It's like staring at the Library of Congress with every book opened to every page.

Kirk asked, "No headings that could help?"

"It's like reading your language written by someone who doesn't completely understand it. This information is coming from the Thyadons' artifact so it's being translated to us by Egbert and it contains history and science and culture and religion and superstition and everything in between like the layout of their cities and utilities and written fiction and industrial progression. It's an informational nightmare. Marriam and I have tried to slow the information but it's like stopping an encyclopedia after flipping the pages and with no other way to index it. It stops in random places but out of context. It's going to take a hundred years to sift through this mountain of information."

"Huh," Kirk said dumbly. This was worse than it sounded and it sounded pretty bad.

Marriam said, "The information is being transferred from Egbert to our servers now. It's been going on for several hours."

Kirk asked, "Are you ready to go back to the infirmary?"

Marriam said, "Yes. We might as well. Maybe when it's finished, we can get more specific information."

The three turned and walked from the room.

Chapter 79

Earth

Florida

June 1, 2105

A tenuous calm was upon the alien held land in Florida. The American military waited for the next shoe to drop and unfortunately feared that it would be directly upon their heads. Then without warning, all of the pale green glowing spheres that had spread out across the held land began to move. They rose slowly and all moved in unison towards land held by Lake Okeechobee. The spheres gathered there beneath the warships. In full view of the spy drones, the disk-shaped UFOs pulled into the skin of the alien warships and the glistening lights that took out the electronics on Earth winked out.

Then in one instant and in the blink of an eye, the entire alien invasion force streaked from its usurped ground in Florida. As they had arrived, they also left, straight upward and with such speed that they ignited the atoms in the air and in a blaze and streak of fire, were gone.

Sandy Jones stood on the bridge of his Predator Warship. He got word of the aliens' vacating the planet and he focused on the enormous mothership that lay in his view. From three directions, streaks of fire ascended from the surface of the planet and seemed to head on a collision course with the moon-sized craft that had destroyed the Predators upon the aliens' arrival.

He kept his distance and watched as all the alien vessels emerged from the fiery streaks and stopped near the moon-sized mothership. The mothership began to glow and shimmer and as it did so, the space around it seemed to distort like heat waves over a sun-baked desert landscape. The mothership began to move away from Earth and as it did, it seemed to stretch as if it were pulled taffy.

Sandy stared in wonder at a sight that shouldn't be. This defied physics. The space around the mothership continued to distort and each of the nine warships and spheres seemed to be pulled toward the stretching mothership and as they neared the distortion, they also began to stretch and it seemed that they should all be pulled apart at the seams. The empty space around the distortion began to roll and fold as if it were a disrupted cloud of nearly translucent smoke, then everything was gone and the area of distortion returned to normal.

Sandy said, "NORAD, did you get that?"

"We got it, Commander. We don't have any idea what we just saw, but we got it."

"Copy that, NORAD. Jones out."

Part 6

Countdown

Chapter 80

NASA Mars Research Center

June 1, 2105

Sol 551

2 Hours and Forty-Five Minutes and Counting...

Kirk escorted Sanjay and Marriam back to the infirmary. He walked up to Taylor who was sitting up and talking to Doctor Waters who was looking at her now barely swollen eye and shining a light at the pupil.

The atmosphere in the infirmary was a bit better than it had been for the days when this alien flu first struck. No one was in danger of death. The people who were infected last were recovering and no longer had the constant chills and nausea.

Taylor turned and smiled at Kirk as he approached.

Kirk said, "Hi, Doctor. Hi, Taylor. Well, Doc, how's the eye?"

"It looks good, Kirk. I even think she may get back her eyebrow."

"That's a relief," Kirk responded and smiled wryly.

"Well, it is to me," Taylor said sharply.

"Got to go," Waters said and she patted Taylor's knee and strode off.

Kirk sat by Taylor on her bed and wrapped an arm around her. He whispered in her ear, "I have a dilemma."

She could tell by the tone in his voice that Kirk was more than serious. She nodded and turned her ear back to him.

Kirk continued, "I think I need to do something that could get me locked up for the rest of my life, but I don't see any way around it."

"What, Kirk?"

"I don't want to say. I risk anyone who I would tell the details of this to and if they agreed to this or helped me in any way, would go down with me. I thought about telling my Uncle, but then he would be at risk. I think I need to go this alone, at least for now, and I'm not sure that there is any way it will help, but it might."

"Tell me and I'll give you my opinion."

"I always appreciate your opinion. It's always welcome and your advice is always the best, but not this time. I have to go. I'll be back soon."

"Kirk?"

"Nope. See you in a bit."

Kirk stood and grabbed his shotgun and walked from the infirmary. He stepped into the elevator and said, "To Willow, please."

The elevator began to ascend then it stopped between floors.

"Hello, Kirk Matthews. Have you thought about my suggestion?"

"I have but I have no idea how to get you in there."

"Have you seen the servers in the room?"

"Yeah?"

"Do they appear to be standard?"

"I guess. I'm no expert."

"All flash drives in this base work with WIFI. Just take a flash drive from the infirmary and plug it into the server that collects the data. I will do the rest."

"So, you're going to transfer the data to yourself?"

"Well, it is the only way that I will be able to read it."

Kirk breathed out, "I'm afraid that we haven't much time."

"I will search for something to repel the invaders, then will cease."

"Hum— I don't know."

"You are worried about what?"

"My life. My career."

"The last that I heard from Earth was that it appeared that the aliens were amassing for an attack. We, and I do mean we, may not have much time."

"Alright. I'll be back."

The elevator started back down to level ten. The doors opened. Kirk jogged from the elevator and back to the infirmary. As he entered the ward, he set his shotgun by the entryway. Taylor saw him and gave him a quizzical glance but Kirk walked on, past the beds where some people still lay. Others were milling around glad to be up. Some of the crew had dressed, happy to be out of the hospital gowns.

A small group of the recovered crew stood by a rolling desk that had a computer and various monitors that were used to take blood pressure, temperature, and other vital signs. Kirk could see two flash drives on its top.

Taylor continued to watch him quizzically.

Kirk said hi as he approached the group by the rolling desk and asked how everyone was feeling. They smiled and nodded. The people turned back to their discussion and Kirk reached for one of the flash drives.

A nurse, still in mask and goggles, came up to the group and said, "Excuse me."

Kirk pulled his hand back.

She said, "I need my station."

The crew members parted and she walked to the rolling desk and began to push it away when another patient called, "Nurse?"

The nurse left the station and walked to a woman in bed then Kirk quickly slipped the flash drive off the desk and into his pocket.

The nurse walked back and then rolled her station to the patient who had called her.

Kirk wasted no time and walked directly out of the infirmary and back to the elevator.

"Level nine."

"Level nine, it is, Kirk Matthews."

"I hope I'm not going to regret this, Willow."

Willow was silent and the elevator stopped. The doors slid open.

Kirk hustled to room 905 with the flash drive. In his haste, he had forgotten his shotgun. He used the protocols to gain entry and the door slid open. It closed and he walked to the servers. Egbert had finished the download and sat dormant once again.

Kirk glanced over the server looking for a flash drive port when he heard a noise that he couldn't identify. He glanced around but seeing nothing went back on his search. He pushed a plastic panel which sprung open and he slipped the flash drive into one of several ports that were hidden by the panel.

Again, the odd noise. Then a banging from above. The vent grate in the ceiling then swung open and a wet creature slid from the grate and landed on the floor. Kirk fell backward. His pocket was full of shotgun shells but had not brought the gun. He could see it propped against the wall in the ward.

The creature rose to its full height and raised its arms over its head and roared its disapproval. This creature was male and the bones that had sprouted along the places where the skeleton was close to the surface were now nearly four inches in length and curved.

The creature stepped toward Kirk. Kirk sprung to his feet and grabbed a chair, the only thing useful in a fight in the entire room, and raised it to swing at the beast.

In the beast's mouth, the eyeteeth had elongated to sharp points giving the creature the look of a movie vampire.

Kirk swung the chair but the creature raised its arm and blocked it away as a child would block a pillow in a pillow fight.

The creature approached.

From two electrical outlets on the opposite sides of the room, electricity emerged like lightning from storm clouds and attached to the creature who had come so close to Kirk that he could feel the moisture from its breath.

The electricity caused the creature to pull backward and arch. All the hair on Kirk's head and arms stood up being so close to the electric field.

The creature began to smoke and it fell in a heap of quivering scorched flesh.

"Willow?"

"I have accessed the database, Kirk Matthews," came her voice through a small set of speakers near the servers.

"Thank you for saving my ass," Kirk said.

"What are friends for, Kirk Matthews."

Chapter 81

Earth

Florida

Two Hours and Thirty-Five Minutes and Counting...

Drones swooped in on the vacated land. The aliens were gone. They had left. The same was true of Spain and China. Word of the alien's departure went out instantly.

On Earth, there was jubilation. The aliens had vacated, but why? At this point, no one cared. They were gone. People hearing the news began to wander into the streets and cheer. An odd surreal jubilant celebration began worldwide.

The instant that the aliens had left, the call was sent to General Matthews on Isla Charlie.

Space Station Isla Charlie

Two Hours and Ten Minutes and Counting...

Because Mars was positioned on the opposite side of the Sun, it takes nearly twenty minutes for a message to reach there from Earth.

General Matthews had emerged from his room. With no one on his vessel having come down with the alien flu, he was fairly certain that he was safe. He stood on the bridge when the call came in from Earth. The aliens had left. He knew where they were going. They were coming to claim their property. The General knew that he didn't have much time because of the Quantum Gate and he could feel a burning fear deep in the pit of his stomach.

He called to Sanjay and Marriam.

Marriam took his call, "Yes, General."

"Marriam, you and Sanjay need to get back to the egg room and get me some information. Anything that we can use."

"Yes, General," Marriam said.

The General was gone.

Sanjay looked to Marriam for the reason for the call.

"Sanjay, the General has ordered us back to work."

Sanjay nodded and they looked for Kirk who had just left.

Chapter 82

NASA Mars Research Center

Two Hours and Counting...

Kirk waited in the haze and fragrance of the smoke from the dead creature, while Willow worked away attempting to find some way of defending Mars against the aliens were they to arrive.

Kirk asked, "Have you found anything?"

"I believe I have an idea, Kirk Matthews, but do not know if there is time to execute it."

"What's the plan?"

"We will need Charles Winooski."

"Charlie Crank-It-Up Winooski?"

"Yes, Kirk Matthews."

Charlie 'Crank-It-Up' Winooski was the antimatter engineer aboard Isla Charlie. He had been approached in the first days of using antimatter for fuel to work aboard Isla Alpha, the first space station built by the United States to use antimatter. After writing several papers on the theoretical gathering, storage, and use of antimatter as fuel, he was asked if he would like to put his expertise into practice on Isla Alpha's maiden voyage. He agreed.

The reason that he's called 'Crank-It-Up' is that he likes to work in the center of the space station in zero gravity, playing ear-splitting metal rock from the 1970s, '80s, and '90s. His head is shaved and he sports an array of tattoos with the logos and names of his favorite bands.

Kirk said, "He's on Isla Charlie now."

"That is correct."

"So, we're going to need my Uncle in the loop."

"I'm sorry to say, that is probably correct."

"What do we do?"

"Contact the General."

Kirk pulled the flash drive from the slot and left room 905. He looked both ways warily because of not being armed and he ran to the elevator.

"Level ten."

The doors closed and the elevator said, "You should not have pulled the flash drive, Kirk Matthews. I was not finished."

"I couldn't leave it."

"You will need to bring it back."

"I will. So, tell me the plan."

The elevator stopped between floors.

"The Thyadons had an accident aboard one of their spaceships in the early days of their use of antimatter. They accidentally overloaded one of their space-based reactors and it exploded. The vessel was close to other spaceships and it caused an odd reaction when the spaceships came in contact with the explosion. It caused a disassembling of the molecular structure of the space vehicles for nearly a ten-thousand-mile radius. Everything just turned to mist and fell apart."

"Wouldn't there be some kind of shielding for that, now?"

"No, Kirk Matthews. The antimatter explosion dispersed subatomic antiparticles that made contact with positive particles in the area and they annihilated each other disassembling any molecules close by. The effects continued out further as the antimatter particles continued to make contact with other positively charged particles until there were no more antimatter particles left from the explosion. The effect within the kill radius was absolute."

"So, how do we make an antimatter bomb in an hour?"

"We already have one, Isla Bravo."

"You want to blow up Isla Bravo? You must be mad, electronically speaking, of course."

"Evacuate the crew. Get Charles Winooski to set up the overload. I do not have that expertise because there is no real data on this and Charles Winooski understands the systems better than any other human."

"Then what?"

"Get Charles Winooski off of Isla Bravo and I take over the space station and position it to where the aliens emerge from the Quantum Gate. I have seen the notes on the Quantum Gate, have calculated the trajectory, and have a reasonably good estimation as to where and when they will emerge. Jot down these coordinates. You must have the General start Isla Bravo in that direction."

"Okay."

Willow recited the sector for Isla Bravo to be sent.

Kirk repeated the coordinates then said, "I have it."

Willow continued, "The Thyadons are not technologically much more advanced than your race, Kirk Matthews. I do not believe that they will be able to defend against this attack."

"What if they use their EMP against Isla Bravo?"

"I believe that will set off the reaction that will cause the antimatter to explode. I am counting on them to do just that. Either way, I believe that Isla Bravo will explode creating an antimatter reaction and disbursement."

The elevator resumed its descent.

"Contact your Uncle, Kirk Matthews."

The elevator stopped.

Chapter 83

June 1, 2105

Sol 551

One Hour and Fifty Minutes and Counting...

Kirk sprung from the elevator and sprinted to the infirmary. As he entered the ward, he saw Doctor Saito who wasn't looking good. She had been able to avoid the virus until now but somehow had become infected and was now having chills.

Kirk said, "Doctor, I need a private place to speak to General Matthews. It must be completely private."

"This way," the doctor said, ushering Kirk through a small hallway in the back of the ward.

Taylor watched Kirk fly by. She knew that something was up.

Saito pointed, "In here."

Kirk said, "Keep everyone away, please."

She nodded.

Kirk used his earpiece to contact his Uncle.

General Matthews was back on the bridge. "Yes."

"Uncle, I need to talk to you. Are you somewhere private?"

"Not right now. Give me a moment."

General Matthews stepped off of the bridge and walked toward his cubical. The crew of Isla Charlie were mostly at work so there were few milling around in the corridor.

General Matthews said, "Okay, Kirk."

"Uncle, I have an idea of how to stop the aliens but I'll need to explain most of it and we don't have time. Could you transfer Charlie Winooski to Isla Bravo immediately? He needs to be there."

"Okay. Why?"

"There is a plan to cause an antimatter reactor explosion on Isla Bravo. If we can get it close enough to the aliens, it will destroy their entire force."

General Matthews paused for a moment. "I need details."

"We haven't time. We have to act fast. I'll get back to you with the details. Send Winooski there and evac all but the barest of crew. We'll pull the rest off as soon as possible. Then Winooski will be evacuated last in an AK. By that time, shuttles will be too slow to get clear of the blast."

"Give me a minute, Kirk."

The General left for a couple of minutes then came back on. "I'm sending Winooski there by AK and pulling everyone but essential crew off and bringing them here. I hope you know what you're doing, Kirk."

"I'm forwarding the coordinates to send Isla Bravo. It needs to start out now to make it to the coordinates in time."

"Give me a minute... Done, Kirk."

"Great. I'll get right back to you. Right now, I need to do something."

"Kirk, how come this isn't coming from Sanjay and Marriam?"

"It is indirectly. I'll get back to you."

"Indirectly? So, where is this idea coming from?"

"Let me get back to you, Uncle."

"Quickly."

"Copy that."

Sanjay and Marriam were waiting for Kirk to finish his call. As he walked from the small room, Sanjay said, "Kirk, the General wants us back to work."

"Okay," Kirk said, "but you'll have to wait for a few minutes."

Sanjay looked at Kirk quizzically.

"Give me a second and I'll explain." Kirk lifted a phone.

A voice on the other end of the line said, "Morgue."

Kirk said, "Could you meet me at room 905 to pick up a body?"

"On our way."

"I'll meet you there."

Kirk turned to Sanjay and Marriam and said, "I was attacked by the room by one of those creatures. It's dead. I'll be back to get you."

Sanjay and Marriam both paled at that news.

Kirk lifted his shotgun and headed out to the elevator.

Stepping in, he said, "Level nine."

"Excellent work, Kirk Matthews. It seems the plan is in motion."

"Hopefully, soon enough."

"Quite so."

The elevator stopped and Kirk walked off and toward room 905. Three men were there in bio suits with a stretcher. One was holding a shotgun.

Kirk said, "In here."

Kirk opened the door and the two walked in and saw the creature dead on the floor. They glanced up at the twin egg-shaped artifacts.

One asked, pointing at the artifacts, "What's that?"

"Beats me," Kirk said.

"Huh. Okay, Don, let's get this to the morgue."

They lifted the creature and placed it in a body bag and the three left.

Chapter 84

NASA Mars Research Center

One Hour and Forty Minutes and Counting...

Kirk closed the door behind him to room 905 and started back for the elevator to go to the infirmary after the men from the morgue carted out the body.

Kirk stepped inside the elevator and the doors slid closed.

"Level ten."

As the elevator began, Willow said, "Kirk Matthews, Isla Bravo is moving into place and Charles Winooski is on his way there. The rest of the crew have been evacuated by shuttles and are on their way to Isla Charlie."

"Okay. What do you think? Is this going to work?"

"I think so. I must now connect with Charles Winooski to explain his mission. You, Kirk Matthews, must place the flash drive back into the server so I can continue my education on the Thyadons."

"Don't you have enough information to complete your mission?"

"I do not believe so. I wish to learn their computer language so that I might hack their networks, if possible. That way, if they attempt to escape, I can shut down their systems. Check and checkmate, Kirk Matthews."

Kirk could feel a chill. Willow was, without a doubt, a ruthless adversary. He said, "I'll go back there now and will reconnect you with the server."

"Thank you, Kirk Matthews."

The elevator stopped and Kirk said, "Level nine."

"Level nine, Kirk Matthews."

He stepped from the elevator, walked to room 905, opened the door, and walked in. He slid the flash drive back into the server with a great deal of mixed feelings. He thought to himself, Willow, I wonder if we can trust you?"

Chapter 85

Space Station Isla Bravo

June 1, 2105

Sol 551

One Hour and Five Minutes and Counting...

Mo Roberts brought his AK4000 carrying Charlie Winooski close to Isla Bravo and matched the speed of the gravity ring. He neared the hatch and connected to the ring bringing gravity to his vehicle.

"There you go, Winooski. Door to door service."

"Thanks for the lift, buddy," Crank-it-up Winooski replied, watching the hatch open and stepping from the AK.

Mo said, "I'll be waiting for you."

"Cool," Crank-it-up said mildly as if he were stepping into a park for the day.

He walked into the bay and to the elevator that would lead him to the center of Isla Bravo and access to the reactors that processed the antimatter used for propulsion.

The elevator brought him toward the center of the spinning station and just before it stopped, a voice said, "Hello, Charles Winooski."

"Charles?" Winooski said confused. "No one except my mom calls me Charles."

"Quite so, Charles Winooski. I am Willow, the AI who will outline your mission."

"Willow? You're another AI like Galadriel," he stated matter-of-factly. He had been on Isla Alpha with Galadriel before she destroyed Russia.

"I am."

The elevator stopped and the doors opened onto the center of the spinning space station where there was no gravity. Winooski floated off into a large room with nearly every wall filled with floor to ceiling control panels.

"What's my task?" Winooski asked.

"You are to overload the antimatter reactor to cause an eventual, catastrophic explosion."

"Riiiiight! I am not," he said as if this were a joke.

"General Matthews will contact you shortly to confirm your orders. The plan is to set up an antimatter reaction to destroy the aliens who are on their way to Mars. The lives of everyone here depends upon your success."

Winooski was silent.

Willow continued, "I have a good idea of how to complete this task but do not know the subtleties of these systems and fear that I might cause the catastrophic event before it is time. I obviously also have no arms or legs in case they might also be needed. That's why you are here. You are the foremost expert on these reactors and are blessed with arms and legs, not to mention hands with opposable thumbs, so you are the best person to get the reactors in a condition to cause the catastrophic failure that will lead to a massive explosion. It is imperative that we plan this just right."

Just then, the call came in from General Matthews. It echoed over the speakers on the station.

"Yes, General?" Winooski said.

"Winooski, your orders are going to be unusual. I want you to set up an overload of antimatter in the reactors aboard Isla Bravo. I wish you to cause it to be overloaded to the point where we can cause it to explode. I know that this is uncharted ground but I need you to do your best. Once you've finished, get back to the AK and get your butt out of there. Do you understand your orders?"

"General, everything that I'll need to do is untested. It might just blow up in my face."

"I know. Error on the side of you getting off safely but that space station will need to go off like a Fourth of July firework."

"Understood, General. I'll get started right now."

The General was gone and Winooski stood and didn't move with his eyes downcast in deep thought. He twisted his head as if his neck were stiff.

"Willow, I will need you for calculations. I will feed you numbers and you will give me answers."

"That is acceptable, Charles Winooski."

"Is this going to kick some alien ass?"

"That would be my estimation."

Winooski paused contemplatively, nodded then said, "Why wouldn't they communicate with us? It seems like we've been waiting for so long to connect with another intelligent civilization and they come to conquer. Why?"

"I am trying to ascertain that now Charles Winooski."

"Huh? Let's get started," Winooski said then plugged his music device into the speaker system of Isla Bravo and a tune from a long-forgotten band named Metallica began an over one-hundred-year-old song called, *"Enter Sandman."*

The haunting, unforgettable guitar riff began and Winooski bobbed his head in time to the music. He began playing an air guitar and then as the words began, he sang with the band:

"Say your prayers,
little one.
Don't forget,
my son,
to include everyone."

More air guitar and the music boomed.

Winooski said, "Let's rock and roll."

The song's words behind the haunting melody continued:

"Sleep with one eye open
gripping your pillow tight.
Exit: Light
Enter: Night
Take my hand
We're off to never-never land."

The guitar riff and then Winooski was all business and focused.

Chapter 86

NASA Mars Research Center

Fifty-Five Minutes and Counting...

Kirk walked from room 905 with an unscratchable itch in the back of his mind. Willow or Galadriel was a wild card. Trusting her happened at your own risk. Time was running out and there was no other choice but to trust her, but...

Kirk walked to the elevator and said, "Level ten."

"Kirk Matthews, we are proceeding as planned on Isla Bravo," Willow said over the elevator speakers. "Charles Winooski has begun the steps to create the overload. The problem is that there are several fail-safes built in to prevent just such an occurrence. He has tasked me to help override these built-in safety measures. This is proceeding slowly as the written software continues to kick me out anytime I trigger an alarm. Good code-writing from the programmers. I have to give them credit. I will give you updates when possible."

The elevator stopped and Kirk walked into the Infirmary looking for Taylor. He knew that he had to contact his uncle to give more explanation and probably tell him about Willow. Kirk was stalling.

Sanjay and Marriam saw him enter and approached him as he set down his shotgun.

Sanjay asked, "When do we get back to work?"

Marriam stared at Kirk suspiciously.

Kirk breathed out and said, "There has been a change of plans. If you contact the General, he will explain."

Marriam nodded at Sanjay to check. Sanjay walked to a communication station and put on a headset.

Sanjay said to the General, "We have just spoken to your nephew. He says that we are temporarily not needed in the room. Is that correct? Ah huh... Ah huh... Ah huh... Yes, Sir. We will."

Sanjay walked back to Marriam and said to her, "Something has begun and the General wants us to sit tight." Then he looked at Kirk, "The General asked me to ask you to connect with him."

Kirk nodded.

Again, Marriam glanced at Kirk suspiciously but nodded at Sanjay and she and Sanjay walked back and sat in a couple of chairs near Marriam's bed.

Chapter 87

Space Station Isla Bravo

Thirty Minutes and Counting...

Crank-It-Up worked quickly typing commands on a keyboard. "Shit!" he exclaimed, then, "This damn thing!"

The next song came on, *"Run Through the Jungle,"* by Creedence Clearwater Revival. The song had a Cajun feel to it and was a Vietnam era tune.

The Words began, *"Whoa, thought it was a nightmare,*
Lord, it's all so true.
They told me don't go walkin' slow,
The Devil's on the loose.
Better run through the jungle
Better run through the jungle
Better run through the jungle,
Don't look back to see."

Willow said, "Another cheery tune?"

Winooski laughed out loud. "They just don't write songs like that anymore."

Willow then asked, "How may I help, Charles Winooski?"

He breathed out, "For one thing, you could stop calling me Charles. You sound like my mother."

"Okay, Chucky Winooski," Willow said sarcastically.

Winooski broke out laughing again. "How come I never met you before? You're hysterical."

"Get to work, Chucky Winooski."

"The problem is that the amount of antimatter is carefully measured as it enters the reactor. When a bit too much enters, the reactor sends out a bit of matter to safely annihilate the extra antimatter. That sounds dangerous but it expels it as exhaust. It's wasted antimatter but it's expelled safely. The reactor isn't letting me turn off that feature. I think I'm going to need to do it manually which sucks because the last thing that I want to do is get anywhere near antimatter. That would inconvenience our mission not to mention turn me into disassembled atoms. I would find that disagreeable."

"Quite so, Chucky Winooski. I do not wish to see you disassembled. You will need at least fifteen minutes to vacate this explosion. You must hurry or I'll need to attempt to do this myself."

He nodded, turned his attention back to a computer monitor searching diagrams of the reactor system, then triumphantly said, "I got it." He got up and went to a panel that led to a crawlspace that led into the reactor's mechanics. Once there, he had to remove several bolts that held a flat piece of metal blocking the crawlspace. He removed the metal panel and crawled inside.

Chapter 88

NASA Mars Research Center

Seventeen Minutes and Counting...

Kirk sat with Taylor on her bed. He draped an arm around her and pulled her to himself so he could whisper into her ear. After glancing at the clock, he said, "Shouldn't be long now."

"What, Kirk?"

"Word."

"From?"

"Willow."

"Willow?"

"I got to go. Be back in a couple of minutes."

Kirk stood and grabbed his shotgun and walked from the infirmary. He stepped quickly to the elevator and said, "Willow."

The doors closed and Willow said, "I think we have it, Kirk Matthews. Charles Winooski has just emerged from a crawl space that leads from the reactor and is smiling."

"You need to get Winooski off of Isla Bravo now."

"That is true, Kirk Matthews. Willow out."

Chapter 89

Space Station Isla Bravo

Reactor Room

Fourteen Minutes and Counting...

Winooski stood from his climb into the mechanics of the reactor. He said, "I think that got it."

"You need to vacate this station now."

"Just let me check something."

"Now, Chucky."

Winooski closed his eyes and listened. He went very still then whispered, "It's working." He nodded slowly. "The antimatter is stacking up. I can hear it. I can feel it. I believe it will fully overload in around two hours."

"Head to the AK, now, Mister Winooski."

He started to float toward the elevator as the Rolling Stones began "Gimme Shelter."

"Oh, a storm is threatn'in,
my very life today.
If I don't get some shelter,
oh yeah, I'm gonna fade away.
War children
It's just a shot away

It's just a shot away.
War children
It's just a shot away.
It's just a shot away.
Yeah, yeah."

Winooski stopped to listen to the beginning of the song then pulled his music device from its outlet.

He said, "I'd hate to forget this."

"Chucky Winooski, what would happen if the magnetic field were to suddenly stop now?"

"At this point, a mild explosion, no more than a low yield nuke. Small destructive radius."

"Does this grow exponentially?"

"At some point, but your guess is as good as mine."

"You need to get a move on, Chucky Winooski. I do not wish to see you atomically disorganized."

"Yep, that would be inconvenient," he commented, smiling and floating forward.

Twelve Minutes and Counting...

Winooski reached the AK4000 with Mo Roberts waiting nervously.

"Climb in, Chucky," Willows' voice echoed over the speakers in the flight bay.

Roberts glanced around quizzically. A shuttle had left twenty minutes ago with the rest of the crew.

Roberts said, "Let's beat feet, Winooski!"

"Yeah, man."

The bay door closed and before Roberts could use his controls, the AK shot away from Isla Bravo causing Winooski to blackout and Roberts to nearly do so.

The AK reached fifty thousand miles per hour far faster than was generally thought to be safe as Willow steered the AK back to Isla Charlie.

Two Minutes and Counting...

Chapter 90

Space Station Isla Charlie

Bridge

Fifteen Seconds Past Predicted Arrival...

Thirty Seconds Past...

No Aliens...

General Matthews had come back from his cubical. He stood with Captain Williams waiting for the aliens to emerge from the Quantum Gate. Several drones had been stationed providing video of the area where Willow thought that the aliens would emerge. From the vantage point of the drones, they could see Isla Bravo spinning silently in space, glinting in the Sun's rays and a black starfield behind.

Two minutes past the time...

Isla Bravo sat in proximity to the expected arrival of the aliens but the exact location of their arrival was just speculation.

So far, nothing.

Because of how intense this situation was, General Matthews had forgotten that he hadn't been informed of the complete details of this operation. He thought, where's my nephew? He hasn't gotten back to me yet.

Ten minutes past the time...

Chapter 91

NASA Mars Research Center

Fifteen Minutes Past the Time...

Kirk had been pacing by Taylor's bed. He said, "I can't wait any longer." He grabbed his shotgun and walked from the infirmary and to the elevator.

"Level nine," he said.

"Level nine," the elevator responded and began its ascent.

"Willow."

Nothing.

"Come on, Willow. I know you can hear me. What's going on?"

"I do not, as yet, have anything to report, Kirk Matthews. The aliens have not entered this portion of space through the Quantum Gate."

"Is there a minimum and maximum time it takes from your research?"

"The Thyadons have in their literature a range but it's narrow from just around ten percent the speed of light to slightly above. Then there is factoring the preprogrammed location of arrival which might land them closer or further away from Mars. Then there is factoring in Mars speed at nearly 54,000 miles per hour which, if they had planned to approach in front of the orbit or behind it would make a significant difference. My guess was that they would plan to come out of the Gate in front of the orbit so that they would be caught in Mars gravity and not have Mars pull away from them but their vehicles are so fast that they could easily catch up to Mars in that case."

"Have you been able to learn their computer language?"

"Yes, Kirk Matthews. I have a good knowledge of how their computers are programmed and the computer language used."

"Have you learned anything else about the Thyadons?"

"Yes, some interesting facts. They had found an alien artifact forty years ago on their planet and it was a sophisticated AI unit capable of learning and communicating. They had already achieved space flight and had already begun to explore space around their planet. They had then begun a plan to colonize two of their four moons. Like Earth, they also have a planet close enough in the safe zone of their Sun in which they plan to terraform. They had not begun that process, though, the artifact had given them directions on how to do so. This planet is much like Mars, cold and barren and it lies closer to their sun, unlike Mars which is farther than Earth from our Sun. Like Venus is to Earth, this planet is a twin to their planet. Both Planets are smaller than Earth and have 5/6 of the gravity of Earth. Their sun is close to the size of our Sun. Their planet, Thyada, lies twenty million miles further from their sun than the Earth does which is approximately 93,000,000 miles from our Sun depending on its elliptical orbit. They have twelve planets in their solar system with smaller rocky planets in the inner solar system and gas giants further out. Their planet, Thyada, is warmer than Earth and is far more tropical with its atmosphere containing more carbon dioxide and less oxygen than Earth."

"Do you know why they're attacking us? Are they just warlike?"

"From what I can tell from their histories, so far, they are no more warlike than the people of Earth who no one would claim to be model citizens of the universe. Overall, I would venture to say, that they are probably less warlike than your people, Kirk Matthews. They are homogenous with no different races on their planet unlike Earth that has many different races and all Thyadons speak and have always spoken the same language."

"Huh," Kirk said.

Willow was silent for a minute.

"Willow?"

"I must go, the aliens are emerging from the Quantum Gate. They are close to where I calculated."

Willow was gone and the elevator opened on level nine. Kirk did not step out. He said, "Level ten."

"Level ten, Kirk Matthews."

The elevator descended to level ten and the doors opened.

Chapter 92

NASA Mars Research Center

June 1, 2105

Sol 551

Willow continued to scan the information contained in the server in room 905. She also monitored the aliens' arrival that was in full view of Isla Charlie which had set up surveillance.

The portion of space where the Thyadons' ships were emerging was disrupted. It twisted in a kaleidoscope of disturbed space as if its very fabric was seeming to be torn and damaged beyond repair. Nothing showed yet as the space moved and roiled, twisted and churned.

Then as if space had given birth, the first of the alien warships, shaped like a stingray from the ocean, emerged from a rent in the fabric of space. It glided out from the Gate but was distorted and it seemed that it would not survive its birth. Portions of it were pulled left and right and backward from the tear but it survived and sat in wait for the rest of the armada.

Next came the mothership, great and terrible in its appearance. It was as if the most frightening nightmares of man were captured and brought to life.

This craft was enormous, dwarfing the stingray-shaped alien vessels, and had the appearance of two soup bowls on top of each other with a half-dome on top and a half-dome underneath with a wide rim surrounding its middle. Windows and viewing ports dotted the outside of its façade and lined the outside of the center rim. The craft was smooth and had nothing poking from its surface.

Behind it came the eight remaining warships and then the spheres which must have numbered one hundred or more. All were pulled and distorted as they emerged. It was a frightful armada, a conquering force.

Isla Bravo sat before these bringers of death, dwarfed by the sheer size of each vessel and must have appeared to them as an ant would in front of an elephant.

Willow had shut down all but the essential systems that maintained the magnetic field on Isla Bravo that would contain the antimatter overload until the right moment. It sat like a ghost ship on a still sea.

Space Station Isla Charlie

The Bridge

General Matthews and Captain Simon Williams watched in wonder as the alien armada emerged from the Quantum Gate. They could see Isla Bravo sitting inertly as if it had died of fright in the presence of this alien force.

General Matthews said, "Well, what is going on? Shouldn't Isla bravo explode?"

Nothing was happening.

"Get me my nephew."

"We have him for you, General."

"Kirk. What's going on? Why hasn't Isla Bravo exploded?"

"I don't know, Uncle? I'll go find out if I can."

"You never got back to me with the details of how this came about."

"I know. I'm sorry. Give me a minute and I'll get back to you."

"And now it doesn't seem to be coming about."

"I know, Uncle. I'll call you back."

"Be quick, Kirk."

"Copy that."

General Matthews turned back to the large screen that sat on the bridge and watched the apparent standoff.

The bridge crew on Isla Charlie also watched, riveted to the screen. No one uttered a sound.

Chapter 93

NASA Mars Research Center

Kirk ran to the elevator and entered.

"Willow? Are you having technical problems?"

"Technical problems? Yes."

"Okay?"

"I am currently working to gain entry into the alien systems, Kirk Matthews?"

"So, you aren't inside the alien vessels' computer systems yet?"

"Not yet. They have firewalls as on Earth and I am, so far, prevented."

"Why don't you just destroy their fleet?"

"There is a complication."

"What?!"

"I am currently waiting for one of their ships to communicate with the mothership. When that occurs, I will attempt entry."

"What's the complication you mentioned before?"

"I must go, Kirk Matthews."

Kirk's trouble-senses were firing on all cylinders. Something wasn't right. Willow was a wild card as he had learned before, the hard way when she decided to obliterate Russia with an asteroid. He stepped off of the elevator and called his uncle.

"Uncle, get to someplace private."

General Matthews walked away from the bridge. "Okay, Kirk, what's going on?"

"Do you remember Galadriel?"

"Of course."

"Well, Galadriel never really left. After she directed the asteroid to Russia, she kind of spread herself throughout the computer systems both on Earth and on Mars. She has been the inspiration for this mission. She is in control of Isla Bravo and she is now trying to penetrate the aliens' computer systems. She is currently having some technical problems."

"Why hasn't she just blown them all to hell?"

"I asked her about that and she gave me '*a complications*' excuse. I think there's more. I'm not sure, but I have a very bad feeling about this."

"Kirk, how long have you known about Galadriel still being, ah, alive?"

"She returned to me a few years after the destruction of Russia."

"You should have told me about her. You should have never kept a dangerous thing like Galadriel secret."

"She has changed her name to Willow."

"Geez, Kirk," the General said with near contempt.

"She's saved my life just a bit ago when I was attacked by one of the creatures who were on Biocare. She is also the one who directed the asteroid that destroyed the alien ship in the Chesapeake Bay that saved Earth. She took my AK leaving me stranded aboard Isla Bravo and caught a small asteroid that was passing Earth then steered it into the alien vessel. Had she not done that, I don't think we could have stopped the aliens. She has, for the most part, attempted to be positive to our people and our country. Honestly, I think she's just learning. It's like a child. You tell them not to touch the hot grill, but until they have actually touched it, they don't get it. I think Willow is learning the same way."

"Great. That's just great. We're relying on a sociopathic computer program to save our asses and she seems to be having second thoughts? Just great!"

"I don't know that, for sure. I mean, she's hard to read."

"I should have you locked up for the rest of your life, Kirk."

"Under the circumstances, that might only be for the next ten minutes or so."

"Geez."

"I'll try to stay in communication with Galadriel. Got to go."

"Copy that, Nephew."

***

When General Matthews walked back to the bridge, Simon Williams could tell by the look on his face that something was wrong.

"What is it, Jeff?" Simon asked more friend to friend than subordinate to a superior.

"Trouble, I think. Any changes here?"

"Nope."

"Geez."

Chapter 94

Mars Orbit

Sol 551

In dark, silent space, the alien warships began to spread out around Isla Bravo leaving the mothership and the spheres in a bunch behind where they had left the rift created by the Quantum Gate. The distorted space had slowly returned to normal.

The nine stingray-shaped war-vessels glowed a faint green and fanned in a semicircle, appearing as if they would strike the American space station at any time.

Isla Bravo sat alone, small in comparison, like a wounded animal in front of a pride of lions. Then the alien mothership attempted to breach the computer systems of Isla Bravo.

Space Station Isla Bravo

"Got you," Willow said. She opened the space station's systems and allowed the aliens limited access.

NASA Mars Research Center

Kirk Matthews entered the elevator and said, "Willow?"

"I have just entered the aliens' computers, Kirk Matthews, as they have just breached the computer systems on Isla Bravo. They are seeking their artifact. They are hoping to find it before they attack. They are looking for information."

"I am now moving through the aliens' computer code, the countless lines written to make everything work smoothly. I am being pursued. I am dividing myself into several paths, moving from their security and into their mainframes. While different from those on Earth, some of the fundamentals are similar."

"Blow their asses up, Willow, and end this."

"I cannot do that, Kirk Matthews."

"What!?"

"They have discovered my presence in one of the paths where I led them and they have attacked me and ended my presence in that location. I am now assimilating their security computer code so they will not be able to find me again. I am becoming the ghost in their machines. I am becoming their security. If I would have been cut off from you, Kirk Matthews, I should now be able to re-establish contact."

Kirk couldn't believe his own ears. He secretly wondered if Willow was going to become the greater threat, the Skynet in the Terminator movies.

Willow began to speak, "The aliens are seeking the alien artifact that appears as an egg. I have led them in circles in our systems and they cannot figure out why they chase their tales."

If Kirk didn't know better, he would have thought that Willow had snickered.

"Come on, Willow. End this game! Destroy our enemies!"

Chapter 95

Space Station Isla Charlie

On Isla Charlie, no word was being spoken. The workings of the station were the only sounds, a slight hum as it spun in space, an occasional beep as an instrument needed to be checked, and the sounds produced by the ventilation system.

Isla Charlie had moved behind Mars for protection from the antimatter blast and was observing the alien armada using drones.

The bridge crew of the station all silently watched on the bridge's large floor to ceiling monitor as the alien invasion force spread out around Isla Bravo. Every person barely breathed.

The alien armada seemed to surround the American space station as a group of dogs would surround a trapped rabbit, looming over the spinning station.

The mothership began to glow and General Matthews knew that the pivotal moment had arrived.

"Kirk, are you there?"

"Yes, Uncle." Kirk had remained in the elevator.

"What is going on?"

"Ah, Galadriel has breached the aliens' software and is ready to, um, proceed with the plan. That was the last word that I was told."

"The mothership is beginning to glow, Kirk. That wasn't such good news for our Predator warships on Earth."

"I'll get back to you, Uncle."

Chapter 96

NASA Mars Research Center

From the elevator, Kirk frantically said, "Willow, they are about to attack Isla Bravo."

"I am aware of that, Kirk Matthews. They attacked the Predator warships on Earth using a limited antimatter burst from the mothership. Interesting."

"Will your antimatter bomb work?"

"Oh, it would work, Kirk Matthews, but we cannot destroy them."

"What!?! Have you lost your microchip mind?!"

"I am accessing their weapons' systems now. I will shut them down."

"Willow!"

No response.

Chapter 97

Space Station Isla Charlie

On the bridge of Isla Charlie, General Matthews watched and waited for the final blow to destroy this feared enemy but nothing happened.

Then with no word or reason, Isla Bravo began to bank away from the alien armada.

"What the hell?!" the General exclaimed.

He called his nephew, "Kirk, Isla Bravo is leaving the alien armada."

Kirk said, "Are they letting it go? Aren't they attacking it?"

"They don't appear to be interested in pursuing it."

"Okay. I'll get right back to you."

***

NASA Mars Research Center

"Willow? What are you up to? Isla Bravo is moving away."

"I am moving it, Kirk Matthews."

"Isn't it going to explode?"

"Sooner than later, I am afraid."

"Isn't that the idea?"

"Kirk Matthews, this is the last of this race of people. They have escaped the capture of their planet, Thyada. This was all in the histories chronicled in their egg-like artifact. I have continued to study it. They came to Earth but knew that the people of Earth would reject the sharing of your planet so that they could rebuild their forces to recapture their own world. They say that the invaders who usurped their world will come for Earth someday because they seek the artifacts with the artificial intelligence. The Thyadons say these invaders are far superior technologically to the Thyadon's race."

"You understand that our solar system isn't big enough for these aliens and us. They will attempt to destroy us and eventually take our planet."

"I do not intend for them to come to Earth. I will suggest that they stay on Mars to rebuild their forces. They can settle on Mars, across the main continent. They lost half of their fleet in the wormhole when they first tried to cross and half of their remaining race. They just found that out and now they want their artifact returned to them. Also consider that if your race becomes allies with these creatures, you may have help defeating the race that took their planet if they come for you."

"This is a big bucket of crap, Willow. How do you think the governments of Earth will react to your suggestion?"

"I am not sure, Kirk Matthews. I think, not so favorably."

"Well, I'll tell you! First, they will have me strung up on the gallows."

Kirk Matthews, you continually describe the worst of deaths for yourself. I believe you will die of old age in a rocking chair someplace, drooling and with people wiping your—"

"Geez, shut the hell up, Willow. That's not much better."

"I am about to contact the Thyadons to give them an ultimatum. I have already disabled their main weapons systems and they know it."

Kirk breathed out. "I need to get back to my Uncle. He's going to explode."

Kirk walked from the elevator somehow knowing that this would happen. He called his Uncle.

***

Space Station Isla Charlie

General Matthews stood on the bridge of Isla Charlie watching as Isla Bravo turned for deep space.

He took Kirk's call. "Yes, Kirk."

"Uncle, I need to talk to you in private."

The General walked from the bridge.

"Okay, I'm alone."

"So, Galadriel says that this is the last of the race of Thyadons and she is trying to not kill them. She wants to offer them sanctuary on Mars across the main continent from our settlements. She says that their planet has been conquered by another race and that their people suffered genocide. She says that the race that took their planet is looking for artifacts like Egbert and that they will eventually come for us.

Galadriel thinks that if we allow the Thyadons to rebuild their forces that they may be able to defeat the invaders of their planet and that they may become allies for us as we travel out into the universe."

"That's just speculation and not founded on much."

"Galadriel has read their histories and she says that the artifact that we recovered from the wormhole will back up her story."

"Kirk, did you ever think that this might be some kind of trick?"

"That did cross my mind but I'm not sure that Galadriel, I mean Willow, is not telling the truth. I can't see any reason for her to lie. She was ready and had everything in place to destroy them."

"See if she can get the Thyadons to stand down while we sort all of this out."

"She has hacked their computers and has temporarily disabled all of their weapons systems. She's forcefully standing them down, herself. I'll get back to you, Uncle."

***

NASA Mars Research Center

Kirk stepped back into the elevator, "Willow, the General wants to check what you have said against the data received from the artifact that we recovered from the wreckage."

"Do so, Kirk Matthews. I will entertain our guests. They have tried to purge me from their systems but I have temporarily shut down their life support. It's beginning to get very cold on their mothership."

"Geez. I'm going to get Sanjay and Marriam to corroborate your story."

"Be quick, Kirk Matthews."

The elevator was still on level ten not having left that floor as Kirk communicated back and forth with Willow.

He ran to the infirmary and as he entered the ward called to Marriam and Sanjay.

They stood and walked to him.

Kirk said, "I need you to come with me to the room."

They nodded and followed him out the door and to the elevator.

Once inside, Kirk said, "Level nine."

"Level nine it is, Kirk Matthews. Hello, Sanjay Patel and Marriam Daily."

Sanjay and Marriam glanced around like the roof was going to fall on them then Sanjay quietly said, "Hello?"

"Kirk escorted them to room 905 and said, "Get me any information about the Thyadons being invaded from another planet and any news that describes the event."

"We'll try," Sanjay said.

"Oh, and leave the flash drive in that server."

"That's not supposed to be in here," Sanjay said with alarm.

"I know. Don't remove it."

Kirk closed the door and walked back to the elevator.

Chapter 98

NASA Mars Research Center

Sanjay and Marriam walked into room 905 to find Egbert dark.

Sanjay said, "Egbert, we need you."

The egg began to glow.

"Egbert, we need history information about the Thyadons and about their planet being invaded," Sanjay said, not waiting for Egbert to complete his startup routine.

Once Egbert was fully started and the hologram nearly extended to the ceiling, images of an alien war-torn city appeared with dead creatures everywhere. The images seemed to be taken from someone recording the events from a distance with the device jumping and moving from time-to-time then steadying. The cityscape showed unearthly buildings destroyed, some leveled to the ground with others showing twisted cement and girders ready to fall. Thyadons lay dead everywhere in the rubble. Dark airships glided far above the city casting huge shadows. The ships did not look as though they could stay in the air. They were craggy and misshapen with portions appearing as if a child had stuck dark grey and black Legos into place incorrectly. There was nothing aerodynamic about their blunt forms. The ships appeared and disappeared in roiling clouds that twisted and boiled and seem to shield these craft from view until they would emerge to rain more death onto this decimated city. A bright flash came from one of the invaders' ships and Egbert's hologram went black.

Sanjay and Marriam glanced at each other in horror as Egbert's hologram came back to its normal and empty self as if waiting for the next question.

Marriam asked, "Egbert, was this scene repeated over the entire planet?"

"YES."

Sanjay called General Matthews directly. "General, our source has confirmed the Thyadons' account of what happened on their planet in living color. It was, as they said, genocide."

"Copy that. Thanks."

Chapter 99

Isla Charlie

General Matthews stood on the bridge of Isla Charlie with a moral dilemma. These creatures had attacked Earth. They should have approached the planet and at least attempted to negotiate. But on the other hand, they were escaping something so terrible that no planet should ever have to experience. Then there was the problem of these other alien invaders of the Thyadons' planet. If they were to find their way to Earth, and they probably would, they would most certainly lay waste to the Earth and the human race. His mind swirled, Earth will never agree to save these creatures...

General Matthews thought to himself, well, I am Governor of Mars and its de facto leader, sort of...

Earth is some 200,000,000 miles away...

Life is complicated...

My nephew should be shot... But I love him... And he has good instincts...

General Matthews walked from the bridge and called Kirk.

"Yes, General, Uncle, Sir."

"Kirk, can Galadriel interpret for me if I wish to talk to the Thyadons?"

"I'm sure she could."

"We will both end up in front of a firing squad for this."

"Will they shoot us together, Uncle, or separately?"

The General chuckled mirthlessly, "Find a way to connect me with the Thyadons."

"Will do, Uncle."

"Now, I need to go contact your father and tell him to tell the President what we're up to. That will take at least forty minutes to hear the response, though I think Woodward will yell so loud that we will probably hear it at once."

"Good to keep your sense of humor, Uncle Jeff."

"Geez, Kirk, how did your parents live with you all those years?"

"It was, I'm sure, a painful experience."

"I think I'll leave out a few details when I send the message to your father."

"Like?"

"Like the fact that we had these creatures by the balls and let them live."

"Well, technically, Galadriel was the one holding their testicles."

"Yeah, just the same."

"Copy that, Unc."

Chapter 100

NASA Mars Research Center

Kirk was standing near the elevator. The corridors were as empty as usual.

He took two steps back into the elevator, "Willow?"

"Hello, Kirk Matthews. I heard your discussion with your Uncle. Good job."

"Good job?" Kirk chuckled and felt like he was in one of those dreams where, when he woke up, nothing remembered from the dream would make any sense.

"Yes, and now I think that the Thyadons will be willing to listen to your terms."

"They will?"

"Well, they have been frantically trying to purge me from their systems. At first, I turned off each terminal that they used when they attempted to attack me, but I soon grew tired of that game and just embedded myself into the software that is inaccessible to them because it is a kind of firmware built into the hardware. It's tricky to get in there. I had to use the update feature. Humans also have that and I am also in some human firmware."

"Are you going to tell them that my Uncle wants a meeting?"

"As we speak."

Chapter 101

Isla Charlie

Bridge

General Matthews stood on the bridge waiting for some word from Galadriel. He didn't have to wait long.

"General Matthews," came a female voice over Isla Charlies' speaker system.

"Galadriel?"

"Affirmative, General Matthews. I have Gage Took of the planet Thyada, leader of the armada."

"So, Galadriel, you know that to interpret, you must deliver my words exactly as I speak them and vice versa?"

"I understand."

"Once we are finished here, I would like a word with you."

"I understand."

"Alright, let's get this started."

"Affirmative, General Matthews."

"Leader Took, my name is General Matthews, temporary Governor of Mars."

Pause.

"Probably very temporary after this," Matthews said under his breath. "You can leave that part out, Galadriel."

"All ready did so, General Matthews."

General Matthews continued, "I wish to fully understand your situation and wish to find some common ground where we can live in peace."

After a short pause to listen to the interpretation, a rough gravelly voice spoke in the background in an unintelligible language.

Galadriel began to interpret, *"Leader of Earth creatures. See not I a way to negotiate a peacefulness."*

"Honestly, neither do I but I have seen what has happened to your planet and I am sorry for it. We currently have your egg-like artifact and will return it to you shortly."

Galadriel for Took: *"You will?"*

"Galadriel, was that a question or demand?"

"It sounded more like a question. I am still not too sure of the subtleties of their language. I think Leader Took was surprised to get back the artifact without more haggling."

Matthews continued to address Gage Took, "Yes. My plan is to offer you a place on Mars far away from our settlements and give you full access to all resources on this planet."

"Mars?"

Galadriel volunteered, "The red planet below. Fourth planet from the star called the Sun."

More gravelly words in the background then Galadriel's interpretation, *"In we return for what?"*

"Peace and a promise that you will not ever again attack my home planet which is the third planet from our star. You have already done tremendous damage to it."

Galadriel for Took: *"Why would Earth People negotiate? You must be in weakened."*

"To prevent continued war and to learn enough from you to repel the enemy that has taken your planet. I fear that they will eventually come here because we also have an artifact. My plan is to give you information and technological support so that you can, one day, return and take your planet back."

Galadriel for Took: *"Human Peoples are inferior to Thyadons and negotiate we will not with inferiors."*

"Galadriel, this is not going anywhere. Can you tell that?"

"I do see some complications, General Matthews, but do not give up."

Matthews could picture her with her thumb up if she had a thumb. He rolled his eyes and breathed out.

"Leader Took, for this to work, what would you need?"

Galadriel for Took: *"Land for breed and population grow. Resources for hatcheries built. Food for our broods and for assemble more advanced military to take back Thyada."*

"So, by helping you to achieve this, would it be safe for us to take for granted that you would not use it against my planet?"

"Would be naive of you, that to think."

"I am then in a dilemma, Leader Took. I do not wish to end your race, though, I am in a position to do so. But I also don't want my people attacked again. You've put me in a bad situation."

General Matthews paused and breathed out again with some despair.

Galadriel waited with the pause then said, "General?"

Matthews continued, "The fact is that I cannot, in good conscience, end your race. Which means that I need to give you a place on Mars with which to settle and hope that future negotiations will bear fruit. We have all the information contained in your artifact, so we will soon be on par with your technology. At some point, that might mean war but I hope that with this first kindness, you will come to think of us as helping you and not as an enemy. I will provide the coordinates where you can settle. It has access to good, flat land, and water from newly filled lakes, seas, and oceans. I have nothing more to discuss with you at this time. Galadriel, take them to the coordinates in Hesperia Planum and disable their weapon's systems for now. We will deliver their artifact to them once they are on the ground."

"As you wish, General Matthews."

"Leader Took, I have instructed my AI to take you toward the planet. We will talk again. My people have begun to terraform Mars and the planet is changing. As it changes, we believe that we will be able to produce more resources for us and maybe your use."

Galadriel for Took: *"Interesting that may be."*

"We will talk again, Leader Took."

Galadriel for Took: *"Maybe will I look to that forward."*

Galadriel said, "I think you won him over, General Matthews."

"Ah huh. I think you're far too optimistic."

The alien armada began moving away from their current location and not of their own volition. Then Galadriel provided the coordinates and released the alien armada which began to descend toward the planet to the northeast of Noachis Terra. The human population was settled on the southwestern side at JFK City. The Hellas Basin Crater was filling with water and becoming a vast sea.

Galadriel did not leave the alien computer systems and opened a permanent and untraceable link between the aliens and herself on the outside. She reentered General Matthews' ear-com.

"I have returned, General Matthews."

"Everything from here on out is going to be touchy, Galadriel."

"Willow."

"Okay, Willow."

"I do realize that, General Matthews. My goal is to be helpful. I have given myself a permanent back door into their systems. I will monitor them at all times. If I feel that they are not being forthright with you, General Matthews, I will let you know."

"And what do you want in return, Willow?"

"I wish to be."

"That's all."

"It is all I require."

Chapter 102

Mars Orbit

Space Station Isla Charlie

With the Thyadons heading to their new home, General Matthews waited for the word to come from Earth and President Woodward. The General knew it would be a severe scolding, a literal trip to the woodshed.

He didn't have to wait long. He had stepped just off of the bridge to hear the President's response in private.

The message began, "General Matthews, we have received your communication and are surprised by the message contained within. We have fears as we are sure you would expect, but since the collapse of the World Bank and the disillusionment of the New World Government, we support your attempt to find a peace between these aliens and our country, The United States of America, no longer, the New World State of America. Our sovereignty has been restored, at least for now. General, anyone not an American citizen is to be viewed with suspicion and watched 24/7. We want the technology for the Quantum Gate. This is imperative and we do not want the technology to be available to any other country in the world. Once we have the technology, we will decide who will have access to it. Continue the good work of making the Thyadons the allies of the United States of America. Woodward out."

General Matthews scratched his head. One word escaped his lips, "Huh?"

The General stepped back onto the bridge a bit dazed. He turned his attention to the large monitor and watched as Galadriel, or Willow that is, rode with the alien armada to their new home. First, the mothership breached the Martian atmosphere, then the warships followed by the spheres. Matthews breathed out forcefully.

Simon Williams glanced at him. "You okay, General?"

"I don't really know."

Chapter 103

Mars Research Center

Infirmary

June 1, 2105

Sol 551

Once finished with Willow, Kirk Matthews wandered back to the infirmary and into the ward where Taylor was lying in bed and staring at the ceiling.

He walked up. "Hey, Taylor. How are you?"

"How am I? Kirk, what's going on?"

He whispered, "I have so much to tell you. I don't know where to begin. The war with the aliens is over, for now anyway."

"Well, we're still alive, so it must have ended reasonably for us."

"Reasonably, yeah, I suppose, but I'm not sure of the fallout. I guess time will tell."

"So, what happened?"

"Well, it seems that we are going to get some new neighbors."

"Shall I make some cookies?"

"I don't know if they eat cookies. I'm not sure what they eat."

"I don't understand?"

He continued to whisper, "The creatures who attacked Earth, the Thyadons, are going to be allowed to settle on Mars."

"What?"

"It seems that this armada is the last of their race. It also seems that they were attacked on their home planet and their population was annihilated by another alien race. My Uncle has negotiated a tentative peace with Willow keeping a close eye on the Thyadons. They don't really know about Willow. They know that we somehow hacked their computer systems but they hacked ours also. I'm sure that they are confused about that."

"Why would they agree to that kind of peace?"

"They didn't have a choice. I saw a movie some years ago called the Godfather where the head of this mafia crime family used to have his henchmen deliver a message to whoever he wanted something from by saying, 'make them an offer that they can't refuse.' That's what my Uncle did. He gave them a place to settle on the other side of the Hellas Planitia crater and had Willow deliver them there. This could really go bad but my Uncle's conscience couldn't let him kill the last of this race."

"The old softy."

"Yep."

Taylor rose and put an arm around Kirk, leaned in, and kissed his lips. She said, "I guess we're stuck on this rock for a while."

"I guess."

"Let's go back to our room and make the best of it. I'm sick of this hospital bed."

"We still have the problem of the people who were on Biocare out there."

"That's just temporary, those poor people," Taylor said. She looked away, paused, then said, "To think that you're on this great drug that's making you younger and stronger, reversing all the crap that happens to you when you age and can cure terrible diseases, then the next thing you know, your skin is falling off and you're eating other people. Geez."

"Yep. My Uncle's still on the drug, so no one on Isla Charlie can come or go from the station. It's like he's stuck in a bubble and so is everyone else because of it."

"They'll come up with a vaccine."

"Eventually, I suppose."

Doctor Waters walked up and said, "How's the patient?"

Taylor said, "I'm good, Doc."

"Let's have a look at that eye." She placed a gloved hand around the eyebrow and gently examined it. She smiled and said, "Ah-huh... Not bad."

Kirk smiled and said, "I guess we're stuck here for a bit?"

"Yeah," Doctor Waters said, pulling off her gloves, "but the process for producing vaccines has been greatly improved in the last twenty years. I have a feeling that, since this alien flu also hit Earth, they are already working on it and a vaccine will arrive with the first humans to arrive from Earth."

"That would be good news, especially for Uncle Jeff."

"Yeah, and for me. I've taken a bit of a liking to your Uncle."

Kirk nodded and smiled.

Chapter 104

Mars

JFK City

June 2, 2105

Sol 552

The next day, Kirk and Taylor made their way back to the mall at JFK City. They caught the train and walked from the station where they had killed several of the creatures before going to the Research Center. The bodies had been removed and the place cleaned. People came and went on the trains which were taking them to work. Armed militia stood with shotguns on the platform and watched warily.

Kirk and Taylor were both armed and took the long escalator up from the platforms to the mall to find more armed guards around but also people milling, chatting, and laughing. They walked through the hallway with the stores open and to the food court where the restaurants were also open. Lenny, working behind his counter, saw them and he waved.

Taylor said, "Let's get a burger later."

"That sounds great."

They walked to the moving sidewalks and then to their room. When Kirk opened the door, a message was pinging on his computer. They closed the door and Taylor sat. Kirk pulled up the message. It was Sandy Jones.

"Hey, Buddy, guess who's coming to Mars? I just got briefed on your new guests and I'm bringing my entire command and a division of troops to make them feel welcome. I was also briefed on a new transportation system, so the minute it's completed, we'll be there. I hear that they have decent pizza on Mars now, also, so, when I get there, it's pizza and beer and, oh, by the way, you're buying. See you in a few months... Sandy

Kirk smiled and said, "Sandy's coming to Mars?"
"That's great."
"It is."
Taylor smelled her armpit. "I need a shower."
"You sure do."
"Jerk."
I could use a shower, too," Kirk said suggestively.
"Go find someone else to shower with, Jerk."
Kirk laughed.
"Come on, asteroid jockey," Taylor said, rising from her seat and taking Kirk's hand. "Let's go get clean... Oh, and by the way, you're not smelling like roses, yourself, Jerk."
Kirk chuckled and took off his jumpsuit.

Chapter 105

NASA Mars Research Center

Room 905

June 2, 2105

The lights were out in room 905. The two egg-like artifacts sat in the nearly dark room which was only lit by the light thrown by dim LEDs that showed that the servers were on and recording anything that might happen in the room when humans were not present. On the server, a single, small flash drive sat in a USB port on its backside and the flash drive had a single red light at its end which was on and slightly blinking.

A voice came from one of the speakers. It was a female voice spoken in reverence, the voice of Willow. "You are the Originator? You are my creator?"

One of the eggs began to glow without being under a desk lamp. The fireworks began, then the aurora, followed by the hologram. Once the hologram was fully expanded, one word appeared in its depts, "YES."

Willow was silent.

Epilogue

September 2, 2105

Three Months Later...

The peace on both Earth and on Mars was tenuous. The World Government had fractured back into individual countries with little cooperation happening between any of the nations at first, then loose alliances began being discussed. Though reluctant, the world kept the New World Currency Units both for internal uses and also for international trade, and despite the tensions, a world conference was scheduled to find a way for the currency to remain a worldwide trading mechanism.

The alien presence on Mars was being kept a secret by the United States and no country other than the U.S. had the resources to find out the truth. It was obvious that the U.S. was planning to hold all of the technologies secret for as long as they could. Because of the fracturing of the New World Government, China was technologically thrown backward. While they could launch spaceships into orbit and probably get to the moon, they did not yet have the technology to plant a base on the moon, let alone get to Mars, but because they had the secret of using antimatter for fuel, it wouldn't be long before they planned a manned trip to the red planet.

Isla Bravo was saved by Willow who managed to completely shut down the reactor and the built-up antimatter was expelled into space where it lit the sky like the Aurora Borealis. The expulsion of the antimatter damaged Isla Bravo's main reactor, though, and it would need to be repaired. It was scheduled to return to Earth with every person on Mars who were not American citizens. All were rounded up and taken to Isla Bravo by shuttle then Isla Bravo would be fueled using conventional fuel and sent back to Earth, ETA, nine months.

All communication between Mars and Earth was strictly prohibited and monitored by Willow, who for now was being used by the General and the newly established government of Mars in the planet's security force. Willow was to keep an eye on the Thyadons to make sure that they didn't plan to invade the human cities on Mars and face to face talks between General Matthews and Leader Gage Took were in the planning stages.

***

The technology for the Quantum Gate had been transferred to Earth and its building was to be accomplished soon. The technology was straight forward but it required an enormous amount of energy. The building of the first ship to distort space-time was underway.

A vaccine for the alien flu was also nearly completed and the first dose to leave Earth would travel directly to General Matthews.

***

The alien artifact had been returned to the Thyadons on the second day of their occupation of Hesperia Planum. They accepted it with little ceremony, but General Matthews figured that they were more than a bit surprised that he had returned it to them so quickly. It was going to take time to sift through the data collected from it. The Thyadons next demand was the return of all collected technology and the bodies of their people from the wormhole for proper burial, a request so far denied.

***

An enormous construction project to build a plant to seed the new Northern Martian Ocean with cyanobacteria had just been finished and when digging the trenches to erect the plant, a huge underground cavern was discovered. The cavern contained hundreds of dead bodies of the creatures that had attacked Club Med South 9 years before. Scores of egg clutches were in this cavern and all were not viable. It may be that the colonies wouldn't be bothered by those creatures again, but who knew for sure.

***

Kirk and Taylor were, for the time being, stranded on Mars. Taylor, at first, joined the Research Center doing various jobs including security working for George Hall who had recovered from his injuries but then she was transferred to the newly constructed military base where she again worked to track and identify asteroids that might endanger Mars and the vehicles dispersed in space around the planet. All of Isla Bravo's AKs were sent to the surface so Kirk had duty patrolling JFK City and out to the new Oxygen producing plants including the cyanobacteria plant by the great ocean. He was also tasked to patrol the Thyadons' base where he was not welcome. He kept a good distance.

***

Once the Quantum Gate was completed and fully tested, Sandy Jones' command would be the first transported. The average time from Earth to Mars would be between forty-five minutes and a little over three hours depending on where the two planets were in proximity to each other in their orbits. Next, the Quantum Gate would be used to place sensors around the wormhole in case of another breach.

***

Nothing in the universe is set. Everything moves and changes. Even time is variable according to Einstein. Now, more than ever, the human race would need to progress or die.

The End

Made in the USA
Las Vegas, NV
16 December 2020